Sagas of the Servants

The book was called SAGAS OF THE SERVANTS. The first story, "The Mirage Warrior," told of a great hero who must destroy a monster created by an evil wizard. At each stage of his journey he was faced with increasingly ferocious adversaries: a two-headed lion, a giant armor-plated scorpion, and a hideous reptilian abomination which spat acid. As he overcame each one, it disappeared into nothingness, returning to the malignant imagination that had spawned it. He was dueling mirages.

Mark read with a growing sense of unease. He knew he had never seen the book before, yet he couldn't shake the feeling that he had already read this story. All the outlandish monsters were oddly familiar and when the hero strode into the castle's central courtyard and confronted the real monster, Mark nearly cried aloud.

He had been here before and he knew what would happen. *He* was the hero!

And he had seen the dragon.

Servants of Ark

BOOK ONE

The
First
Named

JONATHAN
WYLIE

BANTAM BOOKS

TORONTO · NEW YORK · LONDON · SYDNEY · AUCKLAND

THE FIRST NAMED

A Bantam Spectra Book / November 1987

PRINTING HISTORY
Corgi Book edition published in 1987

ISBN 0-553-26953-4

Published simultaneously in the United States and Canada

Bantam Books are published by Bantam Books, Inc. Its trademark, consisting of the words "Bantam Books" and the portrayal of a rooster, is Registered in U.S. Patent and Trademark Office and in other countries. Marca Registrada. Bantam Books, Inc., 666 Fifth Avenue, New York, New York 10103.

PRINTED IN THE UNITED STATES OF AMERICA

KR   0 9 8 7 6 5 4 3 2 1

To Julia   To Mark

To the feline weaver of tales, for inspiration.
To Patrick, for faith.
And to Vince, even if he's not on my team anymore.

From the sea, peril.
From the sea, safety.

From the parts, the whole.
From the whole, strength.

Arkon's heir, first named and last
Must seize his time, else time shall sleep
Arkon's blade shall gather strength
From all around at journey's end.

When vengeance screams, no human sound,
Iron fire sheds light on Arkon's staff.
Two that are one call judgement down.
One that will reign shall strike alone.
When beauty fades and time awakes,
Then fates decide, and battle cease.

Prologue

Darkness came early the night of the storm. Long before the sun sank below the western sea it disappeared behind a towering wall of purple clouds.

"A wizard's sky," the people of the islands muttered as they bolted shutters, though none alive then was old enough to remember the wizards' wars that had torn the sky and changed the face of the land. Surely now after so many years of peace the powers of magic had been diverted to more comfortable ends or perhaps, as some said, real magic was no more, the wizards' spells atrophied by ease and plenty, now reduced to mere showground tricks.

And yet many strange tales came to be told of that night: of the dolphin which leapt into a small boat and refused to be manhandled back into the water until they were in the relative safety of Grayrock Harbor; of the school of whales which beached themselves on the strand near Sealeap, providing the locals with more meat and oil than they knew what to do with; of the luminous sea serpent in the Tirek Strait: of the eagle carrying two unharmed sparrows in its beak, which roosted in the towers of Starhill Castle; of the frogs which fell from the sky on Heald; and many more. Perhaps the stories grew in the telling at countless tavern firesides but even the most sober citizens agreed that it had indeed been a wild night.

*   *   *

The storm blew itself out at dawn. The sun rose brilliant and serene as the bolder folk emerged from their places of shelter.

At their isolated cottage, Avram the fisherman and his wife, Cara, had lain, with their infant son, awake and worrying, as the rain drummed on their thatch, the wind rattled branches against the walls and all but destroyed their garden's hardiest plants, and the thunder roared as if the earth itself were being torn apart. Miraculously, the cottage had withstood the onslaught more or less unscathed. Avram had been afraid that the roof would be torn away entirely but there was not even one minor leak.

Outside it was a different story. Trees had been uprooted, instant cascades from the hills had reshaped the land and completed the destruction of the garden.

Fearfully, Avram walked down to the shore. His boat was his only means of livelihood and although he had drawn it up the shingle far beyond the tide line, the storm did not recognize such boundaries. As the beach came in sight he was overjoyed to see the *Skua* apparently undamaged. In his relief he ran over the sliding stones and breathlessly inspected the boat. Wave-thrown pebbles had scored the hull's paintwork but it was still as sound as ever. The water and seaweed inside could easily be bailed out and, Avram laughed out loud, there was even a huge crab trapped inside which would make a tasty meal and soup for days to come. He caught and killed the crab, putting it in a bucket, then set about putting the *Skua* back in working order.

Three hours later his stomach turned his mind to thoughts of food and, picking up his bucket, Avram set off homeward, following the deep imprints of his earlier run. His eye caught a flash of light ahead and for a moment he felt his light-hearted mood disappear. Walking on, he found, between two of his footprints, so close that he should surely have fallen over it in his haste, a curious and beautiful casket. Immediately, visions of wealth besieged Avram's mind. Pirate gold? Lordly jewels? Such a rich container, its lacquered wood inlaid and cornered with brass, must surely contain untold riches—and what was lost at sea became the property of whoever salvaged it. Kneeling, he tried the clasp but it was locked, of course.

Boat, storm, and crab forgotten, Avram lifted the box,

which was reassuringly heavy, and hurried back to the cottage where, with Cara looking on wide-eyed, he laid it on the table and with hammer and chisel broke off the lock. Inside were layers of rich cloth which Avram eagerly folded back.

Beneath lay a naked baby girl.

Cara gasped, and Avram felt again that sudden chill. So he wasn't to be rich after all, and he would have to bury the child, on land this time.

"It moved," whispered Cara.

I can't believe this, thought Avram, "*but it's true.*" The tiny chest rose and fell, fingers curled and stretched.

Alive?

Cara's maternal instincts took over. "The poor thing," she murmured, touching its forehead—it was warm—and then scooping it out and cradling it to her. "I hope I have enough milk for them both."

Avram rummaged in the box for some explanation of the child's unusual mode of travel or even some money to aid the orphan's future, but there was nothing except the swaddling. Too stunned to talk, or even think, Avram stared at his wife who in turn gazed at the baby's face.

All at once Cara's eyes grew wide with surprise and then terror before they seemed to cloud over, to receding into an unnatural serenity. "What beautiful violet eyes," she said. "Avram, look."

Avram did not want to look. He was afraid. The chill had returned, stronger than ever. *A changeling*, he thought. *This is no business of mine*. And a small voice said, "Kill this abomination before it is too late."

Snatching the baby from the startled Cara, who flailed ineffectually, he made for the door, intent on returning his burden to the sea. But before he was three steps beyond the door he had forgotten why he had come outside. Puzzled, he looked down at the baby in his arms. *What lovely eyes*, he thought and turned back into the cottage, where Cara calmly took charge of her enlarged family.

Avram went back down to the beach to collect the crab, but it had gone, food for seagulls by now.

Chapter 1

*A*ther as a weakling," Amarino said contemptuously, "and his sons are no better—a clod, a lecher, and a feeble boy. What possible threat can they be to us?"

Parokkan looked at his wife, and once again felt slightly perturbed. Of late, she had shown more spirit than he had been used to seeing in her. He wasn't sure whether to be disquieted by this, or to enjoy the new force. She was certainly a beguiling creature and her slender beauty had a way of distracting him from his purpose. Since the drive that had led him to seize the throne of Ark, kill its king, and exile its princes, he had felt a lessening of tension. Sometimes he thought he would prefer to spend his days gazing into Amarino's lovely violet eyes, rather than bother himself with affairs of state. He blessed the day when they had overcome his parents' opposition to their marriage. Amarino was an orphan and, knowing nothing of her forebears, and nothing of the girl's history before her appearance at court two years earlier, they were reluctant to welcome her into their noble family. She had won them over remarkably quickly with a mixture of charm, innate self-assurance, and a bearing which implied that she would be worthy of the highest in the land.

Now, Parokkan thought that if his hitherto serene lady was to acquire the strength and knowledge to help him in his rule, she would ease his burden greatly.

"So, love," Amarino was saying to him. "What plans have you for the *rightful* heirs?" This last was said in a gently mocking tone, as she took an affectionate hold of her husband's arm. "Are you content to leave them in exile, or would you prefer their slaughter?"

"There has been enough of that! No, as you say, they are little threat to us, and have probably left the island by now. Theirs is a small party, and the people of Ark are behind us. They can gain nothing by remaining. We'll leave them be, for the present at least."

Amarino was content. The three boys were little threat, and if events continued on their present course, she knew she was more than capable of countering any opposition that offered itself. Even so, she was pleased that she had been able to make Parokkan think that the decision to leave them alone had been his own.

At the tiny fishing village of Home, on the south coast of Ark, many miles distant from Starhill and its new rulers, the three "boys" and their party sat in gloom.

"We've got to get this situation into perspective, look on the bright side. We're all alive, aren't we? Still got all our limbs? Brains—well, mostly," the wizard Ferragamo said, looking at Eric, and trying to keep a straight face. "But the truth of the matter is that we do have hope, and health, on our side."

Ferragamo was the eldest of the party—by a good degree. For a man past his two hundred and thirtieth birthday, he was remarkably good-looking. With his close-cropped brown hair, he was not at all the picture of a traditional wizard! His often stern face was belied by the twinkle in his piercing green eyes and any sharp words, when necessary, were usually followed by a jest.

His good (and occasionally very bad) lady Koria didn't mind the age difference of two centuries. She supposed he would eventually outgrow her, but they were both happy to keep that prospect well in the mists of the future. Koria was everything Ferragamo wanted in a woman. Though not beautiful, she was very appealing. Her black hair and brown eyes set off a face that could be either as mischievous as a naughty child's, or as seductively lovely as any high-class whore's.

She could conjure up a delicious meal from the most unlikely ingredients, was warmhearted, and if she showed an occasional touch of impatience with Ferragamo's magical dabblings, well, he wasn't complaining. Their relationship was one based on enduring friendship, respect, trust—and a lasting passion. Koria often provided the wizard with the matter-of-fact outlook on life that he sometimes lacked. She also made him laugh. It was an ideal partnership.

Turning again to Eric, the eldest of the late King Ather's sons, Ferragamo said:

"Perhaps you should consider going across to Heald. The lady Fontaine's parents must surely be concerned for her safety, and I am certain we would find a welcome there."

"No," said Eric. "I want to stay and fight. These upstarts can't just come strolling in and take over the kingdom without so much as a by-your-leave." His blue eyes flashed angrily, and he was obviously having difficulty keeping his large muscular frame under control.

"But they can, and have done so," Ferragamo said, struggling to remain patient. "And I am *trying* to offer sane counsel. We can't fight back yet—we have insufficient force—and so should wait until the time is right. We won't do ourselves any good by dashing off and getting ourselves killed."

"Why can't you blast them with your magic?" said Eric. "You're a wizard, aren't you?"

"It is not as simple as that."

"Nothing ever is with wizards," said Brandel, through a mouthful of nuts.

"As I have explained many times before, magic, as you call it, is not something you can throw about like so much earth. To gather any appreciable amount of power is a long and delicate business and storing it is a constant hazard."

"Yes, so you always tell us," said Eric, "but you're hundreds of years old. What have you been doing all that time?"

Koria appeared in the kitchen doorway. "Looking after ungrateful oafs like you, Master Eric; that's what he's been doing. And besides, he's barely over two hundred years old and, as I have cause to know, he is more of a man than you'll ever be!"

Eric grinned and yelled at the now empty doorway, "You should try a young man one day, Koria. You'll give the wizard here a hernia."

He and Brandel exchanged glances, chuckling at this witticism.

"And another thing," she said, reappearing. "Who was it got you out of Starhill Castle when it had enemies all round and no way of escape?"

"Anyone can run down secret passages if they know where they are," said Eric.

"You never would have even reached the secret passages if Ferragamo hadn't cloaked your passage. You'd all have been cut to bits like your father—" She stopped suddenly, aware of the effect her words were having. Eric sat stony-faced, his eyes angry. Brandel had stopped chewing, his pudgy face drained white, and tears were brimming in Mark's eyes, though he was trying to desperately to stop them falling.

"There now, look what you've made me do," she said and, with a sad glance of apology to Ferragamo, she turned back to her baking.

The silence stretched.

Then Eric said, "Well, magic doesn't seem much good to me if all it can do is help us run away." The anger had gone from his eyes, but his tone was still belligerent.

"Eric," the wizard replied. "I have a duty to you and to your father, and what power I have will be at your service when the time is right. But"—with a hand he forestalled the obvious question rising to the prince's lips—"we have to marshal our resources. The people who took your place were well organized. There was no warning and they came in considerable force. You know they had the backing of almost all the army garrison in Starhill."

"Traitors," hissed Eric.

"And even though I do have some powers that men call magic, I can be killed by a sword or spear just as any other. To have resisted the attack then or to rush back now would be suicidal. All is not lost, but we cannot rely on magic alone to solve everything." *When will I ever be able to explain it?* he thought. *Mark is the only one who's ever paid the slightest attention and he's so dreamy I doubt if he remembers a quarter of what I've told him. Look at him now. Miles away!*

In contrast to his fair-haired brothers, Mark had brown hair and eyes and was slightly built. He was indeed miles away, lost in memories of a life which now seemed so remote. But Ferragamo was wrong about how much he had learned in the wizard's cluttered, fascinating room high in the main

tower of Starhill Castle. Mark could recall perfectly the first
lesson of magic which he had coaxed from his tutor as a
reward for diligent study of more mundane matters.

"Magic," Ferragamo had said, his fingertips steepled and
his eyes noting cobwebs on the ceiling, "is a form of energy.
You can split rocks with a hammer but to do so you have to
pick up the hammer and swing it down, give it energy. It's
the energy that splits the rock, not the hammer. The energy
that comes from your arm. Magic is like that but the energy
comes from your mind.

"All men have magical potential, though the amount varies,
but most don't know how to use it. A lot don't even know it's
there at all."

"You mean I could be a wizard?" asked Mark, his eyes
wide.

"With long years of patience and learning, yes. What you
must remember is that although the power that is called
magic is natural to the world, accumulations of such power
are not. There is an automatic leveling out so that the magical
events which occur about us are so small that they materially
affect nothing and are never noticed. The skill of a wizard is
the ability to draw on the power that is all around and to
focus it in such a way that the magical event *is* noticeable. To
do that you need a great deal of knowledge about the true
nature of the world and a good deal of wisdom too."

Seeing unprecedented enthusiasm in his pupil's face,
Ferragamo smiled and went on. "In here you have a mind."
He tapped Mark's forehead. "With it you think, decide upon
and control your actions, remember your lessons and lots of
other information, and, in general, experience the world. But
your mind is more than that. It has an energy, a power, of its
own. The first step to becoming a wizard is to recognize and
then to control that power as easily as you now control your
hand or eyes. The second, far harder step is to learn how to
increase that power by adding to it from outside sources.
There are many hazards in this process and it has been the
downfall of many an overambitious apprentice. Firstly, merely adding to your energy in a haphazard way is dangerous for
you and for those near you. Without proper safeguards the
extra power will be unstable and can shoot off in all directions, causing chaos, or worse still, can rip apart the very
fabric of your mind, leaving something less than human
behind. You could of course gather and store this energy in

some object, my staff for instance, so that you could call upon it when needed without the dangers of carrying it about in your head so to speak. But this has its drawbacks too. Obviously, a staff may be stolen or lost and, in the wrong hands, could be used to do a great deal of damage. Such magical objects can be protected to some degree of course. Pure iron, for perverse reasons known only to the Earth, is impervious to all magic, and so it is often used to contain magical objects. But such measures are temporary at best and any magical power source is, in itself, a potential danger. It can, if not correctly ensorcelled, take on a life of its own and pass beyond all hope of control." Ferragamo shuddered slightly at the vision of an army of lively broomsticks terrorizing the streets of Starhill.

"Where do you gather this power from? Other people's minds?"

"No! Such a thing is unthinkable. You would be destroying their minds, reducing them to less than animals. In the whole history of the world only one wizard has ever dared such an evil and he was destroyed long ago."

"But—"

"There are many sources of magical power. Look about you. There is potential in everything. The world has a mind, of a sort, just as you do. You know that some places, the old places especially, have a strange and powerful atmosphere. That is the legacy of magical history and the reserves to be tapped are vast, unknowable—and that is another trap. By drawing power unwisely you may unbalance some delicate arrangement and unleash forces which you cannot control and which may destroy you totally. Therefore it is better to build power slowly, carefully, until it is as natural a process for you to replenish your mind as to keep your body fed, and to leave the rightful order of the world intact as much as possible as you do it. To keep a balance in all things."

Mark was silent for a while and Ferragamo left him to think. *At least he is like his father in that he listens to what I say,* the wizard mused. *Unlike his brothers. Maybe I am not wasting my time after all.* When Mark broke the silence Ferragamo began to have doubts again.

"Is it true that you can raise the dead?"

The wizard saw the pain and hope behind the question. From Eric or Brandel such a query would have been mere sensational gossip, trying to neddle their tutor into indiscretions. From Mark it was something more. The youngest prince had been profoundly affected by his mother's death. He had been two years old at the time and no one had been able or thought to explain to him what all the fuss was about. All he knew was that something had gone out of his life. Something warm and lovely.

Ferragamo sat down in his big old armchair which was losing its stuffing where Owl's talons had taken their toll. Trying to keep the weariness out of his voice, he said, "No, Mark, I cannot raise the dead and nor can any other wizard. Necromancy is a disreputable branch of wizardry and one which has been much abused by unscrupulous men. When someone dies, their mind's energy does not disappear. Usually what happens is that it dissipates slowly. Some of it goes somewhere of which we have no knowledge, and some becomes part of the world that the person knew when he was alive. It is possible to harness the energy of a person who has died and to use this to re-create a likeness of that person. But that is all it is—a likeness. The real person, mind and body together, cannot be recalled. The men who claim to do so are illusionists, nothing more."

The wizard's heart felt heavy as the import of his words sank home but consoled himself with the thought that Mark was at least getting a true and clear answer to a question which had obviously been preying on his mind. Better that than the garbled nonsense of the marketplace or the lies of fairground charlatans. Watching various expressions cross the prince's face, Ferragamo wondered what difference the new knowledge would make. He saw one hope die and another, subtler thought take its place.

"You said a person's mind becomes part of their surroundings, their things."

"In a way, yes."

"Does that mean that I might be able to feel somebody through something left behind? Something that was dear to her?

"Or him?" he added quickly.

"Yes, that's possible but you mustn't expect too much from any contact like that," said Ferragamo, noticing that Mark was fingering a small silver ring which he wore on a chain round his neck.

"Sometimes I dream when I'm awake," said the prince.

"Yes, I've noticed," replied the wizard, laughing, "usually

when there's work to be done." *We're getting in too deep here,* he thought to himself and was relieved when Mark came out of his reverie, laughed as well, and said, "Tell me a story."

"Enough stories for now. You'll wear my poor old tongue out. Besides, it's time to eat." The wizard stood.

Owl appeared from his daytime hiding place and swooped to his accustomed position on Ferragamo's shoulder.

"He talks to you, doesn't he," said Mark. "I think I can hear him myself sometimes. Is he hungry?"

The owl and the wizard exchanged glances.

"Yes, he's hungry."

They walked down the spiral staircase and across the tree yard and out to the dining hall in companionable silence.

———————————

A rather different meal we're having now, thought Mark. *The food's as good, if not as plentiful, but the surroundings ...* He looked about the cottage, remembering that earlier eating place with the trestle tables, the shields and banners on the wall, and his father in the place of honor at the great round table. By comparison the cottage was a humble dwelling indeed. For some years it had been Ferragamo's summer retreat, where he rested and restored his own internal balance, away from the constant demands of the court. Until now it had been his rule to keep the whereabouts of his second home from all at Starhill, thus ensuring a complete relaxation. Only Koria shared his secret and she had reason enough not to gossip. She had already been on her way to prepare the cottage before the violent events in Starhill had occurred.

Now the cottage and the village of Home in which it stood, fifty leagues to the south of the capital, were being used as a different kind of refuge. The party of exiles had reason to be thankful for Ferragamo's past secrecy.

Eric and the wizard were still arguing, neither having the slightest effect on the other's beliefs, and Brandel was still eating. *Some things never change,* Mark thought.

Chapter 2

Eric was glowering, looking to his two brothers for support, and finding none. Brandel, having finished the nuts, was on the point of falling asleep and would soon be snoring, and Mark was in no mood to take his side.

"*I* don't want to fight," he said petulantly, "and don't see why you should want to. It's much better to remain safe, and stay together. I've had enough traipsing round, sleeping out at night and getting cold. I'd like to stay here for a while, just for a bit of peace and quiet."

After their headlong flight to escape from the besieged city of Starhill the fugitives' journey had indeed been uncomfortable and agonizingly slow. Once they had collected the four horses, that Ferragamo's ancient foresight had provided, the quickest route would have been along the trading road to the island's main port, Grayrock Harbor. However, this was also the most obvious line of escape and thus the party headed in the opposite direction, hoping to avoid any pursuit.

Before too long, this took them onto little used and ill-kept pathways leading into the foothills of the aptly named Windchill Mountains. Their pace was limited by the fact that there was one less horse than was ideal and Fontaine therefore had to be content with riding behind Eric, Ferragamo, and Mark by turns. Brandel's mount was spared the extra weight as he was already carrying by far the heaviest load.

The most unprepossessing in looks of the three princes, Brandel's girth was a source of both amusement and disgust to the rest of his family. Fontaine was openly thankful for his exclusion from the seating arrangements as the second son had wandering hands and was unable to resist even his elder brother's fiancée. Eric, of course, felt that she should ride with him all the time but Ferragamo pointed out that, as he was the second heaviest of the party, it would make more sense to share the work more equally among the horses. Mark, despite his embarrassment at female proximity, saw the sense of this, but the deciding factor was Fontaine herself, who hoisted herself up behind Mark, remarking that if they preferred to stay and be killed while they argued about horses, they could do so without her.

There were two other members of the party but neither of these added much to the horses' load. Owl perched on the wizard's shoulder or flew overhead and Longfur Mousebane, Mark's inseparable feline companion, clung tightly to the saddle in front of him, being careful not to use his claws on the horse's neck, out of respect for a fellow animal.

As evening approached with no sign of pursuit they allowed the pace to drop and began thinking of camping for the night. The nature of their journey meant that they carried minimal supplies and as they climbed into the mountains which soon deprived them of the sun's last rays, it became clear that despite the day's summer heat the night would be unpleasantly cold. In the clear sky the stars began to shine like particles of ice.

That first night they found a secluded vale with a stream and a few trees in which to secrete themselves and their mounts. Even so, they did not dare to light a fire, and none of them slept well despite their weariness. Cold seeped into their limbs and horrible memories invaded their dreams.

They awoke early, feeling cramped and stiff, eager to move on, to warm themselves with exercise and put more leagues between them and the horror of Starhill. Breakfast was cold and unsatisfying. Longfur's attempts at enlarging their meal—with mice and a frog—were not appreciated.

The sun rose and was welcomed by them all. They rode at first, climbing ever higher, with the giant peaks glistening white to the south. Later they came to a stretch of track which zigzagged up a steep slope composed mainly of loose shale and scree. It soon became obvious that they would have to lead the horses, who were beginning to stumble and become fretful.

As they toiled upward, the sun's growing warmth became less welcome. Soon they were all sweating and stops became more frequent. Until now progress had been made in near silence, each person walled up in their own thoughts, but when the strap broke on one of Fontaine's shoes, which were hardly suitable for mountain walking, her temper snapped as well.

"Why are we going this way?" she screeched at Eric. "This mad old charlatan leads us into this awful mess and you just follow, so meekly. We should have stayed in the lowlands where the horses would be of use."

She sat down and Eric walked back to her, at a loss as to how to placate her. He had seen a bit of Fontaine's temper when she didn't get things her own way, and by now he was having his own doubts about Ferragamo's course.

Before he could think of anything to say, Fontaine went on.

"I'm not going on. I think I've sprained my ankle. Don't just stand there gawking. Do something!" She began to cry, covering her face with her hands.

Eric looked round for help. Brandel had lain down, breathing heavily, with sweat staining his clothes. Mark stood quite still, his eyes wide and frightened, close to tears himself. Ferragamo, who was bringing up the rear, walked toward them, handed his horse's reins to Eric, and, kneeling, said gently, "Let me see your ankle."

"No!" Her spread hands shot out in defense. "Keep your hands to yourself." Her face was mottled red and white.

"Fontaine—" the wizard began, but got no further, for at this point, a chunk of rock the size of a fist bounded down the scree slope and caught him on the side of his head. As he collapsed, the rest of the party became aware of the sounds of men and horses on the path above, moving down to meet them.

There was nowhere to hide, nowhere to flee—to ride or even run in this terrain was to invite disaster. There was only one alternative, as even Eric's slow brain realized. Moreover it was one course of action that he, at least, was well equipped to follow. They must wait and, if necessary, fight.

Eric drew his sword, suddenly sure of himself. "Brandy, get up, you pig! Get your sword out. Fontaine, look to

Ferragamo—see if you can bring him round. We need him. Mark, tie the horses together down the path a little, then get up here with me. Stop gawking, boy. Move!"

By some miracle, they obeyed him almost immediately.

Voices from above indicated that the other party was now aware that they were not alone on the trail. Their leaders came into sight at the next hairpin bend above as Mark and Brandel joined Eric, who stood squarely in the center of the path. Both his brothers, Eric noted disgustedly, were shaking with fright.

The others approached steadily, six men leading their horses and giving no outward sign of hostile intent.

As they grew close, Mark exclaimed, "That's Shill! And Orme!" He started to move forward to greet the familiar faces, but a hand on his shoulder stopped him.

Brandel said, "Wait. We don't know whose side they're on."

"Shill? That's ridiculous. We've known him for years."

"Yes," said Eric, catching on, "but there were plenty of familiar faces in the group that attacked the castle."

Mark fell silent, his smile disappearing as quickly as it had arrived. They waited, Eric's sword held out in front of him.

Shill stopped several paces away, his gnarled face creased in puzzlement.

"This is a strange greeting, my lord. What offense have I given?"

"I've been betrayed by many men that I trusted. Forgive my caution, Shill, but much has happened since I saw you last."

"That's obvious, my lord. Why are you here with no escort? I fear our hunting trip was ill-timed."

"It was," said Eric shortly.

"Oh, Shill," blurted Mark, "Father's dead. What are we going to do?"

And so the story came out, as Shill and his party listened with dismay plain upon their faces.

As Mark listened to his brother's voice he found himself back in Starhill Castle amid the dreadful confusion of bloodshed and noise. It had seemed to go on for hours and he still did not understand what was happening when he found himself with several others fleeing into Starbright Tower.

He had heard his father shout, "Ferragamo! Get the boys

and Fontaine away—into the passage. For Ark's sake, man, quickly! We'll guard the door."

Mark had wanted to cry out, and may even have done so, but nobody heard him in the tumult and Ather's expression brooked no argument.

The princes, knowing how desperate their situation was, did as they were bid, and rushed down the secret passageway that led from inside the wizard's tower to a point in the north of the city. Fontaine, her arm held in her fiancé's vise-like grip, was forced to match their pace. Ferragamo, realizing full well that the king, experienced swordsman though he was, would be no match for Parokkan's men, was using a blocking spell to keep the army away from Ather and the two faithful soldiers fighting at his side. Once he saw that the group was far enough down the passageway, he yelled to the king, "My lord! Come away now—they've gone far enough, now we must make *our* escape. I cannot hold this spell much longer."

He was shocked to see the grim, strained expression on Ather's face, as he said, "Ferragamo, I'm not coming. You must get away. There isn't time enough for us both to escape without leading these bastards to Eric and the boys. And Ark knows, you'll be of more use to my sons in the days ahead than I will. Eric is almost fit now to rule—with your guidance." He gave his sword to Ferragamo, and took up another from a fallen guard. "Give this to him. I'm an old man, sick at heart—and lonely for my love. I've missed her greatly all these long years, and shall join her now. You are needed. I am not. Now go!"

The wizard was frantic, knowing the truth his lord spoke, yet desperate for a way to try and save them both. After holding the spell for a few moments more, he saw the struggle to be unequal, gave up—and ran, leaving Ather to close the door to the passageway behind him, and then to turn and face the battle he knew would not be long in coming, once Ferragamo's spell was out of range.

Within moments, Ather, King of Ark, was cut down . . . bloodily.

———————

At the other end of the passageway, what appeared from the street to be the front door of a house opened, and Ferragamo's head peeped out. The street was quiet, though not deserted. Though he feared exposure, he knew they must get away immediately, as Parokkan's men could be only minutes behind. The streets in this part of the city, he was well aware, were jumbled enough to make their getaway easier; it would be very difficult for their would-be captors to follow their trail. Ferragamo knew exactly where to take his charges—and had known for years. Many, many years ago, in what had seemed more troubled times, he had prepared his "Last Resort," a secret tunnel through the city wall with, if his ancient bribe had held, help not too far from the other side.

He led them through the winding lanes, banked by tall houses, to what appeared to be a dead end at the very edge of the city. Leaning heavily against the wall at the end of the lane, Ferragamo showed the group their passage through.

"Come on," he urged. "But go carefully. It is many years since this passageway was used, and it's likely to be more than a little dusty!" He was right, and there were muffled shrieks from Fontaine as they made their way through the mercifully short tunnel. Once again, Ferragamo showed caution at the other end.

"Now," he said, "some years ago, I paid a very large sum of money to one of the out-wall dwellers. He had a well-stocked stable, and was to keep a group of horses prepared for me, to be used in an emergency such as this. You must all wait here, while I find his grandson and see if my plan has worked. Stay quiet." And he slipped away.

Some little time later, he returned. "All is well, I *think*. There are a number of horses in good condition, but no human in sight. Strange, but under *these* circumstances, I don't think we need wait to take our leave!"

"I should have been there," growled Shill as the tale came to its end.

"You will help us, won't you?" ended Mark.

"How could we else, my young lord?"

Shill and Mark stepped forward but halted as Eric said sharply, "Wait! What proof have we that you are not part of that plot? Your absence was very convenient."

"My lord, we have been hunting." He gestured at the

laden horses. "Here are the pelts and furs we were bringing back."

Mark said, "I trust him, Eric. They could easily have beaten us if it came to a fight."

Eric stood undecided.

"Mark is right. There's no treachery in him," said a voice from behind them, "though I could wish he took better care not to dislodge rocks on mountain trails."

"Ferragamo! It is good to see you here."

The wizard had risen, with Fontaine supporting his arm, but now he sat down again, obviously still shaken by the blow. Swords were sheathed and the two parties mingled. Questions were put and answered. The hunters' dismay was sharpened as they learned how thorough and unexpected the attack had been and how many of their comrades in the Castle Guard had fought against their king.

After a while Ferragamo added his voice to the talk and soon expressed his readiness to go on. They learned from the hunters that the precipitous path soon reached a plateau where the easier terrain would make riding and camping possible.

When the entire party reached the top they decided to halt as soon as possible. The Starhill group were all very tired, the afternoon was turning toward dusk, and there was much to discuss. A suitable spot was found and though there was still no sign of any pursuit, Shill posted one of his men to watch from the top of the steep slope while the others built a fire, set up bivouacs, and catered to the horses. The prospect of a second night in the mountains was much easier to face with the new supply of food and equipment, and even Fontaine, who now wore improvised leather boots, was in better spirits.

The hunters however were still in a state of shock. As darkness fell and all possibility of an attack from the east disappeared, the sentry, Richard, rejoined the group to eat. It was he who first voiced thoughts that had occurred to several others. Addressing Ferragamo, he began:

"I do not know where you are bound, Master Wizard, and perhaps it is better that I do not. It is clear that you cannot go back to Starhill but, if my captain permits"—he turned to Shill—"I for one wish to return to the city. I cannot doubt the tales we have heard yet if it is all true then my brother

Gordon is among the traitors. I can't believe *that* unless I see it with my own eyes."

One of the others, named Bonet, spoke. "Me too, Captain. I've no brother but a woman that I love. Orme here has a wife and two sons in the city too. Are we to abandon them?"

Orme said nothing but his eyes were fixed upon his captain's face as Bonet spoke. Shill met his gaze and saw the worry in the expression of his lifelong friend. But it was Ferragamo who broke the silence.

"Dearly though we would like your company, we'll not hold any who come unwillingly. Yet before you set your course hear me out." He paused and set his gaze to the young man who had spoken first.

"Your brother Gordon is among the rebels, Richard. That is the truth. I know him well enough and saw him clearly. So too did Mark." At Richard's glance, Mark lowered his eyes but nodded.

Ferragamo went on. "I do not know what madness has gripped him but there is something very strange about this whole affair. There will always be discontented and ambitious men in any army but there is no sense in the way the Castle Guard divided. The rebellion set friend against friend, even father against son. Many fought loyally and many good men turned traitor but no groupings emerged. It was as if those who rebelled were chosen at random. I fear they were driven by something more than ambition or greed. I am a wizard, of sorts, and not a soldier but I tell you this. That battle was not natural."

"They were bewitched?" said Richard.

"What evil is this?" whispered Shill.

"I do not know. There is something here beyond my understanding. That is all I can say. However"—Ferragamo turned to Bonet—"I can give you some words of hope. Your lady, I believe, lives outside the castle walls. The city saw little fighting. It was indeed strangely quiet. Therefore I think she is likely to be safe. Remember this is no invading army, intent on pillage and destruction. The rebels are of the same stock and if they hope to rule they will curry the favor of the people at large."

Orme could contain himself no longer.

"My family lived within the Castle. What of them, Ferragamo?"

"It's true that within the castle walls the fighting was

fierce but I did not see any women or children involved. Many of the rebels would have had good reason to see the families away from the fighting. Most, I suspect, were well hidden away. You did not fight against them, Orme. They should bear your family no grudges."

"The lads are resourceful," said Shill, "and so is Anna. They will have made good their escape."

"That is easy for you to say. You who have no kin."

Unexpectedly Fontaine spoke. "Anyone with eyes could see that Shill loves Anna almost as dearly as you, Orme. Even if he has no kin he would not lie to you."

The two old warriors looked at her in surprise, then at each other.

"A woman notices some things," Fontaine said quietly, and then was silent.

A log crackled and spat in the fire and the flames brightened as night drew in. A few minutes passed before Ferragamo spoke again.

"Ather was my king and my friend. His murder was an evil deed. But my senses tell me that more is afoot here than meets the eye. The time will come when we can set this island to rights but until we know what we face we have little choice. The princes and I go to a place of safety to learn and to plan for the future. Your help and company will be welcome but only if it is freely given. Sleep on it and decide your paths in the morning."

Essan, who had been silent until now, spoke up.

"No need for sleep, Master Wizard. My decision is easy for I have no direct kin in the city. One day I hope to renew old friendships there but for now my duty is clear. I will come with you."

"That is my mind too," said the last of the hunters, Benfell. "Our greeting in Starhill is uncertain and while Ather's sons live my place is with them. Come with us Richard, Bonet. It's for the best."

"I need to think," said Richard.

"Think on," said Shill.

The morning saw Orme bleary-eyed for lack of sleep but he had found his resolve. Shill knew his old friend's thoughts before he spoke and was glad.

"I will come with you and the princes," Orme said.

"You will not be parted long if I have anything to do with it," replied Shill. He did not need to specify from whom.

Bonet too had decided to stay with the party and Richard sadly admitted that a lone journey would probably help no one, and he dreaded the truth of his brother's treachery.

Thus it was that the entire party set off westward to cross the saddle of the mountain range. By midday they were past the highest point of the trail and that evening they camped on the lower slopes above the west coastal plain.

For the next five days they traveled southward as stealthily as possible, coming eventually to the large village of Sealeap. They made camp in a nearby copse and Orme and Bonet went into the port to investigate the possibility of a passage by boat round the southern tip of the island to Home, where Ferragamo promised they would find welcome. This would be a less obvious mode of travel and would avoid the necessity of traveling through the deep and forbidding forest which covered a huge part of the center of the island. They met with no success at first as there was no boat of sufficient size available and, moreover, the sailors were reluctant to undertake a long coastal journey when the summer fishing was so good so close to port. After three days, however, a coastal trader arrived who, for the right price, was happy to make the journey. His boat was sound but dirty and the rough coastal waters made the trip unpleasant for all but the hardiest stomach. Mark especially spent much of his time leaning over the side wishing that he were dead. Even the nights afforded little relief as the rugged and exposed southwestern coast offered little shelter for their moorings. Everyone was extremely glad when they reached Home.

Two days later Eric had forgotten all the hardship and was eager to move on, to make some positive attempt to avenge his father. No one else agreed.

"Mark's quite right." Ferragamo looked across at Ather's youngest. "We need to regain our strength and learn all we can before making our move."

"I'd like to learn some more about magic," Mark said eagerly.

"That's not quite what I meant," replied Ferragamo, "but I'll see what I can do."

At this Mark's cat looked up from his contemplation of an interesting-looking spider. *It's about time you got round to thinking of something useful. I've got a feeling we could do with a bit more magic round here. It's all very well our being able to communicate like this, but it doesn't seem to serve any really practical purpose, does it?*

Mark grinned. *No, but it's fun. You've hardly said a word since we left the castle. I've been worried that maybe I couldn't hear you any more.*

You know how I hate traveling. And the smell on that boat was enough to strike any self-respecting cat dumb. You didn't like it too much yourself, I recall.

Don't remind me. I'm glad you feel like talking again now. I rather like being able to put one over on the others. Ferragamo knows about us, and so does Koria probably, but Eric and Brandel certainly don't, and as for Fontaine . . .

Fontaine was the betrothed of Eric. The two neighboring islands of Ark and Heald had decided that a marriage between the two royal offspring would be an excellent idea. When Eric first saw Fontaine, he had not been particularly impressed by the small, spotty, red-haired princess, but he knew his duty and, as they didn't actively loathe each other, the marriage plans had been going ahead until the death of King Ather threw the situation into confusion. Fontaine didn't know whether to return home to her family, or to await events with Eric and his small group of followers. For the moment, she stayed with them, grumbling a great deal about the discomfort, the deprivations a lady should not have to experience, and just about anything else she could think of. The only member of the party who had any sympathy for her was Koria, who just felt sorry for her, remembering her own whiny, rebellious teenage years.

Well, you don't need to bother about her—she's Eric's problem. Lucky for you!

———————————

The next morning Mark woke early, feeling restless. Climbing down the ladder from the cramped attic bedroom—the only

room above ground level in the cottage—which he shared
with the still snoring Brandel, he listened for any sounds of
movement from the other rooms. The main room and kitch-
en, he quickly saw, were empty and all was silent in the
sleeping rooms of Ferragamo and Koria, Eric, and the small
room that the wizard called his study, where a bed had been
made up for Fontaine.

Quietly he let himself out of the front door and walked
the short distance to the cluster of houses, some separate and
some terraced, which made up the village. Several of the
fishermen and their wives were already up and about and he
was greeted several times, in a reserved but friendly enough
manner, as he wandered down to the sea. The village inn,
The Mermaid, was shuttered and quiet however. It smelled
of stale beer, an aroma which made Mark vaguely queasy but
gave off an impression of homeliness at the same time. It was
a lively enough place in the evenings apparently but now The
Mermaid, like its landlord, slept.

Continuing down Main Street, if the sloping and pitted
cobble could be glorified by such a name, Mark pondered on
whether to walk south along the cliff path or northeast across
the rocks to the long sandy beach. He had just decided that a
vigorous swim might cure his uneasy restlessness when he
spotted a group of people on the stone-built jetty which stood
in the center of the village harbor, with shingle strands to
either side. Several brightly painted boats bounced gently in
the early morning swell on both sides of the jetty, sheltered
from the prevailing westerlies by the land and from all but
the most severe storms by the rocks which guarded the
natural harbor.

Recognizing two of the group as Shill and Orme, Mark
walked on to join them. He knew that the soldiers had found
billets in an uninhabited cottage and some spare rooms and
were doing as much as they could to be of use to the
villagers. Unlike Ferragamo, who was well-known here and
respected despite his unknown origins, the soldiers had been
greeted with some suspicion. In a few days they had
counteracted this as best they could with a little money, furs
traded from their hunting, and a good deal of hard work.
There were several gardens which would be more productive
this year if they stayed, and though the soldiers knew little of
boats and their care, they made good laborers and learned
quickly. The younger ones had grumbled a bit at such work

but soon saw the sense of it, given their party's precarious position.

News of Ather's death had traveled fast and while the villagers did not concern themselves with such matters they were shrewd enough to know that the arrival of so large a group from the north was probably connected with those events. And though none had been told that the young men staying with the Visitor, as Ferragamo was known, were Ather's sons, there were many heads that nodded wisely when they were discussed. Their natural country courtesy had made the villagers seem aloof to the new arrivals but now some of the barriers were being broken down. When the visitors were not present, of course, the villagers' talk was less restrained. The Mermaid buzzed with gossip of an evening.

As Mark approached, the two men with Shill and Orme turned away and leapt down into a large fishing boat moored to the jetty, casting off as they did so. Shill beckoned to the prince and the three of them walked to the end of the pier and sat down, their legs dangling above the water, which was dazzling in the morning sun. They watched the boat move out to sea.

"They're good men," said Shill.

"Aye, but they'll need greater reasons than we can give to leave their homes," replied his lieutenant.

"Can you blame them for that? Begging your pardon, Mark, but they do not much care who sits on Starhill's throne as long as their lives are not interfered with. They liked Ather well enough but they'll wait to see how the new régime treats them before they judge. They're true enough, but realists."

Trying not to let the lump in his throat affect his voice. Mark said, "What were you talking to them about?"

"They agreed to sail to Stane and perhaps Bark to see if they can gather news from the north. They'll fish along the way of course, the season being so good, but we may learn something. It's little enough, I know, but we have to start somewhere and gauging the mood of the people is as good a place as any."

"Shouldn't someone go to Heald to let Fontaine's parents know what's happened?"

"Indeed they should, Mark. But the fishermen here aren't willing to undertake such a trip at the moment. We'll have to wait for another trader."

Orme added, "King Pabalan has almost certainly sent

someone to Ark himself for news. With luck he'll learn the truth soon enough."

"The other islands may offer us help in due course but they will still be assessing the new situation and at the moment we've got no means of contacting them to find out their thinking."

Shill went on: "We'll send someone north to Starhill in a day or two. That could be dangerous but we need the intelligence from there most of all."

Mark frowned. "I don't think that'll do much good."

"Why?"

"I just have a feeling."

The two soldiers exchanged glances over the prince's head.

"I can't say I'd be sorry to stay here for a while," said Mark.

"That I can understand," said Orme. "Our mode of travel wasn't exactly ideal."

"But we can't stay here forever," said Shill. "Someday we're going back to Starhill," he added, almost to himself.

"That we are," said Orme. "One way or another."

They sat in silence for a while, watching the waves. The fishing boat was now a tiny speck in the distance. Behind them more boats were being readied and Shill was pleased to note Richard on the shingle intent on mending a net under the careful eye of one of the wizened old fishermen.

Mark's stomach rumbled and Shill laughed.

"By the sound of you, you've not eaten yet. Will you join us in some mackerel?"

"Thank you, but I'd better get back to the cottage."

"The lad's got sense. Koria's cooking will beat ours any day," chuckled Orme.

———————

Fontaine was sitting in the main room when Mark let himself back in. She looked up and scowled and the warning was reinforced by a familiar, silent voice.

Tread carefully. Her Royal Highness is in a royal temper. Longfur emerged from behind a chair and rubbed against his human's legs.

"Been fishing?" said Fontaine. "There isn't much else to do here, is there."

Mark said nothing.

"Cat got your tongue?"

I'd make a meal of hers. Gladly.

Mark was unable to suppress a giggle, which infuriated Fontaine.

"What are you laughing at, you fish-eyed weed?"

Sober now but still unable to utter a word, Mark was saved by the appearance of Koria from her bedroom.

"Early birds, I see," she said. "I'd better get you some worms."

"Ugh," said Fontaine. "So that's why dinner tasted so awful last night."

The absolute injustice of this remark took Mark's breath away but did not disconcert Koria at all.

"My, we are in a good mood this morning, aren't we?"

"So would you be if you'd slept three nights in a lumpy, bug-infested heap surrounded by all those horrible books and *things* in jars."

"I'd change places with you but then you'd have to sleep with a lumpy, bug-infested wizard," said Koria.

"That's not funny," wailed Fontaine.

"I'm sorry, dear. It's not even true," Koria said calmly, putting an arm round Fontaine's shoulders, "though he can be a bit lumpy at times. We'll find you somewhere else to sleep. There now. Come and help me get some breakfast."

"What books?" said Mark, but no one paid him any attention. He decided to investigate on his own and went into the study, followed by Longfur.

Ranged along one wall were shelves containing dozens of books, most of them dusty and ancient looking. Some of the titles were indecipherable and some in languages Mark did not even recognize. Though it was a great temptation he did not take any of the volumes down. Mark knew that a wizard's books could be the source of dangerous knowledge and that some of them were ensorcelled and quite able to prevent any unwelcome readings. The thought both excited and frightened him but his habitual timidity, with some common sense, won the argument. He touched nothing.

On the opposite wall was a work bench with more shelves above it, all of which were cluttered with strange objects. Jars containing various powders, liquids, and the unnameable *things* which Fontaine had referred to, were interspersed with an assortment of curios: a piece of bone, a pair of tarnished scissors, a piece of driftwood, several stones, quill

pens and ink pots, some feathers, a small model boat and, up
on the top shelf, a stuffed owl.

Mark jumped as the stuffed owl blinked languorously and
hooted mournfully.

Behind him Ferragamo said, "I'm glad to see you've had
the sense not to touch anything."

The double shock set Mark's heart thumping and for the
second time that morning he was struck dumb. Not so
Longfur.

*Might have known that bird-brain would be here amongst
the exhibits.*

Ferragamo gave the cat a look and Longfur left the room,
his tail defiantly erect.

"In retrospect it was silly to have Fontaine sleep in here.
Not that she needed telling twice not to touch anything, but
there are too many influences for a young mind. I will tell
you about all these things when you're ready but I hardly
remember what is in some of these tomes myself," the wizard
said, seeing the way Mark gazed at the bookshelves.

"For now, have a look at this. It won't teach you any tricks
but there are some splendid tales in here." Ferragamo reached
for a large, leather-bound book, blew the dust off it, making
Mark cough, and handed it to him.

"I can smell breakfast. Bring the book with you."

The meal was of mixed quality as Fontaine's efforts in
helping had been more enthusiastic than effective at first, and
later, after the novelty had worn off, she had been
downright destructive. The smoke was still clearing.

Only Brandel was insensitive enough to complain and he
still gobbled everything put before him and then cleared
everyone else's leftovers. Mark hardly noticed the food and
ate without tasting it. He spent half the time with his neck
twisted over his shoulder to read snatches of the first story in
his book, and as soon as the meal was over he settled down to
read properly.

The book was called *Sagas of the Servants*, which didn't
mean much to Mark. *Servants to whom?* he wondered. Then
he had begun to read and forgot all about that puzzle. The
first story was called "The Mirage Warrior" and told of a great
hero who had the task of destroying a monster created by an
evil wizard. The creature lived within a maze-like castle and
the hero had to find his way in using only his wits and his
sword . . . and something more which was left tantalizingly

vague. At each stage of his journey he was faced with increasingly ferocious adversaries—a two-headed lion, a giant armor-plated scorpion, a hideous reptilian abomination which spat acid, and so on. As he overcame each one they disappeared into nothingness, returning to the malignant imagination that had spawned them. He had been dueling mirages.

Mark read avidly but with a growing sense of unease. He couldn't shake the feeling that he had already read this story, yet he knew he had never seen the book before. All the outlandish monsters were oddly familiar and when the hero strode into the castle's central courtyard and confronted the real monster, Mark nearly cried out aloud.

He had been here before! He knew what would happen! He was the hero!

Am I going mad? he thought.

He shut the book with a snap that raised another cloud of dust. Perspiration sprang out of every pore. He closed his eyes but it was no good. The story kept on telling itself in his mind, like a nightmare from which he could not wake.

Mark had always loved stories, for they gave him all the adventure and excitement he could want without the need to suffer any danger or discomfort. He could be plodding through icy wastes pursued by white wolves and yet still be in a soft fireside chair with Longfur curled on his lap. This was different! He had actually climbed the castle walls, felt the weight of his sword, and grown weary of illusory battles.

And he had seen the dragon.

"Good grief, Mark. What is the matter?"

A gentle hand touched his arm and he cried out in pain.

"It's all right. Look, it's me, Koria. Open your eyes."

Mark opened his eyes and came back to the world. His mouth was full of ashes and his throat burned. He coughed painfully.

"Brandel. Get some water. Go on!"

Heavy footsteps retreated, returned. Mark drank gratefully, feeling relieved but still scared. Was the nightmare really over? He looked down at the book, resting innocently in his lap, and shuddered.

"What happened? Are you feeling better now?" Koria was kneeling in front of his chair, her concern plain on her face.

"Yes. I'm all right now. I don't know what happened. I must have fallen asleep."

Mark glanced at the book again. Koria saw.

"I don't know why Ferragamo gives you these horrid things to read," she said disapprovingly. "Let me take that."

She leaned over and picked it up. Mark was grateful to see it go, then felt a perverse desire to have it back again. He reached out and caught hold of the binding. Surprised, Koria half let go and the book fell open.

A thin piece of parchment, smaller than an ordinary page, fell out and fluttered into Mark's lap. He picked it up, feeling suddenly calm, the book forgotten.

"What is it?" said Brandel indifferently.

"I don't know. It looks like some sort of verse. It's very old. The parchment's brittle and the writing is tiny."

"Read it to us then."

"Mark, wait. At least until Ferragamo's here," said Koria. "Eric's gone to find him." She was obviously worried.

Mark smiled and said, "It's all right, Koria. This isn't like the book. It's just a poem."

"Well, read it then," said Brandel, sitting down at the table.

Mark cleared his throat and read:

> *"From the sea, peril.*
> *From the sea, safety."*

"That doesn't make any sense," said Brandel.

> *"From the parts, the whole.*
> *From the whole, strength."*

"Is it all like that? It's not much of a poem, is it."

"No. The rest is in two longer verses. And it's in the future tense—"

"Spare us the grammar," muttered Brandel.

"—as if it were some sort of prophecy," said Mark excitedly. He read on:

> *"Arkon's heir, first named and last,*
> *Must seize his time, else time shall sleep.*
> *Arkon's blade shall gather strength*
> *From all around at journey's end."*

"It doesn't even rhyme," said Brandel. "And who is this Arkon fellow?"

"You never listened to any of our lessons, did you," said Mark. "Arkon was the first king of Ark. He gave his name to the island. Our ancient ancestor."

"All right, swot. It still doesn't make any sense to me. Is the last verse any better?"

> *When vengeance screams, no human*
> *sound . . .*

"The next line isn't very clear. The parchment's cracked where it was folded, but I think it says:

> *Iron fire sheds light of Arkon's staff . . .*

"Or it might be *on Arkon's staff*. Then it goes on:

> *Two that are one call judgment down,*
> *One that will reign shall strike alone.*
> *When beauty fades and time awakes,*
> *Then fates decide, and battle cease."*

"I think I can live without prophecies," said Brandel. "What a waste of time."

As he was speaking, the front door was flung open and Eric burst in. "I've found him," he panted. "He's just coming."

Looking at Mark, he added, "Are you all right now? You did look queer."

Momentarily Mark was back in the storybook castle but before he had a chance to answer, Ferragamo came in, closely followed by Longfur and Fontaine.

"What's going on here?" demanded the wizard, looking round.

"Mark had some sort of nightmare but he seems to have recovered now," said Koria. Her expression said rather more.

"Never mind that now," said Mark. "I've found an ancient prophecy. What does it mean, Ferragamo? And how long have you had it hidden away in this book?"

With a feeling of dread in the pit of his stomach, the wizard walked over to the boy and took the yellowing piece of parchment from his hands. He scanned the lines, frowning.

"Can you work it out?" asked Mark, standing to look over Ferragamo's shoulder. "It seems to be about us." *Arkon's heir?* he thought. "Or Eric at least," he added.

"Nonsense!" Ferragamo snapped. "I'm sure it's nothing of the sort—just some old scribbling." He turned the paper over in his hands. "Humph. Just as I thought. There's some more doodling on the back." His eyes narrowed.

At the sound of his name Eric had regained his interest in the proceedings.

"Let me see that," he said. "If it's about me, I want to know about it."

Ferragamo ignored him. "Now this is more interesting," he said. "It's a recipe. Sounds quite tasty."

Brandel's ears picked up. "It would certainly be more useful than the rubbish on the other side," he said.

"But what about the prophecy?" said Mark peevishly.

"Yes," said Eric. "Let me see."

Ferragamo handed the parchment to Koria who read through the recipe. As she did so Eric went into a series of convoluted positions to try to read the other side from below.

Fontaine regarded them all with disdain bordering on disbelief.

"Arkon's heir, first named and last," cried Eric triumphantly. "That's me!"

Ferragamo groaned.

Chapter 3

The afternoon was spent discussing Mark's find. Ferragamo had reluctantly admitted that it did look like a prophecy of some sort, but, with no indication of who the author was or when it had been written, he was still inclined not to treat it too seriously. Mark and Eric, however, were eager for their different reasons to interpret the verse, and the wizard was forced to join in if only to keep a check on their wilder speculations. Fontaine and Koria were busy elsewhere and Brandel had already decided that it was a waste of time and took no part in the arguments, apart from an occasional sarcastic comment.

"All right. All right. If you persist in this foolishness, I'll go through the verse with you," said Ferragamo. "But don't expect anything definite. We don't even know what our anonymous poet was writing about. It could be something that's already happened or that is still centuries in the future."

"But then why did I find it now? It must have been there for ages. Maybe I was *meant* to find it now."

"Mark, that's absurd. That book has been here for centuries. It was old when I read it as a boy. And by the look of it the parchment could be even older. Lots of people could have found it in that time."

"Then why was it still hidden? And why didn't you find it?"

"Enough of these questions. Do you want to go through it or not?"

"Yes," said Eric, "especially the bit about Arkon's heir."

"We will start at the beginning," said Ferragamo in schoolmasterly tones. Gently he smoothed the parchment out on the table.

"The first two lines are a complete contradiction, aren't they," said Mark.

"Not necessarily. It's a riddle. Quite a common way of putting a message in code so that only the intended receiver understands." The wizard glanced meaningfully at Mark.

"Do *you* know what it means?"

"No."

"Why are you wasting time with these bits," said Eric, "when the interesting things are in the verses?"

Ferragamo ignored him, and read:

> *"From the parts, the whole.*
> *From the whole, strength."*

"Parts of what?" asked Eric.

"I suspect if we knew that, this whole thing would make more sense."

"Is it part of the same riddle? Or another one?" asked Mark.

"It sounds more like an instruction to me," mused Ferragamo, "or a proverb, perhaps."

"Like 'Many hands make light broth,'" said Eric.

"Something like that."

"People sometimes say that a thing is more than the sum of its parts," said Mark. "Do you think that's what is meant here?"

"Oh, come on," said Eric. "Let's get on with the next bit.

"*Arkon's heir, first named and last,*" he quoted. "That must mean me."

"What makes you think that?" inquired the wizard.

"Well, Arkon was my ancestor, so I'm his heir. I should be king now. I was the first named of us." He indicated Mark and Brandel. "And I am the last in the line of direct descendants at the moment," he concluded smugly.

"Very good, Eric," said Ferragamo and then, as Eric

grinned in surprise, he added, "There's just one problem. At the moment you are, in some senses, Arkon's heir but we can't assume that the writer had you in mind when he wrote this. If your father had found this he could have assumed it meant him and so could any number of others."

"Yes, but they didn't find it. I did. Or at least Mark did."

"That's right, and Mark is Arkon's heir too. So is Brandel, come to that."

"But I come before them," said Eric indignantly.

"And I wouldn't be too sure about *first named and last* either. It sounds too much like another riddle to me," Ferragamo went on. "Your explanation is much too simple."

"I still think it means me."

"Do you? And I suppose you think the next line means you should set off straightaway to regain your throne."

"Yes," said Eric. "*Must seize his time, else time shall sleep.* That's pretty clear, isn't it. If I wait too long I won't get a chance."

"That's a curious phrase—*time shall sleep,*" said Mark.

"Yes it is, and that's why it shouldn't be trusted."

"Oh come on!" exclaimed Eric. "This is poetry."

"I see," said Ferragamo, "so you can take it literally when it suits you and say it's poetic license when it doesn't."

"Well, at least *I'm* trying to work it out," said Eric peevishly. "All *you* seem to be saying is that we can't tell what it means."

"Precisely. Until we can put it in context."

"But the next bit does that. *Arkon's blade*—that's got to be the old sword father wanted me to have; *shall gather strength from all around at journey's end*—that means that the people will rally round me and the sword as the rightful heir; and *journey's end* must be Starhill. Don't you see? By the time I get there I'll have all Ark behind me!"

Ferragamo grimaced. "Even if it *is* your sword—and we have no proof of that, though it is somewhat special, I will admit—and you *are* the one destined to wield it, there are lots of other possible interpretations. *Journey's end,* for instance, could mean death.

"As this is poetry," he added archly.

"Do you think the *strength* is the same as in the second couplet?" Mark asked.

"Who knows?" said the wizard. "But I don't see how a sword can gather parts of anything to make a whole. Rather the opposite." He paused. "The last verse is full of conundrums like that."

"What?" said Eric.

Koria interrupted proceedings at this point by putting a piece of paper in front of Ferragamo and pointing at it. "Have you got any of this?" she asked.

"Good Heavens, no," the wizard replied. "Wait a minute, though." He disappeared into his study and a little while later reappeared with a glass jar, tightly stoppered, containing a small quantity of a fine brown powder.

"This is very valuable," he said. "What do you want . . ." He handed the jar to Koria, having apparently answered his own half-stated question.

"I don't need much," she said.

"Be careful with it."

"I will." Koria returned to the kitchen.

"Now, where were we?" said the wizard, sitting down again.

"The last verse."

Ferragamo read:

> "*When vengeance screams, no human sound,*
> *Iron fire sheds light of Arkon's staff.*
> *Two that are one call judgment down,*
> *One that will reign shall strike alone.*
> *When beauty fades, and time awakes,*
> *Then fates decide, and battle cease.*"

"Well, the first two lines sound like a description of the clash and sparks from a sword in battle. That would make sense, wouldn't it?"

Before Ferragamo could answer, another idea dawned on Eric. "*Two that are one*—that's me and Fontaine! We're as good as married—"

"I wouldn't be too sure of that," said Brandel from the corner of the room. Eric ignored the interruption.

"—so we're two that are as one. It all fits!"

"But what about this bit about striking *alone*?" said Mark. "That contradicts what you said about gathering people around you as you go."

"I'm glad to see one of you is thinking," said the wizard. Eric said nothing.

They had argued backward and forward for some time after that. Shill arrived and Eric had tried to draw him into the discussion but, much to Ferragamo's relief, Shill had said that he was a soldier not an oracle and that word-twisting was no skill of his. Fontaine had reappeared and had been rather alarmed by Eric's theories.

Ferragamo tried to persuade the eldest prince to reason.

"Eric, believe me, I don't think you should go rushing straight off. If you'd been around as long as I have, you would realize that there is *always* more to something like this than first meets the eye. We should spend more time in trying to work out the real meaning behind this, instead of your taking it at face value and plunging headlong into great danger."

Eric didn't look convinced. In fact, he looked positively sullen (as did Fontaine, who felt no great delight at the prospect of returning to Starhill).

"I don't care! I still think it means me, and if I dawdle now, I may lose the chance of gaining the throne—for good!"

Everyone began to speak at once, drowning Eric's further attempts at justification.

"Eric, you really should listen to Ferragamo. He knows what he's talking about," said Mark earnestly.

"I seem to have missed something here. What's going on?" Brandel demanded.

"I'm not going!" shrilled Fontaine. "I've had enough! I'm tired, and fed up, and don't want to go anywhere!"

Ferragamo's contribution was a long-suffering sigh, halted by Koria's requesting that they all simmer down, conserve their energy (this last with a broad wink at Ferragamo), and eat dinner.

In spite of their disagreements and some heated tempers, they all set to and ate heartily. Eric especially had a really good meal, secretly determining that this would be one of his last with the group.

Now, as Brandel cleared up the remnants of the cold meat and salads, Koria smiled at Ferragamo and went out into the kitchen.

Spicy baking aromas wafted out. Appetites were rekindled—except Brandel's, which had never gone out in the first place.

Koria returned carrying a large, flat circular cake which was obviously responsible for the delicious smell.

"This is something new," she said. "I hope you like it."

"I'll have a large slice," said Brandel quickly.

"You will not," said Ferragamo firmly, taking Koria's hand and guiding her knife so that it cut a tiny sliver. "No more than that for anybody," he said to the surprised cook.

"But that's no more than a mouthful!"

"It is more than enough. Just eat it and see!"

They waited politely until everyone had a piece of the cake in front of them, then...

Fontaine nibbled suspiciously; Mark, Shill, Ferragamo, and Koria took small forkfuls; Eric took a healthy mouthful and Brandel stuffed the entire slice into his cavernous maw. For a few seconds there was silence, then...

Brandel's eyes rolled heavenward in bliss. Eric swallowed and quickly refilled his mouth. The others all made appreciative noises.

"Koria, this is delicious!"

"How do you do it?"

"The best thing I've tasted for years."

"More please."

This last, inevitably, from Brandel.

Koria looked at Ferragamo, who shook his head.

"No more for now," he said. "We'll save it for another time."

"But why? We've hardly eaten a third of it."

"There's plenty more."

"What's so special about it anyway?"

Ferragamo held up his hands. "Enough!" he said. "If you'll listen a minute, I'll explain." He paused until he had everyone's attention.

"This, unless I am very much mistaken, is the result of the recipe on the back of your so-called prophecy, Mark." Koria nodded agreement. "And it contains a rather special ingredient."

"The brown powder you fetched from your study!" guessed Mark.

"That's right."

"All the other ingredients are common enough," said Koria. "Flour, butter, and such like. I thought it might be interesting to test the recipe so I copied it before you all got involved in the nonsense on the other side."

"So what is this mysterious ingredient then?" asked Eric.

"Moonberries."

"But they're poisonous!" exclaimed Mark.

"Not exactly," said the wizard.

"They are!" said Brandel. "I remember being told never to pick any from the tree at home."

"I think you'd better explain," said Koria. Everyone looked at Ferragamo expectantly.

"I can see I'll get no peace until I do," he said. "It's quite a long story, and I'm not going to repeat anything, so listen carefully." He paused, gathering his thoughts.

"First of all, moonberries are not poisonous as such, just enormously powerful. Used incorrectly they can do as much damage as a poison fruit. That's why, quite rightly, you were told to leave them alone. I'm sure you were too, Fontaine."

"Yes," the princess replied. "Mother used to scare us with stories of what had happened to anyone who ate any fruit from our tree."

"You have one too, then," said Mark.

"Yes. All the major islands do," said Ferragamo. "I'll come to that in a minute.

"There is an enormous amount of wizard's lore concerning moonberries, though much has been lost, but I'll keep it simple. It has been known for a very long time that in the correct doses moonberries can have surprising and beneficial effects in dealing with some diseases. That's why I had some dried and powdered in my store. The results are unpredictable however, and because of that it hasn't been used much in recent years. It is also well-known that, if abused, moonberries will have the reverse effect, causing fits, visions, even madness and, in extreme cases, death. Over the centuries, many have tried to harness their magic in the hope of gaining miraculous powers. All have come to unfortunate ends. Hence your mother's stories, Fontaine."

"We've all heard some of those," said Eric. "Like Shalli, the hermit."

"Yes, well, some of those stories will have been embroidered in the telling over the years, but they have their basis in truth. On the other hand, there was a time when the berries were used far more frequently. I suspect the recipe you found dates from that earlier era and because of that and the fact that it uses only tiny amounts, I thought it would be safe enough to try it."

"It certainly tastes good," said Mark.

You're right there. Any chance of a bit more? You only gave me a crumb last time. Longfur looked up from beneath Mark's chair.

Ferragamo forestalled Brandel's unasked question and Longfur's private wish by announcing that, despite the small quantities, no one was going to have any more for the moment, at least until he had had a chance to gauge any effects

"But why do they have such a powerful effect?" asked Mark.

"That is another story which comes from a very long time ago. I thought you might have had enough stories like that for one day," said Ferragamo looking at the youngest prince.

Mark paled slightly but said nothing and Eric urged the wizard to tell the tale. Eric sometimes wished he had been born to a life of heroic deeds and glamorous adventures in an age of warfare and wizardry. He had never been able to read well enough to learn more of such times. If he had, he might have romanticized them less.

Ferragamo sipped his glass of water. "Very well," he said "A very long time ago, before even these islands were formed the world was ... different. Put simply, there was more magic around. Some call it the Age of Wizards, some the Golden Age. Certainly it must have been a wonder, a constantly changing world of delight. It is hard to imagine. And it is lost to us now. Whatever power created that world has long since withdrawn, leaving us only the remnants of its glory."

There was a faraway look in the wizard's eye, which said more than his words. He was silent for a moment, then he gathered himself and went on.

"What happened next, so the legends say, is that one sorcerer, unsatisfied by this teeming world, embarked on an ambitious and evil course which, unchecked, would have made him undisputed overlord of the world, and everything, and everyone in it. His plan contradicted every tenet which wizardry holds dear and, as such, it remained undiscovered for many years purely because it was so unthinkable.

"When it was discovered, it was almost too late. The sorcerer had grown enormously powerful through his corrupt schemes and the other wizards individually were no match for him. Moreover they were, by their very nature, individualists unused to acting in unison, and it was some time before

he powers ranged against the would-be despot could be
marshaled into an effective force.

"The confrontation, when it came, was cataclysmic. The
powers involved were beyond our imagining but it was a time
of great heroism as well—for men as well as wizards. There
are many tales of those who fought alongside the wizards.
They called themselves The Servants."

Mark's head jerked up at this. His eyes met Ferragamo's.

"That war, the War of the Wizards as it's generally
known, literally reshaped the world. These islands were
formed then, so it's said. Even now the magical residue of the
conflict is noticeable and can be harnessed in certain places
and through certain objects. However, in general, the world's
magical potential was greatly lessened. What can be done
now, even by the best of my colleagues, is mere child's play
compared to the exploits of those early wizards.

"Eventually the sorcerer was destroyed. He paid a heavy
price for his evil deeds, for he had himself become hideously
corrupted. His passing was not pleasant.

"Legend has it that the ancient circle where he made his
last stand was blasted by such appalling forces that, to this
day, no one can approach it. In fact, we do not even know
where it is.

"He was destroyed, as I say, but his power could not be
wholly eradicated. There are other dark places in the world
where no sensible man ventures and dread relics which are
hidden away beyond their capacity to cause harm. But these
are few and far between and pose no serious threat. Indeed,
they serve as a useful reminder to the present generation of
the folly of greed and the lust for power.

"End of sermon," he added, smiling.

"But how do the moonberries come in to this?" asked
Fontaine.

The ways of wizards are long-winded, misquoted Longfur
in Mark's mind. *She didn't expect a straightforward answer,
did she?*

"I was coming to that," said Ferragamo. "When the war
was over, the most powerful wizard of the new islands decided to try to prevent any possibility of a recurrence of such
evil. He wanted to do this in such a way that his measures
would outlast his own lifespan, and thus it was that he
created the moonberry trees. With spells which are now lost
to us, he implanted the vital laws of wizardry into the seeds

of an ordinary fruit. Then he delivered a single seed to each of the islands where it was planted in a place of honor. He appointed guardians for the trees and these became the first kings of the islands, though they weren't known by that title then.

"Quite how the trees and their fruit are supposed to act or be used to protect the purity of magic is now unclear, and has been so for many generations. At one time, if the old tales are to be believed, the fruit was eaten regularly, in a sort of ceremonial cleansing, but our knowledge and our powers have declined since then. As you know, more recent, injudicious ingestion has been more than the eaters could handle. The ancient power is still there, even if we don't know how to use it.

"And that's why we'll eat no more tonight."

Koria carried the cake out of the room. Several pairs of eyes watched its departure.

Some time later, Ferragamo made the promised revisions to the sleeping arrangements.

"Fontaine, you'll move into Eric's room. It's even more cramped, I'm afraid, but I think you'll find it more amenable. Eric, you can set up the camp bed in here, if we move the table over to one side. As long as Mark or Brandel don't step on you coming down the ladder in the morning, you should be comfortable enough."

No chance of that, thought Eric, smiling to himself.

Chapter 4

*T*hat night, while all lay asleep, including Ferragamo and Koria, who had been awake—for one reason or another—longer than the others, a stealthy figure crept into Fontaine's room, tiptoed over to her bed, and placed a hand on her mouth.

"Shush! It's me, Eric. Now don't yell, Fontaine. Everything's all right, I just don't want you waking everybody up." The princess, who had begun to struggle violently, stopped, and lay looking at her betrothed with frightened eyes.

"Eric! What's the matter?" she whispered. "What on *earth* are you doing in my room in the middle of the night?"

"It's no good, I've decided that we *must* go to Starhill. You, me, and my sword. We're going to regain the kingdom and get rid of that treacherous Parokkan. I know you don't want to come, and I can't really blame you. We might meet some danger on the way, but after all, you *are* going to be my wife, and I'm positive that once we get to the city, we'll have many supporters and will win through. And besides, what will you do if you stay behind? Spend your time having cookery lessons from Koria, listening to that wimp Mark sucking up to Ferragamo all day long, and fending off Brandel's drunken advances. You know what *he's* like—and there's a distinct shortage of feminine comforts in this village. Come with me, *please*, there's a good Fontaine," he finished, wheedlingly.

She thought for a moment, and suddenly, caught up in the sheer adventure of it, agreed, only to back down slightly when she heard that they were to leave immediately.

"But Eric, I haven't had nearly enough sleep. I'm too tired to go traipsing off now. Can't we go in the morning—and get Koria to make us a picnic?" She smiled to emphasize the joke, but it still failed to register with Eric.

"Bloody hell, woman, no! We've got to leave now, before they try to stop us. And we'll find food on the way, from a peasant cottage or whatever. How can you worry about your stomach when such great and momentous events are taking place?" Eric could be quite pompous sometimes. "Come on, up you get—and quietly. I'll be outside, with our horses. Hurry!" He left, slipping softly from the cottage to where the two horses were already saddled and waiting.

Fontaine joined him in a few moments, and the two rode quietly away, in the direction of Stane and the forest, watched only by a pair of large tawny eyes.

It didn't take Fontaine very long to change her mind about the wisdom of their venture. Not that she wanted to go back to the others—Eric had said enough to put her off *that* prospect—but nor did she especially want to trail about Ark, alone with this dim-witted, loudmouthed, and not particularly handsome prince. She hadn't expected him to be the man of her dreams; princesses didn't marry for love, after all, but you couldn't even hold a decent conversation with him!

Of his brothers, Brandel, or Brandy as he was sometimes, and aptly, called, was even worse. Fat and greasy to look at, he was lecherous and lazy, and Fontaine found him quite obnoxious. She pitied the poor woman who'd have to marry *him*. Eric might be stupid, but at least he wasn't too unpleasant.

Mark, she thought, was a bit of a weakling. Not bad looking, though, and more of a dreamer than the other two. Fontaine had a sneaking liking for him, but would never think of letting anyone, especially Mark himself, know this. She was sure he didn't even know she existed, unless her sharp tongue reminded him. Fontaine worried about her tongue, sometimes. It seemed to run away with her, and she would say the cruelest things, without really meaning to. Her brother called her a shrew, which upset her.

And that was another thing. She got upset so quickly these days. Admittedly, things hadn't been easy for her—leaving Heald and her family to move to the palace of her fiancé, then that dreadful battle with the murder of the old King (she'd grown quite fond of him), and their frantic and frightening escape to Home. But *honestly,* if anybody so much as looked at her the wrong way, she wanted to cry. And did sometimes, trying not to let anyone see. Anyway, they were all so busy thinking about themselves, that they wouldn't notice a red-nosed girl, even if it *did* clash with what she privately thought of as her luxuriant auburn hair. Koria was all right, though. Fontaine had even noticed an occasional sympathetic glance in her direction from the older woman. She'd get no sympathy from Eric, that was certain, so she needn't bother being nice to him! And with that thought:

"Are you *quite* sure this is wise, Eric? After all, you are only one man—brave and strong though you are—to face all the might of Parokkan's armies, and who knows what other dangers, before we even get to Starhill. Not that I'm doubting your abilities, of course, but I do just wonder—"

"Shut up, Fontaine!" Eric snapped. "Of *course* I know what I'm doing. The prophecy says so. And it also says that you have to be there, too. Why else do you think I'd have brought you along? Not"—he placated her hurriedly, as she glared at him and drew a long breath—"that I didn't want you along for your own sake, too. I thought, as we're to be married eventually, that this would be a good opportunity to get to know each other. After all, we hadn't seen very much of each other before all this trouble began, and Father was killed. Hardly an auspicious start, eh?"

He was pleased to see the black frown melt away, though it was only replaced with a cynical glance, before Fontaine turned her attention back to their path.

"Huh!" was all she said. The noble prince breathed a sigh of relief.

After they had been riding for some time, they reached the town of Stane. This large town was situated just south of the large forest they would have to cross, and they took the opportunity of resting their horses for a while. Fontaine's horse, Hero, seemed especially weary, as did the princess.

After they had eaten a good meal, and walked around to stretch their legs, Eric and Fontaine resumed their journey. This, too, was the cause of some bickering.

"Can't we spend the night here, Eric, instead of wandering through that huge forest in the dark? I don't want to sleep under a tree."

"Because it's still early, the others are probably hot on our trail, and the sooner we get on our way to Starhill, the sooner the prophecy will be fulfilled. This is a serious quest, Fontaine, not a holiday. We must move *quickly*."

"Huh!"

As the light failed and the forest seemed to draw in on either side of the trail, even Eric's dull brain began to have some doubts about his quest. Fontaine's shrewish tongue had ceased its complaining some hours ago but this only afforded a small relief, as he hadn't been listening anyway. They had only taken on minimal supplies in Stane, and a makeshift shelter amid the gloomy, rustling trees was hardly an attractive prospect.

Behind him, Fontaine said, "Eric, I think—" but before she could continue, five men appeared as if from nowhere and ranged across the path, blocking their way. They pulled their horses to a halt.

Stepping forward, the tall man in the center said slowly, "Well, what have we here?"

Taking the question literally was natural to Eric. Here, he sensed, his quest was beginning in earnest.

"My name is Eric Ather-son. My purpose is to set right a great wrong and claim the throne of Ark for Arkon's House again. Prophecy guides my course and magic guides my hand."

He sat back in his saddle, feeling rather pleased with his speech.

"Since we have reached the stage for introductions, my lord," replied the tall man, "my name is Durc Warthog-son." The men behind him shook silently but the mocking tone was lost on Eric.

"Tell me, Eric Ather-son, why is so great a task not undertaken by an army? Have you misplaced your followers?"

"An ancient wizard's verse foretells my journey and of the

people gathering around me. My army will grow as I travel. Like one of the old heroic tales, really."

"And I suppose you are going to go on to tell us now that the sword at your side has magical properties, that the scrawny bit behind you is a princess"—Fontaine drew in a hasty breath but wisely held her tongue—"and as a consequence you will claim to need good fighting men like us and suggest we join your noble quest." Durc's followers were now laughing aloud.

"Er... yes," said Eric. Somehow this wasn't going quite the way it was supposed to. He needed to regain the initiative. His left leg twitched as the horse moved nervously under him and at once he knew that the sword was sending him a sign. His hand went to its hilt and into the sudden silence he cried, "Arkon's blade shall gather strength!" In his imagination the sword pulsed with clean blue light, perhaps with runes glowing along its length.

"Eric, I wouldn't do that if I were—" Again Fontaine failed to finish a sentence, something which would have amazed the Healdean court, who were used to several more following in rapid succession. This time however even her quick tongue was not quick enough.

Eric drew the sword with a flourish and held it high. He just had time to notice sadly that the blade was only ordinary steel, though it did flash rather well in the last rays of the setting sun, before he became aware of Fontaine screaming. He looked down from the sword and saw, much to his amazement, five or six arrows sticking from his torso. He was still wearing a look of wide-eyed puzzlement when he hit the ground a few moments later, quite dead.

An owl hooted dismally as several other rough-looking characters appeared from the trees, some carrying bows, the others spears or knives. One of them caught and quietened Eric's horse and Durc caught at Hero's bridle to forestall any foolish thoughts of escape.

"Well, princess, would you care to accompany me to my court? Our evening banquet awaits your pleasure."

"Jani's tree-bark stew, a banquet? That's a good one."

Several of the men laughed. Others were investigating saddlebags, but Durc continued to look at Fontaine, a small frown creasing his forehead. "You'll have to walk," he said, dropping all pretense of courtesy. "Zunic, get her off the horse."

Fontaine switched her stare to the man who approached. Putting as much ice in her voice as she could muster, which, given her natural ability and court training, would have frozen over a medium-sized lake, she hissed, "If you so much as touch me you will regret it for the rest of time."

Zunic hesitated and other voices called, "Afraid of the she-cat, Zunic?"

"If what's inside those riding breeches is as poxed as her face, there's some ways of touching you would regret!"

As the men led a subdued Fontaine away (she had decided that a quiet demeanor might be a good idea, for the moment at least), Ferragamo's owl flew swiftly away, back to Home and his master.

———————————

At Home that morning, Koria had discovered that Fontaine was not in her room when she went to awaken her for breakfast. At first she was not unduly worried, thinking that the young girl may have gone for an early morning walk, though she was a little surprised. Fontaine was not one to relish extra exercise.

The worry began to grow when Mark came to report that he couldn't find Eric. *Probably off somewhere practicing his sword-play,* Longfur said to Mark. *I mean, he's got all those muscles to build up, hasn't he?*

Oh, shut up, Longfur, Mark replied irritably. The youngest of the princes was of a singularly nervous and timid disposition and this disruption to his precarious new routine had disturbed him.

As the morning progressed and Ferragamo noted that Owl was missing, the facts began to dawn on the group. Reluctant at first to share their forebodings with the soldiers, they kept to themselves in the cottage.

By lunchtime—a meal which nobody except Brandel felt like eating—Ferragamo was vituperative.

"That stupid blockhead of an idiot prince! He's gone, following some idiot idea in that brain of his—if you can call that maggot-infested organ he's got a brain! I tell you, he's tried my patience too far this time. He deserves anything that happens to him. Stupid, stupid . . . !" And on he raved, almost spitting out the last words.

Koria, disturbed at the mood Ferragamo was creating, moved over to him and put a reassuring arm around his waist.

"Hush, love. It may not be as bad as it seems. They've taken no supplies, and will probably come to their senses very soon and turn back. And at least we believe Owl to be with them."

Her soothing words masked a genuine concern for the missing pair, and especially for Fontaine. The young princess, despite any impression her unruly temper might give, had been delicately reared, and would not take too easily to this wild adventure of Eric's. At least on their long journey from Starhill she had been part of a large, and therefore relatively comforting, group. How would she fare with only Eric beside her? And how, thought Koria ruefully, would *he* fare with *her*?

Mark had been made extremely uncomfortable by Ferragamo's outburst, and hesitated to say what he felt should be said.

"Er, shouldn't we, um, sort of go after them? Ferragamo? They might get hurt, or something..."

While saying this, and realizing that a search party should be mounted, his natural timidity preferred that he remain behind. He wasn't a coward, he thought, just a bit frightened of all that had happened. *After all*, he thought to his cat. *I'm not a hulking great soldier like Eric. I'm more the scholarly type.*

You're a great wet ninny, was Longfur's response.

Perhaps Brandy would go, with Ferragamo? Mark put this idea forward.

"No chance," said Brandel. "Come on, let's be sensible about this. After all, we don't know which direction they've gone in; they could be anywhere by now. How are we supposed to try and find them? Got any bright ideas, Ferragamo?"

They looked questioningly at the wizard. Instead of the wise counsel they had come to rely on from a man of his years and knowledge, all they got were more insulting remarks, aimed mostly at Eric, with a few choice epithets for Heald's princess.

"How could the silly bitch have let him go? *She* should have had more sense, and why, for Ark's sake, did she agree to go with him? Unless he forced her... no, she'd have kicked up enough rumpus to awaken all of Home!"

He stopped suddenly and looked first thoughtful, then pained.

"Oh, you blasted old fool! *Why* didn't you take any notice?" he groaned.

"Any notice of what?" asked Koria, looking puzzled. "You didn't hear anything, did you? If you had, I would have heard it too, and we slept soundly all night."

"No, I didn't *hear* anything, dammit, I *dreamt* it! Two figures, leaving the cottage on horseback in the middle of the night, and a sense of urgency. That must have been Owl trying to tell me, and I'm such a doddering, senile, sleepy old excuse for a wizard that I didn't heed his warning and wake up!"

Following this latest train of thought, Ferragamo looked even more upset. Muttering darkly to himself, he shrugged off Koria's arm and stomped out of the cottage.

"What's eating him?" asked Brandel. "Where's he gone?"

"I don't know," sighed Koria. "We'd all better leave him alone for a while. Especially me." She looked miserable.

"Why especially you?" Mark asked her, dismayed to see tears in her eyes.

"Because it's my fault that he was so tired, and slept so soundly!"

Brandel sniggered, and Mark, fierce for once, told him roundly to shut up and clear off. This he did, and it was a despondent pair that remained.

Mark, you amaze me sometimes, you really do. Longfur's exasperated comment jerked the young boy from his dejection. *Though I suppose you're not the only idiot around here today. Look, we're pretty sure that Owl has followed your brilliant brother and the ferocious Fontaine. So, naturally, he's going to come back and let us know where they've gone. And soon, too. Do you imagine he'd leave Ferragamo in this state? Of course not. He'll come winging back, put his master out of his misery, and then we can start to clear up this mess.*

You're right, Longfur. Mark cast a grateful glance at his furry friend. *I hate having to wait like this, though. I wish we knew what was happening. Oh why doesn't Owl hurry?*

More anxious hours passed, with the tempers of Koria, Brandel, and Mark growing shorter as the day progressed.

Eventually, the wizard's feathered companion returned to the cottage, arriving exactly at the same time as a breathless Ferragamo. Owl's news was as bad as it could be. After the first moment of communication, the wizard's face turned ashen.

"Ferragamo! What is it? What's happened? Why are you looking like that?"

Taking Koria's hand, he gently made her sit down, then placed a hand protectively on her shoulder and looked at the two princes. Mark moved close to Brandel, as if he was aware of the terrible news to come.

"Eric is dead."

There was a stunned silence, then...

"No!" Mark shouted. "It's not true! Oh Ferragamo, *please* say it isn't true—he *can't* be dead. Not Eric!"

"I'm so sorry, Mark, Brandel, but it *is* true. Owl tells me that Eric and Fontaine were on the forest trail to Ashwicken when they were waylaid by outlaws. Eric drew his sword, and they killed him. They've abducted Fontaine."

"Oh no! That poor child! What will they do to her?" Koria paled at the thought.

After a few moments, Ferragamo pulled himself together. "We know roughly where she is. The forest is large and wild but for the moment, at least, she's alive, and we must find her and bring her back to safety. We must go and search for her."

"But Ferragamo, the forest is *immense*," Mark said. "Where are we going to start? She could be absolutely anywhere."

"I've got an idea," muttered the wizard. "Brandy, go and tell the others what's happened and fetch them back here. We must organize something. In the meantime..." His voice trailed off as he went into his library and began poking about on his bookshelves.

"There's *something* here. I'd swear to it. Now, I tried it last year...where did I put it? Oh, where *is* that pesky book...?"

Chapter 5

$\mathscr{A}$t Starhill Castle, Amarino was enjoying a rare moment of rest, and of thoughtfulness. Of late, she had spent most of her time rushing back and forth, both fulfilling her duties as new chatelaine of the castle, and as Parokkan's helpmate, giving him advice (when requested, naturally) and subtle hints on the best way to handle his new authority. Which was just how she wanted it, of course, but occasionally, she had to admit, it was good to get away from it all, to conserve her energy and work out the best way of harnessing other people's to her benefit.

This afternoon, though, her mind would not stick to her plans, but instead wandered back to the day when she and Parokkan, with the late king's army, had taken over the city of Starhill and its castle.

It hadn't taken too much persuasion for Parokkan to come round to the idea that Ark needed a new ruler (and that he would fit the bill perfectly). After all, they had been together for some time and Amarino knew the best way of preparing her manly captain for new ideas. Really, he had been quite useful practice for her.

Of course, getting Parokkan to agree, and then bringing the army round to their way of thinking, hadn't been the end of it. King Ather and his three sons were not about to give up their rule too easily. At the beginning of the fighting they had been supported by some of the Castle Guard and servants, and had held off the forces massed against them for some time. Eventually, though, it had proved too much for them. After much bloody fighting and many deaths, Ather and his family, together with the wizard Ferragamo, and the terrified Fontaine, had been forced into the tree-yard, and eventually, exactly as Amarino had intended, into Starbright Tower. From there they had escaped, all except Ather who had insisted on making an heroic fool of himself.

Amarino smiled to herself. In retrospect it could not have worked out any better.

She was in control now, and would remain so for as long as she wished. With Parokkan as the new ruler, the army firmly behind him, and the people of Starhill acquiescent, the future looked rosy.

As she had hoped, the people of Ark's capital had very quickly realized where the future power lay and had come round to her way of thinking. After an initial short-lived rebellion, a feeling of lethargy had overcome them, and they submitted to the army's demands for free passage. Any battles had been of short duration, and soon the people didn't bother fighting at all; they just returned to their homes, quiet, subdued, but not unhappy.

Amarino had plans for the people, secret plans that she shared with no one, not even Parokkan, who shared all with her.

A surge of energy rushed through her. She got to her feet, took one swift and satisfied look around her, and went to call her maidservants to prepare her for the evening's festivities. Anna filed in with the others and waited meekly for her instructions.

Some time later, when she was alone again, Amarino looked about her and smiled contentedly. Indeed, the lady had cause to be happy with her surroundings. In King Ather's day, Starhill Castle had been well appointed, but functional rather than luxurious. Ather had preferred to expend resources on building ships for trade, constructing better roads and bridges and maintaining Starhill, as well as spending money in the country areas, encouraging his farmers to experiment with new ideas and methods.

Parokkan and Amarino wanted this to continue, but they wanted it *all*—soft and beautiful clothing, luxurious furnishings, scented water for bathing, and the best table to be spread before anyone. Amarino, recruiting more and more of the idle townsfolk, was seeing their dream of power and magnificence begin to come true.

The banquet that evening was being held in honor of Hoban, Ambassador from Peven, an eastern island. As well as putting forward his home-isle's desire for a peaceful treaty with Ark's new rulers, Hoban very much hoped to be able to find out for himself how the people of Ark were taking to the new régime. So far, he had been disappointed. On arrival at Grayrock Harbor, he had found the folk there sullen and quiet, not inclined to talk about recent events and present rulers; at Starhill, he had been greeted briefly by Parokkan and Amarino, the pair arm-in-arm, before being borne away to his apartment by a not at all forthcoming steward.

His chambers were well-furnished, clean and warm, and a servant was waiting there for him, ready to supply him with respectful but *quiet* service. Hoban sighed, and started to prepare himself for the evening, which was to be a social affair only, with any political talk to be saved for the morrow.

Dinner that evening was held in the grand and newly sumptuous dining hall of Starhill Castle, and the table positively groaned under the weight of the food laid upon it. Hoban was most impressed: he could not remember fare such as this in King Ather's day.

Parokkan and Amarino were in fine fettle that evening; Amarino especially kept their visitor amused by her wit and beguiled by her beauty. At first, discussion was as general as it could be, given their circumstances, but eventually talk turned, as it must, to the recent battle and their takeover of Ark.

"Forgive me for asking this, Parokkan, but what made you so sure that you would win both the army and the people of Starhill over to your side?"

There was a slightly uncomfortable pause. Parokkan sat, apparently deep in thought, for a few moments while Amarino fidgeted slightly at his side.

"It was just the right thing to do. I had felt for some time that Ather was losing his touch as supreme ruler of Ark; trade was slowing between us and other islands, our farming methods were becoming too hidebound, not enough new building was taking place. Really, Ark was beginning to go to rack and ruin! And Ather's sons were all useless."

Hoban was more than a little surprised to hear this and had difficulty controlling his expression. On all his previous visits to Ather's island, he had felt the king to have all well under control and flourishing, and the princes had seemed promising young men. He said nothing to contradict his host, however, feeling that this would be less than politic, and changed the subject instead.

"My lord. It has been felt for some time on Peven that things may be seriously amiss on the island of Brogar. Of course, it is some fair distance from *my* home, but trading has completely ceased. We have even some merchants who have not returned home from their last voyage. Naturally, this is most distressing and, well, I wondered whether Ark, as a nearer neighbor, may have heard anything, or have any advice to offer from your own experience with Brogar."

On finishing this request, Hoban looked expectantly at Parokkan who, to his surprise, was looking completely blank.

"Brogar? Er, yes, we seem, er..." Parokkan's voice trailed off.

"What my lord is trying to say, Ambassador Hoban," came the crisp but nonetheless gentle tones of the lovely Amarino, "is that Ark too has lost all contact with Brogar, and we are *most* puzzled as to the reason. We also have a number of missing merchants and ships, but it was not deemed by the late king to be a good idea to send more on a rescue mission for fear he lost them also. We see no reason to disagree with this policy. It is a problem, I must admit, but I fear we are at a loss as to how to deal with it. Parokkan feels that we must give the situation time, and await events. Is that not so, my lord?"

Parokkan seemed firmer of purpose now. "Quite right. We must let time be our judge in this matter. Hoban, would you care for some more of this excellent wine?"

Hoban felt, correctly, that his hosts believed enough to have been said on the matter. *He* did not feel happy though. Something was not quite right, something in Amarino's attitude, perhaps? She had seemed—indeed, they had both seemed—to brush off the subject of Brogar as if it were of little import. This was surely not the case. However, Hoban bowed to the unspoken wish of his hosts and did not pursue the matter any further. Conversation returned to more general topics—the fine summer weather, Hoban's family, his crossing from Peven, and his comments on the increased state of repair of Starhill Castle. At the back of the Ambassador's mind, though, a small worry nagged him, like a dog with a bone.

"You really are the most enchanting creature, Amarino. Our good Ambassador couldn't keep his eyes off you all evening. Nor could I."

"What absolute nonsense! Still, you are sweet to say so, darling Parokkan. I think the evening went very well, don't you? The food was more than passable and the entertainments really very good."

"Yes, all was excellent. Darling, I am constantly surprised by the way you have taken over your role as chatelaine of Starhill Castle. It is so different to anything you can have known before, and yet you have no problems, or seem to have none. I had half expected there to be some opposition to our wants, and to your, *command*, shall we say?" He chuckled. "But really, the castle servants, and those you are beginning to hire from the city, seem only too willing to do as you request. How do you do it? Ah, you must have beguiled them, sweet, as you have beguiled me." With this, Parokkan pulled Amarino onto his lap, where she snuggled down comfortably, entwining her arms around her soldier's neck.

"Beguiled, my love? Don't be silly." The tone of her voice belied the chiding words. "People who are approached with reasonable requests and the promise of adequate compensation will usually do as they are asked."

"Where's my compensation then?" Parokkan asked huskily, and kissed her throat.

Next morning, a tired but happy-looking Parokkan strode from the Royal Quarters to the audience chamber where he was to meet again with Hoban, this time on a more formal footing, to discuss matters between their two islands. Relations between Peven and Ark had always been good, and

both men were anxious that they should remain so. Hoban
was quite amazed to find Parokkan more affable than he had
been the previous evening, but less decisive. On first appearance, the new ruler of Ark had seemed to Hoban to be almost
pompous, in what must be a taxing new role for him.
However, this morning, as soon as their discussion had
turned to specific matters, he became much more pleasant in
his manner, but less likely to agree to any of Hoban's requests, or even to discuss anything in great depth.

After they had floundered on in this manner for some
time, the door opened, and Amarino stood there. The sun
was quite strong that morning and came flooding in through
the windows of the upper landing, providing a golden frame
for her beauty as she stood in the doorway. Hoban tore his
eyes away from her with difficulty, and got to his feet, then
looked in some surprise at Parokkan. He had remained
sitting, gazing at his beloved with an expression of the utmost
fatuousness. A small frown, quickly hidden, crossed the lady's
face, and Parokkan immediately leapt to his feet and, crossing
the room, took her by the hand, leading her to where Hoban
stood.

"Welcome, my dear. Come and join us."

"Are you sure, Parokkan? I would not wish to interrupt
your discussions." Her voice was gentle.

"You are more than welcome," said Hoban. "If you *are* a
distraction to us, you are a most lovely one."

"You flatter me, Ambassador," said Amarino, blushing
prettily at his compliment. "Do, please, carry on with your
talk."

And they did so, Hoban finding in Parokkan a new sense
of firmness, a willingness to discuss trade and treaties to some
purpose. *Perhaps he prefers doing business with his wife
present*, Hoban thought to himself. *Though I'd have thought
him man enough to stand on his own two feet*. He was jerked
rudely from his thoughts by Parokkan's request for his attention.

"Hoban! Good grief, man, you were wool-gathering. Do
you want this talk or not?"

Though this was said with a smile, Hoban was disagree-
ably surprised by the change in Parokkan's manner. The man
now seemed almost curt. *He is strange*, Hoban thought.
*Totally inconsistent in his manner. How is one to deal with
him?* With difficulty, Hoban turned his thoughts back to the
matters before him.

From then on, all went well, both men proffering ideas and exchanges, with Amarino at Parokkan's side agreeing with her husband for the most part, yet lending a sympathetic ear to some of Hoban's wishes. After some time, most matters had been concluded satisfactorily, with only a few left undecided. Hoban requested that they grant him leave to return home and discuss these with Peven's court before coming to a firm decision. This was approved.

As the three left the audience chamber and Hoban returned to his room to begin packing he thought to himself, *those two are like a strong drink—initially pleasant, rather distracting, but leaving a strange taste in one's mouth.*

Shortly after lunch, Hoban and his small retinue were escorted to the city wall by Ark's leaders and a small band of armed men. Amarino had told Hoban just before his departure that his quickest route would be from the castle exit at the Royal Quarters to Sea Gate, from whence his route to Grayrock Harbor would be direct. Though he demurred at first, requesting time to travel through more of Starhill city and observe its populace, he soon felt a curious ennui come over him, and decided that as it did not really matter which way he went, he'd as soon use the quickest route.

After waving farewell, Hoban left Starhill and began his journey back to his ship and home to Peven. The further he traveled from the city, the more he regretted not having insisted that he remain longer. What had become of his usual decisiveness and firmness in argument? Not many people managed to overcome this ambassador's wishes. *How did they do it?* he thought, and could not put the matter from his mind.

Chapter 6

*T*he forest trails used by the outlaws were almost imperceptible to Fontaine but Durc led the party through the maze without hesitation, until Fontaine was hopelessly lost and despaired of ever finding the main road again. Brambles and low branches snagged her clothes and hair at first, but soon she grew more adept at walking through the undergrowth unscathed. Despite her uncertain future and bodily discomfort—she was sore from riding too—Fontaine's spirits were being fueled in her own particular way. She was becoming angry.

Angry at herself for getting caught up in Eric's idiotic adventure; angry at her parents for arranging her betrothal at the wrong time; and angry at the coarse and disrespectful words directed at or about her by her captors. Scrawny bit indeed! She would show him.

In another, the thoughts which went through her mind might have passed for wallowing in self-pity. *Nobody loves me. My parents just use me as a tool of state affairs. My fiancé is . . . was a fool. And now he's got himself killed and left me alone. My legs ache. My back aches. All of me aches. I'm thirsty. My face looks awful with all these spots.* With Fontaine they formed a steely core about which she built her defiance of her fate.

When they finally reached the outlaws' camp, it was so well disguised that, alone, she would have stumbled through

it unaware of anything but natural growth. Looking around as
the men dispersed she saw several huts covered with branches
and plants but, on inspection, solid and dry enough inside.
There were other dwellings, she learned later, perched in the
branches of the bigger trees, out of sight of anyone below and
out of reach of wolves or bears.

Fontaine stood in the small clearing which formed the
center of the camp and waited. No one paid her any attention
and this disregard sharpened her temper. All about her were
hustle and shouts but she was too weary to move.

From one of the huts before her a huge man, one she had
not seen before, emerged. Completely bald and stripped to
the waist, he presented a formidable and frightening figure in
the fading light. The two of them stared at each other for a
few long moments, then Fontaine started as, close behind
her, Durc said, "Don't mind Jani. He's harmless."

The big man went back into the hut, and came out
carrying a large iron pot. This he placed on the ground and
began building a fire. Fontaine turned to Durc. If he thought
she would ask timorously, "What are you going to do with
me?" he was soon to be disabused.

"And you, no doubt, are harmless too," she said, witheringly.
"After all, you have proved how brave you are by filling one
man with arrows and capturing his entire army." She stressed
the last words and spread her arms wide.

"Such a hero! A girl must be safe in such hands."

She curtsied and smiled mockingly. The fire was now
burning brightly, the light of the flames dancing round the
clearing, making shadows jump. Fontaine saw Jani sitting
watching her, as still as a rock, and then realized that the rest
of the camp was quiet too, watching. *Have I gone too far?*
she thought, looking into Durc's unmoving face. *Oh well,
may as well be hung for a sheep . . .*

"Sooner or later it will become obvious, even to your dull
brain, that I am no ordinary scrawny bit, as you so wittily put
it." Her voice sounded loud, even to herself, but she ploughed
on, beginning to be unnerved by the silence.

"If you cannot see from the evidence of my belongings
that I am indeed of royal blood then you are as wooden as
these trees. You will die a painful death if you harm me in
any way. Not," she added, making her meaning plain, "that I
think you are man enough, in any case."

His visage cracked into a snarl and his left hand snaked out and grasped her jacket collar.

"Why, you little slut—" He raised his right hand as if to strike her. "If you were worth it, I'd—"

"That's right, hit me. That's all you're fit for, you foul-mouthed ruffian!"

His hand was slowly lowered and his grip loosened. Then Durc laughed and the tension snapped.

"You are indeed a princess. No one else could be so haughty."

Their eyes met and a flicker of understanding passed between them.

"But here I am king. Nobody will find you in this place, so even if you are as important as you claim, I advise you to bear that in mind. An uncivil tongue in so great a lady is unbecoming." It was his turn to mock.

"Do as I say and you will come to no harm. Now sit and eat."

Jani's pot was now suspended over the fire and the big man was adding ingredients to what was obviously a stew of some sort. *As if the food at Home wasn't plain enough*, thought Fontaine, remembering wistfully the palace meals in Heald. She sat and waited while the activity of the camp returned to normal about her.

Durc, who had disappeared into the trees, returned with the man called Zunic and two others. They sat down near the fire and Durc looked thoughtfully at his prisoner. Others gathered around, bringing bowls and spoons which Jani began to fill.

"Feed the Lady Fontaine, Jani," said Durc, pointing to where she sat.

At the sound of her name, Fontaine looked up sharply.

"I'm not quite as wooden as you thought, perhaps," he said, looking pointedly at the ring on her finger. It bore the coat of arms of the royal family of Heald, transposed over an inscribed F.

She said nothing. Jani rose and offered her a spoon and steaming bowl.

"Thank you." She looked up and smiled at the huge figure.

"Thank him after you've tasted it, lass," said an anonymous voice.

"He won't hear you anyway."

Jani sat down, oblivious to the comments, and started eating.

Durc said, "Jani is deaf and dumb, a bit simple besides, but he's strong and he can cook better than this lot, despite their jibes."

Fontaine looked back to the bald giant, placidly spooning stew, and felt pity and then anger rise.

"So you use him as a slave, a useful animal." Her eyes challenged the outlaws' leader. Durc was unruffled.

"He's not unhappy. The forest is all the home he knows. In the town he'd be shut up in a cell or worse. He's not mistreated here."

"You'd not dare," she retorted, but the fire had gone out of her voice.

She turned her attention to the food and was pleasantly surprised. She could not identify all the ingredients but the mushrooms, root vegetables, nuts and the rest were savory and warming and she was too hungry, once she started, to be particular.

While she ate she was vaguely aware of conversations around her, which she gathered from odd phrases concerned her. Strangely, she did not feel afraid any more. She felt she could deal with any of them singly and she didn't think Durc would allow any mass brutality.

He certainly looked strong enough to hold sway over anyone—indeed, he would not be the leader of such a band of ruffians were he not able to match them physically. He was a tall, lean, well-favored man, his shaggy black hair and beard making him look not a little outlandish. His rough leather jerkin and belt, containing no fewer than four knives, would certainly earn the respect of forest-dwellers. Fontaine, though, was none such, and cared at this moment only for her safety and comfort.

In an effort to convince herself, she thought that now he knew who she was, he would probably be thinking of ransom demands. A living, unharmed princess would be more valuable.

By the time she finished eating she could hardly keep her eyes open. Durc turned to her.

"You'll sleep in my hut," he said, making sure every man could hear him. In the midst of the muttering that followed this statement he added more privately, "You'll be alone."

"Thank you."

"Don't thank me, lady. Thank your parents. They'll be paying well enough for your lodging."

Underneath the gruffness of his words, Fontaine thought she heard a touch of gentleness. *Perhaps I have a friend here after all*, she thought. Then, aware of another pair of eyes resting on her, she looked up to see Jani staring at her, wide-eyed. *Perhaps I have two*.

She smiled and the big man smiled crookedly in reply and came over to collect her dish. She touched his hand as he did so and, looking up, said, "Thank you, Jani. That was delicious," hoping that something of her meaning would be received.

Jani nodded as if in reply and turned to collect other dishes.

I'm so tired, thought Fontaine. *I wonder which is Durc's hut*.

A few steps away, Jani halted, turned round to look at her, then glanced first at Durc and then at one of the nearby dwellings. At that moment Durc said, "Zunic, I'll share your boards if I may."

"Of course, the branches are broad."

"You'll be wanting to sleep, lady. Come." Durc stood. Fontaine rose and was led into one of the huts. Only later, when she was alone in the darkness, did she realize that it was the same hut that Jani had indicated with his glance.

Despite the roughness of her bed Fontaine fell asleep as soon as she lay down. She did not sleep for long, however. Through her dreams she became aware of voices raised outside her door.

"No. Do you challenge me, Deg?"

"I'll not challenge you, Durc, as well you know, but what reason is there in this? I'll wager she's no virgin anyway. You know what these court bitches are like."

"This is no ordinary royal whore. She's a princess," came Zunic's voice.

"Princess or not she's still a woman and we've not seen one of those in months."

"Aye." There were mutters of agreement from several voices.

"It's not just for pissing with."

"Ain't natural, all this time."

Durc's voice overrode the chorus.

"If you're that desperate you can leave for Ashwicken. Though what welcome you'd get in the whorehouses there I'd not like to say. This one's valuable and any man who touches her will answer to me."

"No more!" he said as muttered protests rose again. "Go to your beds."

"You could always snare a wild sow, Deg," called a new voice.

"Aye, Or bore a hole in a tree." Laughter spread.

"She'd not be worth the taking anyway."

There were sounds of men dispersing.

"Fools," muttered Zunic. "Can't they see the chance we've got to get out of this forest for good?"

"They're only human, old friend."

"Aye. And so not to be trusted, eh!"

"Perhaps. We'll leave Jani on the door to make sure."

All was quiet once more and sleep reclaimed the subject of the argument.

Durc set Jani by the door of his hut and signed to him to let no one enter. The big man nodded, rolled himself in a blanket, and set his back against the door. He showed no surprise or resentment at being given this assignment. Whatever thoughts, if any, went on within his isolated mind were hidden from the outside world. He slept, but lightly.

Durc and Zunic climbed to their squirrel's nest.

In one of the ground dwellings, three men sat drinking by the light of an oil lamp, burning low. The talk went round with the flagon but always came back to the same subject.

"He's a hard bastard, that Durc. I'd not like to cross him."

"Huh. He's probably saving her for himself."

"No, he's scared of the rough edge of her tongue!" They laughed.

"She's not much to look at either."

"A woman's body, hasn't she? It's not her face I'm interested in."

"We know what you're interested in, Deg, but how do you get it?"

"Aye, with Jani blocking up the door and Durc to explain to afterward."

"I'll think of something," said Deg. "Pass the bottle."

Time passed and the flagon grew lighter.

"There'sh the ranshom to think about too."

"Clowery, you're as dumb as an ox. What difference would a few games make? They'll just cover it up. Make out it was that royal boyfriend of hers we knocked off, or something. Hey! That's the last of the drink. Give me that."

Reluctantly the nearly empty flagon was handed over. Deg drained it and wiped his lips on his sleeve.

"Besides, I reckon there's not much hope of money for the bitch."

"Aye. They'd probably pay ush to keep her with that tongue in her head," said Dunn.

Deg sighed with exaggerated patience.

"I meant she's on the run. There's a new king in Ark—or haven't you heard? How are the people from Heald going to find her here? I doubt if relations are too good at the moment."

"Sho the bitsch ish worthlesh and Durc won't even let ush have her for our own profit."

"Wonders will never cease," said Deg. "Understanding has dawned."

He looked at his two drunken friends with mild disgust. *Why do I bother,* he thought. Then slowly a smile spread over his face.

"I have it," he said. "We have two problems, right? Jani and Durc. We use one to best the other. All we have to do is persuade Jani to go into her. After that there can't be any objection to our following him in—if you understand me."

"But Jani'sh not like that. He'sh never been with a woman!"

"He's an animal, isn't he? You saw him staring at her like she was a ripe peach. And even if he doesn't do anything we can say he did. He can't gainsay us, can he!"

The two drunkards looked doubtful.

"You are men, aren't you? Durc won't blame Jani. He's too soft on the dumb brute. And it leaves us clear. What can we lose? And you gain a night's pleasure. We've earned that these months, haven't we?" Deg was silent for a minute to let the idea settle, then said, "Well?"

In their fevered and befuddled state Dunn and Clowery could find no fault in Deg's logic and their bodies demanded satisfaction now. The morning could take care of itself. The longer they thought about it the better an idea it seemed.

"Lesh go," said Dunn, and the other nodded.

Stumbling and cursing, the three crossed the open space to Durc's hut. As they sat down around Jani, Deg produced a smaller bottle from inside his jerkin. He unstoppered it and offered it to Jani, who sniffed it and took a small mouthful. He nearly choked, coughed, and, eyes watering, handed the bottle back to Deg.

"Giss a shwig, Deg."

"You've had enough. This is for our friend."

The conversation that followed, if such it can be called, would have appeared very strange and comic to an observer. Deg used words, though he knew they were useless, and increasingly crude sign language to try to convey his message. His companions were no help, interjecting helpful suggestions, such as, "Why don't you fondle it for him?" and "What a lovely mover," and so on; or more often collapsing into fits of giggles which Deg had to quieten hastily for fear of wakening the whole camp.

Jani merely watched everything curiously, drinking when the bottle was offered, while Deg grew more and more frustrated. Finally Deg stood and put his hand on the latch of the door. Instantly Jani rose and pushed him away so that Deg staggered back and fell into the ashes of the old fireplace. He sat there swearing quietly.

Then, before the others had had time to move, Jani turned, unlatched the door, stepped inside, and closed it behind him.

The three stared, unbelieving. Had he really got the idea? They sat in silence for a while, then Deg stood up abruptly and ran off in the direction of the stream. Dunn and Clowery fell together in an uncontrollable fit of laughter. The moonlight had quite clearly shown them that, as Deg beat his hasty retreat, his trousers had been smoldering.

Inside the hut, Fontaine had been aware of voices and laughter intruding into her dreams but it was not until the door opened and closed quietly that she woke up. In that brief moment, the moonlight had shown her the massive bulk of Jani's shoulders as he stooped to pass under the lintel. Now in darkness again terror crept into her heart.

I could handle any of them, even Durc, she thought, *but this one—he's so big—what hope have I got? How could I have mistaken the way he looked at me?*

She thought of screaming but the memory of Jani's deafness somehow rendered her as mute as he.

Only the unheeded sounds of the nocturnal forest animals disturbed the vigil of the three men. Deg had returned, his clothes cold and wet, and silenced his companions' laughter with a glare. Now they waited, listening for any indication of Jani's progress. All within the hut was silent.

Eventually Deg's patience wore out.

"If he hasn't done it by now he never will," he said, standing. Unlatching the door, he pushed. It didn't budge.

"They've wedged it." He pushed harder, to no avail, then turned to the others. "Come on. Give us a hand."

Before they could, however, the door opened, seemingly of its own accord, and Deg almost stumbled in. What prevented him from doing so was the large fist which came through the doorway in the opposite direction, catching him just below his left eye. The blow was so powerful that it practically lifted him off the ground and sent him sprawling backward to land on his back, completely unconscious.

"Mind the fire, Deg," giggled Dunn.

The door closed and neither of the remaining would-be intruders felt any inclination to risk opening it again. They half-carried, half-dragged the inert Deg back to their hut where they too lost consciousness, in more gentle fashion.

Despite her strange surroundings, Fontaine woke with a feeling of security that even the dawn coldness could not disperse. As her eyes grew accustomed to the light, she made out the sleeping form of Jani, curled at the foot of the door, making it quite impossible for it to be opened from the outside.

I didn't mistake the look in his eyes, she thought. *One friend at least.*

She stretched her stiff limbs. Jani stirred, opened his eyes, and they smiled at each other. Then, just as if it were a perfectly normal start to a day, Jani rose and went out to build a fire and prepare breakfast. After a few minutes he returned to the hut and handed her a mug of hot liquid which looked like tea but smelled and tasted unlike anything she'd encountered before.

Fortified, she wrapped her cloak around her and went outside. The camp was already astir and she followed the noise of running water to the stream. She found one of the men on all fours by the stream with his face and most of his head ducked under the water.

Clowery was attempting to ease the effects of a formidable hangover without much success. He came up for air and groaned.

"What a night," he moaned to himself, unaware of his audience. "And all for nothing, now that the bitch has put a spell on Jani. Oh, my head!"

He lowered it back into the water. Fontaine came up behind him, planted her boot on his backside, and shoved so that he sprawled full length in the water. When he came up drenched and spluttering, she said, "The bitch will put far worse a spell on you, little man, if you don't watch your language. Now get out of here so I can wash."

Despite his tender head, Clowery hurried to obey.

"She's a wildcat, that one," he complained to no one in particular as he came into the clearing.

Fontaine splashed her face and arms, then found the horses and satisfied herself that they were well tended.

"You'd not get far on a horse in this forest," said Durc behind her.

"I have no intention of riding off," she shot back. "If you have any sense you'll escort me back to my family and friends. It will be so much the worse for you if you don't."

"For someone in your position, you make rather impressive demands."

"I'm not afraid of you."

"I don't believe you are, but you will stay here until I say you go. If they agree to pay my price you will indeed be escorted back to your family."

"And what price do you put on my head?"

"That's for me to say. Come and eat."

Most of the outlaws were again seated around the fire, where Jani stirred nut porridge. Both Dunn and Clowery were holding their heads in their hands and Deg was sporting a spectacular black eye, which caused considerable ribaldry among his fellows.

"No one troubled you in the night, I trust," said Durc as they sat down. Fontaine hesitated, then replied, "No one."

She smiled up at Jani, who served her first of all.

Chapter 7

"*A*ll we have is rumor and hearsay," said Pabalan, King of Heald. "We cannot act on that."

"But we can't just do nothing!" responded his son Ansar. They were walking in the grounds of Ramsport Palace with Rehan, a trusted courtier, discussing the news from Ark.

"Father, my sister—*your daughter*—is missing. Some tales we've heard say she's dead but I won't believe that, and if she has escaped then we must try to find her. And if she is imprisoned there is all the more reason for swift action."

"You need not remind me of my paternal duties, Ansar. I will do all that is possible within the bounds of reason. But we cannot rush in blindly. You know as well as I that we cannot match the military forces of Ark, and until we know what has happened to Fontaine and how this Parokkan means to treat with us, any action we take could make matters worse."

Ansar was about to speak again, his eyes burning angrily in his agitated, rugged face, when Rehan interposed.

"My lord," he said, "may I make a suggestion?"

"Of course. Your counsel is welcome, as always."

"We cannot, as you say, move in force but we can move by stealth. The news we have received from Ark is unreliable, confused, and contradictory. We need first-hand reports, from men we can rely on."

"I will go today!" said Ansar.

"No, my lord," said Rehan. "I do not doubt your cunning or your bravery," he lied, "but your face is too well known. We do not know whether the new ruler of Ark—and from all reports we have to accept Parokkan as such—will be antagonistic to us. You could not hope to pass unremarked and obtain the intelligence we so desperately need."

"The insult to my sister is enough to show how he regards us," said Ansar huffily, "but I don't like this waiting around. There must be something I can do."

"My lord," said Rehan, speaking to the king. "I have never been to Ark. My face is not well known there and I believe I could pass myself off as a merchant quite well." He smiled. "I am not a bad judge of jewels—or of men. Let me travel in disguise to Starhill. There surely is where the answers to our riddles lie."

Pabalan pondered this for a moment.

"It makes sense," he said. "At the very least you should be able to give us a decent report on how the new régime is running things, and with a bit of luck you will find out where Fontaine is."

"And if it is politic, I may be able to bargain for her release—if she is held captive."

"Go then. With my blessing." The king laid one large hand on his advisor's shoulder.

"While I sit here, chasing my own shadow, I suppose," grumbled Ansar.

Rehan turned to the prince.

"I think it would be of great value for us to send a party to Ark. That way we could cross-check my information and perhaps obtain other news. The southern part of the island is remote from the capital and unlikely to be heavily guarded. Might I suggest that you sail there and see what you can learn." *At least it should keep the impetuous fool out of trouble,* he thought.

"Gladly. What do you say, Father?"

Pabalan smiled. "I do not think I could put up with your pacing and prating if I refused," he said. "You can go if you give me your word that you will learn what you can in the south and then return swiftly. No one-man rescue attempts."

"Of course not." Ansar looked hurt for a moment, then brightened at the thought of some action. Even a tame jaunt like this was better than chafing away at home.

Rehan only hoped that Ansar would keep himself out of trouble for a few days. It was very unlikely he would learn anything useful, but one never knew. The prince was undoubtedly brave but he was also used to having his own way and, unfortunately, royal blood did not guarantee any great degree of intelligence.

Some days later, Rehan stood in the bows of a merchant ship, relishing the sea breeze and the flying spray, his slender frame braced against the swell. He stared ahead, trying to catch a glimpse of the fabled Grayrock Shoot, the entrance to Ark's main port, Grayrock Harbor. Gradually, as the coastline drew nearer, he discerned the "sea gate," the entrance to the massive natural harbor which could provide completely sheltered anchorage for an entire fleet—or two!

The Shoot was an impressive sight even to Rehan, whose sharp face and midnight-blue eyes indicated a shrewd and knowledgeable mind. Huge gray cliffs rose on either side of the entrance, which was about four hundred paces wide. Whatever strange fault in the rock formation had created this coastline had also ensured the future prosperity of the harbor by making the straits deep and except in the most appalling storm, easily navigable. This convenience had been enhanced by the citizens of Grayrock Harbor who had built light towers on either side of the Shoot, making it possible to make a safe passage even at night. The seamen of the islands took all this for granted, appreciating the practical arrangement perhaps, but ignoring the grandeur of the place in favor of more pragmatic considerations.

Nevertheless, it was an awesome feeling to sail for the first time between those lights, the sky seeming to shrink and the ship, however large, being dwarfed by the granite bastions on either side. For a time, Rehan forgot the nature of his mission and gazed about him in wonder. However, once inside the harbor, which stretched west and north a half league in each direction, his thoughts returned to the part he must play for the next few days. The captain and crew of the trading ship, which hailed from Strallen, had accepted him readily enough as what he claimed to be: a merchant from Arlon trading in silks, cloth, and jewelery. The goods he brought with him were ample proof of his occupation should anyone have been suspicious enough to inspect his cargo. He had paid a fair but not too generous price for his passage, which made him an acceptable and unremarkable passenger for the ship's master and his crew, who were well versed in the ways of trade. They lived by the profit of their travel and cared little for the politics of any island unless it affected them directly. Thus they had thought nothing of sailing from Heald to Ark despite the rift between these two communities, caused by the new régime in Ark and the uncertain fate of Heald's princess. That an Arlon merchant should wish to make the same trip caused a similar lack of surprise.

Now as his ship nosed toward its mooring, Rehan braced himself for the task ahead. It was one he relished. He was no stranger to intrigue and he had no doubts about his own ability as a spy. And whichever way events turned he was determined that he would gain by it. He was in his element.

Two hours later, Rehan sat in the tap room of The North Star, the best tavern in Grayrock, enjoying lunch and listening to the talk of the other diners. He had felt a strange and vaguely frightening tremor as he had stepped off the ship onto dry land but this had only heightened his feeling of excitement and anticipation. Now, after having made arrangements for the storage of his merchandise and his lodging for the night, he was ready to start gathering information in earnest. Life in Grayrock seemed to be going on much as would be expected in a busy port. From the scenes in the docks with its ingenious cranes and pulleys and seemingly chaotic bustle it was obvious that trade was thriving. *Kings may come and go but business will always be with us,* thought Rehan, sipping his beer. There was no lack of prosperity either, judging from the amount and variety of goods he had already seen being unloaded in the docks or on offer in the markets and trading halls of the town.

It's not many places that would support a place like this either, he thought, looking round the comfortable and well-furnished room, with most of its tables occupied by well-to-do merchants and such like. Fragments of conversation reached his ears but it was mostly business matters and he gleaned nothing interesting.

The landlord came to his table to see if he required anything else.

"No thank you. I am replete. You set a good table," Rehan replied. *Too good*, he thought to himself, eyeing the man's large, flabby bulk with distaste.

At that moment there were sounds of a commotion from the tavern's hallway and a red-faced but important looking gentleman burst through the doors.

"Heaven help me," he exclaimed to no one in particular. "Landlord, a tankard of your best, please. I need it."

As the large man hurried off to draw the ale, Rehan rose and offered a chair to the newcomer.

"Please join me, if you will. You seem to be having some trouble. If I may be of any assistance..."

The gentleman slumped gratefully into the proffered seat.

"Thank you, sir," he said. "Sometimes I despair of the porters here. Recently they seem to have no minds of their own. You have to spell every instruction out for them or your luggage will end up on six different ships, like as not."

The landlord returned with a filled tankard.

"I will deal with the porters, Your Excellency. Please excuse their clumsiness."

"Just makes sure *all* the cases are aboard the *Dolphin* in one hour. And don't let them drop anything again."

"Of course, Your Excellency." The landlord strode off purposefully.

Rehan said, "My apologies, Your Excellency. I took you for a mere trader like myself. I am honored. Which island do you represent?"

"Please don't apologize. It is a pleasure to have some civilized company. My name is Hoban. Peven is my home-isle and I'll not be sorry to be on my way back there soon."

"I am Palmar, a merchant from Arlon," said Rehan as the two men shook hands. "Every man loves his home-isle but is Ark not hospitable? True, this is my first visit here but it seems so to me."

"Oh, I'll not deny the welcome, for all the trouble there's been here recently, but I've not got a good feeling from this visit of mine. Though I got as much as I could have wanted, I suppose." He looked puzzled at his own inability to explain himself better.

"I've heard some tales, of course," said Rehan, eager to

make use of his new source, "but I'd welcome some solid facts about the new king. It was a sudden thing, I hear."

"It was, and most surprising in many ways." Hoban's voice dropped to a more private tone. "News came fast to Peven for some of our ships were here at the time and they fled, fearing the violence, but as far as I can see there was no vast amount of bloodshed. The takeover was very thorough and totally successful—and there seems to have been no warning. Ather was not unpopular, we all supposed, but his overthrow doesn't seem to bother anyone too much. Even so, it is odd that there were no signs of unrest before it happened."

"Ather was killed?"

"Yes, that's sure."

"And his family?"

"No one seems to know. Or at least no one seems to be willing to talk about it. I've heard bits of gossip of course, but I don't know whether that is worth heeding. The most common story is that Ather's three sons escaped and are now probably on another island, but no one has seen them and it is possible that they're either dead as well, or in Starhill Castle's dungeons. Either way the new king doesn't seem worried about them. But then he's an odd fellow."

"You've met him then?"

"Aye, I have. Though I don't know what to make of him."

"He was an army captain, was he not, of noble blood?"

"Yes on both counts, but yet I can't see what he has that put him where he is now. He has a very changeable nature. He made me feel uneasy, though it's difficult to explain why. Ever since I left Starhill I have kept remembering more oddities in his behavior which I never noticed at the time."

The ambassador paused, puzzled again, then grinned and said, "I think I must have been dazzled by the new queen. By all the Wizards, she is a beauty! It was difficult to think straight when she was in the room." He laughed. "Anyone would think I was an inexperienced youth again, to be so distracted by a pretty face."

Aware that time was running out but trying not to appear too eager, Rehan said, "Wasn't there a princess in the castle at the time? The fiancée of the eldest son or something?"

"Yes, Princess Fontaine of Heald. She was there but, like the boys, she's disappeared. There's all sorts of tales of who escaped with the princes. Wild stuff about the court wizard spiriting them all away invisibly and such like. Most say the princess escaped with them but I don't know how much credence to give a rumor like that."

"Doesn't that make relations with Heald rather awkward? After all, it is Ark's nearest neighbor."

"You would think so, wouldn't you, but Parokkan—the new king—doesn't seem to care at all. He's just not interested."

"But trade—"

"Oh, he's interested in trade all right. He made that plain enough. They live very well in Starhill Castle. If you have luxuries to sell I'd wager you'll find a good price there. It's just that Heald seems to have been discounted. It's all very odd."

At that moment a young man's head appeared round the door to the hallway.

"Your Excellency, we should be going, the tide will be right in a half hour or so."

"Thank you, Andrew. I'm on my way." Hoban turned back to Rehan. "Good luck with your ventures here, Palmar, and thank you for the company. I feel fit to face the sea again now."

Both men stood.

"Thank you for your company. And your news. May the *Dolphin's* journey be safe and speedy."

"Thank you, my friend. Fare you well."

"Farewell."

Rehan watched the ambassador's broad back disappear, then sat down again to ponder all he had learned. It was a good deal more than he had any right to expect so soon, but it was not nearly enough. One thing was certain. The sooner he got to Starhill, the better.

Rehan spent that afternoon walking around the town, talking with any who would spare the time and gradually turning each conversation to the new king and the fate of those he had deposed. He detected a certain reticence to talk about these matters but that, he decided, was only natural, especially with a stranger. Even so, he confirmed for himself the gist of Hoban's report. Most people believed that the princes had escaped and Fontaine with them. There was also a general level of agreement that the new régime was an improvement on the old, though no evidence was offered to justify this belief. At worst, the feeling shown toward Parokkan was of indifference. No one seemed to be opposed to or resent his overthrow of Ather. Or at least no one was prepared to say so outright.

In the course of his wanderings Rehan also made arrangements for his transportation to the capital, starting the next morning. He returned to The North Star that evening pleased with his day's work and eager for the next stage. He was beginning to feel more hopeful about Fontaine's escape—rumor usually has some grain of truth at its core, after all—and the prospect of seeing the great city of Starhill appealed to Rehan. Not the least of its attractions was the fact that, once within, he intended to meet this strange new king.

And his queen.

Although it was only some ten leagues from Grayrock to Starhill, and most of that on a good wide road, the journey took most of the next day to complete. The carriage, in which Rehan and two other travelers rode, was accompanied by three baggage carts and it was these that determined the party's pace. Moreover, the way led mostly uphill as the road left the coastal plain and climbed into the hilly region where Starhill lay.

At the midday halt Rehan, who had become weary of the carriage's stuffiness and the relatively uninteresting conversation of his fellow travelers, suggested to the coachman that he would like to ride alongside him on the driver's seat. What this position lacked in comfort it made up for in airiness and the view it provided of the surrounding country. The driver was a gruff man who grew steadily more taciturn as the day wore on but Rehan was content to ride in silence for the most part and to use his eyes.

As with Grayrock, all appeared normal to him. Farming and village life did not seem to have been affected by the upheaval in the capital. *It's almost as if nothing had happened,* mused Rehan, but this thought did not strike him as at all odd. Life was going on as it should. He felt relaxed and confident and he awaited his arrival at the city with a pleasurable glow.

They were still more than a league distant when Rehan first glimpsed Starhill. The city was sited on top of a hill. The

huge stone walls which enclosed it formed a great circle and
had been built in an earlier age with a precision and skill
which had subsequently been lost. Within the walls the
highest point of the city was the center and it was here that
Starhill Castle stood, topped by the immensely tall and
elegant Starbright Tower, more commonly known as the
Wizard's Tower. Much of the upper part of the castle was
easily visible from outside the city walls and, even from afar,
it was an impressive sight, with the distant Windchill Mountains as its backdrop.

Rehan watched closely as the city grew in his vision
and details emerged. He picked out the large towers that
interspaced the gates of the city, which were themselves
flanked by smaller defensive towers. He recalled from charts
he had studied before he left Heald that there were five
towers and five gates equally spaced along the circumference
of the city wall. Facing due north was the Star Gate. The next
gate, the one which Rehan's party was approaching, faced just
north of east and was known, for obvious reasons, as the
Seaward or Sea Gate. Continuing round, there was the Field
Gate, the Mountain Gate, and the Stone Gate. From each of
these entrances a broad thoroughfare ran inward to the
center like the spokes of a wheel. The wheel's hub was
Starhill Castle. The symmetry of this arrangement, Rehan
was to learn, did not extend to the five sectors divided by
these roads, which in defiance of all logic were known as
"quarters." Each area had a character of its own. In some
places the jumble of streets was like a maze in which the
unwary traveler could become hopelessly lost. Elsewhere
buildings were more ordered and well-spaced and, in the
more prosperous neighborhoods, parks and gardens added
beauty and fragrance to the environment.

The Sea Gate stood open, apparently unguarded, and, as
they passed within, Rehan felt a weariness out of all propor-
tion to the exertions of the day. This lethargy seemed to have
spread to all the members of the party and it seemed to take
an age before his goods were unloaded and stored, and
lodging organized for himself. He stayed at one of the many
hostelries that formed an important part of the merchants'
quarter, the section between Sea Gate and Field Gate.

Rehan retired very early, finding himself more in need of
sleep than food, and happily postponing any investigations
until the morrow.

Chapter 8

"*F*erragamo, what *are* you up to? Shill and Orme are here and want to know what they're supposed to be doing. And you're buried in your study, being no help to anyone."

The wizard, muttering incantations to himself, looked up from the dusty book on his lap.

"I'm *trying*," he said with exaggerated patience, "to locate the spell for searching."

"Why?" asked Brandel, unaware of the irony of Ferragamo's statement.

"Oh, Arkon, give me strength. Because we have to have a better idea of where Fontaine is being held before we all go charging off to that *rather* large forest. Or have you got any better ideas? Eh?"

A slightly shamefaced Brandel admitted that perhaps Ferragamo was employing himself toward a useful end after all, and left the study, closing the door quietly behind him.

"He's a bit busy just at the moment. I don't think you should disturb him."

"So we just sit here and wait for him to come up with ideas? Is that it?" Mark sounded a little frustrated. Although he wasn't too keen on the idea of rushing off, he didn't mind the thought of the others doing so, and would prefer the matter resolved sooner rather than later.

Nobody took any notice of his petulance, and Shill and

Orme soon left, having decided to go ahead and get supplies for the trip to find Fontaine, to be ready whenever Ferragamo decided to emerge.

A little while later, Koria walked into the room, brandishing a large black hat, liberally festooned with dust, old onionskins, and not a little mold.

"Where's Ferragamo?" she asked.

"Good grief, Koria, what *have* you got there? It looks revolting!"

"Um, yes, it does rather. It's Ferragamo's old hat. He's been looking for it for the last couple of years. I suddenly discovered it peeping out from behind the stove. I thought—" and at this she paused and grinned wickedly—"that I'd just go and see whether it still fits or not!"

"Oh, yuk! Koria, you can't possibly think of putting that thing on someone's head," Mark admonished her.

"Oh, but Ferragamo's not just somebody, is he? We *all* know that. And *I* know that he'll be perfectly delighted to get his rotten old hat back. He made enough fuss when he lost it. Now, where is he?"

"In his study. And I must say, his head did look remarkably bare." Brandel grinned, looking almost as wicked as Koria, who was already striding purposefully toward the study door. As she opened it, she said, in her most dulcet tones, "Ferragamo, my love. Do put that book down for a moment and look at what I've got for you."

They heard Ferragamo's roar of laughter break off suddenly.

"Where did you get that?"

"I found it in the kitchen."

He groaned. "It's not working properly. I *knew* it wasn't. Why can I do anything right these days?"

"What are you trying to do?" Koria asked him.

"Get this searching spell to work, to find Fontaine, so that we can't get a better idea of where she is. And all I've managed to do is turn up my mangy old hat."

Just as he finished speaking, the cottage door burst open, and Mark yelled. The sounds of thumping and crashing from the main room brought Ferragamo and Koria rushing to see what was happening.

"Help! Somebody help me! Get it away, for heaven's sake. Oooh!"

Mark was being chased round the room by a rather large, but underfed, pig.

"It likes you!" Brandel was laughing so much he nearly fell off his chair. "It just wants a cuddle!"

"I'll *give* it a cuddle if it would just stop chasing me! Do something, someone. Ferragamo, please!"

Ferragamo, one arm round Koria's shoulders, shouted, "Desist!"

Looking puzzled, the pig came to an abrupt halt, as did the red-faced and panting Mark.

"Phew, thanks, Ferragamo. What on earth is that pig doing in here anyway?"

"If I remember rightly, your friend there went missing a few months ago. The Mermaid's landlord told me about it. It would appear that my attempts to use the searching spell have had *another* use."

After sending Brandel to The Mermaid with the pig, Ferragamo, Koria, and Mark sat at the table, trying to think of a way to make the spell work as it should. They were beginning to get impatient, realizing that the longer they delayed, the longer Fontaine would be in her captors' hands. This thought pleased no one.

Mark found himself worrying more and more about the obnoxious young princess. *She's not that bad*, he thought. *And I wouldn't wish her predicament on anyone.*

Well, I would, came the response from Longfur. *How about wishing it on Parokkan!*

Mark fell to musing again.

"This is ridiculous," said Ferragamo. "There should be a way of making the spell more specific." *I'm losing my touch*, he added silently.

"Yes," said Koria. "There are some things I'd rather you didn't find again."

"Don't remind me," the wizard replied. "Do you remember that little house made of shells with "A Present from Lugg" inscribed round the base?"

"Truly tasteless," laughed Koria. "Who was it who gave it to you?"

"I forget, thank goodness. I don't think they'd want to be connected with it now."

Ferragamo stopped laughing and looked at Mark. "You're very quiet," he said. "It wasn't you, was it?"

"No." Mark paused, his face creased in thought. "But something you said . . ."

Koria became serious again. "This isn't getting us very far."

"Scent," said Mark suddenly.

"What?"

"Like a dog."

"But I had a bath yesterday!" said Ferragamo, feigning offense. Koria pretended to hit him over the head. "Let him speak," she said.

"Do you think that you could . . . No, it's silly."

Spit it out, blockhead. It can't be any sillier than long-lost pigs!

"Tell us," said Koria.

"I just thought, maybe, if you had something of Fontaine's, something she was attached to, then you could use it to sort of . . . focus the spell," said Mark. "Like—"

"Giving a dog a scent," completed Koria. She saw the look dawning in Ferragamo's eyes and was already half-way out of the room before he spoke.

"Of course. Why didn't I think of that?"

Koria came back with a silk handkerchief, which she gave to the wizard.

"She liked this."

Ferragamo sat very still, holding the delicate scrap of cloth tightly. He closed his eyes and mumbled a few syllables.

Mark and Koria held their breath.

A short while later he opened his eyes and said quietly, with great satisfaction, "That's it."

"Did you find her? Is she all right?" asked Mark excitedly.

"She's unharmed for the moment," said Ferragamo, "and I *also* think we stand a good chance of being able to find her. She seems to be in some sort of well-established camp, so provided her captors don't move off again too soon, we should be able to track it down. There is a stream nearby and Owl told me that she was taken off eastward from the trail somewhere midway between Stane and Ashwicken. I believe if we follow the river through the forest, we should come close to where she is."

"He looks quite pleased, doesn't he?" said the grinning Mark.

"And so he should," Koria replied proudly. "Mind, it was your idea about the handkerchief that helped him. Well done!"

Mark glowed, feeling as if he'd been of use for once. It was a good feeling.

After their initial euphoria had worn off, the three sat down to discuss what to do next. It was decided that they would need to borrow, or hire, a large fishing boat from one of Home's men, in which they could sail around the coastline to Stane, and a rowboat, which could be carried aboard, and then used on the river through the forest. Shill and Orme returned, bearing provisions for the anticipated journey.

The next decision to be made was who would go. Ferragamo said they would *all* go, except Koria, and Richard, who would remain behind to guard her. Mark felt surprised by the fact that he wasn't scared of being included in the search party. Rather, he felt pleased.

Perhaps you're growing up at last.

Longfur! I don't know why I put up with you and your snide remarks. I wouldn't take them from anyone else.

Ah, but you know I love you. That's why.

And Longfur Mousebane purred contentedly at Mark's feet as the boy bent down and rubbed his cat's head.

"Where's Brandel?" Ferragamo asked suddenly.

"You sent him to The Mermaid, don't you remember?"

"That was some time ago. He should be back by now," said the wizard. "I want everybody here so that we can get organized."

"If he's gone to The Mermaid, he'll be gone for some time," Koria laughed. "Mark, run and fetch him. Tell him dinner is nearly ready. That'll bring him soon enough."

"And I think that, as no one has shown any ill effects after two days, we can all have a bit more of that rather special cake."

———————

After dinner, it was decided that early to bed was a good idea. It meant that they would awake in good time in the morning, refreshed and ready.

There was some discussion between Ferragamo and Shill as to precisely where Fontaine was. Ferragamo pointed out that while he didn't know *exactly* where she was, he had a fairly good idea, and was sure that as soon as they got reasonably close they'd be able to pinpoint her location. He also found himself having to reassure Mark, who lingered behind after the others had gone to bed, about the nature of the forest.

"It is a dangerous place, Mark. No one with any sense would deny that. It is huge, and more or less untamed. Few people venture through it, though the trail is adequate, because of those very outlaws that killed Eric and took Fontaine. Their reputation has long been an evil one. And that is why *we* must venture into it. We cannot leave her there, though she appears safe for the moment, and should remain so for a while. It seems probable that they will think of some sort of ransom, but she is still in great danger. The temper of these men is not likely to be gentle, and Fontaine's nature is such that she may aggravate her own dire situation. And they would ignore her youth and royal station, if the mood took them for . . ." At this, his voice trailed off.

"Well, she seems safe enough for tonight, and I'm sure we'll reach her soon. *Then* all we have to do is think of a way of getting her away without getting us all killed in the process!"

Mark paled, and Ferragamo cursed himself for his thoughtlessness. He hastily tried to make amends.

"Mark, do you honestly believe that I'd be the slightest bit flippant if I thought the situation was hopeless? It will be dangerous, it's true, but there are quite a few of us, you know, and our party will include trained soldiers and one reasonably well trained wizard. Between us, we should manage something. Haven't we got this far?"

Mark nodded, still looking rather glum. With a quiet "goodnight" he went to his room, followed by Longfur.

He got into his bed, Longfur settling himself in the curve of Mark's legs, shifting slightly until he was assured of the most comfortable position. Sensing Mark's distress, the cat asked:

What is it? Are you frightened by having to go with the search party? Don't worry, it's only natural to be scared, especially after what you've been through.

No, it's not that. Though I thank you for your sympathetic attitude. No, I'm just wondering how Fontaine is feeling at the moment.

Oh, she'll be all right.

How can you be sure?

Because that tongue of hers is enough to keep anyone at

bay. She hasn't exactly endeared herself to any of us, has she? She's a vixen.

Is she? Mark wondered. *Sometimes we forget how young she is, and she's been made to come and live in a foreign land, away from her family and the people she knows well. I know I still miss my own mother dreadfully, and she died when I was almost too young to remember her. All I have left of her is this ring.* He briefly touched the chain round his neck. *I sometimes wonder what Father would have been like had she been with us all these years. Ah well, who knows. But Fontaine—the awful things that have happened must have affected her as badly as any of us. If not more. After all, she's only a girl!*

You're working yourself up into a real state, aren't you? Stop thinking about it, and get some sleep. You'll be more useful tomorrow that way!

Sometimes, Longfur, you can be really heartless. You go to sleep. Just leave me alone.

Huffed, the cat did as he was told, whiskers twitching, and Mark was alone with his miserable thoughts. It seemed to the young boy that he lay awake in the dark for hours, his mind going over and over Fontaine's plight.

Fontaine, please be all right. I'm thinking of you.

And with that thought, Mark fell asleep, a tear making its silent way down his cheek.

It was a remarkably refreshed group that met at the breakfast table the following morning. Even Brandel, normally a sluggish lie-abed until hunger pangs forced him into action, was up bright and early. Only Mark seemed quiet as he emerged from his room. Koria, noticing the dark rings under his eyes, and his listless state, went over and gave him a quick hug, whispering, "It'll be all right. You'll see."

He ventured a smile, appreciating her efforts. "Thanks, Koria."

Joining the others, he noticed the air of restlessness that had everyone in its grip. They seemed as though they could hardly wait to get started organizing the search party and on their way. Their mood was infectious, and it wasn't long before Mark, his natural good humor reasserting itself, joined in the chatter.

After serving everyone with a hearty meal, Koria bustled around in the kitchen for some time, preparing food for them to take. She soon discovered that she had insufficient supplies and Brandel, as the largest eater in the group, was sent to the village and harbor to acquire more.

Ferragamo and Mark were not far behind him. It had been decided that Ferragamo, as the natural spokesman for their party, should approach the fishermen for the hire of the required boats. He was determined to keep Mark by his side, and soon, by means of banter and general good humor and optimism, managed to reinforce the cheering up of the lad. It was a smiling pair that arrived at the harbor.

"Now, we must find Derwent. He's got the biggest boat, and his wife is heavy with child, so he's leaving later in the morning than usual at present. If we offer to pay him well enough for the loan of his boat, he may be glad of the opportunity to stay at home for a while."

They located the man's cottage easily, and the transaction was soon completed to everyone's satisfaction, especially that of Derwent's wife, who did indeed seem pleased at the thought of her husband's company. Two rowing boats were included in the deal, as was Derwent's assistant Birn, a brawny young man who was to sail the fishing boat to Stane with the searchers.

Ferragamo, satisfied at the lifting of Mark's depression, sent him scurrying back to the cottage to find Richard and two other junior soldiers to assist in loading and preparing the boat.

By early afternoon, by dint of a good deal of hard work, they were almost ready to set sail. The entire search party were on or near the jetty, with Koria and Richard waiting to see them off. Everyone was glad at least at the prospect of some action and the boat's crew especially were in high spirits. They regarded this voyage as something of a holiday compared to fishing and an adventure into the bargain. They were making last-minute adjustments to rigging and stowing the last of the supplies when a sail was sighted out to sea, distant but obviously heading toward them.

Everyone turned and watched the approaching vessel but the varied speculation as to the nature of the visit was silent until Birn said, "She's not showing any colors, but from the set of her sails I'd say she was from Heald."

Several of the older fisherman nodded agreement.

"Merchant most like," said one. "We don't see many here but—"

"After recent events they'll be careful in their approaches to Ark," finished Birn for him.

"It's not big enough to carry troops in any number," said Orme, voicing the thoughts of several of the group. "I don't think she poses any great threat."

"Then let us await their arrival," said Ferragamo. "It makes sense that Pabalan would try to find out what's happening but he is a cautious man. He might well try an approach like this."

"Let's hope so," said Koria. "We can send them some news then at least. Adesina must be very worried."

"Fontaine's mother is made of sterner stuff," replied the wizard.

"That's a surprise," said Brandel sarcastically. "She must be, to have survived her daughter," he added unnecessarily.

"Shut up, you pig," said Mark angrily.

"Sorry, I'm sure," said Brandel, feigning shocked contriteness. "What's eating you?"

"I trust Pabalan has an understanding nature," interrupted Shill. "Having to rescue Fontaine once is fair enough, but twice could be construed as carelessness," he added drily.

"You have a point," said Ferragamo.

"She's hoving to," said Birn.

Her sails furled, the boat was now approaching the jetty slowly, with oars providing guidance. About fifty paces out the reversed oars brought her to a halt broadside on, and a large, weather-beaten man standing at the side of the raised stern hailed them.

"Greetings, friends!" he yelled. "I would have news of Ark. Strange tales are being voiced. We wish to trade but are uncertain of our welcome."

Ferragamo replied, and though he did not seem to raise his voice, everyone ashore and at sea heard him clearly.

"You have nothing to fear here, captain. If, as I judge by your accent, you are from Heald, you will be most welcome. And news we can supply in quantity."

Before the sailor could reply there was movement behind

him and another man appeared at his side. Ferragamo smiled at the sight of the newcomer.

"Well met, Ansar," he said.

"I thought I knew that voice. Ferragamo, by the heavens, is it really you?" the other yelled back.

"Can you doubt it?" laughed the wizard. "Tell the good captain to bring his ship alongside the jetty. We have much to discuss."

"Fontaine, is she with you?"

"Not precisely. Come ashore."

"Is she all right?"

"Yes, but come ashore. Talking is easier than shouting."

The men on the boat exchanged a few words and soon the boat was gliding slowly to her mooring.

"That's Fontaine's brother, isn't it?" asked Mark.

"Yes," said Ferragamo quietly. "We'll have to be careful how we tell our story or he'll race off as recklessly as Eric. The two of them were quite alike in some ways. Ansar spent much time at Starhill as a boy."

"I remember him," said Brandel. "He and Eric were always fighting battles and causing havoc."

"From what I've heard he hasn't changed much," said the wizard.

After the boat was tied up introductions were made. Ansar's only companion, apart from the captain and his crew, was a thin, intelligent looking courtier named Laurent. The departure of the search party was delayed while these two joined Ferragamo and the others at the cottage. The sailors retired to The Mermaid with their fellow seamen from Home to learn the news in their own fashion.

Tactfully Ferragamo related the events of the three weeks since their flight from Starhill. Ansar's first concern was for his sister, but Eric's death obviously distressed him a great deal. With help from Laurent, who had obviously been a shrewd choice as Ansar's traveling companion, the wizard convinced Ansar that they were doing everything they could and kept the discussion reasonably calm. The Healdean prince even grew cheerful when he learned of the proposed expedition to find his sister. It was obvious from the start that he had every intention of going with them and no one saw any reason to try to dissuade him. However, it was obvious that the latest news had to be taken back to Heald and it was decided that Laurent would sail back there immediately.

Ansar in turn told his news of the mood in Heald and of Rehan's mission to Starhill.

"He left before me and should be almost at Grayrock Harbor by now."

"I know of him by reputation," said Ferragamo.

"He has many skills," said Laurent, a slightly antagonistic inflection marking his words. "He will discover as much as any man could."

"But *we* will find Fontaine and bring her back!" said Ansar. He spoke proudly as if the deed were already accomplished. Ferragamo and Laurent exchanged a glance which spoke volumes.

Chapter 9

*T*he *Seahawk*, as Derwent's boat had been somewhat optimistically named, sailed in the early afternoon. Fortunately, the weather was fine and even the more delicate of the passengers suffered little from seasickness. As they sailed northward, intending to make Stane by nightfall if possible, Ferragamo took the opportunity to test out how Mark was feeling about his unnerving experience with *Sagas of the Servants*, a subject which had been avoided or superseded by other events until now. The wizard was curious and a little disturbed by his pupil's reactions and by the coincidence of finding the ancient parchment at the same time.

Even with no one else within earshot, Mark was reticent at first but Ferragamo persisted, knowing that talking about it would help them both in the end.

"It was very strange," the prince said, a faraway look in his eyes. "I know I've never seen that book before but as I read on I began to anticipate things."

"Well, you're a bright lad—sometimes," replied the wizard, as Mark looked up in surprise. "Some stories are very predictable."

"No, it wasn't like that. It was almost as if I were *in* the story. I kept imagining myself as the Mirage Warrior. He doesn't have a name in the story, does he?"

Unnoticed by Mark, who was by now staring out to sea

again, the expression on Ferragamo's face went through a number of rapid changes and it was with an effort that he replied evenly.

"No, he doesn't." After a moment he added, "You could have read something similar in another book, you know. Those are very old stories and they've been copied and adapted countless times over the centuries. Even the version you read may not be the original tale."

"But it did happen that way. I just know it did." Mark shuddered. Ferragamo eyed him narrowly but before he could ask the young prince anything, Mark spoke again.

"You said The Servants were the men who helped the good wizards in The War of the Wizards."

"Yes, although strictly speaking The Servants continued in existence long after the war was over."

"Does that mean that the Mirage Warrior was one of The Servants and the story comes from the war?"

"Yes, to both questions."

"It seems a funny name for heroes to choose for themselves— The Servants."

"Not really. They were great men but they chose to dedicate themselves to serving something greater."

Ferragamo let Mark mull that over for a while then he asked gently, "Why did the story frighten you so?"

"I wasn't really—" Mark hesitated. "Yes," he finally admitted, "I was frightened. It was as if I couldn't control things. I tried to stop reading but—"

"What the eye didn't see the imagination more than made up for?"

"Yes, but it wasn't imagination. More like a memory I didn't know I had. I've had dreams like that before. Almost as if I was watching a piece of history through someone else's eyes. But none of them has ever been like this one. They were always comforting somehow."

"Do you remember any of them?"

"Not really. I've never thought about them much."

"But this one was different?"

"Yes. I wanted to stop it. I knew I was awake after all. But I couldn't. How can that be?"

"I don't know."

"You know how the story ends?"

"Yes."

"So do I," said Mark, "but I didn't read that far. I started

feeling strange and the next thing I knew Koria was asking
me if I was all right. I must have fainted. Sort of," he added
lamely.

"Well, I think you should get enough excitement in the
next few days so that you won't need any stories," said the
wizard as jovially as possible.

"It's funny, isn't it," Mark replied, brightening. "For a
long time your stories and tricks—I mean spells," he cor-
rected himself rapidly as the wizard's brows darkened, "were
the most exciting thing in my life. Now here I am in the
middle of an adventure of my own and it doesn't seem like
the ones I've read in books at all."

"They rarely do. Scribes and storytellers have a nasty
habit of leaving all the unpleasant, uncomfortable, or just
boring bits out of their tales."

"And the worry," said the prince. "In a story things don't
matter. But this does. We've *got* to find Fontaine, haven't
we?"

"We will."

"Yes, we will," said Mark, his face displaying uncharacteristic fierceness.

At this point their conversation was rudely interrupted by
a loud shout of surprise from the stern. They looked round
quickly just in time to see a pair of legs, the wrong way up,
disappearing over the back railing. At the same time the boat
heeled round, causing everyone to stagger and the sails to
flap wildly.

There was a loud splash and then the air was filled with
curses and Birn's voice yelling orders to his three crewmen.
The rigging was rapidly brought under control and the boat
steadied as Birn took control of the tiller.

Mark ran back to the stern. Brandel emerged from the
below-decks cabin where he'd been resting.

"What's going on?" he asked.

"Someone's fallen overboard," said Mark on his way
past.

"It's Ansar," said Orme. "He was at the tiller."

Mark reached the stern rail and saw the Healdean prince,
now some way behind, splashing and spluttering in the lazy
swell.

"Bloody idiot nearly capsized us," muttered Birn, bringing the boat round smoothly. "We'll have to fish him out
quick."

"He can swim all right," said Mark.

"Yes, but that water's terrible cold. If it gets to his bones, he'll die sure as if he drowned."

Mark, who until then had found the whole scene rather comic, grew serious and kept out of Birn's way as he brought the boat round in a circle and organized ropes to be thrown to the unfortunate Ansar.

Everyone was now on deck watching the proceedings and there were plenty of willing hands to haul in their unusual catch and to help him climb on board, where he was hurried below decks to be warmed and change his clothes.

"I'm sorry, sir," said Birn to Ferragamo when the boat was back on course. "He said he'd sailed before and asked to take the tiller. I was reluctant but he all but ordered me. I'm not used to dealing with nobility." His voice trailed off sheepishly.

"Birn, as far as I am concerned, you are sole master of this vessel. Where sailing is concerned *you* give the orders—to anybody and everybody. I will explain this fact to our young friend."

Ferragamo went below, a stern expression on his face.

"What happened?" asked Mark.

"He tried to change tack without letting anyone know. The wind and swell caught him short and the tiller knocked him over," answered Birn shortly, adding a few uncomplimentary epithets. "It'll not happen again."

"Will he be all right?"

"Aye. We got him out quick enough. He'll be cold for a while though," Birn added with grim satisfaction.

It was a chastened and subdued Ansar who emerged some time later. His apology to Birn, while it had quite obviously been ordered by Ferragamo, was none the less sincere and was accepted gruffly.

The rest of the afternoon passed uneventfully and at sunset they anchored near Stane. Two of the sailors rowed Ferragamo, Shill, and Bonet ashore while the others prepared for a cramped night on board. The shore party returned an hour or so later with little to report.

"We heard a few horror stories about the forest," said Shill, "but no one seems to have any idea where the outlaws' camp might be. Some people reckon there's more than one band."

"And there's no news from further north either, as far as

we can glean," added Ferragamo, "though there were plenty of rumors about us! I think we're safer on board tonight. And it'll mean we can go on at first light."

The *Seahawk* boasted few home comforts and was not usually at sea overnight, and there were more than twice as many people on board as usual so space was at a premium. Fortunately it was a warm night so that most of them slept on deck rolled in cloaks or blankets, but even so the only ones who were truly comfortable were probably Owl, who roosted in the rigging, and Longfur, who curled happily within a coil of rope close to where Mark lay looking at the stars. Only the sound of Brandel's snoring was audible above the slap and gurgle of water on the hull and the creaking of rigging and anchor chains as the *Seahawk* shifted in the breeze.

He doesn't have any trouble sleeping, does he? came Longfur's comment.

Brandy never does.

Unlike you, he doesn't let anything as ephemeral as thought or imagination interfere with his bodily comforts. All he cares about is eating, drinking, and sleeping.

He would have made a good cat.

If I thought you meant that I would sulk. Outrage dripped from Longfur's every word. *As it is I'm glad to find you in the mood for joking,* he added pompously. *You've been very quiet recently.*

Have I?

Inside you have. I didn't like it when you went funny over that book. It was as if you weren't there.

I think I was trying to hide. The idea had only just occurred to Mark. *And that's the only way I could do it.*

Hide from what?

I don't want to think about it.

That's as silly as trying to forget about something. You have to remember what something is in order to forget it!

You don't understand.

You're still hiding, aren't you? You've never been like this with me before. We've never had any secrets. Longfur sounded huffy.

I'm not doing it deliberately, Longfur. There's a part of me I don't seem able to control.

The cat's thoughts formed the feline equivalent of shrugging shoulders and left it at that. A while later he spoke again. *If you don't go to sleep soon the sun will be rising. Shall I sing to you?*

No! replied Mark, laughing silently. *I've heard your singing.*

Among those who appreciate such things I am considered to have a very fine voice, the cat retorted.

You'd more likely be thrown overboard.

Nonsense. Every sailor knows a ship's not complete without a cat. They're lucky. Unlike bird-brain up there. He glanced up at Owl. *Goodness knows what the seagulls make of him.*

How can I go to sleep if you keep chattering? asked Mark, smiling to himself.

With that they lapsed into mutual silence and the two of them went their separate dreaming ways. Longfur purred in his sleep.

They weighed anchor at sunrise and by noon had reached the mouth of the River Greenwater. Although for most of its length the river flowed through the great southern forest its source was further north in the Windchill Mountains and even in summer a large volume of water flowed into the sea. At its mouth the Greenwater was wide and placid and the *Seahawk* had little difficulty in navigation for the first league or so. After that the river narrowed and the forest closed in on either side of them. The combined effect of the faster current and the shelter from the wind made progress much slower and soon it seemed to Mark that he could have walked into the forest more quickly. Then he considered the dense growth which clustered beneath the trees on the river bank and decided that maybe this way was better after all.

By late afternoon they reached the place which Birn said was as far as the river was navigable for the big boat. The spot was marked by a wooden landing stage, long fallen into disrepair, which the sailors said had been used at one time by hunters to send their furs to Stane or Bark. The *Seahawk* was moored and the two small boats were prepared to continue the journey upstream.

Birn and his crew agreed to stay with the boat until noon two days later. After that it would be up to the sailors whether they waited any longer or departed leaving the

search party to make their way home as best they could.
They were already making plans for hunting trips into the
forest and were in quite a playful mood, in contrast to the
wizard's party who loaded supplies in determined silence.

Anxious to make the most of the remaining daylight,
Ferragamo hurried everyone along and organized the crewing
of the small boats. The wizard, Mark, Orme, and Bonet
would travel in one boat, with Ansar entrusted with the tiller
after his plea for a second chance, while Brandel, Shill, and
the other two soldiers would sail the other.

They made better time than the *Seahawk* would have
done, but even so they frequently had to resort to rowing
when the current grew too strong for the small sails to
overcome, and all of them were glad when Ferragamo called
for the boats to be moored at a clear stretch of the western
bank. They set up camp and collected wood for a fire while
the wizard prepared to try and pinpoint Fontaine's location
more accurately with his searching spell.

"Mark, come here. I want to try something."

Mark stacked his armful of firewood and came over to the
wizard as he sat a little apart from the activity.

"Do you know how a searching spell works?"

"I think so. You told me about it once. That was a long
time ago, though."

"Well, it doesn't really matter. The important thing is that
I want to find out where Fontaine is, how far away and in
which direction. It would also help if we knew a few landmarks, either where she is or on the way there."

Ferragamo took out the princess's handkerchief and laid it
on the ground between them.

"When I tell you, place your left hand on this, touching
mine, and repeat the words that I say. I hope you will be able
to see what I do and your eyes are sharper than mine. Try to
remember every detail."

"What are the words I have to say?"

"In themselves they're not important. They just happen
to be the keys to this spell which are locked in my mind.
They won't even make sense to you. Put your hand on mine.
Now shut your eyes, relax, and try to empty your mind of all
thought."

For a few moments Mark's mind tumbled over in a
mixture of confusion, excitement, and trepidation but then he
controlled his thoughts by concentrating on the gentle rip-

pling noise of the nearby river. Eventually even this became an abstract sensation and faded into nonexistence. He felt very calm.

Then Ferragamo said just three words, which Mark repeated and then instantly forgot, unaware of whether he had whispered, shouted, or even just thought the strange syllables.

Immediately, he was almost overwhelmed by a rush of images. Though still aware of the river bank underneath him it was as if he were flying, soaring over the treetops at a dizzying pace. The river shone to his right; an unusually shaped fir tree which stood above its neighbors flashed by; and he noted a small treeless hill half a league to his left. Then the sensation of movement slowed and, fighting vertigo, he seemed to plunge into the trees, coming to rest at the level of the lowest branches of an ancient oak. Before him was the outlaw camp. And there in their midst was Fontaine, helping a huge bald man serve out some kind of stew, and looking quite at home. She was even smiling as she moved among the rough-looking men.

As Mark remembered the purpose of his "visit" and began to count the men he could see and take note of the details of the camp, Fontaine paused on her way back to the cooking fire and then looked up, seemingly straight into Mark's eyes. There was a puzzled expression on her face. Then she shrugged and sat down, cross-legged, on the floor.

"Eat up," Mark heard her say. "There's plenty more."

She turned to the giant seated beside her and smiled. He smiled back and Mark felt an odd quiver of jealousy.

Then the scene began to waver, as if it were under water, and abruptly he was back by the river, listening to its small sounds. Mark opened his eyes to find Ferragamo looking at him questioningly.

"Which direction would you say?" the wizard asked.

Unhesitatingly Mark pointed into the forest, in a line just behind his left shoulder, almost due west.

"Good lad! Exactly what I thought. How far?"

"About two leagues?"

"Nearer three I would say but still close enough." He sounded pleased.

"Ferragamo, that was amazing. It was like flying!"

"Yes, well, we'll talk about that later. I'm glad it worked, but right now we have plans to make."

For some time the two of them compared notes from their

joint vision and then discussed their conclusions with the others. The river turned north at this point and so it was decided to leave the boats where they were now and continue on foot at first light. With the element of surprise on their side they hoped that even if it came to a fight they had a good chance against the fifteen or so men that Mark and Ferragamo had seen.

"Finding them shouldn't be too much problem," said Shill. "We can spread out in a line of sight and move slowly until we see them. Then we can spy out the situation and make any last-minute plans on the spot."

"I'll send Owl out later," said Ferragamo, "just to confirm their position and to see if we can spot where Fontaine is sleeping."

"I'm going to enjoy this," said Ansar.

Mark didn't sleep much that night.

They were up at dawn the next day and, leaving most of their gear behind, set off westward. They were all armed. Even Mark had been given a spare sword, though Ferragamo emphasized that it was to be used only for self-defense.

"If it comes to a fight, leave it to the people who know what they're doing," the wizard said, "though I hope we won't need any bloodshed. I have a few tricks up my sleeve."

Mark was secretly relieved at the advice. The sword felt heavy and awkward in his hand. *I'm more likely to injure myself than anyone else*, he thought.

Practice on a few trees, came Longfur's comment. *They should be big enough to hit and they don't move too much.*

Just keep out of my way. I might practice on you!

Not a chance, came the reply. *Besides, I had better stay close to keep you out of trouble.*

You're the smuggest person I've ever met.

With good reason, Longfur replied smugly.

With Owl flying above and relaying information to Ferragamo about their course and various landmarks, the party made reasonable progress. Even though it was still gloomy beneath the thick roof of leaves, and the occasional impenetrable patch of undergrowth made some detours necessary, they were able to travel in a more or less direct line westward.

They kept together with the older members of the group

curbing Ansar's enthusiastic tendency to get ahead of everyone else. When it was judged that they were getting close to the camp, they spread out, with Orme and Shill at either end and Mark and the wizard in the center. The others were ranged in between and it was arranged so that everyone could see at least two people on either side at any one time. They advanced separately, as cautiously and as quietly as possible.

After a few minutes Mark thought he recognized the lie of the land. Signaling to Ferragamo, he pointed to the small stream and the large oak beyond it. The wizard nodded and they regrouped. As the first rays of the sun filtered through the greenery they were able to pick out the various dwellings which at first sight appeared to be no more than undergrowth of an unusually dense nature.

"There are some platforms in the trees as well," said Mark. "We'll have to watch out for men above us."

"For outdoorsmen they're late risers," said Shill. "There's no sign of activity at all."

"Let's hope they all had too much to drink last night," joked Orme quietly. "We might get away without a fight at all."

Ansar was unable to hide an expression of disappointment, and watching him, Mark had to stifle a nervous giggle.

"There were horses tethered over there recently," said Essan, "but there's none around now."

"Do you have any idea which one of those huts Fontaine is in?" asked Shill.

"No," said Mark.

"Not really," said Ferragamo, "but we can guess that it's likely to be one near the center of the camp."

"The big one nearest the fire perhaps?"

I'll go and find out, said an unexpected voice in Mark's head, and Longfur trotted off gaily toward the camp.

One of the soldiers noticed and made a grab for the cat which was avoided with contemptuous ease.

"Stop him," hissed Orme.

"No," said Mark, quietly but commandingly. "Let him go. He knows what he's doing." *Be careful,* he added silently.

Of course, came the jaunty reply. *Keep your humans quiet.*

Ferragamo was smiling broadly but the rest of the party

divided their attention between Longfur and Mark, both of whom they regarded with a good deal of suspicion.

Mark watched anxiously as Longfur padded silently into the camp. Keeping a careful watch about him he went straight up to the large hut, stood up on his hind legs, and pushed at the door which opened with a creak. Everyone tensed at the sound but still nothing stirred. Longfur disappeared inside.

It's empty, came the cat's report, *but she was in here recently. I can scent her. I'll try the next one.*

Longfur reappeared and tried the next hut. The door didn't move.

"What's going on?" whispered Shill. Mark was grateful when Ferragamo answered, "I don't think she's in there. Divide up into pairs and take one hut each. At my signal we all go in but keep it quiet if possible. There are still the tree houses to consider. And no unnecessary violence," he said, looking at Ansar. "Knock people out if you have to but no killings. We're not here for that."

Mark was still watching Longfur while these arrangements were being made. The cat had tried several huts but none of the doors would budge.

We're coming in, Mark told him.

Wait a bit, Longfur replied. *I just want to try something.* And with that, he climbed rapidly up one of the largest trees. To delay things a moment Mark asked, "What am I going to do?"

"Come with me," said Shill. "We'll circle round and take that hut over there." He pointed.

Mark looked questioningly at Ferragamo.

"Go ahead," said the wizard, "but mind you do exactly as Shill says."

Longfur's voice came again. *The ones in this tree are asleep.*

Well, don't wake them up then, Mark replied.

No chance of that. I just walked across the chest of one of them and licked his nose. He still didn't wake up!

Mark's abstracted air made Shill and Ferragamo look at him curiously.

"Wait a moment," said the prince. "There's something strange going on here."

"That's an understatement," said Shill. He looked at Ferragamo and the wizard motioned him to leave the two of them alone. When the others were out of earshot, Mark told the wizard what Longfur had said. He had just finished when the cat spoke again.

The lot in the next tree are just the same. I bit one and he just kept snoring.

"They're all fast asleep. Are they under an enchantment?"

"Something a little more prosaic, I think," replied the wizard. More loudly he said, "Stay cautious, but we may have had some help from outside. They seem to be having difficulty waking up!"

"Let's go," ordered Shill, and the looks of puzzlement about him were replaced by those of professional determination.

Stealthily they took up their positions. At Ferragamo's sign, four doors were thrust open and men moved quickly inside, swords at the ready. Mark stayed by the door at Shill's instruction as the soldier went in. A few moments later he emerged, a curious smile on his face.

"There are two of them in here, dead to the world. Even a sword point to the throat didn't rouse them."

Others were coming out of the huts with expressions that told that they had found the same thing.

Ferragamo walked into the center of the glade and everyone looked automatically to him.

"Check the other huts," he said, "including the ones in the trees. I don't think we'll meet any opposition but it pays to be careful."

Soldiers moved off purposefully.

"But where's Fontaine!" cried Ansar.

"I would have thought that was obvious," replied the wizard. "She's escaped. Probably by drugging her captors and simply walking out. That's why the horses have gone."

Ansar stared at him openmouthed then moved off to help with the final search. Following a hunch, Mark also went round all the huts, on and above the ground, checking on the occupants.

A few minutes later they all grouped at the center of the camp.

"Fourteen men in all," said Shill, "but no Fontaine."

"The big bald man isn't here either," said Mark.

"What man?" said Ansar.

"It looks like one of the outlaws has gone with her," replied Ferragamo.

"You mean he's carried her off for himself?"

"I don't think so. They seemed to be friends."

"How do you know?"

"I'm a wizard," Ferragamo said shortly.

Ansar looked skeptical but said nothing. After a few moments' silence, Orme asked, "What do we do now?"

"I knew that girl was trouble," said Brandel. "She hasn't even got the patience to be rescued properly."

Even Mark had to laugh at that.

Chapter 10

*A*fter a hot and satisfying breakfast, Fontaine began to wonder about her situation. Escape seemed out of the question, for the moment at least. Although not closely guarded, there were too many interested eyes about for her to risk any untoward movements, such as leaping on to a horse, yelling, "I'm off!" and thundering away into the forest. On the other hand, as she was not restricted, she was reasonably free to do as she wished. In spite of her treatment of Clowery at the river and her sharp-tongued advice to him, she decided that she would prefer to keep her distance from the three revelers of the previous night. Durc and Zunic sat together by the fire, heads close in talk, and the only reasonably friendly face around was Jani's. He was still serving hot porridge to others of the outlaw group, and Fontaine watched him closely.

From her vantage point on the ground, he seemed enormous, far bigger than any of the other men.

He'd be a good size to have as a friend, she thought, not having previously considered men much for their physical attributes. The young and haughty princess was more used to considering a person's attitude toward herself when deciding her likes and dislikes. *And he saved me last night, without even thinking of the harm he could have done to me. It wasn't just because Durc warned him to guard me, I'm sure. I rather think I like this fellow.*

This fellow turned from serving the last outlaw, the ever-so-slightly dampened Clowery, and grinned at Fontaine.

He likes me too, she thought, pleased, and got up and went over to the bald giant.

"I'll help you clear up," she said, knowing that he couldn't hear her, but at the same time making movements as though she were cleaning dishes. Jani understood, and gently pushed her in the direction of the river, following her with dirty pots and a cloth for scouring them clean.

If, a short while later, Durc found the scene of the proud princess of Heald—on her knees on the river bank, scrubbing dishes and humming—an unusual sight, he wisely did not show it. His slight experience of the girl's temper and attitudes warned him that it was all too easy to tip her over the edge into shrewishness. He didn't wish to repeat the experience—a happy captive would be easier to deal with.

"Good day to you again," he said. Fontaine started, then said, "Oh, it's you. You made me jump, creeping up on me like that."

"I beg your pardon. I didn't mean to startle you, but to inform you that I will be sending a messenger to Heald today with a ransom note, and believe that the matter could be brought to a swifter and more satisfying conclusion to all, were you to give the man directions for his journey and the best way for him to gain admittance to your parents' court and hearing. Don't you agree?"

"Yes, I do," she said sharply. "Though no doubt they will object to hearing news of me this way, at least they'll know I'm alive. The sooner your man gets there, the sooner I'll be free." A doubtful look passed over her face.

"You *will* free me, won't you? How do I know that I can trust you, after what you've done. You killed Eric!"

"He was as likely to have killed *me*, the way he was brandishing that sword around! He wasn't playing with it! For my word and honor, you'll just have to trust me. I haven't harmed you yet, nor have my men."

"Though they'd have liked to," she retorted bitterly. "It was only Jani who saved me from a fate worse than death last night." She shuddered.

"Yes, well, as to that, you may be relieved to hear that at least one of the troublemakers is to depart the camp soon. I'm sending Deg to Heald. He's not always as stupid as he seemed last night—yes," he said, as she looked up in surprise, "I heard all about your little commotion from one of my men."

"Not Jani, surely," Fontaine said.

"No, he cannot speak, as you know. Another of my men, who, while not wanting to take arms against Deg and his merry men last night, still thought it better that I should know about the episode. It won't happen again. I'm amazed, though, that you did not tell me of this yourself."

"I would have done," she said. "I was just so relieved to awaken unharmed this morning, that I had not pulled my thoughts together." She paused. "So Deg is to be the ransom demander. Can you trust him? Will he bring an answer and the ransom straight back to you? How do you know he won't make off with the money?"

"Do you honestly think your parents would hand over a payment, without a sight of you alive, and unharmed? No, Deg will arrange a rendezvous. We'll meet your parents' emissary in Bark, on a date to be arranged. You should prepare yourself for a lengthy stay, though. However quickly Deg can travel and persuade your father that he tells the truth, it will be quite some time before he returns and you take your leave of us. Still, you seem to have found a protector—and employer, of sorts—in Jani. You should be safe enough, and we'll try to make sure you don't get bored."

She looked sharply at him, looking for the malice behind his words. Finding none, she sighed. The thought of spending any time at all in the camp was a depressing one to someone used to ease and comfort, and respect of sorts. To Fontaine it seemed a heavy sentence for her brief desire for adventure.

"Well, the sooner I brief Deg on the best route, the sooner I can hope"—with a gentle stress on the word—"to get out of here. Will you help me carry these dishes back to Jani?"

If Durc's men were surprised to see him walking meekly beside Fontaine with his arms full of clean dishes, they had more sense than to show it. His look dared them not to.

Deg's briefing from Fontaine was short—and curt. The girl had no liking for the man who, as well as being the ringleader of her previous night's fear, was also a thoroughly disreputable-looking character. His shifty eyes, greasy hair, and dirty fingernails were among his most prepossessing characteristics, and Fontaine wanted their interview to be as short as possible. She told him of the quickest route to her parents' palace, and advised him on how to win their ear, giving him her ring. Her parents would know it for hers, and that, combined with the note she had written for them, would convince them of the genuineness of the ransom demand. Durc's note would convince them of its urgency.

Deg himself was glad to be sent on this errand. On his way through Bark, he fully intended availing himself of some longed-for female company. It was a minor port with major attractions, as far as he was concerned, in the form of the local ale and the local whorehouses. Besides, his reputation, since the trouser-singeing episode, could do with some boosting, and if he managed to obtain for the outlaws the enormous amount of money Durc was demanding, his ego would grow, as would his reputation as a cunning emissary.

So Deg's going suited everyone, and he was sent on his way in the early afternoon. Jani, as well as Fontaine, heaved a sigh of relief to see him go. That was one less threat to deal with.

In fact many years would pass before Fontaine learned what became of Deg, and when her ring was eventually returned to her family it would be in circumstances even stranger than those she found herself in now.

Left much to her own devices that afternoon, Fontaine's mood was a pensive one. Pensive, soon turning to rebellious. *I wish I wasn't stuck here all on my own,* she thought, not counting a camp full of outlaws as company. *I want to be back home with my family and friends.* This thought stopped her in her tracks, as she realized that those she considered her friends were Koria, Mark, and Ferragamo. At this distance and in these circumstances, even Brandel looked appealing. They might be rude to her sometimes, but they were better than a bunch of fawning courtiers. Another thought struck her. What would happen to her now that Eric was dead? Would they want to marry her to Brandel? She shuddered. Or send her back to her parents' court until the situation stabilized or another suitor showed his face? This time her shudder was more of a shiver, realizing that neither option appealed to her. Grimly, jaw set, she decided that when she was freed, she wanted to go back to Home (and not marry anyone!) if they wanted her with them after her stupid behavior. Koria would intercede on her behalf, Fontaine was sure; her words might have some effect on Ferragamo. And Mark could be kind, too, sometimes.

Her mood brightened for a moment at this, and then sank back into despair at the prospect of days—or even *months*—held as a captive with a bunch of hardened criminals. Deg might have gone, but that still left a large number of men who could be lecherously inclined. And she could count on only two as possible friends; Durc—who would protect his investment—and Jani. She thought about Jani. At times, she was sure, there seemed to be almost an understanding between them, as if he could sense her thoughts. Strange for such a frightening-looking man to be the most gentle. She needed all the friends she could get. She'd never had that many, her sharp tongue and unpleasant manner had seen to that, and the thought that in the big man she had found an ally was sweet.

But her mood, as it was wont to do, changed swiftly. Impatience at her helplessness grew in her until she could have cried from vexation. The worst thing of all, she decided, was the inability to do anything herself. Biting on her lip, she could feel the frustration welling up inside her, until she almost wanted to bang her head against a very hard tree in order to stop herself thinking.

If she could hope that help was on its way, that someone cared enough about her to take her away from this peril, she decided, she would never ask any boon from life again. And, as she bitterly doubted that anyone *did* care enough, or even if they did that they would be able to find her in this impenetrable forest, she decided she was on her own. She'd just have to take matters into her own hands. With this resolve, though with no firm idea as to what she was taking on, Fontaine looked up from the ground, at which she'd been glaring fixedly for some time, to see Jani, standing near her, with an expression of mingled worry and doubt on his large-boned face. He looked at the girl, puzzled, then his expression cleared, as if he'd made up his mind about something, and coming over to her, knelt down and took one of her hands in both of his. Amazed, Fontaine could only stare at him. No one, but no one, had ever dared lay a hand on the princess of Heald's person. Familiarity was not something encouraged by that young lady. To her surprise, she found herself liking the touch of his hands; it was almost comforting. She could feel a

strength about him that she suddenly realized was intended
for her. A happiness surged up inside her—someone *cared*!

Jani grinned at the lightening of her expression, squeezed
her hand as if to say, "Don't worry," and pulled her onto her
feet.

He walked back to where he had been preparing the
camp's evening meal and, leaving Fontaine there and signing
his request for her help in chopping vegetables, walked away
to his own hut.

I wonder what he's up to? Fontaine thought, but wasn't
left to puzzle for long. Jani soon returned, carrying a handful
of what looked like spice powder. This he added to the
cooking pot, then stirred, raising the spoon to his nose in a
pantomime of delight. She laughed, causing Durc and Zunic,
who were once again in close consultation, to raise their
brows.

"That smells very good, Jani," Fontaine chuckled. "I'm
sure we're all going to enjoy our dinner."

Enjoy it they all did. Worn out by her afternoon's troubled musings, Fontaine sleepily sought her bed not more
than an hour after she'd finished eating, and fell immediately
into a deep and dreamless sleep.

On wakening the next morning, she looked to see if Jani was
at his post at her door and saw, somewhat to her surprise,
that he wasn't. Getting up, she went outside, almost to fall
over her large friend sitting by the door. He was watching the
men as they gradually awoke and went about their day's
business, a satisfied—and rather smug—look on his face.
Fontaine ascribed this to the fact that there had obviously
been no would-be intruders during the night and, smiling at
him in passing, walked sleepily down to the river, where she
hoped the clear, cold water would wash away some of the
cobwebs in her brain. *I wish I could wake up properly,* she
thought. *I need to work out what to do.* But the gentle
lassitude that was with her remained for the rest of that day,
and she dozed in the shade of a tree, rousing herself only
when it was time once again to help Jani cook dinner.

"You're bright and breezy this evening," she said to him
and smiled. He smiled back and, laying down his paring
knife, went into his hut, beckoning her to follow. Puzzled,

she nevertheless did so, occasioning some ribald comments and whistles from the outlaws who had seen this exchange.

Trying to ignore the flush that crept up her face, she looked at Jani, wondering at the reason for the summons. He rummaged around in some pots, then held up more of the spice used in the meal the previous day. Pointing to it with one hand, he pillowed his head on the other, feigning sleep for a few moments. Then, picking up a larger handful, he repeated the pantomime, only this time, he pretended to sleep for a while longer.

Puzzled, Fontaine could only stare at him. Then understanding dawned.

"By all the heavens, Jani, you drugged us! Last night's *was* a heavy sleep!"

As the realization hit her of what his signaling had meant, she gave a little squeal and jumped up and down a few times, before hugging him—being careful not to spill any of the precious power. Then she collected herself and quieted down, not wanting anyone outside to hear her.

And you'll drug them again tonight, but with a heavier dose, and while they're asleep, we can get away. On horseback, we'll be miles away before they wake up and discover I'm missing. Why, I feel as fearless as any heroine!

A thought struck her and she looked at Jani. "You *are* coming with me, aren't you?" she whispered, pointing to herself, and then to him, and then using her fingers to signify walking away. He nodded, put an arm around her shoulders, gave her a hug, and then pushed her back toward the door. Her jaunty step, which she tried to curb with difficulty, led the men to nudge each other and chuckle.

Rude pigs! See if I care. I'll be out of here soon!

It was a happy Fontaine who helped Jani serve that evening's meal to the outlaws, though she did her best to appear unperturbed. At one point, making her way back to the fire, she had the oddest sensation—almost as if she were being watched. It wasn't a worrying feeling, but a friendly one. With a slightly inquiring frown, she looked up into the trees, but saw nothing and, shrugging, sat down and pretended to eat her own portion.

"You're not eating much, girl. Not hungry after all your exercise?" A raggedy-looking man leered at her.

"Don't be so impertinent, fellow! The doings of a royal lady should be no concern of yours." Her haughty manner softened somewhat as she continued, "No, I'm not very hungry, but you should eat up. There's plenty more."

Looking around at Jani, who had sat down next to her, she smiled.

The outlaws ate heartily. Except, of course, for Jani and Fontaine; she feigned lack of appetite, while the big man only pretended to gobble up his meal with the rest of them.

It was early to bed for the whole camp, and the resonant sounds of a large group of men snoring out of tune soon filled the forest for some distance. After listening to these beautiful sounds for nearly thirty minutes Jani and Fontaine, alone in their hut, decided that perhaps the coast was clear, and made their way to where the horses which Fontaine and Eric had ridden were tethered. They arranged their few supplies and Jani handed the princess a dagger, indicating that he too was armed. She accepted it gratefully and thought, *I do hope I don't have to use it. I don't know how good I'd be in a fight, but it is reassuring.* She cursed suddenly. *Damnation! How could I be so stupid! The sword—Eric's sword, Arkon's blade he'd called it—I mustn't leave that behind!* Taking hold of Jani's arm, she mimed the drawing of a large blade, pointed back to the camp, and looked pleadingly at him. He nodded and ran off quietly, returning very shortly with the sword that Eric had drawn just before his death. Fontaine was surprised at the jolt it gave her. Eric may have been, in her eyes, a bit of a fool, but he *had* been intended for her husband, and she had got to know him quite well over the last few months. She had few enough friends that she could afford not to mourn the loss of one who should have been her closest. She thought of breaking the news of his death to Mark, and her heart sank.

Jani, seeing her gloomy expression, put a finger under her chin, tilted her face up to his, and with his other arm, made a sweeping gesture of "Let's go!" She gave herself a mental shake, and they went, leading the horses. The forest all around the camp was dense, almost impenetrable in places. The camp's site had been chosen deliberately; only a few knew the paths of access, which meant that discovery was unlikely. It also meant that Fontaine and Jani could not ride away, but must lead their horses for some time.

The quiet pace suited Fontaine for a while. Her thoughts were excited, racing ahead to what she would do when she was safe again, and the walk soothed her. She and Jani walked on, with her new friend leading the way. He constantly looked back over his shoulder, as if to check that she was all right, and she smiled reassuringly, his care warming her heart.

She wondered about what course her life was going to take if—when—they reached Home safely. How would Ferragamo, Mark, and Brandel welcome a man who had been part of the outlaw band which had killed Eric? But she was sure that Jani was gentle, and wouldn't hurt anyone. Following this train of thought, she became agitated and was amazed when Jani stopped his horse and quickly walked back to her. His frustration at not being able to speak was evident, and he took her hand. She was quite surprised at the way he had known of her changed mood, looked at him ruefully and squeezed his hand. They went on. After some time, though, she began to get tired, and almost envied her ruffian captors their drugged sleep. She wondered what Durc's reaction would be on awakening and finding them gone. She shivered. *Best to put a good distance between us,* she thought. This conquered her sleepiness for some time. The path through the forest eventually became clearer, and she and Jani were able to mount their horses and ride, though not at speed.

Some hours later, Jani felt that they were far enough away from the camp to be reasonably safe, and motioned Fontaine to stop. They dismounted, and while Fontaine stretched her tired limbs, Jani prepared them a speedy but nourishing meal. He did not light a fire, and Fontaine was cold, so she went and sat by him as they ate. At first, she felt slightly awkward and, sensing this, he looked at her appraisingly, then put an arm around her shoulders and pulled her closer to him. After a moment, she relaxed and enjoyed the sensation of closeness. After what the weary girl thought was all too short a rest, they were off again, on horseback, riding through the still dark forest in what she hoped was the general direction of Stane.

Daylight came eventually, and with it, welcome sleep. Fontaine and Jani both knew that to travel during the day would be foolhardy and dangerous. They could not hide the horses completely, but Jani rigged a shelter so that the animals would be partly hidden from view. Then a little further down the path, but set back slightly from it, he did the same thing for himself and his royal charge. They took their packs and arms into their makeshift hut and settled themselves.

Fontaine awoke some considerable time later to find that Jani still slept. His face looked as peaceful in repose as it did when he was awake, and she smiled. They were lying close together, having huddled together for warmth in their morning's sleep, but she did not feel embarrassed. Indeed, she found their relationship a source of some amazement. She could not recall ever having felt such a liking for anyone, nor so in tune with anyone as she did with Jani. In spite of his muteness, they communicated with remarkable ease, almost as if each one knew what the other was thinking. And she knew that his proximity was no danger to her; on the contrary, he was her protection. On this comforting thought, she drew her cloak up to her neck and snuggled back down to sleep again.

They spent all that day at rest in their little hut, Jani occasionally venturing forth to check that their horses were all right. Nobody had found them and they set off once darkness had fallen. They rode through the night, and slept again the next morning. After a short sleep, Fontaine awoke, full of impatience to press on. She longed for the company of her erstwhile companions. *Surely Durc would have found us by now if he was going to,* she thought. *We must be safe— and I do so want to get back to Home.* She persuaded Jani that they were far enough from Durc and danger for it to be safe for them to travel in daylight, and so once again they mounted their horses. Fontaine's sore behind didn't bother her too much on this journey. She knew where she was going and would suffer any discomfort to get there quickly.

Alas, the poor princess was to suffer more than discomfort! Durc and his men were not the only outlaws in the forest, and an even more vicious group spotted the pair of travelers that afternoon. Rustlings from the trees aroused Fontaine's attention from her dream of Koria's cooking—and soothing words—but it was too late. She and Jani were surrounded by a bunch of filthy, evil-looking men, all armed to the teeth.

"Oh *no,* not *again!*" she wailed.

Chapter 11

*T*hree days after his arrival in Starhill, Rehan had not advanced his cause very much. It did not bother him unduly. He was enjoying the generally lazy pace of the city life and if he had learned nothing definite he had at least received further reassurance, albeit inconclusive, that the princes and Fontaine had escaped. People in the city were, if anything, even more reluctant to speak of these matters than those in Grayrock, which Rehan thought was only right and proper.

His main aim now was to obtain an audience with Parokkan and to this end he had made several useful contacts in trade and court circles which he hoped would eventually bring him and his merchandise to the king's attention.

Every so often, something about the people around him struck him as odd, although he was quite unable to put his finger on the reason for this. Uncomfortably, he recalled Hoban's words. *I've not got a good feeling from this visit of mine.* However, the moments soon passed and he was content to spend his time in conversation and a little exploration when he felt more energetic.

In the evening of his third day in the city Rehan was sitting at a table outside one of the better taverns in the company of a group of local merchants and craftsmen.

A tailor who was most interested in Rehan's merchandise, but who had been unable to persuade him to even show any of his wares, was getting slightly drunk and becoming more talkative than usual.

"We're well rid of them," he said, to general nods of agreement. "What did Ather ever do for trade, eh? I'll tell you. Nothing. Nothing at all. We're well rid of them. At least this new lot spend a bit of money." He jingled coins in his pocket.

"Aye," said another, "the queen's got an eye for a nice bit of stuff."

"She's a nice bit of stuff herself from what I hear."

"And they're not afraid to try a few new things. Ather was so set in his ways I thought he'd turn to stone."

"His sons were a poor lot too, I'll tell you. We're better off with Parokkan by far."

"Here's to King Parokkan."

"And Queen Amarino."

Toasts were drunk and more wine called for.

Rehan sat silently, enjoying the drink and content to let events take their course.

"And another thing," went on the tailor, "they've cleared the city of the vermin—the tramps and beggars. You don't see them around any more these days, do you?"

"That's right," replied another. "The streets are safer now for decent folk."

There was a chorus of agreement. A question began to form in Rehan's mind but disappeared, forgotten, before he came close to voicing it. He picked up his goblet instead. As he did so the tailor spotted a passerby and called out "Captain Luca, well met!" He was not so drunk to miss the trick of promoting the royal guard beyond his actual station.

"What news from the Castle? Has our royal lady chosen from the designs I submitted? I am eager to be of service."

The soldier walked up, eyeing the group somewhat contemptuously.

"I am sure *all* of you are only too eager to be of service. But take care, gentlemen. The queen is as shrewd as any of you and will not be taken in by your flattering tongues."

"We doubt it not, captain. But put us to the test. If we do not offer true value then we will be rightly spurned." His face was the picture of false humility.

"You'll get your chance, merchant. The queen is looking for new apparel for the coronation. Naturally the old, traditional robes are not to be used. She commands any who can offer cloth, garments, or adornments of sufficient worth to submit them for examination by her treasury officials tomorrow morning. Those found to be worthy she will inspect herself, later in the day. *If* you have anything suitable then there is your opportunity. I wish you luck, gentlemen." *You'll* need it, his manner implied. "Good night." He strode away, leaving a momentarily silent group behind him.

Soon afterward the merchants went their separate ways and Rehan returned to the inn where he was lodging, secretly rejoicing—for he knew the worth of what he had to offer—but with a nervous sensation in his stomach which was not entirely due to the wine.

When Rehan arrived at the City Square outside the main gate of the castle the next morning, there was already a crush of people waiting for admittance. Word of the impending royal audience had spread like forest fire so that now half the city seemed to be clustered around the gateway, vying for precedence and proclaiming the superiority of their goods. All sorts of merchants were there, from the richest, surrounded by an escort of servants and carriers, to the humblest artisans protectively clutching the finest examples of their craft. Many had little or no chance of even being admitted to the treasury and must have known it to be so, but all had been drawn by the lure of royal patronage and all the wealth and status that implied.

Others in the crowd had different reasons for being there. Some had come to trade with the traders; winesellers who knew that some ill-provisioned people would be here all day and would need drink to sustain and later to console them; bakers' boys with cakes and breakfast rolls; old women selling good-luck charms which would *guarantee* a gullible merchant's success. Then there were those whose trade involved no selling but the removal of other people's goods—or purses. Lastly there were those who could have given no good reason for being there at all but who had been caught up in the hectic atmosphere and irresistibly drawn into the mêlée.

The gates were still fast shut and from the guard house towers on either side, and from the parapet above, soldiers watched the throng with detached amusement. It was a colorful and noisy scene.

Rehan saw no need to join the scramble for admittance and sat instead at a wine-shop table on the far side of the square, feeling the reassuringly heavy weight of the soft leather pouch stowed inside his jerkin. He ordered sparkling wine and cakes and awaited developments.

Before too long a door inset into the large gate was opened from within and two soldiers came out. Immediately those in the crowd who knew them set up a chorus of requests.

"Gordon, I've been waiting to see you."

"You know my worth, Luca. Let me proceed, I beg you."

"Over here, captain!"

Stoically the soldiers ignored everyone and one of them climbed onto a stone block at the base of the nearest guard tower so that he could see over, and be seen by, the crowd. He waited patiently for silence and then spoke in a voice which carried easily to all corners of the square.

"Patience, my friends. You will all get your chance to prove yourselves and your goods worthy of admittance. But no one will enter until there is some order here. First of all, please move back from the gates."

There was a general muttering and shuffling and gradually a space cleared. As it did so, more soldiers emerged from the door and stood, well-muscled arms folded across uniformed chests. They did not look to be men any sensible person would wish to antagonize. The captain spoke again.

"Remain where you are until called by one of the guards here. I repeat, everyone will get his chance, but we can only admit a small number at a time."

Stepping down, he waved aside a new chorus of shouts and said quietly to his lieutenant, "See that we do not admit anyone who has nothing of worth, Luca."

"The men were not chosen for their size alone," replied Luca, smiling.

"Good. We would be here all day otherwise. Let's get started."

And so the procession began. The main gates were opened but no one was foolish enough to try to enter uninvited. Under the guards' supervision, a steady stream went in. Most reappeared shortly afterward, still in possession of their goods and wearing expressions which would have curdled milk. They disappeared or joined the early wine-shop customers to drown their sorrows. A few emerged empty handed, with smug looks, too pleased to notice the envious and even malevolent glances cast their way by those still waiting.

Rehan watched the crowd thin out, enjoying the sunshine and his leisurely breakfast. He was about to rise and make his petition when a disturbance caught his attention. A merchant wearing a fur-lined cape despite the summer heat shouted and pointed at a poorly dressed and skinny child who was nimbly skipping away between the groups of people.

"Stop, thief!"

A guard moved with surprising agility for such a burly man and collared the young pickpocket. He removed a small bag and tossed it to the merchant who hurried up, white-faced and breathing hard.

"Your gems, merchant?"

"My gems," wheezed the man. "My thanks to you, soldier."

"Save them," the guard replied gruffly. "Come, my foolish lad." The wide-eyed boy squealed and pleaded, struggling hopelessly in the soldier's iron grip. Then abruptly he was calm, his eyes narrowed, and he was led away, as obedient as a well-trained dog. All life had gone out of him.

"We'll not see that young tyke again for a while," said a man at a table next to Rehan.

"Good riddance," replied his companion sourly.

The incident was soon forgotten and Rehan decided to make his move. He went forward and caught the eye of one of the soldiers who approached and raised his eyebrows in question. Rehan took a pair of sapphire earrings from his pocket and held them in his palm. At the sight of them the guard's attitude became more respectful and he handed Rehan a small wooden token inscribed with a strange device and said, "Give this to the captain on the gate and tell him you want to see Corzen. He'll agree if you show him those."

Corzen was the court's Chief Treasurer. Rehan smiled, thinking that if the least pieces in his offering produced this effect then he could not fail. Not that he had ever thought that he would.

A few minutes later he walked under the archway of the main gates, passed the guard houses and turned, as directed, into a chamber on the left. From here he was directed to another room where Corzen sat at a plain table, attended by two assistants who were packing and labeling other items before storing them in the next chamber.

Corzen motioned for Rehan to sit opposite him. "I hope

you are not wasting my time. Our good soldiers sometimes find it difficult to distinguish between genuine jewels and fake glitter."

Without a word Rehan took out the pouch and removed from it a necklace and two rings, all carefully wrapped. These he spread out on the table and added the earrings to the set.

Corzen was too experienced and worldly-wise to show any reaction but his assistants' eyes widened and one all but gasped in amazement. Sapphires and opals winked darkly in their silver settings. The necklace especially was an intricate and beautiful example of the silversmith's art. Rehan sat back, his composed face masking his confidence.

"You are willing to leave these in my custody until this afternoon's audience." The treasurer's unaccented words formed a statement rather than a question. He was already filling out a receipt.

"Of course."

"Your name?"

"Palmar of Arlon."

Corzen handed him a small piece of card.

"Return to the main gates in four hours' time. Show this to the guard."

"Thank you."

That afternoon, as he joined the select group, who greeted each other with a mixture of comradeship and suspicion, Rehan wondered briefly at his own motives for being here. Was he really likely to learn anything more of the fate of Fontaine and those idiot boys she was supposed to be with? He doubted it. Far more urgent, he admitted to himself, was his own desire to see this fabulous creature, Amarino. *I should be more nervous than I am*, he thought as he showed his card and was admitted by the small door.

The audience was held in what was obviously used more frequently as a dining hall. At one end of the room a vast circular table was arrayed with jewelry and other valuable items. Chairs which usually stood beside the table were ranged along the walls and on these were rolls of silk and other materials as well as larger ornaments and sculpture. In other parts, clothes were displayed on special racks with their creators fussing over their arrangement.

It was like walking into a treasure house. The tapestries and banners which decorated the walls seemed drab by comparison.

The afternoon sunshine streamed in the large windows which faced out onto the castle courtyard, bringing to the room an almost incandescent glow.

Like many others, Rehan first checked on the arrangement of his own offering and then inspected what he unconsciously thought of as "the opposition." There was nothing to match his stones or silverwork.

Soon a hush of anticipation fell over the gathering. All eyes turned to an inner door from which an immaculately dressed servant had just emerged. In a clear, high voice he announced, "Gentlemen, the King and Queen."

Parokkan, with Amarino on his arm, stepped into the room. Everyone present bowed, but even as he joined them, Rehan's mind was reeling from that first glimpse.

The queen was undoubtedly the most beautiful woman he had ever seen. She was small and slim, her elegant form clothed in a simple light blue dress which set off her pale gold hair perfectly. Her oval face was a dream of loveliness, highlighted by large, violet-colored eyes which swept the room, taking in—or so it seemed—everything and everyone she saw. Her gaze lingered for a few seconds on some of the faces about her and, before he realized it, Rehan's eyes were locked to hers. Entranced, he was unable to look away, and felt a tremor run through his whole body. He felt naked.

Amarino smiled then and looked elsewhere but Rehan remained uncomfortable. When Parokkan spoke, it came as a shock to Rehan, who had forgotten he was there. The king was a muscular, handsome man of military bearing with light brown hair and clear blue eyes. Yet beside his queen, who was obviously some years younger, he was an insignificant creature.

"Gentlemen, you are welcome. As you know, our coronation is set for seven days' time. There is much that we need, to make the ceremonies worthy of the occasion and of my lovely queen." He glanced devotedly at Amarino, who smiled in response. *No wonder he's besotted,* thought Rehan.

"We thank you for your trouble in bringing these things before us. You will find we are not ungenerous if any of your goods meet with our requirements, but you will forgive me if

I leave the choice almost entirely to my queen. She has so much better taste in these matters than I."

There was a round of polite laughter.

"My dear."

With Parokkan and Corzen dancing attendance, albeit discreetly, Amarino began her round of inspection. Whenever something caught her attention, the chief treasurer called for the item's owner to come forward to answer any questions and, if all proved satisfactory, handed the merchant over to one of his trusted assistants to complete the transaction. Parokkan talked amiably but, true to his word, left the choosing to his lady.

Rehan waited, hardly daring to breathe as she approached the round table. Her eyes rested briefly on his pieces and she glanced quickly up at him. He was about to step forward when she looked down again and walked on round the table to judge some other jewelry.

Rehan was aghast. *Surely not*, his thoughts screamed. *There is nothing here to touch them. Surely she cannot just ignore them!* He watched her as she continued her tour. While talking to another merchant, she glanced briefly at Rehan, looking directly at his agitated face, and smiled again.

Was she playing with him? He felt again that disconcerting tremor and fought against the irrational fear that the queen knew his real identity. Despite the sunlit warmth of the hall, Rehan began to shiver.

And still he couldn't take his eyes off her. Surely she would reconsider his offering.

It was a considerable time before Amarino completed her circuit of the table. By the time she did so Rehan felt himself on the verge of collapse. Every nerve in his body was jangling.

The queen looked again at the sapphire and opal necklace. She said nothing for a while. Rehan held his breath.

"These are very fine," she said at last. "I can't imagine how I missed them earlier." Her voice was soft and mellifluous.

"To whom do they belong?"

"Palmar of Arlon, my lady," said Corzen, beckoning to Rehan, who recovered enough self-control to step forward and bow. She met and held his gaze as he straightened up. Close to, her eyes were even more extraordinary. Rehan wondered briefly if he were being hypnotized and with fresh resolve gathered his wits about him.

"Tell me, Palmar"—was that slight accent on his name deliberate? "—is this your own work? It is finely crafted."

"No, my lady. That skill is beyond me, but I am a fair judge of such things. It is the work of the finest silversmith of my home isle."

"Arlon?" A slight questioning note.

"Yes, my lady. The opals..." he went on hesitantly, "...were mined there too and I believe the sapphires are of a quality... unmatched in all the isles." He looked to Corzen for confirmation but the wizened, sharp-featured face betrayed no feelings or opinion on the matter.

"And what price do you ask for the necklace, Palmar?"

"Only that it should rest upon your lovely neck, my lady."

Amarino laughed. "That is a price easily met. Come, fasten it for me."

With trembling hands, Rehan picked up the necklace and opened the clasp. The queen turned away from him and he slipped it round her neck and fastened it. He fought an almost irresistible desire to kiss the back of her neck as he did so. She turned back to face him and as he adjusted the necklace's position, she said, "If you wish to meet me alone come to the kitchen gate of the castle an hour after sunset."

Rehan froze, unable to believe his ears. He glanced quickly about him but, although she had apparently spoken quite openly, no one seemed to have heard the astonishing invitation. Even Corzen and Parokkan, who stood close by, had noticed nothing out of the ordinary.

Amarino smiled and said, "You will come, *Palmar*?" This time the accent on his name was unmistakable.

"Yes, my lady," he croaked.

"Good." She turned to Parokkan and said, "What do you think, my love? How do these gems suit me?"

"Perfectly, my dear. Your colors exactly."

"And it is paid for already!" Smiling, she turned back to Rehan. "You have a pretty way with words, merchant, but I cannot allow you to be so generous. If I accepted such as this, few merchants would offer me their best goods for fear of my demanding equal generosity from them. And besides, it is not good for a queen to be in debt to anyone. Corzen here will see you get a fair price for the entire set. It will grace our coronation."

"Thank you, my lady," was all that Rehan felt able to say.

Soon after this the royal couple left the hall, their business completed. With their departure, the atmosphere became noticeably more relaxed and the volume of conversation rose. Rehan remained silent, despite the congratulations of several colleagues, and as soon as he had completed arrangements with Corzen for payment, he left quickly and returned to his room and lay down.

He felt drained, utterly weary, yet was quite unable to sleep, or even to think straight. A small part of his mind nagged at his uneasiness. *What is happening to me? What am I getting involved in? I should leave the city now, forget the gold due to me.*

Yet in truth he knew that an hour after sunset he would be at the kitchen gate.

The small door inset into the castle's kitchen gate was opened from within a few moments after Rehan arrived.

Wondering at his own boldness, he stepped inside. Two soldiers stood nearby at the guard post door. Rehan shrank back but they showed no sign of noticing his presence, and continued talking in low voices, ignoring him completely.

Amarino appeared from a doorway on the right and beckoned. His heart pounding, Rehan walked toward her. As he did so, one of the guards stepped forward and absent-mindedly closed the door behind him, still ignoring the visitor entirely.

Once inside Amarino led him along several corridors and eventually into a luxuriously appointed drawing room. She bade him sit and fetched him a glass of wine. Then she settled into another chair with her own wine and smiled at her guest.

"A toast," she said. "To honest trade." She raised her glass.

"And to you, my lady, whom trade adorns." Rehan was surprised at the steadiness of his voice. "Not," he added, "that any adornment is necessary."

"A pretty way with words indeed." They sipped.

"Forgive me," she said, "I have never visited Arlon. I was unaware of the craftsmanship of your home-isle until today. The jewelwork is remarkable."

Surely she did not invite me here to talk about jewelry, he thought. *What did she invite me for? Be careful!*

"It is a remote island, my lady, but not without merit."

"Obviously. Did you call at any other islands on your journey northward? Heald for instance?"

It took all of Rehan's considerable diplomatic skill to keep his face calm as he replied, "The ship on which I sailed came via Strallen, my lady, not Heald."

"But a seasoned traveler such as yourself would have visited Heald before, no doubt?"

"Yes, but not for some time."

"I ask because, as it is our nearest neighbor, we are anxious to reestablish relations with Heald. However, there are certain . . . difficulties."

"My lady?" For the first time in his life Rehan felt totally out of his depth. *She knows*, he thought. Then, *how can she?*

"Come, Palmar, you are not so ill-informed that you can be unaware that Princess Fontaine of Heald was here until recently as the betrothed of the previous heir to the throne. Since the situation changed, her whereabouts have been uncertain."

"I have heard rumors, my lady, but pay them little heed."

"A man of sense as well as courtesy, I see. I find my liking for you growing greater still."

Rehan's heart leapt into his throat, strangling any words.

"Tell me, Palmar, is the admiration mutual?"

He gazed, transfixed and, for a moment, clearly saw the breathtaking vision of her perfect body entirely naked. Suddenly he felt weak. Sweat started to trickle down his back.

Huskily he said, "You are beyond question the loveliest thing beneath the sky."

"And would you see more of me?"

Mutely he nodded.

"And I of you." She smiled. "But first I have a favor to ask of you."

"Anything," he whispered, rejecting the warnings of the tiny corner of his mind not yet beguiled.

"I need you to travel to Heald. A merchant of your repute should have no difficulty in gaining access to court circles there . . ." She paused as Rehan struggled with the implications of this latest development. ". . . And I need to know certain information about how we are regarded now in Heald. What are their plans? Has the princess returned there? And if so, who accompanied her? And so on."

Then it's true, a small thought crossed Rehan's mind. *Fontaine did escape. . . .*

"If you would agree to undertake this mission for me, I would be most appreciative. In more settled times I will ask you to return here. And you will find I am not ungenerous to those who serve me well."

This last was said in a sultry tone which sent shivers through Rehan's whole body. Her echo of her husband's earlier words held entirely different connotations. He was defenseless and gladly so, but an inconsistency in her proposal nagged at his mind.

"Of course I accept," he said, "but surely I would need to return sooner than you suggest to bring you the intelligence you require. Besides, I would not want to prolong my stay away from you."

"I shall not enjoy the separation either," she replied, "but it is necessary. We will have ample opportunity for more pleasurable times together when this matter is concluded."

"But how . . . ? I would not want to entrust such information to a messenger."

"Let me explain," Amarino said. She stood, walked over to a wallside desk, and took a small object from one of its drawers. This she placed in Rehan's hands before sitting down again. Rehan studied the object. It was a featureless glass sphere, milky-white in color and about the size of his palm. It was heavier than he had expected.

"Look into the glass and call to me with your thoughts."

What witchcraft is this? he wondered, doing as he was bid. In moments, the glass changed, became less opaque and then a miniature image of Amarino's face appeared.

"No witchcraft," said the vision.

Tearing his eyes away, Rehan looked up at the real person who sat smiling a few paces away.

"It is a seeing-stone," she said. "Few of them have survived, for they were made in the Age of Wizards, long years ago. With it we can contact each other across huge distances and then speak as freely and privately as if we were in the same room."

Rehan struggled with this new concept.

"A word of caution," said the queen. "Do not try to use the seeing-stone to contact anyone other than me. It would not work."

"You trust me with a valuable possession. But it pains me to know it will lengthen the time we are apart."

"The sooner you begin your task, the sooner it will end and then I will call for you."

"I will leave on the morrow."

"Good. It grows late. I think it best that you take your leave now."

"Of course." Rehan stood, recovering some of his customary poise, and pocketed the seeing-stone, which was milky-white once more.

Amarino led him back to the lane which led to the kitchen gate and walked with him to the doorway. Once again the guards appeared not to notice either of them.

Amarino opened the door, then reached up and kissed Rehan lightly on the lips. Even in the poor light her eyes, when seen close to, were bright and entrancing.

"Do not fail me, Rehan," she said.

A vision of darkness and damp, of pain and despair in unfathomable dungeons flickered briefly in his mind's eye. He quailed, terrified, then went limp with relief as the nightmare was replaced by Amarino's smiling face.

"Until we meet again," she said, ushering him outside and closing the door.

Rehan was halfway back to his lodgings before he realized that Amarino had used his real name.

Chapter 12

"*P*lease let me explain, my lord."

"It had better be good, Laurent. I expressly sent you with my son to make sure the young fool didn't get himself into more trouble than his usual quota. Now you've returned alone and tell me he's still on Ark!"

"Ansar is in good hands, my lord, and it was necessary for one of us to return with the news I bear."

"What news is that?" Queen Adesina looked up from her needlework with renewed interest in her clear green eyes.

"Princess Fontaine escaped from Starhill when the overthrow took place."

"Thank the stars!" exclaimed Pabalan. "You're sure of this?"

"Yes. She traveled to the south of the island in the company of Ather's three sons and the court wizard."

"Ferragamo?"

"Yes, my lady."

"I might have expected that old schemer would get away," said the queen. "You don't grow to be that ancient without *some* ability."

"His ability didn't stretch to foreseeing his king's death, did it?" remarked Pabalan acidly. "Ather *is* dead, isn't he?"

"Yes, my lord. The early reports were quite correct in that."

"You met with Ferragamo and the others?"

"Yes, in the village called Home. Our landfall was most fortunate."

The queen, who was calmly continuing with her embroidery, said, "Forgive me for asking, Laurent, but there is something I do not quite understand. If all is as you say, why did Ansar and Fontaine not return with you from Home?"

"Yes," said Pabalan. "Where are they?" He stopped his restless pacing to stare at the courtier.

"There's more to the tale, I'm afraid."

"You're afraid!" Pabalan shouted. "What's happened?"

"Let him speak, dear," said Adesina mildly, but her eyes betrayed her anxiety.

"It seems that Fontaine became party, whether by choice or by coercion I do not know, to a feather-brained scheme of Eric, Ather's eldest son."

"I know who he is, man. She was going to marry the boy next year."

"That won't be possible now. He's dead."

"How?"

"He and Fontaine were ambushed in the southern forest by outlaws."

"He *and* Fontaine?"

"Yes, my lord. She had gone with him to regain his throne."

"She did what!" Pabalan bellowed.

"Shouting at Laurent will not solve anything," said the queen. She was fighting her own inner battle to stay calm.

"You keep out of this. Whatever possessed them?"

"It seems there was a prophecy of some sorts which prompted the escapade."

"And where is Fontaine now?" asked Adesina, as her husband picked up a goblet and drained the contents.

"She was captured by the outlaws and is being held in the forest. As I left, Ferragamo was organizing a search party to rescue her. Ansar insisted on going with them, of course."

"Stars!" said Pabalan, red wine dripping from his chin. "What a mess."

"Wipe your face, dear," said the queen, handing him a handkerchief. The king gave no indication of having heard her but nonetheless took the cloth and did as he was bid.

"When did all this happen?" he asked in a more normal voice.

"I left Ark four days ago. The search party set out the same afternoon. With luck they will have found her by now. Ferragamo is, as my lady says, a resourceful character and he has some good men with him."

There was a pause.

"Do you wish me to return to Ark, my lord?" asked Laurent hesitantly.

"There wouldn't seem much point at the moment," the queen said. "If Ferragamo's talents and the local men cannot find Fontaine I do not see that anyone from here will be of much use."

"I agree, my lady. Ansar will get a message to us as soon as there is any definite news, I'm sure, and any boat from here might miss one coming in the other direction."

"If you two have finished deciding state policy—"

"It is your decision, of course, dear."

"Don't call me that in public, Adesina."

"Laurent is not public, Pabalan."

"Hmph. You're right, of course. I mean about not going back. Until we hear more, you stay here."

"Yes, my lord."

"But make sure you have boats and men ready in case we need to move fast."

"That is already in hand."

"Good. Go and get some rest. You look as though you could use it."

Thankfully, Laurent went to the door. As he went out he heard Pabalan say, "Stars. Now where's that wine?"

"In the bottle, dear," his queen replied, and then, as the door closed, she abruptly began to cry quietly, her eyes squeezed shut against the tears. Pabalan was nonplussed for a moment, then, his face a picture of contrition, he swiftly knelt before his wife and held her until the sobs subsided. All the while he murmured softly into her ear and gently stroked her hair.

Outside, Laurent breathed a deep sigh of relief. Another courtier waiting outside greeted his friend.

"What was all that about?" he asked. "I thought I saw steam coming under the door."

"I'll tell you in a while," said Laurent. "Right now I need a drink." .

Eight days later Rehan arrived back in Heald. He did not go immediately to the palace, however. The sharp-faced courtier went first to his own house in the island's seaport capital. There he secreted the seeing-stone and made arrangements with his servants to stow the gold he had received in Ark in the royal treasury. Then he spent a short while composing himself and rehearsing what he would say to the king.

As he had ridden from Starhill to Grayrock the morning after his meeting with Amarino, Rehan had felt conflicting emotions. He was clear-eyed enough to know that his infatuation with Amarino was not natural, but he was still unable to do anything about it. Part of him clamored to turn his horse around and go back to her. However, he was certain that he must not do so, even though he was now unsure of the reason for this. Curiously, he had forgotten that Amarino knew his real name.

The weight of the seeing-stone in his pocket had acted as a constant reminder of his mission and by the time he reached the port his mind was made up. He would do exactly as she had asked and wait for the day she called for him again.

He had found a ship leaving for Heald on the first tide of the morrow and had booked his passage. As soon as he had gone on board it was as if his mind had cleared. He had felt more of his old confidence return and had begun to relish this new game in which he was a leading player. He could not lose. A double agent can always become a triple agent, he mused, yet he knew that Amarino now ruled his fate.

The journey southward had seemed endless at times. He longed to be back in Heald, for the next round of the game to begin. He resisted the temptation to use the seeing-stone to contact Amarino, as he knew intuitively that it should not be used frivolously.

Now back in his home-isle, his mind resolved, Rehan made his way to the palace and was immediately called to the royal apartments. Laurent was already with the king and queen when he was shown in.

They greeted each other and Rehan was asked to give his report. This he did, beginning naturally with the rumors concerning Fontaine. At this point Pabalan and Laurent told him the latest news of the princess and her companions, which Rehan filed away for his eagerly awaited first message to Amarino. He then went on to more general matters such as the state of Ark's armed forces, the fortification of Grayrock and Starhill and such matters. Part of this he made up as he realized that he had not been as observant as he usually was, especially in the capital. The overall picture of strength was accurate enough however.

"How are the people taking to their new rulers?" asked the queen.

"They seem contented enough. Life goes on almost as if nothing has happened. Though they were naturally somewhat reticent, the people I talked to seemed unanimous in their opinion that it was a change for the better. The takeover seems to have been so swift and efficient, with relatively little bloodshed, that most people weren't even aware of it until after the event."

"Remarkable," said Pabalan. "What's he like, this Parokkan?"

"From all the reports I had, he is a most able man. Strong, decisive, and energetic. Certainly the business community is much impressed. And his queen is a pretty thing. They make a handsome couple and the general populace will get a fine show with their coronation." He made a mental calculation. "Which is today."

"You sold the jewelry?" asked Laurent.

"Yes. For a good price but a fair one. Parokkan's shrewd but he wants to encourage trade. He's acquisitive. My merchant's guise would work again if needed."

"Did you meet the royal couple?" asked Adesina.

Rehan felt momentarily uneasy under the queen's shrewd gaze. "Not personally, my lady. Though I saw them from a distance. My dealings were with the treasury officials."

"And how is Heald regarded?" Pabalan eyed his advisor narrowly.

"They are unsure of their position, my lord, for obvious reasons. They would like to resume normal relations, I am sure. As near neighbors, trade is virtually essential, but the situation is a little delicate. Nobody in Starhill is aware of the whereabouts of the princess." *Though they soon will be*, he added to himself. "And until some understanding is reached on this matter, they are content to wait."

"Knowing full well that we are not strong enough to avenge the insult in any case," muttered Pabalan darkly.

Hoping for an order which would enable him to follow his

own desire rather than Amarino's wishes, Rehan asked, "Do
you want me to return to Ark, my lord?"

The king looked quickly at his queen and Laurent and
said, "No. Until we hear from Ansar, no one goes anywhere.
When my daughter is safe, we'll think again."

"As you wish," said Rehan.

That evening Rehan had little stomach for dinner and retired
to his bedchamber earlier than normal. His servants assumed
this to be a reaction to a long and tiring journey, but nothing
could have been further from the truth.

Immediately he was alone, he took the bag containing the
seeing-stone from its locked drawer. He did not, however,
take the stone out straightaway. Knowing that, Amarino would
be busy on the day of her coronation, he forced himself to
wait until later in the evening. Finally, when his nerves could
no longer stand the strain, he carefully removed the stone
and cradled it reverently in his hands. Staring at its milk-
white surface, he cried out silently to Amarino. So fast that
for a moment he was taken aback as the glass cleared and
shifted and the incomparably lovely image of Amarino's face
appeared. A simple silver coronet adorned her head and the
sapphire and opal necklace glittered at her throat. Rehan was
struck dumb by her beauty.

"Well, aren't you going to say anything?" the vision asked.
"I've had a very busy day."

"I'm sorry," he murmured. "You have bewitched me."

"Of course," she replied in a more gentle tone and with a
brilliant smile. "Do you have some news for me?"

Rehan recovered his poise sufficiently to give a more-or-
less lucid account of the journeyings and plight of Fontaine
and of Ferragamo and the princes. Eric's death seemed to
annoy Amarino but she found Fontaine's fate amusing. Rehan
told her of the plans being made to rescue her and watched
her mental calculations about the timing of this.

"You have done well, Palmar."

"Thank you, my lady."

"Call me Amarino."

"I would dearly like to do so in person."

"Not yet, Palmar, though that time will come soon enough.
But you would not leave a job undone, surely? I need you to

tell me when there is further news of the princess and also of the others who fled from here. I am especially concerned about Ferragamo. He could prove to be a nuisance."

She sounded oddly eager, Rehan thought.

"I will do as you wish, my . . . Amarino. Though I would rather be on my way back to you."

"I know I can rely on you," she replied. "And now I must go. It has been a long day and my lord is waiting."

Rehan groaned, racked with jealousy.

"Farewell, Palmar. Till we meet again."

"Farewell, Amarino."

For some time Rehan sat staring at the now opaque surface of the seeing-stone. Then, moving slowly like a man underwater, he replaced the stone in its hiding place and went to bed.

Rehan had never married and scorned the foolishness of others who felt themselves in love. He had never met a woman who had attracted him for more than a few days and certainly never one he could think of as his equal.

Now all that had changed dramatically. It was nearly dawn when he finally fell into a restless sleep.

Chapter 13

"*F*arewell, Palmar. Till we meet again."

"Farewell, Amarino."

She cut the contact and immediately Rehan's anguished image faded from her mind. Once she would have needed a second stone to establish a link over such a distance. She recalled her conversations with the man she thought of as her father, the man who had shaped her infant mind so many years before. She had regarded him with a mixture of affection and awe, tinged with fear, and had generally been glad when his image faded from the stone. But that had been a long time ago. Now all that she needed was her own growing power—and one seeing-stone.

She dwelt for a moment on Rehan's sharp features and deep blue eyes. *He will make an amusing plaything,* she thought. Then she returned to present concerns. Rehan's report had been interesting but hardly a revelation. That Ferragamo and the princes had been staying in the south of Ark came as no surprise. Even when she had tested her mind over the whole island a few days ago she had not been able to detect their presence. That meant that if they were still on Ark, they must be to the south of the great forest, the only part of the island not under her influence to some extent. This was exactly what she had hoped for when she allowed them to escape, keeping her knowledge of the secret passages to herself. That had not been the time to face Ferragamo. The wizard would have learned too much about her and the uprising and she had not been strong enough then to confront him openly.

Eric's death was an annoyance. He had been a dunce but his blood carried its own potency and she begrudged its loss. However, the kidnapping of Fontaine would keep the others occupied. In the time that gave her she would continue to grow, knowing that every day brought her closer to invincibility. Very soon she would welcome the inevitable confrontation with Ferragamo, confident that he would soon be in her thrall.

It had not always been so. Her current situation was the result of a great deal of painstaking planning. Parokkan's overthrow of the throne had been the last and most important stage. That had achieved several things. Firstly it had, one way or another, rid her of the formidable threat posed by Ferragamo's talents. It had also dispersed and disabled the natural power of the royal bloodline which, though fallen into dormancy through decades of peace, could still have menaced her ambitions. Lastly, the revolt had placed her in a position of power which needed no reinforcement from her special abilities. When that other matter in the castle had been taken care of—she didn't like to think about that very much—everything had been set for her to utilize the natural resources all about her.

A month later she now knew that her nascent power which had fueled Parokkan's rise to the kingship had been nothing compared to the energies she now controlled. *Soon,* she thought, *I won't need anybody, not Parokkan, not the army. Just a few servants and playthings.* She smiled at the idea. It was impossible for her not to despise her husband king, attractive though he was in many ways. Blissful in his ignorance and besotted with his new queen he made an impressive figurehead but he would soon realize where the power behind the throne really lay.

Seated in her private chamber, Amarino allowed herself to gloat over this prospect for a few moments. Then she roused herself and summoned one of the captains of the guard. He arrived promptly, unable to hide his surprise at the lateness of the summons, or at the fact that the queen was still attired in her coronation robes. However, as soon as she outlined what she wanted, his military professionalism took over and he strode out to round up his platoon and keep them from getting too drunk in the evening's revels.

Alone again, Amarino began her preparations for retiring, musing as she did so. She was glad that the time for action, albeit cautious, had arrived. It had been a great temptation to send soldiers or spies to search out Ferragamo and his companions before this. However the far-ranging nature of such expeditions would, until now, have stretched her infant powers of control over the soldiers to breaking point. Now it was different.

Her thoughts turned to the day's ceremonies. It had been a frivolous but worthwhile entertainment. Her hold over the people of Ark, and Starhill in particular, would be easier to maintain if they were contented enough to begin with, and the coronation had provided the perfect excuse for a good deal of celebration. The popular emotional appeal of the event combined with a generous provision of food and drink had ensured the day's success. And if a few poor souls never made it home again after the night's revelry, who would be surprised? And who would care?

Soon this sort of charade would not be necessary. But not yet. The effort involved in spreading her power over the whole island had been so great that she had become exhausted after a day or so. Much of the process was becoming simplicity itself, as unthinking as breathing. As she spread her net wider and wider, Amarino could choose to regard the human potential within her range either as an amorphous mass to be used as she pleased or as an infinite collection of individual possibilities. She had begun to amuse herself by sampling images of what she already considered her realm, as seen by various ordinary citizens. However, the novelty of this soon palled as, to her, the lives of farmers, shepherds, sailors, merchants, and all those engaged in the island's multifarious occupations seemed petty and she was unmoved by their concerns. The island itself also failed to hold her attention. The awesome beauty of the mountains, the rugged coastline, the bustling market towns and sleepy hamlets, the green rolling pasture and the mysterious forest depths meant little after her initial curiosity was assuaged.

Of far more immediate interest was the process of molding the people to her uses. But her ultimate goal was, as yet, unattainable beyond a certain range. It had been a sobering but informative experiment which promised much for the not too distant future. For the time being she was concentrating on particularly useful people and on the capital and its environs, widening and strengthening her power base. It was an endeavor she enjoyed for its inexorable progress.

Her mood as she made her way to her husband's bed was one of triumph. *Father,* she thought, *you old goat. It's working!*

Far away, laughter sounded hollowly.

Early the next morning a platoon of guards left the castle and rode out toward Field Gate. The blank look upon their faces was not wholly due to ill-tended hangovers. The captain and his men passed through the city like men in a trance noticing little of what went on around them.

A more keen-eyed observer would have noted several strange items. There were less people about than had been normal recently. It had been known for some time that the vagabonds and beggars who used to haunt the city streets had disappeared. Most were heartily pleased with this, for the relatively well-off are never glad of disturbances to their consciences, and they spoke admiringly of the improvement in the policing of Starhill.

Now, however, the phenomenon had spread to other parts of the community. A few decent citizens failed to return to their homes. Nobody knew where they went.

The strangest thing of all was that life went on as normal.

As the troop rode past his shop that morning, a baker wondered idly, and without any concern, about what had happened to his wife and two small daughters. He hadn't seen them for three days. Still, there was work to be done, and soon his mind turned to more important matters. Bread was essential after all.

It seemed that no one who was really needed disappeared. Trade went on, food and drink were as plentiful as ever, and regular deliveries were still made to the castle. All was as it should be.

Chapter 14

"They have horses but they won't be able to move fast in this forest," said Orme, "especially if they set off in darkness. We can't be too far behind."

"They shouldn't be difficult to track," said Essan. "The leaf mold is quite soft. As long as it's light the trail should be clear enough. We know they started off more or less westward."

"Let's go then!" Ansar looked impatiently at his companions. "What are we waiting for?"

"Peace, Ansar," replied Ferragamo. "We can't all go after them. Someone has to take the boats back, and besides, we don't have enough supplies for a party this size. We know which way they're headed. Presumably they are making for the trail and then Stane, but it could be days before we catch up with them."

The wizard held up his hands to forestall Ansar's retort.

"A few moments' thought now will repay us later." He turned to Essan. "You can track them?"

"Yes," replied the soldier confidently.

"He's your best man for that," said Shill, "but I've a nasty feeling you're going to want me back on the boats."

"Well, apart from Ansar, you are the only experienced sailor here. How many men will you need?"

"Two for each boat."

"I'll go," said Brandel. "I wouldn't be much use on a long

journey on foot." *Especially if food is going to be short,* he
added to himself.

"Benfell and Bonet can manage the other boat," said
Shill. "Unless Mark . . ."

Mark shook his head. "I'm going on," he said firmly.

Oh good, interjected Longfur. *I could do with the exercise.*

"That only leaves five of us," said Orme. "We won't be
able to cover much ground."

Six actually.

"I hope we won't need to," replied the wizard. "If we
haven't found them by the time we reach the forest trail, we'll
assume they've turned south, and follow. By the time they
reach Stane, Shill and the others should be waiting for them."

"If we arrive before they do, someone can ride north to
help the search," added Shill, glad of the possibility of more
positive action.

"Good," said Ferragamo. "Now, before we set off, let's see
if we can find some more supplies in this camp. If we have to
spend time hunting, it'll slow us down."

"Just don't eat any stew!" said Mark, "or you won't wake
up till tomorrow."

Ferragamo nodded, smiling. He had examined a couple of
the slumbering outlaws. From the look of their eyes when he
had lifted their lids he guessed that they would sleep for
several hours yet.

Quickly, they gathered what food they could find and
Orme emerged from one hut with a crossbow and a quiver of
bolts. With the loads distributed they set off, much to Ansar's
evident relief.

"See you in Stane!" shouted Brandel, as he and the boats'
crews disappeared into the trees.

All that day Essan led them on at a good pace, though it
wasn't fast enough for Ansar. Only occasionally was the trail
so indistinct that Essan needed to study the ground closely,
and in some places it was so clear that even Mark saw that
Fontaine and the big man had obviously been walking beside
their horses.

They ate sparingly as they trudged along to make full use
of the daylight, but as evening drew on Essan was forced to
halt more and more often and eventually they agreed to stop,
as to go on was to risk losing the trail altogether. Had they
known it, they were less than half a league from where, at

that time, Fontaine and Jani were preparing to leave their makeshift shelter.

Mark was very tired after the day's march, and after a quick meal and the minimum of camp preparations he was glad to wrap himself in his cloak and sleep. Longfur for once was not talkative but even so Mark took comfort from his warm presence and gentle purring. The cat seemed none the worse for his unaccustomed day's exercise. Indeed, true to his word, he had reveled in the display of his physical prowess.

As he drifted off into sleep, Mark was aware of Owl's return, but he obviously had nothing important to report as Ferragamo said nothing, even to Ansar, but lay down and was soon asleep.

They rose at first light, eager to move on, if only to ease their cold and stiff muscles. The forest seemed less dense here and they made good time as the trail was clear and walking easy.

Ferragamo cursed and Ansar swore bitterly when they came upon the makeshift shelter and realized just how close they must have been to their quarry. They hurried on and by noon all of them were slick with sweat despite the almost constant shade.

Essan judged that the latest hoof-prints were quite fresh, and new hope kept their pace going. Ansar took to yelling Fontaine's name but grew hoarse and eventually silent. Owl was sent off on reconnaissance again and soon afterwards Ferragamo called a halt.

"I'm getting a message from Owl," he said, as the other four looked at him expectantly, "but he's quite a way off, and it's not clear. Wait a moment."

They were all silent, watching as the wizard stood with his head cocked to one side, his eyes closed. There was no doubting the urgency in his look when he opened them again.

"He's seen her. As near as I can judge she's about half a league on. She's with a big man but Owl says there are several others around them. I don't know what that means."

"Well, I'm going to find out," said Ansar and he set off at a run, drawing his sword as he went. The others glanced at each other and, all coming to the same conclusion, set off after the prince as fast as they could go.

Despite his tiredness, Mark found new reserves of strength

and ran swiftly, with Longfur bounding effortlessly along beside him. Afterward, he found it almost impossible to recall everything that occurred in the next few minutes because it all happened so fast. Before he caught sight of anyone ahead of him he heard a familiar voice say quite clearly, "Oh *no!* Not *again!*" and after that came the sounds of a scuffle. Then, breathing heavily and with sweat stinging his eyes, Mark emerged into an open area among pine trees.

Evidently Fontaine and her companion had been attacked by another band of outlaws—it couldn't be the same ones—and had tried to flee on horseback. They had not gone far. Both horses were now riderless and one had run away in panic. The other, which Mark recognized as Eric's, was rearing and lashing out with its forelegs at three nasty-looking men ranged about it.

The big man that Mark had seen with Fontaine was nearby, wielding a huge wooden stave against four men with swords and clubs. Despite the blood streaming from a broken arrow shaft in his arm, he was holding his assailants at bay, but obviously he could only hold out for so long. Behind him, Mark caught sight of Fontaine and his heart lurched. She was struggling between two men, swearing and kicking, but unable to break free. Ansar had made straight for her and was now engaged in a sword fight with two more outlaws.

Without realizing how it got there, Mark found that his own borrowed sword was in his hand and he plunged forward without thought for his own safety or the odds against him.

Eric's horse had flattened one of the men trying to control him and the other two had fled from him before he galloped away. Mark was almost upon them before they realized he was there but shouts from the others warned them and Mark hesitated. That was his undoing. One of the men had a sword and swept it at Mark, who came to life just in time to parry the blow which would have split his skull. The clash jarred his arm horribly and when the other man swung a wooden club at him he was helpless to avoid it. He stumbled and fell, his sword flying out of his hand. He had the presence of mind to roll away but even so he would surely have been killed had Essan not come crashing in, felling the swordsman with one stroke and turning on the other instantly.

Mark had a fleeting vision of Longfur, his tail bristling to twice its normal size. Spitting and hissing, the cat launched himself at one of the bald man's assailants, scrabbling up his clothes and clawing at his face so that he was forced to break off to rid himself of his hellish tormentor. Then his own plight became Mark's immediate priority.

The unexpected new arrivals had caused some consternation among the outlaws but now they were recovering from the shock and organizing themselves for a serious fight. Looking up, Mark saw that Fontaine had been flung to the ground and her captors were joining in the fray. One of Ansar's opponents now lay prone but the other was soon to be reinforced. Two of the men around the still undefeated but tiring big man had left him and were advancing on Essan and Mark.

The young prince looked round frantically for his sword but could not see it. In desperation he picked up a fallen branch and rose to face his adversaries. The first of these was almost upon him when he collapsed with a crossbow bolt buried in his chest, announcing that Orme had joined the fray. In the moment of surprise and stillness that followed, Mark became aware of a voice calling his name. He looked round and saw Fontaine holding a sword which she promptly threw toward him. Snatching it up he felt a surge of confidence and wheeled to meet the other outlaw. The sword felt surprisingly light and he lashed out with it so fast that his attacker's weapon spun out of his hand.

"Help Ansar!" Fontaine was yelling and Mark saw that the Healdean prince was being driven back by three opponents and was obviously wounded. As Mark ran toward them one of them turned to him, sword at the ready. The man smiled at him evilly.

"Well, laddie. You've come to learn how to fight?"

Stung by the other's sneering look, Mark leapt forward. His thrust was turned aside but he recovered and parried the riposte. He attacked again, in a fury now, but somehow still calm. His opponent was obviously surprised at the vehemence and fluidity of the attack, for his expression changed and he fought in earnest. Backward and forward they moved, watching each other like hawks, but by necessity trying to stay aware of what was happening about them. Thus Mark was vaguely aware of Fontaine's companion finally succumbing to a blow on the head and of Fontaine herself setting upon his vanquisher like an avenging fury, dagger in hand. That almost made him falter but a sharp pain in his side brought his attention back to more immediate matters. He just glimpsed Orme, his crossbow discarded because of the closeness of the combat, joining Fontaine over her fallen companion, sword in hand.

Mark's opponent drove him back and again aimed for the gap in his guard through which he'd drawn blood. This time Mark was waiting for it and sidestepped neatly, making his own thrust at the same time. It would have fallen short but the outlaw half tripped over something on the ground and could not draw back in time. With an ease which appalled Mark his blade slid into the other man's chest. His eyes went wide and he fell forward, taking Mark to the ground with him.

At the same moment there was a terrifying crash and what seemed like a miniature lightning bolt lifted one of the outlaws engaged with the tiring Essan and slammed him bodily against a pine trunk. Ferragamo had arrived.

After all the earlier surprises, this last attack was too much for the remaining outlaws, and to a man they turned and fled. Ansar pursued for a few paces but then even he gave in to exhaustion and joined the others.

Mark extricated himself from his fallen opponent and got gingerly to his feet, only to be nearly knocked down again as Fontaine rushed to embrace him.

"Oh, you're alive!" she said joyfully. "I thought . . ."

Bemused but pleased, Mark returned her hug, wincing as the cut on his ribs reacted. Then abruptly she was gone and his face colored as he saw Orme looking at him and smiling. He turned round to look at the man on the ground. Sightless eyes stared at the leaves above and there was a small red mark on the front of his jerkin. The man must have died very quickly as there was little blood in evidence.

A few moments later the reality of what he had done dawned on Mark. He doubled up, fell to his knees, and was violently sick.

Some time later Mark sat by their camp fire. Despite the warmth of the evening, he was shivering, and the soup in his bowl went untasted despite his stomach's aching emptiness. Ferragamo watched him, trying to judge when would be the best time to try to bring him round from the shock.

The wizard had taken charge after the last of the outlaws had fled. After her initial jubilation at her rescue, Fontaine had quickly grown serious and helped him tend the wounds of the others in the party. Ansar and Essan both had nasty gashes on their arms and Mark's cut, while not serious, needed careful bandaging. It was very painful but he hardly noticed it. More worrying was the plight of Fontaine's companion whose name, she informed them, was Jani. He was still unconscious and could not be roused. Fortunately, the blow on his head had been from a wooden club and not a sword, but the egg-sized lump it had raised stood out obscenely on his bald pate. His left arm too was a bloody mess after the arrowhead had been removed and it would take a great deal of care to ensure it did not become infected. Ferragamo had bound some herb leaves into the bandaging but kept muttering about things he didn't have with him and should have thought to bring.

Meanwhile Orme, who had remained relatively unscathed, had checked on the outlaws. Of the six bodies, four had been killed outright, and another died shortly afterward despite efforts to staunch his bleeding. The sixth man, the one Ferragamo's magic had accounted for, was still unconscious but his breathing and pulse were strong, if slow, and he would obviously come to in time.

Orme had started the laborious process of burying the dead and later Ansar had helped him, despite warnings not to disturb or dirty his dressings.

They had set up camp a few hundred paces away from the scene of the battle and between them arranged fire and food. The horses had returned of their own free will though Fontaine's still shivered and rolled its eyes until the princess went to talk to him.

Now as the evening drew in they were all seated round the fire. Reaction to the day's exertions and excitement had set in and there was little talk. Fontaine gave out soup in the two bowls she and Jani had brought with them and tried to be bright and cheerful but did not get much response. Even Ansar was unusually quiet as he watched over the unconscious outlaw and listened for any movement in the forest. No one thought the outlaws would attack again after the beating they had taken but Ansar was taking no chances. Ferragamo might trust his owl to stand guard at night but Ansar had no intention of doing so. Once, soon after the fight was over, he had seen someone or something moving among the trees in the direction from which they had arrived. It had moved away however and he had put it out of his mind.

Gradually food and rest brought their voices back and they exchanged tales with Fontaine. She was immensely relieved that they already knew of Eric's death as she had been dreading breaking that piece of news. She knew that she could have prevented his mad escapade and thus his death. In front of Ferragamo and Mark especially the guilt she felt was acute and, although she didn't quite understand how they knew, she was glad she only had to give a brief description of what had happened.

She related events at the outlaws' camp and inevitably it was Jani who caused the most curiosity in her listeners.

"He's deaf and dumb," she said. "I don't think Durc was cruel to him, but no one treated him like a real person before me. They just used him. I know it sounds silly, but we understand each other, honestly we do. As soon as I was taken to their camp, he was my ally—as if he recognized something in me. He likes me, and it was his idea to drug Durc and the others." Glancing around quickly, she went on: "Oh, you probably think I'm going on a lot about nothing, and I'm sorry, but he *is* my friend and I care about what happens to him." She sounded almost fierce. "I *do* hope he's going to be all right!"

Somewhat taken aback by this lengthy speech from the princess, everyone looked at the slumbering giant.

"I think he will," said Ferragamo, "but all we can do now is wait. We could all do with some rest."

He glanced at Mark but the young prince was still sunk in his private reverie and did not react.

Soon afterward they made preparations for sleeping.

"What do we do about him?" said Ansar, indicating the outlaw.

"I don't think he's much danger," said Ferragamo.

"Tie him up anyway," said Orme. "Better safe than sorry."

Ansar looked relieved. "I'll stand first watch," he said. "I don't think I could sleep anyway."

"Wake me when you've had enough," replied Orme.

The fire was damped and capes and blankets spread. Ansar finished tying the captive and sat with his back to a tree. Only Mark and Ferragamo stayed where they were.

"Do you want to talk about it?" said the wizard quietly.

Mark stared at the fire, looking into flames that were no longer there. After a while he said, "No," softly and relapsed into silence.

"You have to come to terms with it. You can't mope for ever."

The prince's eyes snapped up. "I'm not moping."

Yes you are, came the caustic comment in his head. Ferragamo saw Mark look sharply at the cat and smiled, thinking that Longfur would probably be better at talking Mark round than he was. At least Longfur had got a reaction out of him. Aloud he said, "We'll talk in the morning then. Try to get some sleep. Goodnight."

"Goodnight," said Mark absently, but he made no move to lie down and remained sitting hunched up, his arms wrapped round his knees.

You'll get a cramp if you stay like that much longer.

Go away, Longfur.

Charming, came the reply. *Here I am, looking out for your welfare, and that is all the thanks I get.*

Leave me alone. I don't want to talk now.

Well, listen then!

No! Mark turned away but the cat didn't give up.

You can't hide from me now, he said. *What you're doing is very silly.*

But I killed a man!

Don't shout so, replied Longfur in a pained voice, though no sound had disturbed the camp. *I know you killed him*, he went on. *If you hadn't, he would have killed you. Perhaps you would have preferred that.*

Mark was silent.

If he had killed you, do you think he would be grieving as you are now? He'd be laughing.

I don't ever want to be like that. It's barbaric.

I'm glad you feel that way, came the reply and for once there was no trace of sarcasm in Longfur's tone, *but what you did was right! What else could you have done? Just left them to butcher your friends and use Fontaine any way they wanted?*

Mark shuddered at the images implanted in his brain.

But you don't know what it's like. You weren't even there. His thoughts were anguished.

Oh, wasn't I? Who do you think tripped him up?

Mark looked round at Longfur, his eyes wide. "You?" he exclaimed.

You don't think I'd let you get into a mess like that on your own, do you? said the cat, meeting his gaze.

After a moment Mark said, *Then you're just as much responsible as—*

Yes, came the reply. *I'm not proud of it but I'm not ashamed either. We had to do something.*

After some reflection Mark said, *I suppose so. I don't have to like it though.*

Nobody who is even slightly intelligent does.

Ansar seems to.

He likes the excitement. But he was very quiet after it was all over, wasn't he?

There must be a better way to settle things between men.

Well, your kind have yet to find it, said Longfur, so pompously that Mark had to smile. *You don't find animals behaving like that.*

I'm sorry we don't come up to your standards. He was only half joking.

You're better than most, but you've got to see the world the way it is, not the way you'd like it to be.

Well, I'm going to change it if I can.

That, if I may say so, is a commendable attitude. But don't set your heart on it.

Thank you, sage.

A pleasure. Shall we sleep now?

I am very tired.

Goodnight.

Goodnight, Longfur.

Mark awoke late the next morning and was surprised to see that several others were also still in their bedrolls. Ferragamo had decreed that it would be better not to move Jani for a while and, as most of the others in the party would benefit from a prolonged rest, he had decided that they would stay where they were for the morning at least.

Orme had retrieved the crossbow and set off hunting to replenish their dwindling provisions but apart from him only the wizard and Fontaine, whose sleeping patterns were confused already were up and about. Ferragamo was sitting beside Jani muttering to himself, while the princess tended a steaming pot suspended over the fire. When she saw that Mark was awake, she poured some of the liquid into a bowl and brought it over to him.

"Drink this. It'll do you good."

"What is it?" Mark sniffed the herbal fumes suspiciously.

"One of Jani's recipes. How are your ribs?"

"Sore," he replied, resisting the urge to stretch. He sipped the hot liquid and made a face. "If it tastes this bad it must do me some good. How is Jani?"

Fontaine's face clouded over. "There's no change. Ferragamo's worried, although he won't admit it. I think there's something he doesn't understand limiting his healing abilities."

"Poison?"

"No. The arrow was clean enough. Oh, I wish he'd wake up!"

"Give him some of this," said Mark, handing her back the empty bowl. "It's enough to wake the dead."

Immediately he wished he'd bitten his tongue off. Fontaine looked stricken. "I'm sorry—" he said, but she had already turned away.

Oh, Stars, he thought. *What made me say that?*

Don't worry about her, came Longfur's voice. *She's tougher than you think.*

If only Jani would be all right.

He will be. He's coming to now in fact.

Mark looked across and saw Ferragamo smile as Jani's eyelids fluttered. Mark rose and went across to where he lay but Fontaine was there before him, kneeling and taking Jani's right hand in her own. His look of bewilderment was emphasized by his dilated pupils as he opened his eyes. He gazed first at Fontaine, who smiled encouragement, and then at Longfur who had sidled up beside Mark. An odd look passed over his face and then he closed his eyes again and fell asleep once more.

Ferragamo rose, radiating satisfaction. "He's on the mend," he said. "It'll take a while, but he'll be as good as new."

Fontaine looked up at him. "That's wonderful," she said. "Thank you."

Mark felt somehow excluded and Longfur caught his mood.

Let's go and see if there are any fish in that stream, the cat said, and the two of them walked away.

In the end they stayed at the camp all that day and the following night. Nobody objected to the enforced idleness.

Fontaine stayed by Jani for most of the time. Ferragamo was pleasantly surprised by the care the princess was showing for someone other than herself. Jani's periods of waking became more frequent and prolonged and he was able to drink some of the herbal brew and some soup. Although the stream had proved far too small to contain any worthwhile fish—a fact which Mark suspected Longfur knew all the time—Orme had returned with three game birds and a rabbit so no one went hungry. They would have to move on soon, though, for the sake of the horses. The last of their grain was gone and there was little grass beneath the pines in this part of the forest. Owl confirmed Ferragamo's feeling that the great forest track was only a league or so to the west and it was decided that they would head for that in the morning.

Almost unnoticed amid the general concern for Jani, another member of the party regained consciousness during the day. The outlaw awoke, feeling vaguely surprised that he was still alive. He stayed very still for some time, watching his captors through half-closed lids. The soldiers he saw were daunting enough but having been on the wrong end of Ferragamo's wrath he feared the old man even more.

He could see no likelihood of immediate escape and soon his thirst forced him to make his awareness known.

"Water," he croaked, as piteously as he could.

Ansar brought him some which he drank gratefully then pretended to lapse into oblivion again. He had no wish to be questioned, especially by this violent-looking young man.

In the evening his hands were untied and he was given food. He ate quickly under the careful scrutiny of several pairs of eyes before being bound again. Apart from this the captive was more or less ignored and was happy to be so.

Ansar took the last watch that night, but soon after Essan woke him, the lack of sleep from the past few nights caught up with him. He dozed, convincing himself that he would be fully alert at the slightest noise.

When he awoke at dawn his heart thudded suddenly. He sprang to his feet with a cry, looking around wildly.

The outlaw was gone.

Chapter 15

*S*oon afterward, everyone was awake. To Ansar's immense relief, no one was harmed and nothing had been stolen.

"He was obviously only too happy to get away," said Orme.

"But he could have cut all our throats," said Ansar, aghast at the thought.

"Well, he didn't," said Ferragamo. "There's no harm done, so forget about it."

Ansar said nothing but his sense of shame and self-directed anger showed in his stony face. In compensation he worked absurdly hard, gathering far more firewood than was necessary for breakfast and rubbing down the horses as well as practically begging for errands from everyone.

"It helps him not to think, I suppose," said Fontaine quietly, as she watched her brother stride off to fill water bottles at the stream.

"He'll get over it," replied Mark, knowing that in Ansar's place he would be having nightmares for a week.

As a result of all this industry they set off when the day was still quite young.

At first their progress was painfully slow. The pines gave way to more mixed growth and several detours became necessary, even in the short distance from their camp to the track. Jani was awake most of the time now but still very weak. He sat slumped on Hero's back, strapped to the saddle, with Orme and Ansar on either side in case he slipped. Essan and Ferragamo led the way, with Mark and Fontaine guiding the two horses.

Strangely, as they were still heading away from the river, this part of the forest was quite damp with several pools which made perfect breeding ground for biting insects. Even the horses' ears twitched and their tails flicked constantly. They were all glad when, at last, soon after midday, they reached the great track. Here at least there was some wind and the ground was firmer.

The road at the center was hard-packed stones and dried mud. The forest had been cleared on either side so that in all the trail's width was close to fifty paces, not wide enough to keep men and horses safe from bowmen in the trees, but sufficient to give warning of wild animals and to give most travelers a sense of security. The road was not used sufficiently to justify the work in widening the clearing and even now the forest was moving to reclaim its own in places.

The party rested, leaving the horses to graze. Ferragamo inspected Jani and the others' various hurts and pronounced himself satisfied with their progress.

For the rest of that day and for all of the next two they traveled south. They met no one and Orme wondered aloud about where Shill and the others had got to. They considered sending someone on ahead with one of the horses but decided against it as Jani was still not capable of walking and the other horse was being used to carry all their gear and occasionally one of their number if anyone felt especially weary.

The weather remained fine and the heat discouraged haste. Confined as they were to a walking pace and with frequent stops to replenish supplies and water their progress was very slow. Longfur took to riding with the baggage and spent a large part of the time asleep. At night he went off on his own hunting trips. As a consequence Mark found himself without his usual companion and sought out others to talk to. Surprisingly he quite often found himself walking alongside Fontaine. The princess's moods varied considerably. At one moment she would be chattering on about some part of her time in the forest, and the next she would be fretting over Jani's condition, or sunk in despondency when she remembered Eric's death. Mark found it hard to keep up with her.

"Poor Jani," she said as they trudged along. "He still doesn't look very well, does he? I wish I could do something more to help him. He's been so good to me, and I'd like to repay him, but all I can do is sit back and watch. What do you think of him?"

While Fontaine was obviously hoping for a complimentary remark for her new friend, Mark found it difficult to know what to say.

"Um, well, I'm sure he's very nice, when you get to know him." Inwardly he cringed at the ineptness of his comment, and floundered on, trying to put things right.

"But, I mean, well, it's a bit difficult to tell at the moment, isn't it? After all, he's been unconscious a lot of the time—and it's hard to judge a person's character when they're in that state."

Fontaine, while acknowledging the reasonableness of Mark's comment, obviously felt that it wasn't good enough.

"Well, *I* think he's wonderful. And you will too. You know, he's helped me such a lot in these last few days—more than by escaping from Durc, I mean. Knowing that he cared about what happened to me made me feel that I could cope better, instead of just sitting around and moping. I actually felt quite brave and independent for a while. You never know, I might have got used to life in the forest!" She laughed. "I tell you one thing about all this, though. I'm going to find it difficult to go back to being a lady at court, wearing dresses and powdering my face." Automatically her hand went up to touch her cheek and she colored slightly. Mark pretended not to notice.

"I know what you mean," he said. "So much has happened I can't really remember what it was like living in Starhill."

"Ansar doesn't like me dressed like this," she went on. "He always was a stuck-up pig. I'm sure he thinks all women should be pretty and keep in their places!"

Mark looked at Fontaine's brother as he walked beside Jani's horse, then back at Fontaine. With a shock he recalled her first appearance in Starhill. *She's a different person now,* he thought. *Prettier too somehow.*

"I think you look all right as you are," he said hesitantly.

Something of Fontaine's royal blood reasserted itself. *All right?* she thought, but she caught her own haughty response and remained silent. *We have a long way to walk,* she thought, *and talking to this naive young prince is better than nothing.*

Unaware of the response his words had provoked, Mark quickly tried to hide his confusion. "I know what older brothers can be like," he said.

"It's worse when you're a girl. Nobody pays you any attention except the idiots who mistake flattery for conversation. It was all so dull."

"Well, you can't say that now."

"That's true. Too much seems to happen to me now. And all I seem to do is cause trouble." Her face fell.

"That's not true."

"Yes it is. You've all had to run after me. And fight and get hurt." She glanced at his side. "And I could have prevented it all if I hadn't run off like that. And then Eric wouldn't—"

She stopped abruptly, swallowing her words so that she half choked. Mark looked at her but she refused to meet his gaze. Tears that were a mixture of contrition and self-pity were brimming in her eyes. Gingerly he stretched out an arm and put it round her shoulders. He gave her a quick hug then withdrew, feeling embarrassed.

"We're all all right now," he said quickly, as she looked up at him. "What's done is done. Eric caused his own . . . downfall. You mustn't blame yourself."

Mark still felt the death of his brother keenly. Eric had always seemed somehow invincible but even Mark had to admit that he had also been impetuous and downright stupid at times. Perhaps Fontaine could have talked some sense into him or foiled his plans, but Mark knew from personal experience just how forceful Eric could be.

He carefully looked away as Fontaine dabbed at her eyes with her hand. When he turned back she was smiling and he felt a small glow of pleasure somewhere deep inside him.

"Being a girl does have its advantage sometimes," she said. "You can get away with lots of things a boy couldn't." She grinned mischievously. "Perhaps that's why Ansar resents me sometimes."

Mark could not think of a prudent reply to that so he waited silently for her to go on. Soon they were happily exchanging tales of childhood pranks and discussing the relevant merits of their former homes. Mark grew gloomy when the talk turned to their parents. His father had always been a remote figure, preferring his more active elder sons, and he hardly remembered his mother, but their absence was still a cold ache in his heart. Fontaine, sensing his unease, reversed their earlier roles and tried to cheer him up. She coaxed him to talk about Ferragamo, realizing that in a way he was the prince's real father figure, and soon Mark was describing his lessons, magical and otherwise, and admitting to past blunders which ordinarily he would have been ashamed to mention. Fontaine's quick mind grasped the underlying principles of magic as Mark carefully related them to her and then surprised him by saying, "You never hear of any wizardesses, do you? I wonder why."

"I've never thought of that. I'll have to ask Ferragamo."

"He's very old, isn't he?"

"Only in time. He explained it to me once but I didn't understand all he said. Wizards don't work quite like ordinary men."

"Koria seems to find he works all right," said Fontaine, taking a faintly malicious amusement in Mark's discomfort at this statement.

"They love each other," he said simply.

"I didn't think wizards were supposed to . . . be like that."

"I think that's an idea spread by wizards to keep their apprentices paying attention to their studies," said Mark, blushing furiously.

Resisting the temptation to tease him further, Fontaine said, "You like Koria, don't you."

"I love them both," he replied solemnly.

"I don't think I treated her very well sometimes," said Fontaine. "I kept thinking of her like one of the servants at home. I'll have to make it up to her when we get back."

Their pace was still slow but the talk speeded up the day and they were both surprised when Ferragamo called a halt and started organizing their night's camp.

"We should reach Stane tomorrow," said the wizard.

"And Home the day after," added Orme.

It was a thought they all approved of, especially Ferragamo, who was finding the responsibility of looking after the group just a bit wearying. He decided that he was definitely looking forward to the rest that he could only find in Koria's arms.

Later that evening, as they prepared to sleep, Mark felt a familiar furry presence.

Not hunting tonight?

The reply was untranslatable. If it had been a human sound it might have come out something like *Huhnn.*

What's the matter?

You've been ignoring me all day.

You were asleep!

I was not. I was resting. What were you talking about all that time anyway?

You wouldn't be jealous, would you? Mark put as much mock astonishment into the thought as possible.

Don't be silly, came the contemptuous retort.

She's all right, you know, really.

She's been horribly spoiled and doesn't know the first thing about cats.

You mean she doesn't spoil you? Mark laughed.

There was no reply.

Don't sulk. I think she's learned a lot in the last few days. She'll be different now, I'm sure.

I'm not sulking and I hope so. You're not going soft on her, are you?

Now you're being silly!

Good. Do you think I could have some peace and quiet so that I can go to sleep?

Mark lay back and wondered.

Soon after they set off the next morning they passed through the southern fringes of the forest. Their spirits rose as they realized that this meant they were within two leagues of Stane and meeting their friends. A partial reunion came even sooner however.

"Horses coming up behind," said Essan. "Only two, I'd say," he added a few moments later as they all looked back.

"It's Shill," said Mark delightedly.

"Aye, and Bonet," confirmed Orme.

They waited until the two riders drew up and dismounted. There was a good deal of hugging and smiling as Fontaine and the others told their stories to the newcomers. Jani received several appraising glances. He had dismounted without help, and stood watching intently, seemingly content but wary.

Then it was Shill's turn to relate his actions.

"Aye," he said, "our tale's not as grand as yours, but it

bears repeating. Young Bonet here has been through some rough times."

"You exaggerate, Captain. I'm fine now." Nonetheless his smile seemed to Mark to be slightly uneasy.

"Maybe so now, lad. It was different in Ashwicken."

Bonet was silent, looking embarrassed.

"Ashwicken? You've ridden hard then. Let's hear your story?"

Shill turned to the wizard.

"We reached Stane four days ago. The others and the boat should still be there."

"Good," said Ferragamo. "We've done enough walking."

"I thought we'd ride north along the trail in the hope of meeting up with some or all of you," continued Shill. "So I hired these horses and Bonet and I set off. When we reached the fork we realized that we'd almost certainly missed you, so rather than wander about blindly, I decided we'd go on to Ashwicken to see if we could gather any information from the north."

He paused. "This is where it gets strange," he said. "On the second day, Bonet started feeling ill. He complained of being dizzy and sleepy. I thought it was a reaction to being back on horseback after being at sea and that it would pass, but when we came out of the forest and crossed the ford just south of Ashwicken, he near fell off his horse. We stopped and rested but there was nothing wrong that I could recognize. But I had a wizard's job—begging your pardon, Ferragamo—getting him back on his horse and into the town."

He looked at the young man and asked, "Do you want to tell them what it felt like, lad?"

Bonet, who had been studying his boots while the captain talked, looked up, cleared his throat, then said, "I just felt very lazy. As if nothing was worth the effort of doing it."

"That's not like you," said Orme.

"No aches or pains?" asked Ferragamo.

"No, none."

"He'd eaten nothing different from me," added Shill before resuming his tale.

"We stopped the night at the first tavern we came to. Dozy lot they were. Food was awful too, not that Bonet here took any notice of that. He slept solid for half a day and when he did come to he wasn't interested in anything. I didn't like to draw attention to us, not being sure where loyalties lay in the town, so I decided to get us back here somehow, hoping we'd find you." He looked at Ferragamo.

"I practically had to tie him to his horse when he left, but later on he started perking up and complaining of hunger. He's been on the mend ever since, till now he says there's nothing wrong at all. And I'm still none the wiser."

"Hmm. Let's have a look at you, young man," said the wizard.

"I'm fine," repeated Bonet, but he allowed Ferragamo to draw him aside, peer into his eyes, and listen to his heart, while the others stood about and talked.

The wizard rejoined them and looked to Shill again.

"You felt all right the whole time?"

"Me?" replied the soldier. "Of course."

"Is he all right?" asked Mark.

"There's nothing wrong with him at all, as far as I can see."

"I told you," said Bonet, joining the group. "I half think we both imagined it all."

"That we did not," said Shill firmly. "I almost had to carry you out of Ashwicken."

"I don't like the sound of that place," said Ansar.

Mark noticed Ferragamo glance quickly at the Healdean prince, his eyes narrowing slightly, but Ansar's face held no secrets.

"Come on," said Orme. "Let's get to Stane and on our way home."

With four horses between them and the promise of food and rest in civilized surroundings so close, they made good time, and were in Stane well before midday. They found they were all eager to continue their Homeward journey so they collected Brandel and Benfell and then, after a quick meal, joined Birn and his crew on board the *Seahawk*. They set sail almost immediately and by navigating by the stars overnight arrived at the familiar jetty of Home late in the following morning.

Koria was already waiting for them as they docked, having been alerted to their arrival by one of the sharp-eyed village children who already knew of the excellence of her cooking and guessed, correctly, that the bearer of good news would not go unrewarded. She hugged them all as they came ashore and made just the right amount of fuss over the rescued princess.

Ansar, meanwhile, was already engaged in negotiations with Birn which led, later in the day, to the boat and its crew setting sail again, this time for Heald. Birn was reveling in his new, if temporary, captaincy, and enjoying the variety of his recent employment. He carried a message for King Pabalan from his son, properly sealed. The message stated that Fontaine was safe once more—unharmed—and that they should therefore ignore the ransom demand which would be put to them by a certain ring-bearing gentleman by the name of Deg, and deal with him as they thought fit. Birn was also given enough money to make the trip and stay on Heald worthwhile.

Mark watched them sail away, feeling oddly restless. The last few days had been so full of purpose and adventure that suddenly everything seemed very flat. He sat on the end of the jetty and watched the lazy swell below his feet. The water was so clear he could see starfish on the sea bed.

What do we do now? he wondered. Although he had not consciously projected the thought a familiar voice replied, *Ferragamo will think of something. Until then, how about some fishing?*

Chapter 16

Pabalan's secretary was peeved. The well-ordered running of the court, which was his only real joy, had been disrupted too often in the last month. Only yesterday, Rehan's return from Ark had caused unavoidable changes in his carefully planned schedule, and now, on the very morning he had set aside for discussion of the latest acquisition of supplies for the palace, there had been not one but two unforeseen arrivals. The secretary disliked people who did not make appointments.

At the king's summons the secretary entered the royal apartments. Pabalan sat beside his queen. She was reading. He was staring into space, drumming his fingers on the arm of the settle.

"Morning, Fluke. What's the plan?" the king asked without any great enthusiasm.

The secretary winced inwardly at his master's informality, but of course nothing of this showed in his face.

"Good morning, my Lord. Good morning, my Lady," he said, bowing. Adesina nodded in reply, but continued to read. Fluke tried to make out the book's title but was unable to do so. He hoped it was suitable. Fluke noticed with some distaste that, despite the earliness of the hour, there was a glass and an open wine bottle at Pabalan's side.

"Your majesty has no official appointments until luncheon."

"Good."

"I had hoped to discuss the production reports from the southern estates. We need to agree on shipments to the capital and advise on schedules."

"I am sure you can arrange that satisfactorily, Fluke. I'll leave it to you."

"It is necessary that you countersign the consignment documents, my Lord. I felt it only proper that you should be cognizant of their contents.

"However," Fluke went on before the king could deflect him, "it may be necessary for our discussion to be temporarily delayed."

Pabalan looked up, unable to keep from smiling. "Why?" he asked.

"There are two matters which should be brought to your attention. Firstly, there is a young man from Ark who appears to carry a message from Prince Ansar. He refuses to part with it to anyone but yourself. I have no way of ensuring that it is genuine but the seal appears to be your son's."

Both the royal couple were regarding him intently.

"I have tried to reason with him but he is most insistent."

"Bring him to me."

"His attire is not entirely suitable, my Lord. He says he is a fisherman." Fluke's nose wrinkled in refined distaste.

"Just get him in here."

"Yes, my Lord."

"Wait. Is he armed?"

"Not openly. Do you wish me to have him searched?"

"No. From the sound of it he'd not take kindly to the idea."

"As you wish," said Fluke stiffly.

"Bring him here. What's his name?"

"Birn, my Lord."

"While you're about it fetch Rehan and Laurent. I want them to hear what this chap has to say."

"At once, my Lord."

Fluke turned to go, only for the queen's quiet voice to call him back. The king, now standing, looked at his wife, then at his secretary.

"You said there were two matters, Fluke. What is the other?"

"Moroski is back in the capital, my Lady."

"Moroski!" said the king. "About time too. Get him in here as well."

"Yes, my Lord," said Fluke, unable to hide his disapproval. He withdrew.

"I wonder where he'd been hiding all this time," mused Adesina.

"Just when we could have used him, too."

"You make him sound like a tool."

"You know what I mean. I don't have much time for wizards usually—"

"But they do have their uses."

"Yes."

"Well, I'm glad he's back. He's a good deal more entertaining than Fluke. How do you suffer that man?"

"I know he's a pompous windbag but he's good at his job. He can organize anything. Most of my court can't organize their own thoughts!"

There was a knock at the door.

"Enter."

A tall dark man entered, his eyes gleaming with pleasure. He bowed slightly, which caused the small falcon perched on his shoulder to tighten her grip on the padded leather.

Adesina rose and crossed to the newcomer. Taking his hands, she stood on tiptoe and kissed his cheek.

"We've missed you, Moroski."

"And I you, my Lady," he replied, smiling. "My Lord," he added, turning to the king.

"You know what's been going on on Ark?" said Pabalan.

"Yes. It was that which brought me back to the city."

"Where have you been?"

"Traveling. Here and there."

"You never could decide whether you were a court wizard or a vagabond, could you," said the queen.

"There are advantages to both," replied the wizard.

"And disadvantages too," she mocked him gently. "I'm glad you're back."

Their reunion was interrupted by Rehan and Laurent who arrived together, having obviously made some haste. They had time only for the briefest of greetings before Fluke reappeared and introduced Birn. An armed guard was stationed pointedly outside the door.

The sailor looked round the assembled company and nervously cleared his throat.

"You have a message for me, I gather," said Pabalan with uncharacteristic gentleness.

Birn bowed awkwardly. "Yes, Your Majesty. That is if... if you are the king."

"If...!" exclaimed Pabalan, then quieted down and replied, "I am Pabalan. Most people reckon me king of Heald, though sometimes I wonder. This is my queen and these are my closest advisors."

Birn's eyes flicked round the room.

Recovering some of his nerve, he said, "Forgive my caution, sir. Ansar was most insistent that I give this letter to the king and no other."

"I am he."

"I do not doubt it, sir. I see the likeness now."

The queen said, "Your news is good, I hope, Birn." She was smiling but the concern was obvious in her voice.

"It is, my Lady. Here." He withdrew a folded parchment from his jacket and handed it to the king.

Pabalan studied the seal for a moment then broke it open and read the letter. A smile spread over his face and he handed the parchment to his wife.

"Good news indeed," he said. "Fontaine is safe and apparently none the worse for a few days in the woods."

"He doesn't tell us much though, does he," said Adesina. "That's just like Ansar."

"Where are they now?" asked Laurent.

Pabalan looked to Birn who said, "At Home, sir," and added, "the village, that is," when the possible misinterpretation of his words sank in.

"Ferragamo and the princes are safe too?" asked the queen.

"Yes, my Lady."

"Why didn't Ansar and Fontaine return to Heald with you?" asked Rehan.

"I don't know, sir. They were all in need of rest and Ansar was anxious that a message be sent as soon as possible. And... my boat's not very luxurious, sir."

"I wonder what they're planning to do now," said Laurent. "Ferragamo and the princes, I mean. Should we invite them to Heald, my Lord?"

"Gentlemen," interposed the queen. "If you are to have a prolonged discussion perhaps some refreshment is in order."

"Good idea," said the king.

Chairs were gathered round the table and wine and

glasses produced. Laurent fetched a map of Ark and showed Pabalan where Home was.

"They'll be safe enough where they are," ventured Birn on being asked. "We rarely see anyone from Starhill that far south. We've seen no soldiery and no one there knew of the visitor's cottage."

"The visitor?"

Birn glanced uneasily at the dark man whose falcon now stood on a window ledge.

"Ferragamo, sir, the wizard."

"So that's where he sloped off to every year."

"When will you return to Ark?" asked Pabalan.

"With your permission, sir, on the first tide. We've been away a few days now."

"Do you want me to go with them?" said Laurent.

"I don't know yet."

The discussion went backward and forward for some time. It was late morning when they broke up. Laurent set off with Birn toward the harbor.

"Give my regards to Ferragamo," called Moroski before he and Adesina turned to each other, looking forward to a long and pleasant conversation. The king would have joined them but as he moved to do so Fluke reappeared with two large ledgers.

"My Lord, about those reports. I think we just have time to go through them before the Guildmen arrive."

Pabalan groaned.

"Let's get it over with then," he said.

Rehan left and went his own way.

At home he collected the seeing-stone then went to his study leaving strict instructions that he was not to be disturbed. Reverently he weighed the bag in his hand. Surely Amarino would not mind him using the stone again so soon after the last message. Had it only been yesterday? It seemed ages since he had seen her beautiful face.

Trembling with anticipation he took out the stone and cradled it in his hands. Its coolness calmed him. He marshaled his thoughts and called out, staring into the milky depths.

The glass shivered, cleared, then wavered again. Rehan gasped in horror. He almost dropped the globe but found he could neither move nor look away.

Instead of the lovely visage he had been expecting he

found he was looking at a gnarled and hideously ugly face, most of which was covered with an unruly black beard. The eyes were nearly colorless and they radiated an almost palpable evil.

"Well, what have we here?" said the vision. He laughed and Rehan shuddered at the sight of discolored, broken teeth.

"My little girl has been playing, I see. I wondered what she was up to when the stone awoke yesterday. Now I know."

Transfixed, like a rabbit before a snake, Rehan was helpless. He could not even blink.

"Of course this interference will irritate her." The vision laughed again. "But she was foolish to allow an unskilled novice to handle a stone. She must learn by her mistakes. Not that it will matter in the end."

The man moved and with a sweeping gesture of his silver and black robe revealed the scene behind him.

"Behold your future, weakling."

As the scope of the vision expanded, Rehan caught a brief glimpse of a grim circle of stones. Beyond that, mountain slopes and lowland regions of some unknown island flashed in front of his eyes. It was a scene of utter desolation. Blackness dominated everything. Polluted waves slapped at stained and jagged rocks. Stunted, dying trees stood amid diseased and wilting crops. No flowers grew, no birds sang, no life knew joy.

It was a land blasted by something more terrible than Rehan could ever imagine. He saw it all in a few moments and his heart quailed.

Then the face reappeared, filling the globe.

"Drowning will be easy by comparison," it said and laughed.

Although no longer constrained, Rehan sat immobile for a long time, his eyes staring at the innocent white surface of the stone, seeing nothing.

Finally he stirred and fumbled hurriedly as he put the stone back in its bag. Locking it away lessened his fear slightly and he was able to start thinking rationally again. Nothing in all the islands would induce him to attempt to use the seeing-stone again. But that left him with the problem of how to communicate the latest news to Amarino. He deliberately let his thoughts dwell on her, letting her remembered radiance wash away his terror. The passion he held for her was undiminished, a fact his body told him as clearly as his mind. Surely now he had the excuse he wanted to return to Starhill. It was the only way he could let her know what was going on. She would accept that, wouldn't she? Rehan was sure that he could persuade Pabalan to let him go now that Fontaine was safe. It all fitted. The idea filled him with pleasure fueled by a fantasy in which all things were possible. He ignored the tiny part of his mind that writhed in terror.

Resolute now, he left his house and set off for the palace.

The next day he set sail for Grayrock Harbor.

Chapter 17

$\mathcal{L}$ike any self-respecting cat, Longfur was not averse to allowing humans to feed him, preferably with fish, and spending most of the time in between meals asleep, preferably in the sun. However, Longfur, as he would have been the first to admit, was no ordinary cat. Even if his unruly black and white hair did stick out at peculiar angles sometimes he knew he was not to be compared to a common village cat. Moreover, the last few days had given him a taste for travel and adventure which he would not have dreamt of before.

Thus it was, on the evening of the day after the party arrived back in Home, that Longfur went in search of entertainment. Mark was preoccupied and uncommunicative and Longfur, who had always thought of his human as almost feline, began to have his doubts.

He left the cottage and padded silently into the village.

The scene inside The Mermaid was brightly lit and cheerful. Derwent's wife had given birth to a healthy baby boy that morning, and although his closest friends were absent, sailing with his boat to Heald, there were plenty of the villagers eager to help him celebrate the event. In addition, a trading vessel had docked that afternoon, which was a rare event in a village as small as Home. The captain of this ship and his crew had evidently done well in their recent travels for they were keen to sample The Mermaid's excellent beer and had plenty of money to do so. Soon the sailors were included in the general celebration as if they moored at Home every week.

As the evening drew on, tongues were loosened and the talk turned inevitably to the events in Starhill. The merchant captain enjoyed an audience and was happy to tell his version of the tale to a new set of listeners.

"I've not been to Starhill, mind," he said. "We're sea men and Grayrock's our port of call, but I can tell you there's some strange business going on. Ever since that army man took over there's been some wild tales. Ather's dead of course but no one knows what happened to his sons."

The villagers looked knowingly at each other but said nothing and the sailor went on, "And now they say there's magic at work. Life's so good in the capital there's folk heading there from all over. None of 'em's come back so it must be someways true. Not that I hold with that stuff meself. There's always folk'll believe city streets is paved with gold."

The captain paused and took a swig of beer. One of his crew spoke up.

"Grayrock's changed too, eh cap'n? It don't feel right somehow."

"Aye, that's true enough. I can't say exactly why but it's odd. You feel it the moment your feet touch land."

"It's like you're half asleep."

"Everyone there's in a dreamworld, I'd reckon."

"The trade's good enough. That's what counts," added another crewman, jingling coins in his pocket.

"Aye, we can't complain. The merchants are eager enough," said his captain, "but I was happy to be back at sea. And happier still to be here," he added, draining his mug, "This beer's the best we've had all summer, eh lads?"

There was a chorus of agreement. The landlord was already moving round with jugs to keep the party going.

Nobody noticed a black and white cat slip out into the night.

———————

Ferragamo was worried. It was not necessary to be as close to him as Koria was to realize that. He had hardly touched his lunch, which was unusual enough on its own, but moreover he could not keep still and would not meet her eyes. He spoke little and anything said to him usually had to be repeated before he responded.

After the meal, Koria contrived to be alone with him in the kitchen. Holding him firmly so that he could not escape her question, she said, "I would appreciate it if you would share it with me. At least then I would know why you're acting like a cornered rabbit."

"Is it that obvious?" His eyes were sad.

"Yes," she said. "Don't look like that. Tell me about it."

"Come for a walk with me," he said, taking her hands. "I need your common sense to tell me whether I'm being a senile old fool."

"I'll come for a walk, but you're never that."

"Hear me first," he replied.

Some time later they were sitting side by side on the grass above the cliffs to the south of the village. They were gazing out to sea. Koria's face was uncharacteristically serious. The wizard's was animated.

"So you see," he said, "it's not any one thing but all of them put together that worry me." He turned to look at her. "Tell me I'm crazy."

"You're not crazy, as you well know."

"Then you agree?"

"Not so fast. Let me see if I've got this right. First of all, there was what happened to Bonet in Ashwicken."

"Yes."

"That could have a perfectly natural explanation."

"It could, but I can't think of one, and neither can Shill."

"All right. Then there was the time when Jani was hurt and you found that something hindered your healing."

"Yes, there was something wrong. I had to get around it before I could get to him. I've never encountered anything like it before. And that was the same time as Bonet was ill in Ashwicken."

"Jani is a strange one. Are you sure it wasn't something in him blocking you?"

"I don't know. I don't think so." Koria was about to go on when Ferragamo exclaimed, "Wait a minute, I've just thought of something else. We all slept late that day but the next night Ansar fell asleep on watch. That doesn't seem like him, does it?"

"No, it doesn't, but anyone can get tired. You'd all been through a lot in a short time."

"But we keep coming back to this business of feeling sleepy, or half-asleep, which is exactly what those seamen were talking about in The Mermaid last night."

"But that was at Grayrock, not Ashwicken!"

"Well, maybe this thing—whatever it is—moves from place to place."

"If there is a thing."

Ferragamo said nothing.

"Can you trust a story from Longfur?" Koria asked after a while.

"Mark's not easy to fool. If he believes him, so do I."

"It's still only hearsay."

The wizard recalled the frustration of the morning's strange threeway conversation. Longfur had quite obviously been able to hear him but the wizard could only catch tantalizing snatches of the cat's replies, which Mark relayed. He had been unwilling to admit the full extent of Longfur's abilities— or Mark's—before, but now he had no doubts. After another pause, he spoke again.

"I keep going back to the day Ather was killed. I cannot escape the feeling that more than swords was used that day. It has nagged at my mind ever since but I can't recall any specific sign of magic at all. Yet—"

"Don't start imagining things," Koria smiled. "We've enough to think about without that."

"You know what worries me most?"

"What?"

"That Shill wasn't affected in Ashwicken when Bonet was."

"Why? Surely that is an argument against this magical theory you've been building up."

"It would be but for one thing."

Koria waited.

"This is going to sound silly," said Ferragamo.

"Out with it, my love. I'll judge whether it's silly."

"Shill ate some of the cake. Bonet didn't."

The absurdity of this statement left Koria feeling cold. It sounded so ridiculous that she was sure it wasn't.

"The one from that old recipe?"

"Yes."

"What made you think of that?"

"Something Mark said this morning. It's uncanny the way he happens to trigger off lines of thought sometimes. This time it was the idea that perhaps he should try to eat moonberries, that we could do with a powerful new hero."

"And you think the moonberries in that cake somehow counteract this thing in Ashwicken?"

"I hope not," he replied.

"Why?"

"Because moonberries would only be effective against one sort of magic." He paused.

"And I don't even want to think about that."

By the end of the afternoon Ferragamo had made a decision. The idea stemmed from Koria who, practical as ever, had suggested that if there were something in Ashwicken and if the cake was protection against its influence then there was a simple way of proving it. The wizard had caught her drift at this point and now as they sat down to their evening meal it was merely a question of whom to send. It was not an easy choice but by the time they were ready for dessert he was resolved. He nodded to Koria who went off into the kitchen. Looking round the crowded table, the wizard wondered how much he should tell them. All the soldiers were eating with them this night and at least one of them would be asked to put himself deliberately at risk. Ferragamo cleared his throat.

"There are some special arrangements I'd like to make for the rest of the meal," he said.

Everyone looked at him expectantly.

"It concerns the cake we . . ." he began but got no further. Koria reappeared in the kitchen doorway.

"It's gone!" she said. "All of it."

"Oh no! Are you sure? Where are you going, Brandel?"

The prince was quietly moving toward the door. He stopped at the wizard's sharp words and turned. The expression on his face made it obvious what had happened to the cake.

Ferragamo stood, his fists clenched by his sides.

"Brandel, if you've eaten it all, you deserve to be horsewhipped or worse. Your gluttony will be the death of me—and you probably."

"But I got so hungry," whined the prince, "and it was such a small piece really. After I started I just couldn't seem to stop. I'm sorry."

Ferragamo sat down again with a bump while everyone else looked embarrassed.

"Oh well," said the wizard, "I suppose we can make some more."

"Er . . . no, we can't," said Koria. "That cake used all there was."

"But I told you only to use a little bit."

"There was only a little bit," she said firmly.

"You know what this means?" Ferragamo groaned.

"Yes."

"Will somebody please explain what on Ark you're talking about," said Orme.

"I'm not going to go mad, am I?" Brandel had gone quite pale.

"No, you're not going mad," said Ferragamo. "You're going to Ashwicken."

Later that night Mark lay in his attic bed, listening to Brandel snoring. *How can he sleep?* he thought.

I've explained that before, came Longfur's silent reply.

But tonight, with what's happening tomorrow! I can't sleep. How can he?

His body rules his mind, not the other way round like you.

Do you think the cake will have affected him?

There's a lot of him to affect. All that flesh must spread it out a bit. Ferragamo didn't seem worried about that, did he, so there's no need for you to.

He didn't want him to go though, did he?

No.

That's because he feels responsible for us, Ather's . . . my father's sons, I mean. Eric's dead already and now he has to risk Brandel.

There wasn't much choice though, was there?

No. Even those of us who'd had some of the cake had had so little that its effect might have worn off by now. I wish we could send more than one other person with him though.

Benfell's a good man and besides we've been through all that. If anyone other than Brandel is going to fall asleep as soon as they get near Ashwicken, how would he cope?

I know.

After a pause Mark went on, *I don't envy Benfell.*

I noticed Bonet was none too keen to go north again despite his protests that his attack was really nothing.

Ferragamo thinks that some people may be more sensitive to this thing than others. Maybe Bonet is one of those.

Well, I hope for Benfell's sake that he isn't. I don't think Brandy would make a very good nursemaid.

They looked over at the slumbering figure.

You could be right there, said Mark.

I usually am, replied Longfur complacently.

———————

The next morning Ferragamo gave Brandel and Benfell their last-minute instructions.

"I don't want you two taking any risks," he said. "Take it slowly between here and Stane to keep the spare horses fresh but once you're in the forest move fast and keep moving. No heroics. If you see anyone, run away!"

"That's fine by me," said Brandel. "I hope my horse agrees."

Benfell smiled. "We'll be careful," he said.

"As soon as you feel anything strange, Benfell—if you do—then turn back. I don't want you going on until you collapse just to prove a point."

"No, sir."

"And Brandel, you keep an eye on Benfell. If he starts nodding off or turning green, turn him round."

Brandel nodded, appreciating the wizard's feeble attempt to lighten the mood.

"Off you go then."

They mounted up, together with Shill and Orme who had persuaded the wizard to let them accompany the two as far as

Stane. From there they would return with the spare horses so
that Brandel and Benfell could continue on fresh mounts.

"Good luck!" called Mark as the riders set off.

"Come back soon," added Koria.

"For your cooking—of course!" returned Brandel, laughing despite, or perhaps because of, his nervousness.

Ferragamo stomped off into the cottage, muttering quietly
about doing something in his study. The rest of them
watched until the riders were out of sight then went their
ways.

Closeted in his study, the wizard made sure that he could
not be observed, and then took out the parchment from its
hiding place. The current relevance of the recipe had started
him thinking about it again. He wanted to dismiss it as
inconsequential nonsense but all his wizardly instincts cried
out against this.

Now as he read it through again he found himself drawn
back to the first two couplets. His mind insisted on putting a
particular interpretation on the words each time he read
them. He tried to clear his thoughts and approach them anew
but it was impossible.

> From the sea, peril.
> From the sea, safety.

The first, his thoughts insisted, meant that the threat, if
threat there was, came from the sea. From another island?
The disquieting memory of the mysterious isolation of Brogar
jumped unbidden into his head. He shuddered at the thought
that Ark might be doomed to follow that path. The implications of that were horrendous.

The second line surely was a reference to the well-known
fact that magical power was unable to be used effectively over
moving water. The sea would therefore provide safety from
most magical threats, which would fit in with the sea captain's
tale that Longfur had overheard.

There must be other interpretations, he thought, but his
brain refused to countenance any.

The second couplet worried him even more.

> From the parts, the whole.
> From the whole, strength.

If, as he suspected, it referred to the recipe, it meant that
perhaps, just perhaps, the whole thing did refer to the

present situation. Because if his theory was correct about the cake then that was horribly relevant to what was happening now. And it *was* a coincidence that Mark had found the prophecy just after his nasty experience with the old tale.

And if all that were true, he ought to be taking the rest of the verses seriously. In fact, he already was. He had read the whole thing through several times and considered it from every angle.

And still he could not make head nor tail of it.

————————————

Ferragamo emerged from his study in the late morning. The cottage was deserted so he set off to walk down to the village. He found Ansar at the jetty talking to the sea captain who, with his crew's full approval, had decided to stay another day. As the wizard walked to join them he saw Mark, Fontaine, Koria, and Jani sitting on the shingle nearby. As he watched they laughed. Even Jani smiled broadly. It was a sight the wizard needed after his almost fruitless morning.

He wanted to talk to the sailor about Grayrock but decided against it and when he joined the conversation it was for a more practical purpose. Ansar had already ascertained that the merchant ship would be sailing from Home to Heald, as was only natural, and he had thought that Fontaine could perhaps go with them.

"If the captain is willing," said Ferragamo, "I would like you to go as well. There are a lot of things I don't understand about what's going on but it pays to be prepared. There are certain arrangements I'd like you to make."

"Of course," said Ansar and looked to the seaman.

"The more the merrier. We sail on the next tide though, so you'd best make your plans quick."

"Good," said Ansar. "I'll go and tell Fontaine."

Ferragamo fell into step beside the Healdean prince.

"I've written several letters," the wizard said. "One is to your father. It asks that he mobilizes your army and has ships available to bring them to Ark when it is time. On no account are they to set sail or land on Ark before more discussion has taken place. I just want them ready, that's all."

Ansar looked at him.

"You're taking this seriously then?"

"I am. I hope I'm wrong but I fear that something evil i
at work on Ark and if it is we will have to act quickly."

"The other letters?"

"They are to various colleagues of mine on other islands.
If you can find ships to take them on speedily it will be a
great help. We don't have any available here."

"That shouldn't be a problem. What do you say in the
letters?"

"It's a request for help basically. Ships and men if we
need them, but more importantly, for moonberries."

"I'm still not very clear about that," said Ansar.

"You don't need to be," replied the wizard. "We need
them, that's all. And that's what I want you to do."

"Collect berries?"

"The ones from your own tree on Heald, yes. Pick all but
two or three of the fruit and keep them sealed. And if there
are any dried or preserved supplies, bring them too. I've put
all that in my letter to Pabalan."

"So you want me to come back here," said Ansar, unable
to hide his pleasure at not leaving the action after all.

"Yes," said the wizard, "and by the way, I'd like you and
Mark to sign the letters as well so call him up when you tell
Fontaine."

"Right," said Ansar and jumped down onto the shingle.

"I'm not going!"

"You're being ridiculous," retorted Ansar, glaring at his
sister.

"I don't care. I am not an object to be sent here and there
at your whim."

"But Heald is your home."

"Father didn't seem to care about that when he sent me
off here, did he? Ark is my home now. My friends are here."

"There could be war here, Fontaine."

"Then I'll learn to fight!"

"I give up," said Ansar, looking around the cottage. "Can't
any of you talk some sense into her?"

Mark looked at the floor. Jani, as silent as ever, looked
backward and forward between Fontaine and her brother, a
worried expression on his face.

Ferragamo spoke. "I think that this is one argument

you're going to lose, Ansar," he said softly. "Right or wrong, you might as well give in gracefully. Your ship is on the point of sailing."

Fontaine smiled at the wizard gratefully. Country life must suit her, he thought. She looked much healthier now.

"All right," said Ansar resignedly, "but the stars know what I'm going to tell Father."

That evening, Mark determined to put his time in Home to good use. He felt singularly restless. Part of the reason for this was that most of the others were actively engaged in the events that were engulfing them all while he was without purpose. The other part was due to the feelings that had flowed through him while Ansar and Fontaine had argued. He had desperately wanted to speak up at the time but had known that, confused as he was, he would have been hopelessly tongue-tied. The decision that she was to stay had caused a momentary elation which soon turned to anxiety about the possible consequences and about his own motives. Ansar's mention of war had shaken him more then he cared to admit.

He had not touched the sword, Eric's sword as he still thought of it, since he had returned to the cottage. Now, before he went to bed, he drew it from its scabbard and balanced it in his hand. Again he was surprised by its lightness. *Tomorrow,* he thought, *I'll ask one of the soldiers to give me some lessons*. The memory of his clumsiness in the fight in the forest still brought him out in a cold sweat and he vowed that next time—if there had to be a next time—he would not be a danger to himself or a liability to his friends.

That night his dreams were full of vague images of violence and confused with these was the face of Fontaine alternatively mocking him and smiling as she had done after the fight. Although he recalled none of this clearly, it made him all the more determined to learn the skills of combat as quickly as he could, and he went in search of a tutor. Richard proved a willing and able teacher and offered to show him how to use a crossbow as well as the rudiments of swordsmanship.

Mark became so engrossed in the training that it was some time before he realized that they had an audience. Fontaine stood nearby, her arms folded, watching closely.

"Could I try that?" she asked.

———————

On the afternoon of their second day's riding, Brandel and Benfell were moving quickly, aware that they were nearing the forest's northern edge. From there it was only a matter of fording the Greenwater River and riding a further half-league, and they would be in Ashwicken.

Benfell had felt nothing untoward, aside from a little queasiness which he put down to nerves, and they were both feeling that the whole journey looked like being a waste of time.

They reached the ford as it was growing dark and debated whether to cross straightaway or camp on the forest side. In the end they decided to ford the river but camp on the bank ready for a quick look at the town and then the journey back to Home.

Brandel felt a slight twinge of anxiety as their horses splashed through the shallow water but it soon passed. They went upstream a way and settled for the night. Their evening meal was cold for they didn't care to attract attention with a fire. They had seen no one since leaving Stane, but Ferragamo's exhortations about stealth had been taken to heart.

They sat and talked quietly in the moonlight, growing accustomed to the little night sounds of the river bank.

"I'm tired," said Benfell eventually.

Brandel looked at him quickly.

"Quite normally, I mean," added the soldier. "We might as well try to sleep now and set off at first light tomorrow."

"That makes sense," said Brandel. "That way we can be in Ashwicken before most people are up and about."

"And gone again before they know it."

"Goodnight then."

"Goodnight."

Despite his rudimentary bed, it was not long before Brandel was snoring. Benfell was just dozing off when an unusual sound made him sit up with a start. He peered into the darkness, but saw nothing and was just convincing himself that his imagination was getting the better of him when several men appeared. Moonlight glinted on unsheathed steel. Benfell grabbed his own sword and struggled to rise. His feet tangled in his bedding and despite his wild attempts he had no chance to defend himself against a three-way attack. A sword caught him in the stomach and he gasped in anguish before a second blow ended his pain permanently.

Brandel was by now wide awake but unmoving. He looked up with wide eyes at the man whose sword point rested lightly on his throat.

Another man spoke. "You fools, we're supposed to take them alive—all of them."

"He came at us, captain."

"And it was beyond all three of you to disarm him without killing him, I suppose," came the contemptuous reply. "Throw him in the river."

The leader appeared in Brandel's range of vision.

"At least we got the important one," he said. "This is a face I couldn't forget."

It had only been three days now, thought Mark, but already his days were beginning to follow a pattern. In the morning he trained with his sword and then with either crossbow or staff. Fontaine had insisted on joining in and had surprised both Richard and Shill, who had now returned from Stane, with her dexterity and speed. What she lacked in strength she made up for with timing and agility. The other soldiers sometimes came to watch and add their comments and advice. Not all of their words were complimentary or even serious and Mark often felt awkward under their scrutiny. Fontaine, however, gave as good as she got, proving to be as spirited with her tongue as with a light sword.

Jani, who was now fully recovered, was also an occasional observer. He at least was silent. Later, he also played his part acting as a formidable opponent when Richard suggested combat with staves. That was one exercise Fontaine was happy to watch. She came to the conclusion that she quite enjoyed watching Mark fight, and not just because she admired his growing prowess with sword and stave. She also found herself admiring the sight of the young prince stripped to the waist, a feeling which surprised her as much as it would have embarrassed Mark had he known of her thoughts.

In the afternoons Mark and Fontaine would relax and go for a walk or just sit and talk before the evening meal, which was followed by more general conversation. Mark was work-

ing on Ferragamo to start teaching him some more magic but
the wizard was currently too preoccupied. Now as he lay in
the afternoon sun on the beach to the north of the village,
Mark wondered idly if he should try again this evening.
Fontaine sat beside him, staring out to sea.

"It's hot," she said. "I'm going for a swim." She was
already stripping off her clothes. "Coming?"

"No, I'll stay here, I think," he said, despising himself for
his cowardice. "You go ahead." He shut his eyes and resolutely
refused to look at the girl as she walked down to the water.

It was hot and he was weary from the morning's exertions.
He dozed.

Afterward he could not say when the nightmare had
caught him up again. He was not even sure whether he
fought those hideous mirages again. He only knew that he
was weary beyond words when, at last, he faced the dragon
and knew it for his real opponent.

The baleful yellow eyes stared at him. He knew he must
avoid falling into their hypnotic depths or the duel would be
lost before it was begun.

The dragon's voice spoke like thunder in his mind.

*What's this? This puny morsel dares to challenge my
citadel? Begone before I sear your flesh from your bones.*

Crying his defiance the man hurled himself forward. He
was met by a blast of fire which no mirage could produce.
Instantly his armor turned into an oven, scalding his skin and
drying his nose and throat in moments. Still he ran on. The
fire came again and the acrid smell of burning hair filled his
nostrils. His shield, which he held before him, blazed red hot
but his hand was clamped insanely to the smoldering strap-
ping. Blinded now, the sulfurous fire his only reality, he
plunged forward at the beast.

His sword glanced off a steely scale then slipped between
and plunged into the black heart of the dragon. Its scream rent
the sky and blood like acid splattered all around.

He lay knowing that he had won but unable to move. His
armor's joints had fused with the heat. He would lie here until
someone came—if they came—and cut him free. He knew
too the disfigurement that had been the cost of victory. Too
tired and agonized to do more than live he lay and waited for
someone to come to his aid.

"Mark, Mark! Wake up!" Hands shook his shoulders.

Green eyes, wide in fright, stared into his. "You did frighten me," she said.

"You were yelling and screaming and then you went all quiet. Are you all right now?"

He nodded feebly.

"You look awful."

"Thanks," he croaked. He was drenched in sweat, burning as if he had a fever.

"I'd better fetch Ferragamo," said Fontaine. "Will you be all right for a few moments?"

He nodded again and she sped off, heedless of the fact that she wore only her sea-drenched undertunic.

Mark sat up, waited for a wave of nausea to pass, then rose and staggered down to the water. Fully clothed, he plunged in and let the cool salt water wash away the dread.

Last time this happened Eric was killed, he thought. *Please let Brandel be all right.*

Chapter 18

*F*ollowing his capture, Brandel was marched into Ashwicken. There he was thrown into a small, dank cellar with no windows, whose only entrance was a securely locked door. He heard the muttering of guards outside and gave up any hope of escape. Even he found it difficult to sleep that night.

In the morning he learned that his captors were a platoon of Castle Guards from Starhill. There were several faces that he recognized, though none he could put a name to, but he could elicit no response from the seemingly emotionless soldiers.

Soon he was taken out and put on a horse. For the whole of that day and most of the next he rode north, surrounded by eight soldiers. The rest of the platoon remained in Ashwicken.

Brandel soon abandoned his forlorn hopes of escape and wished fervently for some help from his friends. He knew in his heart however that he was beyond their aid.

By the afternoon of the second day out of Ashwicken he was so sick of being in the saddle that he was glad to see the walls of Starhill come into sight. Despite the ominous nature of his arrival he was glad that at least the journey and waiting were over.

They entered the city by Field Gate in the late afternoon. Immediately, Brandel was struck by the wrongness of the place. It was a few moments before he realized that the streets were less crowded than he remembered them. Those people he did see seemed intent on their business. There were no idlers, no groups gossiping on street corners, no children shouting. Empty expressions marked their progress and nobody took much interest in the soldiers' prisoner.

Apart from the unaccustomed space and quiet there was nothing specific that Brandel could point to as being wrong. The streets were clean. There were no signs of any violence or looting which might have followed the uprising. There were no broken windows, no burnt-out buildings. Yet the very normalcy of everything around him turned Brandel's stomach. His danger-heightened awareness cried out that the city's very atmosphere was steeped in dread.

His escort obviously saw nothing odd in the scenes around them and rode directly to the castle without any orders being necessary. They had spoken little for the whole of the journey and now the sound of their horses' shoes on the cobbled street sounded loudly amid the strangely silent city.

They entered the castle by the main gate, which swung open without any need for the captain to announce his company's presence. In the central courtyard they dismounted and Brandel was led immediately around the inner wall and into what had been the royal apartments. He felt a lump in his throat as the familiarity of the place sank in. Yet somehow everything was different.

The room into which he was led was one he had known from childhood but the furnishings had been altered considerably. He disliked the new design. His guards withdrew, leaving him alone. *What now?* he wondered, looking around.

A woman entered from another door. She looked momentarily surprised, then her eyes narrowed and regarded him curiously. Slowly a frown creased her lovely face.

Brandel had no doubt that this was Amarino and was vaguely surprised to be brought before her—and alone—rather than Parokkan.

Abruptly she spoke.

"Where are your brother and the wizard?"

"I don't know and I wouldn't tell you if I did."

She stared at him disbelievingly.

"Where are they?" she demanded.

Brandel remained silent.

"Still in Home?"

He tried to keep his face impassive.

"Where's that?" he said.

Anger showed in her eyes.

"Sit down," she said. "I can see we will have to have a long talk."

"I'd rather stand." Somehow his disobedience gave him inordinate satisfaction. "I don't think we have anything to talk about."

Amarino's face was now contorted with fury and there was something else too. Fear perhaps? He decided to find out.

Taking a step toward her he said, "You and your friends murdered my father. Aren't you afraid I might do the same to you? I could reach you before the guards arrive."

There was no mistaking the fear now. He took another step. The air about Amarino began to shimmer and sparkle.

He moved forward again as the door burst open. Lunging for her, Brandel found himself kept back by an invisible force and almost lost his balance. He just had time to wonder how the guards had known that they were required when something hit the side of his head and the world went black.

The two soldiers looked at their queen who stood white faced, looking down at the bulky figure on the floor. Her features showed her internal struggle as she fought to contain the panic which had threatened to overwhelm her.

"Take him to the vaults and have him killed," she said shortly.

If the soldiers had any qualms about these orders none showed in their faces. They grasped the prince under each arm and dragged him away.

Amarino turned away. *That's not the way it's supposed to happen,* she thought. *What have I missed?*

Coming to in the corridor outside, Brandel thought he heard the sound of several babies crying, but paid the noise no attention. He was still trying to get in touch with his legs which seemed strangely uncooperative. Besides, the throbbing pain in his head made thinking next to impossible.

By the time they reached the top of the stairs, he was able to walk on his own, albeit unsteadily. Even had he been in a state to contemplate sudden movement, the four armed men about him discouraged any ideas of that sort. The door was unbolted and they went down the dark steps into the extensive vaults, which had been more or less unused for as long as Brandel could remember. The stairs turned a corner at the bottom and they emerged into the first of the caverns. Brandel gasped in horror. By the smoky light of a few torches on the walls he saw that the floor of the cavern was covered with bodies. Hundreds of them.

Bile rose in his throat. Such slaughter. And of women and children too. Even infants. All were laid out in neat rows. Most were poorly dressed. There were several tramps and crippled beggars. How had they become involved in the fighting? It was horrible, horrible. Then something else registered in Brandel's numbed mind and his heart turned even colder.

At first he had thought they were dead, for the eyes which stared at the ceiling were sightless, but there were no wounds on them, no sign of disease and no smell of corruption. Then he saw with a shock that they still breathed. Slowly but regularly the chests of the prone men and women rose and fell.

"What is this?" Brandel croaked. "What have you done to them all?"

"What's he talking about?" asked one of the soldiers.

"These people, what happened to them?" He was terrified, revolted.

"What people?" The man's voice sounded genuinely puzzled.

Brandel gestured wildly, making his head spin. "All around you!" he cried. "Don't you see them?"

"He's mad."

"Let's get this over with. He gives me the creeps."

They drew their swords and the awful reality of the situation crashed down on Brandel.

"No!" he yelled, and lunged at one of the men, who went down under the prince's not inconsiderable weight. His breath was knocked out of him and he gasped painfully for air.

Grabbing the fallen man's sword, Brandel whirled round. His eyesight was blurred but he lashed out in desperation and heard his blow strike home. Blood splattered as a soldier went down clutching his ruined neck. Another wild swing was parried but still sent the soldier staggering back to crash into the stone wall and slide slowly to the floor. Desperation had hold of Brandel now and he swung again but he was naturally clumsy and, as his blow went wide, the last soldier thrust forward, reducing Brandel's left shoulder to bloody ruin. He lurched backward, his senses reeling from the excruciating pain. As he did so he caught sight of his friend

Darin, Orme's elder son, lying amid the ranks of the living dead.

"No!" he screamed, uncomprehending.

The soldier was on him again and Brandel struggled to raise his sword to protect himself only to have the fiery red agony erupt again between his shoulder blades. The previously winded man had regained his feet and drawn the dagger which he now twisted viciously in Brandel's back. He staggered and fell to the floor, cursing, as night closed in.

The two soldiers looked at each other with grim satisfaction. Then, as one, their expressions changed to one of alarm.

"Stars! She's changed her mind. She wants him back alive," said one.

The other knelt quickly beside the fallen prince. "Too late," he said.

Chapter 19

"**I**'m beginning to think she doesn't want to come back," said Pabalan.

Ansar took a deep breath.

"She doesn't," he said.

"Oh," said Adesina quietly while, for once, her husband's astonishment was silent.

Ansar went on to give as tactful a version of Fontaine's reasons as he could manage.

"Well," said the queen, "it seems our little girl has decided to grow up faster than we guessed. It had to happen some time."

"She's with good people," added the prince.

Pabalan was silent for a while. At last he said, "Well, at least she's safe. It seems that must be enough for now. What is the rest of the news?"

"There's quite a lot, Father. I think this letter will explain most of it."

He took Ferragamo's missive and handed it to the king. As Pabalan was reading, there was a knock at the door and Moroski entered. He and Ansar exchanged greetings.

"Where is Laurent?" asked Ansar.

"He sailed back to Ark with Birn three days ago," replied the queen. "They must be almost there by now."

"I hope he has the sense to stay there, or we could keep missing each other at this rate. Is Rehan back from Starhill?"

"He was back for a day or so but he's on his way again by now." Adesina started to give Ansar an abbreviated version of Rehan's report when Pabalan interrupted.

"But this is ridiculous!" he said, waving the letter. "Here you are telling me Fontaine's in safe hands and then you hand me this which tells me to prepare for war. Have you gone mad?"

Ansar was unable to meet his father's face.

"I think," said Adesina, as always the more perceptive of the pair, "that we have to accept that Fontaine has made her decision, dear. And you know how stubborn she can be."

"May I read the letter, my Lord?" said Moroski.

"Of course," said the king, handing it over. "Perhaps you can work out what Ferragamo's going on about. Half of it is gibberish to me."

They waited in silence while the wizard read. At one point Moroski's eyes widened in shock and thereafter his expression was grim.

"Well?" said Pabalan, when he reached the end.

"I think we had better treat this seriously. Ferragamo is not one to panic and if he thinks these measures are necessary, then I believe they are."

"You trust his judgment then?"

"I do."

"Laurent did too," put in Adesina.

"I've known him a very long time, my Lord," said Moroski.

"I'm sure," said Pabalan, eyeing the wizard narrowly. "All right, so we'll raise our army, pitifully small though it is, and have transport ready. That much I understand but what was all that about berries?"

"That is what convinces me that his requests should be taken completely seriously," replied the wizard, wondering how much to tell his king. He still had not considered all the implications himself. "Put simply, it means that Ferragamo believes there is magic being used in Ark for evil purposes. It implies that such magic was used in Ather's overthrow. The berries are needed to combat this magic and to stop the evil spreading."

"He doesn't know for sure," said Ansar, "but Ferragamo is making certain we're prepared for the worst if it's true."

Adesina had taken the letter and she too was now aware of its contents.

"I'll pick the fruit myself," she said, "and then we'll check the stores for any preserves."

"Fluke will know where it is if we have any," said Pabalan. "I told you he had his uses."

Moroski turned to Ansar. "The other letters?" he asked.

"I took the liberty, Father, of speaking to the harbor commander. He said he would arrange fast ships to take the letters on as quickly as possible. I thought it best not to waste any time."

"And talking to me would obviously be a waste of time," said Pabalan, but he was smiling as he spoke.

"You trained him to use his initiative, my Lord."

"So I have only myself to blame, eh?" chuckled the king. "I'll leave you three to sort out this nonsense with *fruit*," he went on. "I'm going to talk to my commander. We'll gather the troops on the north coast at Marviel. That's the nearest point to Ark and they have a good harbor there. We'll gather supplies and wait for the next message. Any objections?"

There were none and the king strode out purposefully. They heard him shouting instructions as he went.

Adesina looked after him. "I haven't seen him so animated in years," she said quietly. "Maybe something good will come out of this after all. He's been very bored for a long time now." The affection in her voice was that of a partner who loves her other half despite being quite well aware of his faults. The others were silent.

"I'm sorry," she said. "We won't achieve much standing here. Pabalan can take care of the military arrangements. We can start on the moonberries. Ansar, why don't you go and rest. You must be tired after all your traveling."

"I'm fine," he replied, "but I could use a long hot soak. I've forgotten what it's like!"

He went to the door, then paused and turning to Moroski said, "I've just realized what it is that's odd about you."

The wizard laughed. "Most wizards are pretty odd," he said.

"I don't mean it like that," said Ansar. "I mean I've never seen you before without that hawk of yours being somewhere about. Is she all right?"

"Oh yes. Atlanta's off somewhere on business of her own. Enjoy your bath."

"I will," said Ansar and was gone.

Moroski and Adesina looked at each other.

"You're worried, aren't you?" she said.

He nodded. "If Ferragamo is right then it's a very bad business indeed. I would like to explain further but you would need to be trained in magic to realize how bad."

"You're going to go back to Ark with Ansar, aren't you?"

"Sometimes I think you can read my mind."

"Without any magic too." She smiled, then frowned as she saw his expression.

"I'm sorry, did I say something—"

"No, no, of course not. Forgive me. I am being stupid!"

"Look out for Fontaine for me."

"Of course. Though from the sound of things she is well able to look out for herself."

"I hope so," said the queen.

Two days later Ansar and Moroski set sail for Ark. Adesina was at the quayside to see them off. Pabalan was already in Marvel.

"We're going back and forth like shuttles!"

Laurent had just stepped ashore at Home and been greeted with the news that Ansar had left on the reverse journey five days ago.

"Aye," said Shill, "but he'll be back."

The soldier went on to outline the developments and the plans which Ansar was helping to set in motion. Laurent listened grimly.

"I don't like the sound of this magic," he said.

"There's more," said Shill, and told Laurent of Brandel's journey north. "He's been gone five days now. Time enough to get to Ashwicken and back. Yesterday Ferragamo tried a searching spell to find him. It failed. He says the whole of the north of the island was like an impenetrable fog. Brandel was in there somewhere but he had no idea where. And there was no sign of Benfell."

Laurent frowned.

"He won't say so, but Ferragamo thinks he's dead," said Shill. "What's more, the effort nearly wore the wizard out. He slept solidly for half a day afterward."

Two days later, far to the north, another traveler stepped ashore. Rehan almost stumbled at the shock of walking on solid ground again. His mind was in turmoil the moment he left the ship but shortly afterward he became unnaturally calm and moved with quiet deliberation. Before very long he had acquired a good horse to carry him on to Starhill and he made haste to continue his journey. The compulsion he felt to see *her* again was stronger than ever. He rode hard, looking only ahead, and thus did not see the falcon far above whose shadow followed his trail.

Three days after his arrival in Home, Laurent was watching Mark sparring with Richard and admiring the boy's quickness and natural, if unrefined, style. Suddenly aware that he was himself watched, Laurent turned and saw Fontaine eyeing him curiously.

"Princess," he said, bowing slightly.

"You needn't be formal, Laurent," she said quietly. "As you can see, I'm hardly dressed for the court." She was wearing breeches and a simple shirt. Her feet were bare. Even so she looked more attractive than he remembered her.

"Have you come to watch?"

"No," she said. "I've come to fight." So saying, she went forward and, taking up a short sword, took Mark's place in the practice area. Laurent stared, unbelieving.

"She's better than I am," said Mark as he sat down beside Laurent. His voice was deliberately rueful but the Healdean caught the underlying pride in the comment. *There is something between these two,* he thought.

Aloud he said, "How long has this been going on?"

"Oh, a few days."

"She learned quickly then."

"Yes," said Mark. "Don't you approve?"

"It's hardly my place . . ."

"Stop being so diplomatic."

Laurent looked at the prince in surprise. He had not known him to be so forthright.

"Whatever's coming you won't keep her out of it," Mark went on. "She thought Pabalan had sent you to fetch her back to Heald."

Laurent shook his head. "I don't think I could succeed where Ansar failed."

"That's not what I heard," said Mark, smiling. "You have quite a reputation."

It was Laurent's turn to smile. "Perhaps," he said, "but I have yet to win an argument with either of the royal ladies."

"I can understand that."

The next morning another traveler reached the village. Her presence was announced by Owl. Ferragamo came out of the cottage and stared at the small falcon which sat unconcernedly on a nearby fence-post. The bird finished preening her wing feathers, then looked at the wizard with piercing eyes.

"Well, Atlanta," said Ferragamo, "and where is Moroski?"

The falcon regarded him solemnly.

Chapter 20

The following day Atlanta was still there, apparently content to wait. There was no sign of her usual companion but Ferragamo hoped that the falcon's arrival heralded the wizard's. Thus when it was reported that a military looking vessel was approaching he hurried down to the jetty.

The ship, however, was from Strallen, the island that stood nearly a hundred leagues to the southwest. On board were some twenty soldiers led by a captain called Lomax. He led his men ashore and came straight to Ferragamo.

"Sir Wizard, I bring greetings from Saronno and King Illva. They received your letter and send this reply." He handed Ferragamo a rolled parchment.

"You have made excellent time."

"The navy has its uses," replied the army captain, "and haste was deemed necessary."

Ferragamo read the letter with evident pleasure. "Excellent," he said. "You have the supplies?"

"Yes," replied Lomax, indicating a small chest carried by one of his men.

"Come up to my cottage when your men are organized and I'll give you all the details."

"Yes, Sir Wizard."

"I've never bothered with titles. My name is Ferragamo."

Two more ships arrived that afternoon. The little jetty was fully occupied, so rowing boats ferried the new arrivals ashore. Ansar and Moroski were among the first to step out onto the shingle. Shortly afterward, Atlanta was back in her accustomed position on the wizard's shoulder. His expression grew stern at their evident conversation, and the greetings between Moroski and Ferragamo, while warm, were quickly set aside as the two wizards went to the cottage for a private conference.

Ansar meanwhile exchanged news with Laurent and others and supervised the bringing ashore of the precious supplies of Healdean moonberries. Both naval vessels had full crews but carried no extra soldiers. The army, as requested, was waiting with the main fleet in Marviel.

Speculation was rife about the meaning of Moroski's arrival and the wizards' discussions. A sense of foreboding settled over the village.

As evening approached, Ferragamo and Moroski were still closeted in the study. They had been talking for a long time and now sat silently, lost in their own thoughts.

"You agree then?" said Ferragamo eventually.

"Yes. It's the best we can do."

"We'll gather them all here tonight and outline our plans."

They were silent again for a while.

"We've been too lax."

"Now we have to consider the unthinkable again."

The main room of the Visitor's cottage was quite large but that night it was crowded. The two wizards sat at the table and around them, sitting or standing where they could, were Mark, Ansar, Fontaine, Laurent, Shill, and the other four soldiers, Koria, Jani, Lomax, and, representing the villagers, Birn. Even the rafters were occupied. Owl and Atlanta looked down at the assembled company. Longfur was curled in Mark's lap.

As soon as everyone was settled, Ferragamo looked at the young fisherman.

"Birn, I've asked you to be here tonight because you've proved you have a level head and I can trust you to report what's said accurately to the people of Home. You've all been very good to us and you deserve to know what's going on. I hope none of you need be involved in our plans but, one way or another, what we decide here will affect your village."

Birn nodded acknowledgment but said nothing.

Looking around, Ferragamo went on, "You all know, I think, about the letters I sent off with Ansar to Heald and the other islands. At the time I hoped it was only a precaution against an extremely unlikely event. Since then, several events have combined to convince me of the seriousness of the situation. Even if it is not the thing that I feared, there is something evil at work on Ark."

He paused. The room was very quiet.

"Some of you will have to forgive me if I go over things that you know already." Occasionally asking for confirmation from others, the wizard went on to detail his suspicions about Ather's overthrow, of Bonet and Shill's experience in Ashwicken and of the merchant's tale from The Mermaid, and his own difficulty in healing Jani in the forest. Then he told them of the unsuccessful attempt to locate Brandel and the reactions he had felt from that spell.

"Finally," he said, "we have had a first-hand report from someone who has been in Starhill only a few days ago."

Moroski spoke for the first time.

"When I arrived back at court in Heald I was curious to know what was happening on Ark. Ferragamo's letter worried me and I was suspicious about the eagerness of a courtier named Rehan to return to Starhill."

The wizard ignored Ansar's indrawn breath and continued. "So I decided to send Altanta here with him. He traveled, as expected, to Grayrock and then rode to Starhill in a great hurry. There he went straight to the castle and remained there, at least until Atlanta left. That in itself doesn't fit in with what he told us in Heald and Rehan has always been reliable before. But the more immediate facts that Atlanta reports concern the city itself."

The picture that he painted, despite its bird's eye view, was substantially the same as the sights which had so be-mused Brandel a few days earlier. So convincing were his

words that it brought a chill to each and every heart, and
even those unused to the link between wizards and their
familiars felt no reason to doubt his story.

Ferragamo did not allow anyone time to brood. As soon as
Moroski finished talking, he said, "All this adds up to one
thing. There is a magical power in Starhill which will destroy
this island if it is not itself destroyed."

"Brogar!" Laurent exclaimed.

Everyone turned to look at him.

"It could be," said Ferragamo, "and we ignored the
warning."

"To our cost," added Moroski.

"I thought you said the power was in Ashwicken," said
Orme.

"That's because I couldn't conceive of anything so powerful that it could affect someone from a far greater distance,"
answered Ferragamo. "Now, I'm not so sure. I've had a taste
of it," he added ruefully.

"It could be that there are other places it stems from as
well," said Moroski, "but all the evidence points to Starhill."

"But that's twenty leagues from Ashwicken!" said Bonet,
aghast. "That's incredible." He shuddered from first-hand
knowledge.

"And you think the moonberry cake is some sort of
antidote to this magic?" asked Shill.

"More a sort of protection," said Ferragamo, "like magical
chain mail." He smiled but only briefly.

"Brandel's dead, isn't he?" said Mark suddenly.

There was silence. The same thought had occurred to all
of them at one time or another, but no one had wanted to
voice it. Mark however sounded certain.

"We don't know that. If we're right then he was safe
against the magic and he could be anywhere by now."

"Then if he hasn't been taken by magic, he's been taken
by force. We should never have let him go." There was the
suspicion of tears in Mark's eyes.

"We've been through all that," said Ferragamo defensively.

"Well, the sooner we're in Starhill, the sooner we'll
know," said Ansar, provoking several nods of agreement.

"Yes," said Ferragamo, "that's what we all want—"

"It's what *it* wants too." Mark's voice was quiet but something in his tone froze everyone in the room. He was staring
at the floor, his eyes unfocused. After a moment's silence he

said, "Whatever this *thing* in Starhill is, it's waiting. It wants us to go to it. Otherwise, if it's so powerful, why hasn't it driven us off Ark? It could have easily by now." He looked up at Ferragamo.

"I've been wondering about that too," the wizard said, "but it doesn't alter the fact that we have to go back to Starhill."

"Aye," said Orme, his feelings written plainly on his face.

"However," said Moroski, "we need to be careful and plan thoroughly."

"Yes," said Ferragamo. "Even if, as I suspect, this power we face is growing stronger every day, a few days of preparation are still necessary."

Moroski then went on to outline the plan which he and Ferragamo had devised that afternoon. Recognizing that, even with help from Strallen, the Healdean army was no match for the forces now controlled from Starhill, no large-scale invasion was envisaged. Indeed, if the wizards were correct, and the magic they faced was as potent as they feared, it would be the height of foolishness to land an army. At best they would promptly go to sleep and at worst could possibly be controlled to such an extent that they became effectively part of the enemy. Ferragamo believed that some people would be more susceptible to the magical influence than others and Bonet acknowledged grudgingly that he could be one of those.

"Also," said Ferragamo, "I think the strength of this power is not necessarily constant. It is as if whoever is controlling it is testing his strength every so often. One thing is certain though. The closer we get to Starhill the stronger the effects will be."

"But the berries—" began Ansar.

"Yes, the berries are the key," said Ferragamo. "I hope," he added.

"This is what we propose," said Moroski. "We can't countenance a direct attack. We don't have the forces and we don't have sufficient protection. Therefore a small group of us will try to get into the city and find the source of this evil. Even the most powerful wizard can be destroyed by sword or arrow."

"Each member of the party will be given supplies of the moonberry cake to last as long as we'll need," said Ferragamo. "In fact we'll start eating it as soon as we can so that we build

up our immunity. That's another reason why the group has to
be a small one."

"But how can a small group hope to get past the whole of
Ark's army?" said Shill. "We couldn't even match the Castle
Guard."

"First of all, we'll approach from the west, over the
mountains," said Ferragamo. "That seems the most unlikely
route and hopefully it won't be watched so closely. But
secondly, and more importantly, we hope the army will be
well occupied a long way away."

"It will take a little time to organize," went on Moroski,
"but we should, between Heald, Strallen"—he nodded to
Lomax—"and Ark be able to put together quite a sizable
fleet. When we're ready this will sail up the east coast of Ark,
making itself as noticeable as possible. In that way we hope
that the army will be directed to Grayrock and the coast to
wait for an invasion that will never come."

"And while they're looking out to sea, we'll sneak in the
back door," finished Shill.

"It doesn't even matter if the ships do not carry any
troops," added Moroski, "as long as they *look* as if they do.
I'll be doing my bit to add to the illusion."

"I thought magic didn't work over moving water," said
Mark.

"I'll pretend the ships are mobile bits of land," answered
the wizard, smiling.

Lomax spoke for the first time. "I'd better return to
Strallen and advise them of this plan. Otherwise they may
well head for Ark directly."

"With your permission, captain, I'd rather you stayed
here," said Moroski. "Your soldiers have a part to play in our
plan and as we intend to do the first part of the journey north
by sea your ship would be useful too. I am shortly going to
sail back to Heald in one of our two vessels. If one of your
men will accompany me, a ship will be provided to take him
on to Strallen so that he can divert your fleet to Heald."

Lomax nodded. "Agreed," he said.

Laurent said, "You're going to have a hard time persuad-
ing Pabalan to this plan. He won't want to stay at sea."

Ansar coughed and Laurent glanced at him. "Your pardon, Prince."

"No, you're right," said Ansar. "Once he gets the bit

between his teeth . . ." He trailed off as if he had just realized
something. "I'd be just the same," he added.

Moroski smiled. "Perhaps, Laurent, it might be wise if
you accompanied me. I could use your organizational abilities
and Pabalan's more likely to listen to you than me."

"All right. I was getting tired of dry land anyway," came
the ironic reply.

After that, as it was growing late, most of the group went
their own ways. Mark waited for his opportunity and then
cornered Ferragamo in his study.

"Are we going to do anything about Brandel?" he asked.

"I don't see what we can do."

"There must be something."

"All right. When we set off north—and that won't be for
some days—a few of us will ride to Ashwicken. That way we'll
gather what information we can and then meet up with the
others on the west coast somewhere. Will that satisfy you?"

It seemed little enough but Mark knew they were not
ready for anything more ambitious. Koria had already said
that preparing the raw moonberries and producing the cake
in the sort of quantities needed would take several days. And
until then, any expedition would be very foolhardy. He
nodded and turned to leave. At the door, he paused.

"I'm sorry about interrupting this evening. I didn't help,
did I?"

"You must follow your nature, Mark."

The young prince paused, then looked up at the wizard
with an odd mixture of fear and knowledge in his eyes.
When he spoke, it was so softly that Ferragamo had to
strain to hear him.

"This is the start of the Second War of the Wizards,
isn't it," he said.

And then he was gone.

Chapter 21

*T*he next morning, Koria threw everyone out of the cottage. The first stage of preparing the berries was a delicate operation and she wanted no distractions. She had already made a list of the other ingredients which she would need and dispatched various people to help secure them. These supplies would not be needed for a day or two, which was lucky, as she doubted whether there was enough in Home to meet her demands, and journeys to Stane might be necessary. Richard was one of those so occupied and therefore Mark and Fontaine found themselves without a tutor.

In fact neither of them felt like training anyway and instead they set off to the beach.

"I won't fall asleep this time," said Mark.

Fontaine glanced at him anxiously but saw that he was grinning.

For several days after his second attack Mark had been afraid to go to sleep. His resistance had finally been defeated by exhaustion and now he seemed to be returning to normal. The memory of that afternoon still haunted Fontaine however.

"I should think not," she said as brightly as possible. "It is terribly bad manners to fall asleep in company."

"I can't help it if your conversation makes me somnolent," he replied and ducked the blow she aimed at his head.

Fontaine chased him across the headland and onto the dunes where the shifting sand made further running impossible.

Three pairs of eyes watched them leave the village, each showing conflicting emotions. Jani and Longfur sat together, finding a measure of solace in each other's company. If ever a cat looked rueful, Longfur did, perhaps regretting his often harsh words about the princess. Jani's eyes showed a mixture of sympathy for his feline friend, whose chin he scratched gently, and approval of the blossoming relationship.

Further away, Ferragamo also watched, looking both amused and troubled.

———————

The attack, as everyone thought of it afterward, came in the early afternoon. It lasted only an hour but in that time almost everyone in the village felt its effects one way or another. A few fell asleep where they were. Others found even simple tasks beyond their abilities. Those of them that had eaten the moonberry cake merely felt uneasy. Mark described it afterward as a sort of probing in his head, something he was aware of but which offered no immediate threat.

There were no serious repercussions of the attack beyond the inconvenience of a few stiff muscles, bruises, and some badly mended nets, but it served to confirm the wizards' theory and the urgency of the situation. Nothing had been felt in Home before, which indicated that the attacks were growing in strength. As Starhill was over thirty leagues away the fact that it was felt at all was frightening and made the prospect of the next few days' waiting even less appealing.

Jani, who had proved competent to help in the kitchen, was with Koria when the magic struck. She merely felt dizzy for a few seconds but thought nothing of it until Jani collapsed. He was seated at the table, carefully slicing the thumbnail-size berries. As Koria steadied herself, he fell forward, scattering some of the fruit. His head hit the table with a thump. Koria went quickly to him, fighting a sudden dread, and found him to be asleep. She shook him and he woke but his eyes were vacant and she laid him down again. Soon he was snoring gently. Koria went down on her hands and knees and gathered up the precious berries. She washed them and returned them to the bowl and then went out to find Ferragamo who was in the village with Shill, observing the effects of the attack on the various inhabitants. He was talking calmly enough but Koria heard the tension beneath his words.

Shill went off to check on others as she approached.

"It's the magic, isn't it?"

"Yes," he replied. "Are you all right?"

"I'm fine but Jani's fast asleep."

"So are quite a few others. If it weren't for my wizard's vanity I'd be panicking now."

Even in jest she did not like to hear him talking that way.

"Where are Mark and Fontaine?"

A cloud passed across the wizard's face.

"They went to the beach. They should be all right."

"Then why the long face?"

Ferragamo looked embarrassed. Koria waited. Finally, he said, "They seem to be spending an awful lot of time together."

"So?"

"He's my responsibility. So is she, come to that. I just wouldn't want anything . . . improper to happen. Perhaps I'm too free with them."

Koria stared at him. The wizard recognized her attitude and looked sheepish.

"That's what Pabalan would say," he said.

"Eric's gone," said Koria. "She could do worse than Mark. Leave them alone."

"He's important, Koria. He's the last of the line."

"You think Brandel's dead then?"

"Yes." Ferragamo paused, then said, "I feel Mark has a role to play in what's happening now. I don't want him distracted."

"You're turning into a sour old man. What's happening now may get him—or her—killed! What right have you to deny them a little joy? They're of an age and I don't think they'll have a chance to be young again once this is over."

Ferragamo spread his arms in surrender and moved closer, hugging her to him. Then he laughed and at her quizzical look said, "I'm not sour, my love. I'm crazy! Here we are with half the world falling asleep or going daft about us and all I can argue about is court etiquette."

After that they went round the village making sure, where possible, that no accidents occurred to the magic's victims, and hoping fervently that things would soon return to normal. Fortunately that was what happened and when it became obvious they hurried back to the cottage to see how Jani was.

He was still sitting at the kitchen table but was awake. A puzzled expression covered his large face. Koria smiled at him and made signs of drawing water. Jani rose and went out to the well. Koria followed to ensure that he was all right. The blankness had gone from his eyes but she wanted to make sure.

As he followed them out Ferragamo noticed a whole moonberry which had rolled into the main room, collecting a coating of dust as it went. He picked it up and pocketed it, then went outside and promptly forgot about it.

Mark and Fontaine were walking up the path toward them and he was sure that they had been hand in hand until the moment he saw them.

Arkon's heir, first named and last, thought the wizard. *I wonder.*

————————————

That night, as Ferragamo and Koria lay in bed, he found himself unable to sleep. After a while, Koria grew concerned about his tossing and turning. She put an arm around him and said:

"What is it, love? Still fretting?"

"I'm sorry. Am I keeping you awake?"

"Of course you are, you fool. Do you think I could sleep knowing that you're lying there worrying? Are you still upset about Mark and Fontaine?"

"I'm not *upset*. More uneasy, really. I think the prophecy does concern what's happening now, and *if* it does, then Mark... If Brandel *is* dead—and somehow I'm sure he is—then Mark is the last of Arkon's line. And Arkon's first son was also called Mark."

"*Arkon's heir, first named and last.*"

"That's right. So you see, *he's* the one who *must seize his time*—and he won't be able to do that if he's got his head in the clouds over Fontaine. There's more at stake here than a pair of love-struck youngsters. The future of Ark could depend on him."

Koria said nothing for a while as she thought about the implications. Then:

"You never used to be such a pessimist. Haven't you noticed the change in that girl recently? She's much nicer to be around, somehow. She's easier with people, *much* more willing to pull her weight—and she smiles a lot, too. If there is something going on, it can only do them both good. It'll strengthen them and make them more able to face whatever's coming. They'll have each other to care for, and you *know* that's good for a person."

He laughed. "You're so right, Koria sweetheart. You always are. Look at us! If it hadn't been for you, I'd have got myself into a right mess sometimes."

"And as for this afternoon, describing what you thought was happening as improper . . . Well, if I didn't know better, I'd say you were turning into an old fogey."

"Old fogey! Me!"

Pulling her closer, Ferragamo showed Iconia, in the nicest possible way, that he was anything but.

———————

The days passed very slowly after Moroski's departure. There was plenty to do, with preparations to make and supplies to gather, and the training now had a more definite objective. Yet everyone was on edge, waiting for the next attack and wondering if the newly distributed rations of cake would prove an effective ward.

Mark found the waiting difficult enough but Ansar's impatience was awesome to behold. Unable to remain still for a moment he was forever throwing himself into unnecessary tasks only to find that something new needed attention shortly afterward. He also practiced his weapon skills with fanatical dedication, but very soon found that nobody was willing to cross swords with him, as he was apt to forget it was only a training exercise.

The whole situation was becoming intolerable. Even Koria's calm nature was affected. Only Jani seemed unperturbed, but whether this was because of his naturally placid nature, or whether he was simply unaware of the dangers that were looming over them nobody knew.

It was thus a great relief when after some seven days a messenger arrived from Heald. Moroski sent word that they should set out as planned immediately The fleet was expected to be ready to sail in eight days or so.

The bulk of the party would sail around the southern tip of the island and head for Deerhide Bay, some five leagues north of Sealeap. On board the two ships, apart from the crews, would be Ansar, Lomax and his men, Orme and the other three soldiers, and Jani. At Deerhide they would wait to meet the others, who were to travel overland via Ashwicken in the hopes of learning Brandel's fate and any other useful intelligence.

There had been a good deal of argument about who should be in this group. In the end the fact that some of them had eaten moonberry cake earlier, and thus presumably built up a greater immunity, was used to make their decision. Ferragamo and Shill were obvious choices for their individual skills and, although the wizard was clearly unhappy about it, Mark soon made it clear that he would not be left behind. The journey to Ashwicken had been at his insistence after all. Fontaine had then declared that she was going too. Her newly found martial abilities, the logic of her magical immunity, and, above all, her inborn stubbornness gradually wore down all the opposition until it was accepted that she too would ride north.

Ansar was clearly vexed by this and by his own exclusion but was mollified by being given the command of the other group. Privately Ferragamo made it very clear to Orme and Lomax that they were to ensure that the prince did nothing rash. As the ships would be traveling directly to Deerhide Bay and no one knew how long the investigations in Ashwicken would take, it was decided that Ferragamo and his group would set off at first light the next day, but Ansar would not sail for another three days. Five days after that, provided all went well, they would be at the rendezvous.

At dawn the next day the sun rose on a great deal of activity. The horses had been led up from the stables in the village. Saddlebags had been packed and provisions of the moonberry cake carefully measured out. Weapons were being checked. Even those not traveling were fully occupied.

In the general bustle it was not until they were almost ready to mount up that anyone noticed that five horses, not four, had been saddled. Jani hoisted himself into place and sat looking down on all around him. His face was quite calm, and he obviously meant business. Strapped to his saddle were his staff and a large, iron-headed axe.

Ferragamo was about to remonstrate with him when Koria

laid a hand on his arm and said, "I had a feeling he wouldn't let them go alone."

The wizard looked at her. He didn't need to ask to whom she was referring. Fontaine was beaming, delighted that the two people she cared about most would be with her on the journey. Mark was smiling too, despite a distracted air. In fact, he was getting a no-nonsense talking-to by Longfur.

He'll come with you whether you like it or not, the cat declared. *You'd have to keep him chained up to prevent it. And I'd like to see you manage that. It's as much as you can do to handle that girl. Speaking of which*, he went on without allowing Mark to get a thought in edgeways, *you should be grateful for Jani's company. I don't think you would have enjoyed the last few days quite as much as if it hadn't been for him.*

What do you mean? Mark asked nervously, his face reddening, but Longfur refused to be drawn. Instead he sprang up to Jani's leg, climbed up his leather breeches, and settled at the front of the big man's saddle. A large hand reached out gently to stroke Longfur's head.

Shill looked at Ferragamo uncertainly but the wizard merely shrugged and mounted his own horse. Owl flew overhead as the five horses rode out on the northern trail.

That night they stayed at an inn in Stane and the next day they rode into the forest. Memories welled up in each of them and most of the day passed in an uneasy silence. They camped that night just south of where the trail divided between the routes to Ashwicken and Sealeap.

An owl-hoot awakened Ferragamo at dawn. Immediately he felt that something was wrong. Bleary-eyed, he reached out for his staff. Before his fingers could close on it however, a booted foot came down heavily on the wood. The wizard looked up blinking, to stare into the smiling face of the outlaw who, briefly, had been their captive. He held a loaded crossbow pointed unwaveringly at Ferragamo's heart.

"If you so much as mutter, old man, or twitch a finger, you're dead."

Unable to move, Ferragamo sensed rather than saw what happened to the others. Fontaine was on her feet but held fast from behind, a knife pressed to her throat. Shill and Jani stood frozen, sword and staff in hand, unable to help their comrades. Mark was still rolled in his cloak on the ground, an outlaw sword point resting on his chest.

"I think," said their former captive, "that your friends had better drop their weapons or . . ."

Shill and Jani, having no choice, obeyed.

"That's better. I've been looking forward to this meeting." The outlaw was obviously enjoying himself. "I have a little score to settle." The crossbow remained steady.

"Knock him out and tie him up. And gag him," the outlaw said to an unseen fellow. Ferragamo slumped to the ground again as a club caught him behind the ear. Fontaine tried to cry out and began to struggle but was soon quieted by the steel at her throat.

"Now we can deal with the rest," said the outlaw's leader. "Search the saddlebags. And bring *her* over here."

Mark started up but was forced down again as Fontaine was manhandled by a grinning ruffian.

At this point the thunder of galloping horses became audible from the nearby trail. Everyone turned to see and a few moments later a small troop of Starhill Castle Guards swept into view, their swords already drawn. Shouts sounded over the pounding hooves.

"They're the ones we want!"

"Take them alive!"

Chaos reigned. The outlaws turned to meet this new threat and one of the soldiers fell with a crossbow bolt in his chest. Then the horses were amongst them and in the mêlée each of the group from Home, except the unconscious wizard, made their bids for freedom. The man holding Fontaine received a crack on his shins and then collapsed as her knee slammed into his groin. Mark rolled away from his man and struggled to find his sword. Shill and Jani each dived for their discarded weapons, aware that they were unlikely to fare any better as captives of the soldiers than of the outlaws, most of whom were shortly either dead or had taken to flight.

The eight remaining soldiers had by now dismounted and were intent on wearing down Mark and his companions who fought on, not wanting to exchange one set of captors for another. They were losing ground steadily, being forced into tight corners, and it would only be a matter of time before they were disarmed or disabled.

Then one of the soldiers yelled, "They're coming back. Look out!" A group of outlaws joined the fight. Fontaine felt a jolt of recognition as one of them swept past her and sent one

of the soldiers spinning in a spray of red. The unexpected aid
had come from Durc.

Shortly afterward, two of the soldiers reached their horses
and galloped off. The rest of them lay dead in the gruesome
debris of the conflict.

Mark, Jani, and Shill stood, breathing heavily, still holding their bloody weapons. Facing them were Durc, Zunic,
Clowery, and three other outlaws from Durc's band.

"Thank you," said Mark simply.

Durc bowed slightly. His eyes flicked to Jani whose face
was impassive.

"To what do we owe this pleasure?" said Shill.

"I would hate to see so fair a lady fall into the hands of
those rough troopers," said Durc.

Fontaine, who was kneeling beside Ferragamo, cradling
his head in her arms, mouthed an obscenity which caused
even Shill to blanch. Durc laughed.

"She still has her gentle tongue, I see."

"I hope you slept well," she said. "I thought I'd seen the
last of your ugly face when I drugged all you clever men."

"With Jani's help," Durc reminded her.

"What do you want?" said Mark.

"What can you offer?"

"We can offer not to knock your heads off," said Shill.

"There are more of us than you," Durc pointed out
evenly.

"Wait a moment," said Mark wearily. "I've had enough
fighting. You helped us. Why?"

"One favor deserves another," said Durc.

"And maybe you can help us," added Zunic.

"How?"

"We've been having a few problems recently," said Durc,
"and Zunic here was quite impressed by your last performance against our old friends from the other side of the trail.
He was especially impressed by the talents of your fallen
friend there."

Mark glanced round at the wizard.

"Is he all right?" he said over his shoulder.

"I don't know. He's alive," said Fontaine. "I thought you
were all asleep when that happened," she added, looking at
Zunic.

"I wasn't hungry that night," the outlaw replied.

"Where are the rest of you?"

"Dead or taken," replied Durc. "That's another problem.
There's so many soldiers round here it's nigh on impossible
for a decent outlaw to make a living. Now I think we know
why. You must be important if they want you alive."

"You still haven't said how we can help you."

"It's the wizard's help we need. There's things happened
recently that don't bear too much examination. We're a match
for any soldiers but we can't fight magic."

Mark and Shill exchanged glances.

"Aye, I think you know what I mean," said Durc. "We've
been falling asleep a little too often in the last few days, and
not because of what we've eaten either. If someone's putting a
spell on us, he can take it off again. If anyone can."

"He's coming round," said Fontaine.

Mark went to the wizard's side. Ferragamo's eyelids fluttered
open. "What's going on?" he croaked.

"Er... it's a little complicated," said Mark.

Some time later the two groups still kept apart but they were
sitting and swords had been sheathed. Gradually the facts of
Ark's predicament had emerged and Ferragamo, who was
recovering rapidly, had outlined their intentions to Durc and
his followers. The wizard's frankness had astonished Shill and
Fontaine who were both still extremely skeptical about the
outlaws' motives.

"Why should we trust them?" said Fontaine at one point.

"They have as much to lose as we do," replied the wizard.
"No one can face the prospect of mindlessness easily."

"But they killed Eric!"

"In ignorance, yes. They could kill us too, no doubt, but if
they did they'd be worse off than ever."

"What's to stop them handing us over to the soldiers in
the hope of some reward?" said Shill.

Mark saw Durc flinch slightly at this question and wondered if the outlaw had indeed considered this possibility.

Fontaine was scathing. "Oh, he's a *great* one for rewards,
he is! What about the ransom he demanded for me?"

"We've no love of those soldiers," said Zunic, ignoring
her, "as our numbers testify."

"You're scared!" said Fontaine. "Great big men like you.
Scared!"

"Aye, my lady," replied Durc, "any man would be. And that's why we ask your trust. You journey north so you must have some sort of protection from this evil magic. If you would extend that protection to us we'd repay you in service."

"Service?" laughed Fontaine. "You?"

"Aye, lady. We can fight. It seems to me you'll need some men for that before this is through."

"We've men enough."

"The five of you?"

"We meet others," said Mark.

"Where?" said Durc, looking round.

"Further north."

"And until then?"

"We'll prove our worth," added Zunic.

"What do you say?" said Durc.

"This is crazy," said Fontaine. "These people are criminals."

"They did help us out though," said Mark.

"If you can keep me from being hit on the head," said Ferragamo, "I will keep an eye on them. They know a little of my powers. I say they can come with us. They'll know the island better than Lomax and his men and I don't doubt their fighting ability."

Durc smiled. Hope dawned in the other outlaws' faces.

———————————————

That day they continued north, the outlaws riding the dead soldiers' horses with varying degrees of skill. By evening they had reached the edge of the forest and made camp just within the shelter of the trees. It was a long night, with the uneasy nature of the alliance emphasized by two people being on watch at any one time.

In the morning it was decided that Ferragamo, Mark, and Zunic would go into Ashwicken. Some time was spent in exchanging clothes and disguising faces, then when the wizard was satisfied, they crossed the ford and rode with two other outlaws to a small copse half a league from the town. From there the three continued on foot.

At first the town seemed normal enough but somehow the atmosphere was subdued. The market square was less noisy than it should have been. As strangers they received a few incurious glances but no more.

Ferragamo said, "We'll split up and try the taverns.

hey're the best place for gossip. You two stay together and eep your ears and eyes open. We'll meet back here at noon."

The reason for the town's quietness became plain soon fterward. As they went their separate ways, two contingents f soldiers entered the square. All of them wore the uniforms f Castle Guards and Mark was careful to keep well out of heir way. He and Zunic found a tavern which was already uite full despite the early hour and ordered drinks, but ardly touched them as they listened to the talk around hem. They learned nothing and were about to try their luck lsewhere, when Zunic's hand on his shoulder and urgent vhisper stopped Mark in the act of rising.

"Stay put," the outlaw hissed.

Four soldiers had entered the room, which had suddenly rown quiet. Two of them stayed by the door while the others valked round looking at the drinkers.

Mark and Zunic's turn came for inspection and the prince owered as the oddly vacant eyes rested on him for a moment r two. Then the soldier moved on and shortly afterward all our left the tavern.

Mark let out a long breath and exchanged looks with Zunic, who smiled briefly. Around them, conversations started p again.

"What right have they?"

"Soldiers everywhere these days."

"Cold fish, ain't they?"

"Aye, wouldn't like to be that fat boy they took off north ome time back."

"He'll lose a bit of that weight in Starhill, I'll wager."

"Reminded me of someone, he did."

"Aye, your wife's been putting on a bit of weight . . ."

The men laughed and turned to more congenial topics. Mark and Zunic listened a while longer but learned nothing nore. They left and went to another tavern, then wandered n the market waiting for Ferragamo. A cold feeling in the pit of his stomach reflected Mark's belief that the fat boy had een Brandel.

As noon approached they moved toward the prearranged neeting place, only for Zunic to abruptly pull Mark aside and nto an alleyway. A large body of soldiers marched into the quare. In their midst, two burly men half led, half carried omeone whose head was bent down upon his chest and vhose legs seemed to be acting independently of each other.

As the group went past, the prisoner's face was visible briefl
and Mark stiffened, his hand groping for his knife, but Zuni
held him back. The odds were hopeless.

When the soldiers had gone, Mark nearly collapsed. H
sank down on his haunches and tried not to be sick.

That Ferragamo should have been captured was ba
enough, but it was the horribly barren look in the wizard'
eyes that had set Mark's stomach churning.

Chapter 22

*A*nsar's two ships arrived at Deerhide Bay a day early for the rendezvous. The day before, they had put Essan and Richard ashore at Sealeap, but had not lingered and their journey had been uneventful. The weather was still good despite the approach of autumn. They anchored off shore and left signal lights burning in case Ferragamo and his party arrived during the night. It was unlikely that anyone else would see them on this uninhabited part of the coastline and, even if they did, the chances were they would be taken for fishermen.

There was no sign of the wizard's party that night or the next morning. Ansar paced the deck anxiously and suggested going ashore but Orme counseled patience and the day passed slowly.

In the early afternoon there was some excitement as movement was seen on the shore but this turned out to be Essan and Richard, who had completed their horse-buying expedition satisfactorily, and ridden north with their purchases. Orme rowed ashore and spoke to the two soldiers. They reported no ill effects from their time ashore and were happy to remain on land with the horses. They were corralled in a secluded spot and were unlikely to be discovered.

Ferragamo and his group still did not arrive and by nightfall even Orme was becoming worried, but by then there was nothing for it but to set the lights, and try to sleep out another night.

In the morning there was still no sign of the others and Orme agreed that they should go ashore. If nothing untoward happened they could set up camp and wait in relative comfort. There was little else they could do.

While this was being arranged with men and supplies being ferried ashore a falcon swooped down from the sky and settled on the railing near Ansar and Orme. It was Atlanta. At first they were bemused by this unexpected arrival but then Orme noticed something tied to the bird's leg. She allowed him to detach the thin, tightly curled parchment which he handed to Ansar. The message was, obviously, from Moroski and told them that there had been some considerable delays in putting together a sufficiently impressive looking fleet and consequently that they should delay their journey north. He asked that they set up camp and wait for a further message.

"We don't have much choice, do we," said Ansar. "We've got no one to go north *with*!"

He wrote out a reply acknowledging Moroski's message and telling him that Ferragamo had not arrived but that as they were only a day late so far there was no immediate cause for concern. He only wished he could believe his own message.

The soldier looked down at the two men squatting in the alley. The older of the two looked up.

"Young 'un can't hold his drink," he said.

"Well, get him off the street then or it'll be the worse for both of you." The soldier's contempt was obvious, even if his face was expressionless.

"Yes, sir. Thank you, sir."

Zunic sighed with relief as the soldier walked off. He pulled Mark to his feet. They left the town by the back streets. By the time they reached the horses Mark had recovered from his nausea but was in shock. The despair he felt showed in his face as they rode back to his companions. He could not accept what had happened. Ferragamo was their undisputed leader, the only one knowledgeable and clever enough to organize a plan like this. With him gone . . . Mark's mind refused to function. All he could think of was the fact that if the wizard had fallen prey to the evil that haunted Ark then the moonberries were no protection at all. They were all doomed.

When, late that afternoon, they reached the forest camp it was Zunic who told the others what had happened. Fontaine and Shill were aghast and in the wizard's fate the outlaws saw the downfall of their only hope of salvation. An enervating depression settled over them all. Durc and Shill made an effort to raise their spirits and to plan what to do next but it was obvious that their hearts were not in it and they soon gave up. No one could be bothered to set a watch that night.

Fontaine lay awake, curled up in her cloak. She was worrying about Mark, knowing what he felt for Ferragamo, and how he must be suffering now. After some time, she realized that she was not going to get any sleep, and wondered whether Mark was awake too.

She got up and, taking care not to disturb the sleeping camp, went over to him. He lay on his back, with his eyes open, staring at the sky, and started slightly at her quiet arrival. Crouching down beside him, she whispered:

"Are you all right? Do you want to talk about it?"

"No."

"Oh."

Nonplussed, but determined not to give up easily, she sat down. Saying nothing to Mark, she looked at the silver ring she now wore. Her own ring had gone with Deg, and this new one had been given to her by Mark while they were in Home.

"It was my mother's," he had explained. "I've worn it on a chain round my neck ever since she died." He had paused, his face going bright red. "I'd like you to have it." He had slipped it onto her finger, then looked away, fighting back tears. Fontaine had said nothing, just hugged him.

Looking at the ring now, Fontaine thought about what it meant to her, what her new-found love meant, and made up her mind.

"Come on," she said quietly, tapping his shoulder. "We're going for a walk."

"No."

"Yes. Or I'll shout and wake everybody up. And they need their sleep. Up you get."

Muttering something about her always wanting her own way, Mark got to his feet and they walked away from the camp. Once out of earshot, Fontaine started.

"Look, I know how you're feeling and *you* should know how that makes *me* feel. I can't just sit back and do nothing when you're hurting so much. Please talk to me. You never know, it may even help."

"I know, and I'm sorry, but sometimes the words just won't come," Mark replied.

There was a short silence.

"Can't you try?" she asked.

He sighed, partly in exasperation at her persistence, and partly at his own frustration.

"When I saw Ferragamo being hauled off by those soldiers, it was all I could do not to run after him. I would have, if Zunic hadn't held me back. It wasn't just because I love Ferragamo. I felt as though *everything* had fallen to pieces. He's been so strong for us all, leading us, telling us what to do, and now he's gone. I'm *scared*, Fontaine. I don't know how to cope!"

"But you've got friends with you! We'll all help. You're not going to be fighting this battle on your own. I know you're the prince, but you've got good soldiers—and even those rotten outlaws may be of some use—and Jani, and me, and..." She hesitated. "I love you, Mark, and I've got faith in you. I know you're not perfect—nobody is, but"—and she grinned at him, trying to lighten the mood—"with the love of a good woman behind you, there's no telling what you'll be capable of."

Mark laughed. "All right," he said. "You've got a point there. And it won't help anyone if I just sit around moping." He became sober once more. "Nor will it help anyone if we're incapable of anything tomorrow because we're half asleep. Come on, back to bed."

The next day they made a belated and forlorn attempt to find the wizard. Riding into town in small groups from various different directions, they soon discovered that most of the soldiers had left and Ferragamo had been with them. The reported size of his escort made pursuit unthinkable even if it weren't for the fact that their cake supplies would run out very quickly if they attempted to share it out among all of the group. So far the outlaws had not been given any. Mark now seriously doubted the cake's efficacy; in isolation it seemed such a silly idea; but it was one more reason not to attempt any foolhardy action.

In the end they made the only choice open to them and

decided to go on to the rendezvous without the wizard. As they rode westward Mark hardly spoke. Despair lodged once more in his throat like a fishhook. Even Fontaine could not rouse him from his self-imposed depths.

It should have been impossible for the situation to get worse but the next day it did.

The awesome power which they sought to oppose chose this time to flex its muscles. Mark, Fontaine, and Shill felt various symptoms—buzzing in the ears, a sudden lassitude, and in, Mark's case, the uncanny notion that he was being looked for. No one knew what Jani felt but he did not seem unduly concerned. The effect on the outlaws was far more dramatic however. Each one slumped as the magic asserted itself. Three of them immediately fell off their mounts. The others were luckier in that they fell asleep but stayed in their saddles.

For most of the day the outlaws snored or stared vaguely at the sky while the four from Home made them as comfortable as possible. They felt helpless, but rejected the thought of abandoning their new colleagues to this unnatural fate. They could only wait and hope the attack would abate as the earlier ones had done.

Strangely, this setback restored a measure of Mark's confidence. At least now they knew that the moonberries *did* have a beneficial effect. It didn't explain what had happened to Ferragamo but it did give them a little bit of hope for their mission. They resolved to give each of the outlaws as much of the cake as they could spare when—if—they awoke.

At some time in the night the outlaws' sleep turned to the natural variety and in the morning they awoke, bemused by this latest attack which was by far the strongest they had yet experienced. There were many strange glances cast and they were not unnaturally suspicious of the cake they were offered, especially as Fontaine was the one to distribute it. They all ate it in the end, and however, and expressed amazement at how it cleared their heads.

After that they hurried on to Deerhide Bay. They were already behind schedule for the meeting and did not want to lose any more time. But their route took them first through marshland and then rough, rock-strewn hills before they reached the coastal plain, and it was another four days until they reached Ansar's camp.

The relief of those waiting there turned sour when they

learned of Ferragamo's absence, and Durc and his men were the object of many suspicious glances.

If the waiting at Home had been bad, the waiting at Deerhide Bay was worse. The whole group felt their lack of action to be a necessary evil but that did not make it any more bearable. Their communal sense of helplessness was emphasized by worries about Ferragamo and the seeming inevitability of another, even stronger magical attack. There was nothing they could do about either, and they were left kicking their heels. To make matters worse, the weather turned sour with rain squalls and gusty westerly winds, making their makeshift quarters uncomfortable and damp. Halfhearted attempts were made to build more solid shelters but no one had the patience to do a good job when each hoped they would be leaving in the next hour or the next day.

Before too long another problem arose. With their expanded numbers and the delay stretching to several days the supply of moonberry cake was shrinking rapidly. It become obvious that some men would have to go back to the safety of the boats. Nobody was keen to volunteer, having come this far, and in the end Mark, as the nominal head of the party, was forced into making a decision. He called Shill, Lomax, and Durc to him and explained his reasoning.

"Lomax, some of your men will have to go aboard ship. You know why."

"But my men are trained soldiers," the Strallenese captain replied, glancing at Durc.

"I know," said Mark, "but this won't be a normal battle we're going to fight. I don't doubt the worth of your men but if we spread our resources too far we could all end up helpless."

"Ark *is* my home-isle," said Durc.

"You've not served it too well up until now," said Lomax.

"Peace," said Mark anxiously. "Durc and his men *do* know Ark better than you. I want them to have their chance. Ferragamo promised them that."

Lomax accepted defeat. "I would like to stay with a few of my men," he said. "My lieutenant can take charge of the rest at sea."

"Of course," said Mark. "Pick three of your best men.

The rest can sail back to Home and perhaps join the fleet as it sails north. That way they will be as much a part of this battle as we will."

"Agreed, my Lord. I'll make arrangements." Lomax strode off.

"Thank you," said Durc.

"Thank me when this is over," replied the prince. "You may regret not going to sea."

"We're no sailors. Just looking at the sea gives me the shakes."

Durc went off to tell his men the news.

"A motley crew we'll be and no mistake," said Shill.

"Do you think I was wrong?"

"No. And even if you were that's the price of leadership. You'll learn that fast enough."

"I feel lost without Ferragamo."

"So do we all."

Chapter 23

*T*he unlooked-for appearance of Rehan had annoyed Amarino initially, and she had punished him by secreting him away in a chamber in a little-used corridor of the castle. He was virtually a prisoner there, under orders to stay where he was, and with a guard on hand to bring him food and keep an eye on him.

Now, however, she smiled as she recalled his arrival. His haste had been such that he had still been sweaty from riding hard when he furtively entered the castle. The wretched man had looked ridiculous.

Why couldn't he have done as she asked and stayed on Heald as her spy? No, one look at her father's face in the seeing-stone and he'd come running back to her like a whipped dog. Perhaps she couldn't blame him entirely. The old man Alzedo was enough to frighten anyone, except her of course. Meddling old fool.

After leaving Rehan alone for a few days, Amarino had relented and gone to see him. She rather enjoyed the experience. He was, as she had predicted, an amusing plaything, one of the few she would consider keeping when she achieved her ultimate goal. Unlike most men, he combined a splendid physique with an astute mind. No match for her, of course, but attractive nonetheless. She had begun to pay him regular visits.

This was only one of many pleasurable activities she

enjoyed at the moment. Her plans were progressing admirably, and even her tests of power over the whole island were becoming less wearying every time. Her reserve of strength from Starhill grew constantly. The city was completely under her control.

Rehan's information had proved useful, if unsurprising. That Ansar and Laurent were in Home with Ferragamo and Fontaine made it likely that, when the inevitable attack came, she would be facing forces from Heald as well as the few from Ark not already subjugated. She had expected that. *The more the merrier*, she thought. *By the time they get here they'll just be yet another source of power for me.* Her confidence grew with every day.

The only fly in the ointment was the incident with Brandel. She was still puzzled about that. Having him killed had been a mistake. She had tried to prevent it but had changed her mind too late. In trying to read the prince's mind she had met only an unnatural blankness. It had frightened her momentarily and she had panicked. Instead of biding her time and learning what she needed to know from him by other means, she had become so angry that she had put an end to him. It was regrettable but it couldn't be helped.

He was small fry. It was the wizard she wanted.

At first, Rehan had chafed against Amarino's annoyance and his restriction, but soon realized that if he wished to grow in her regard, he must be patient. She would recognize the benefits of his company sooner or later, he was sure. For a while he enjoyed a restful existence.

When, after a few days, she had still not come, he began to be frightened that her anger at his return was deeper than he had thought. He fretted and could not eat.

And then she came.

At the beginning she would only stay with him for a few moments, but as time passed, the visits would last some hours—and Rehan knew that he would do anything to make sure those times were repeated. He was dazzled by her and seemed almost magically under the spell of her beauty, overwhelmed by his desire for her.

He thought it nothing short of miraculous when she let him know, in no uncertain terms, that she felt much the same way about him. As long as she kept coming to him and proving her regard, he was happy to wait in his secluded cell.

Chapter 24

For eleven days Mark and his friends had waited for Moroski's message. On the twelfth day it arrived. Atlanta dived from the sky and this time they wasted no time in removing the tiny scroll from her leg.

They had half hoped that it would give them news of Ferragamo, that somehow the two wizards might have been in touch, but Moroski gave no indication of any knowledge of Ferragamo's fate. The message was simple and to the point.

The fleet will sail in two days. Grayrock six or seven days later. On your way! Moroski.

"That's it then," said Ansar.

"Aye. It's probably too late to stop them sailing, even with Atlanta's help," said Shill.

"What would be the point anyway?" said Mark, looking round. "If Ferragamo had escaped he would be here by now."

He did not need to say any more. All of them had assumed that the wizard was in Starhill by now, therefore either a prisoner or, quite possibly, dead. Nobody felt like voicing such thoughts, however.

"The plan is still the best chance we've got," said Orme. "We have the berries and, with luck, we have the element of surprise."

"With the fleet on its way we're committed," said Shill, "otherwise all their effort will be wasted."

"And they could be in danger, too," added Lomax. "They can't stay at sea for ever."

"We go to Starhill then?" said Orme, unable to conceal his eagerness.

"Yes," Mark replied, surprising himself with the firmness of his words. "We set off first thing tomorrow."

They went to start the final preparations, leaving Mark alone. Almost alone, that is.

You're learning. At least you make decisions and stick to them now.

Oh Longfur, I don't want to make decisions! I wish Ferragamo was here.

Well, he's not. And, like it or not, these people are looking to you now.

I know, and it scares me.

You're backsliding. Here I am boosting your confidence and all I get is doubts.

I have to talk to someone.

I'm honored. For a long time you only spoke to her.

That's different, Longfur.

How?

Mark looked round as if to check that no one else was near enough to hear his thoughts.

She's special.

Humph.

Don't be cross, Longfur. I never really knew her before. Now . . . His train of thought trailed off.

She's prettier than when she first arrived. I'll admit that.

Do you think so? I wondered if it was only my imagination.

After a pause, Mark said, *I love her, Longfur.*

You think.

I know.

Huh. Humans always know things that are unknowable. Just make sure you concentrate on the job in hand.

Longfur stalked off.

Mark watched him go. *He's jealous!* he thought, feeling suddenly bewildered. *Oh Longfur!*

Next morning the entire party set off, taking the spare horses with them as baggage animals. Atlanta had already been sent

ahead to give Moroski the news of Ferragamo's disappearance
and of their intention to carry on without him.

They rode north along the coastal plain, making reasonable time, although their route was sometimes winding as
they tried to avoid villages or farmhouses wherever possible.
The autumn rains were now upon them and, as they were on
the exposed western side of Ark, it proved to be a very wet
day indeed.

The next day they rode on, still going north. This brought
them into the first of the foothills on the Windchill Mountains. The morning was overcast but dry and the view to the
east was imposing. Several members of the party began to
wonder about the advisability of trying to cross that formidable range of mountains, whose highest peaks were invisible in
the clouds.

The sun broke through shortly before noon, providing
some welcome warmth and making the distant snow-capped
mountains glitter. Against the whiteness a speck appeared.
Mark watched as it drew nearer and nearer, obviously heading straight toward them. When, finally, he recognized the
bird, it caused a flutter of hope in his chest.

Owl alighted on a nearby branch.

To Mark's utter astonishment, Owl then spoke to him in
the way that Longfur did. His mind was still reeling from
this—Owl had only ever been able to communicate with his
wizard before—and from the ambiguous message, when with
a shock he realized that he recognized the "voice" which had
spoken to him.

It was Ferragamo's.

———————————

The fleet which set out from Marviel was a most impressive
sight. Almost every seaworthy boat on Heald, of whatever
size, had been pressed into service and these were augment-
ed with ten naval clippers from Strallen. These last carried a
full complement of soldiers as well as their crews, but elsewhere the ships were less heavily manned. From the shore
that would not be obvious, however, and with banners and
shields showing their colors, they made a brave sight, despite
the gray weather which attended their departure.

Aboard the Healdean flagship, the *Ram*, Pabalan, Moroski,
and Laurent stood on the bridge, looking north.

The wizard's emphasis on the serious nature of their mission had finally had an effect on his king, but Pabalan was unable to contain his excitement as, after all the pettifogging delays, they finally set sail. Indeed, he seemed made for such adventures. Clad in his armor, which was topped with emblazoned silk on chest and back, he looked every inch the conquering hero. Even if he had reluctantly accepted that he would conquer nothing but a measure of the sea, he saw no reason why he should not do so in style.

As they left their various moorings, the soldiers of his small army cheered him. There was not one amongst them who had not heard and seen his king in the last few days, such had been Pabalan's enthusiastic diligence, and they respected him for it.

Laurent and Moroski, less noticeably dressed, watched the king as he acknowledged the cheers and smiled to each other. If truth were told these two were the real admirals of the fleet but it would be Pabalan who voiced the orders.

Traveling at the speed of the slowest vessel, they crossed the straits that day, and by dusk were in sight of the southern tip of Ark. As expected, two more vessels joined them from Home.

The next day found them rounding Bark Tine and sailing slowly up the east coast of Ark. The intention was to make it appear that they were looking for landing sites and, at the same time, ensure that any observers on the island got a good look at both the misleading size of the fleet and at the variety of standards they were flying. Prominent among these were Ather's royal colors but Heald and Strallen were also represented.

Shortly after noon, Atlanta returned to her master. She swooped down, causing consternation among the gulls which were following the *Ram*'s progress. Already aware that all was not well from his immediate contact with the falcon's mind, Moroski read the message with some misgivings. Ferragamo's capture shook him more than he was prepared to admit, though Laurent, as shrewd as ever, recognized the signs in his face.

"Bad news?"

"Yes. Ferragamo's been taken by Starhill guards."

"Oh." Even the courtier was temporarily at a loss for words. Then he asked, "How did it happen?"

"Mark doesn't say."

"They're going on without him?"

"Yes. There's nothing else they could do and they knew it."

"Well," said Pabalan, who had been listening to the conversation, "maybe it'll come down to fighting after all. I never did hold with this magic business."

Behind him, Laurent rolled his eyes skyward.

———————

Two days later, the fleet anchored in the shallow waters off Ironmouth. Moroski was gratified to note that the town was obviously garrisoned and that they were being closely watched. All the ships were put on alert but the forces on the shore showed no signs of putting to sea, despite the presence of several warships in the harbor and riverside docks. That fitted with the wizards' theory and Moroski smiled grimly to himself as the two forces faced each other across a short span of water which neither of them had any intention of crossing.

———————

Mark stared at Owl. Just when he began to think that he had imagined the whole thing, the bird spoke again, repeating exactly the same message in Ferragamo's voice.

Then Fontaine brought him back to the world.

"What's going on? What's he doing here?"

A much more familiar silent voice added, *If you'd care to stop impersonating a fly-trap and use your mouth to make the noises that pass for human speech, there are several people here who would like to know what is happening.*

"Are you all right?" asked Ansar.

Mark found his voice.

"Owl just spoke to me," he said.

"I thought he could only speak to Ferragamo," said Fontaine. "Are you a wizard too?"

"He spoke with Ferragamo's voice."

"What?" said Durc. "I didn't hear anything."

"It's not like that," said Mark.

Never mind that. Tell them what he said! interjected Longfur.

"Wait a minute," said Mark.

He turned back to Owl who blinked slowly. Mark projected

his thoughts toward the bird, trying to make the link which came so naturally with Longfur. *Where is Ferragamo?* he said, but knew immediately that his question wasn't getting through. *Help us,* he pleaded silently. Ferragamo's voice sounded once again in his mind but it was only a repetition of the message he had already heard. Even the inflections were exactly the same.

I am alive. I will join you if I can but this may not be possible. Carry on the mission as planned. Don't worry about me. Good luck. Remember the source.

Though it was unmistakably the wizard's, Ferragamo's "voice," even given the unusual circumstances, sounded weak and strange.

"It's no good. I can't get any more out of him," said Mark, looking at the faces of those gathered round him. He almost laughed at the variety of expressions, which ranged from Fontaine's awe through Ansar's exasperation to Durc's total incomprehension.

"Owl brings a message from Ferragamo," he said and then repeated the message word for word.

"Don't ask me any questions," he added. "That's all there is. Your guess is as good as mine about some of its meaning."

"He's alive. That's the main thing," said Shill.

"But why might it not be possible for him to join us?" said Ansar.

"Who knows?"

"That last bit was odd," said Lomax. "What's this 'source'?"

There was silence for a while. Then Mark said, "We can think about that as we ride. One thing that was very clear is that he wants us to go on to Starhill. We won't get any closer sitting here."

There's hope for you yet, came Longfur's comment. *Perhaps some of my tuition hasn't been wasted after all.*

Mark smiled as the horses moved off again, spreading into a long line, two abreast. The news about the wizard's curious message was passed to those who had not heard all that had been said. For himself, Mark felt almost lighthearted. The message, while puzzling, had renewed his hope.

They camped in the foothills that night and there was a great deal of talk around the fires. Speculation on the meaning and method of the wizard's message was the most common topic but there was also discussion of passes over the mountains and approaches to Starhill thereafter, as well as the inevitable discussion about the weather.

After they had eaten and the cake had been carefully distributed and consumed, a light drizzle began to fall and the party retired early to their bivouac shelters.

Mark lay awake, staring into space. Without being aware of how he came to a conclusion about Ferragamo's message, he suddenly knew what the 'source' was. He had a vivid mental picture of the moonberry tree in the courtyard of Starhill Castle. It was clearly a source of power. He wondered why he had never realized that before. It all fitted. Then his vision clouded and went black, as though a veil had been passed over his eyes. He shivered involuntarily.

"Can I come and keep you warm?" said a voice in the darkness. Fontaine's lithe form wriggled into his tent and snuggled up against him. Mark was glad of her company but still felt awkward.

"Did anyone see you come in here?" he asked.

"Only Jani, and he wouldn't say anything even if he could," she replied. "He's kept watch for us before, you know."

"Longfur said as much," whispered Mark. "I didn't know."

"In any case," she said, "are you ashamed of me or something?"

"Oh no!" he said. "It's just that—"

"Besides, we need to share our warmth."

Fontaine giggled.

———————————

The next day they turned eastward and began the climb in earnest. Owl flew off ahead of them and did not return. Mark strained to see where he went but it was impossible after a while as the weather had taken another turn for the worse. Rain fell intermittently and it was distinctly colder. Strong westerly winds pushed the clouds from the sea and by mid-afternoon the rain had turned to stinging hail.

"It'll be snow higher up," said Orme gloomily.

"Look on the bright side," said Shill. "It'll disguise our approach. Nobody will expect us to come down from the mountains in this weather."

"If we don't all freeze to death first!" added Durc.

Chapter 25

"*T*ime for some fun and games, I think," said Moroski. "Ask the captain to send the signals please, Laurent."

"Right."

"What's going on?" Pabalan asked.

"We're going to make the forces in Ironmouth think we're preparing to land."

"Keep them guessing eh?"

"That's right."

Their conversation was interrupted by an unearthly metallic crashing as aboard every vessel shields were beaten with swords or other implements. Gradually one rhythm came to dominate the cacophony and its slow beat rolled ominously across the water. Moroski's special talents were turned to amplifying and directing this noise so that the onshore defenders received its full impact.

Then smaller boats were let down from the sides of the troop ships and soldiers clambered down the rope ladders. They cast off and milled around in all directions, though they remained carefully outside of the range of the crossbows and catapults in the town.

Flag signals were sent between ships. Most of them were meaningless. Others were the latest naval jokes. Anyone on Ark would have had difficulty following them all, let alone deciphering them, which was precisely what Moroski intended. He watched with a mixture of amusement and satisfaction as the army units on land hurried to and fro in response to each movement at sea.

They kept up these bogus maneuvers until dusk, when all the small boats were recalled. They hoped by this that the defenders would be left in a state of alert anxiety all night. There had been no sign of any attempt by the defenders to put to sea and force the fleet to fight, and Moroski expected none. Nevertheless, guards were posted. The vast majority of those aboard slept soundly.

The next morning they weighed anchor and set off north again. They were rounding the promontory known as The Anvil when a lookout shouted to say that sails were in sight. Soon it became obvious that a sizable fleet, military in appearance, was heading toward Ark from the east.

Moroski ordered his ships to change course in order to intercept them.

Over the next three days Mark and the odd assortment who followed him found the going increasingly hard. It wasn't just the changing nature of the landscape which lost the green softness of the coastal plain and became more and more rugged and rock-strewn. It wasn't just the bleakness of the view; the distant cold gray sea behind them and the mist-enshrouded mountains ahead. There was a sense of uncertainty, almost of dread, which had been growing ever since Ferragamo was lost and which, in these dismal surroundings, seemed to increase with every step. To make matters worse, as predicted, snow began to fall intermittently and the prevailing westerly winds grew colder as they climbed. The trail also added to their difficulties as, in places, it was steep and winding so that horses had to be led. In the highest part of the pass even the relatively level stretches held their own pitfalls because here the snow lay inches deep and both men and horses trod warily.

The morning of the fourth day dawned clear, with the sun turning the massive peaks to either side into dazzling spectacles. Although they were still surrounded by mountains, the party was now moving downhill and looking forward to crossing the snow line.

As had become his habit, Mark rode at the head of the

slow-moving column. Thus it was he who first saw an extraordinary sight which held him, and subsequently everyone
else, mesmerized.

About a hundred paces ahead the trail curved sharply to
the right to avoid a sheer rock pinnacle which stuck out from
the mountainside. Mark was just thinking that it would
provide an ideal lookout post for the pass, if only one could
climb it, when a man appeared on the top. If he were a
sentry however he was a very strange one. He stood in full
view, arms stretched out as if in welcome, and he made no
move to report his sighting of the party to any unseen force
behind him. He had long white hair and a beard, and his
clothes were most peculiar.

As the others began to bunch up behind Mark, all of them
gazing up at the strange apparition which seemed to have
materialized out of thin air, he became aware that the man
was speaking.

"Quiet!" he yelled, and the mutter of conversation behind
him fell into silence.

It soon became clear that the man before them was
making a speech, using the rock pinnacle as a fantastic pulpit.
Not all of his words reached their ears for, though the sky was
clear, the wind was still strong. Even so there was a hypnotic
quality to the oration which neither the dramatic setting nor
the flailing arms could explain. Men and horses were still and
silent.

"The old ways are forgotten. This cannot be allowed. My
king...but I dared. Now I have proof! Behold. Men can
only...forward. My duty cannot be done until all have
heard. Carry my tale so that others may believe. Tell the
wizards to remember the source..."

Mark's eyes widened at the repetition of Ferragamo's
obscure message.

"...the court grows old. Will it fall? I fly among the stars
and I have seen...So many years, so little done. Men do not
learn, they must be taught, shown! Armies march but no
battles can...and steel can melt. I have seen. A doom is
upon this isle. It groans like a lost thing in the endless dark.
It moans."

The last word was a long drawn-out wail which sent
shivers down several spines. The silence which followed
lasted several moments. Even the wind grew quiet. Then the

man spoke again. Curiously, although it seemed to be said in conversational tones, the next sentence was heard clearly by everyone.

Cocking his head to one side with his hands clasped meekly before him, he looked directly at Mark and asked, "Shall I shut up now?"

Mark gasped. "It can't be!"

Shill said, "I thought he was only a legend."

"I don't believe this," said Durc. "Did he say what I think he said?"

Nobody answered but several of the other Arkans nodded.

"What's going on here?" said Lomax, looking bemused.

"Yes, what are you all talking about?" added Fontaine.

Mark turned to her and said, "There is an old story told on Ark about a wizard who tried to eat moonberries to prove his ability and their power. Unlike many others he survived the experiment but it's said he went mad. He is supposed to have wandered off, traveling around the island preaching sermons which nobody could understand. Then he disappeared to become a hermit. Every so often travelers told of being waylaid by this madman who made speeches to them. These speeches always ended with 'Shall I shut up now?'"

"Oh," said Fontaine.

"That's why in the stories he's called Shalli," said Shill.

"But that all happened centuries ago," said Mark.

"He's speaking again," said Orme.

Everybody returned their attention to Shalli.

Before any of his words could register however, a bird appeared and settled on his outstretched arm. Mark's heart leapt.

It was Owl.

Chapter 26

$\mathcal{A}$gain they could only catch part of what the hermit said.

"My brother comes. His heart is white. This I had foreseen... else time shall sleep. Together... too are white. That is good. The bringers of doom should be so. We are all servants... my home. Storm comes. It is better here."

At the mention of storms, several people glanced backward. Sure enough, huge black clouds were rolling in from the west. They shivered at the thought of the blizzard to come.

Shalli, if indeed it was him, was now gesturing urgently. Owl had flown up into the air to avoid the windmill of arms. "You come!" shouted the hermit. His invitation was unmistakable.

"Up there?" said Ansar. "We can't climb that!"

"I think he wants us to circle round. Maybe there's an easier route the other side," said Shill.

"If nothing else, the rock should give a bit of shelter," said Orme, glancing pointedly westward.

"Let's go then," said Mark.

The horses moved forward again, continuing along the trail. Fontaine drew level with Mark and said, "That's Owl up there, isn't it?"

"Do you think...?"

"I hope so," he replied.

Contrary to all their expectations, the far side of the rock buttress proved to be a steep but climbable grassy bank. It was almost clear of snow and the bright green seemed incomparably rich after so much white.

They dismounted and Mark, Ansar, and Shill led their horses up, doubling back and forth to make the climb less steep. Above them, Shalli continued to wave his welcome but he no longer spoke. When they reached him they found themselves on a surprisingly broad grassy plateau. To their left rose the rock pinnacle which had been so much more impressive from the other side. Ahead of them, the mountain climbed into the sky. Shalli indicated a cave entrance on the far side of the plateau and said, simply, "Shelter. Storm comes."

The white-haired old man, who was dressed in a patchwork of goatskins, rolled his eyes before gesticulating at the approaching clouds and then at the horsemen still on the trail.

"Get them up here," said Mark to Shill. "I'll go and have a look at this cave."

Shalli, who until then had been looking mostly at Shill and Ansar, the two larger men, now regarded Mark with undisguised interest. His eyes flickered to the prince's sword and grew round. Mark met his subsequent stare and was uncomfortably aware of the scrutiny. There was something approaching awe in the hermit's gaze.

"And last," he said.

"What?" said Mark.

"Cave," said Shalli, pointing. "Shelter. Horses too."

"It must be a big cave," said Mark, smiling as he walked toward its entrance. Owl swooped past them and disappeared into the darkness.

"Is there a man with the owl?" said Mark. "A wizard?"

"My brother," said Shalli. "His heart is white."

"Your brother? Where is he?"

Shalli said nothing. He looked back to make sure that the others were on their way up, then led the way into the cave.

"Horse too," he said, as Mark hesitated.

Certainly the cave was high enough to accommodate a horse but Mark feared that the floor would be treacherous in darkness. Caves do not normally make good stables.

Shalli mumbled a few words which were even less intelligible than usual and instantly Mark's fears disappeared. It was as if the very rock had become luminescent and the cave was revealed to his rapidly readjusting eyes. It was indeed a big cave. It went deep into the mountainside, sloping slightly upward, and the main cave had several side entrances leading from it. What was more, the floor was more or less flat, with sand and stones packed down between the larger rocks.

Mark led his horse inside, looking about him in wonder. The light was stronger in some places than others and the different rock formations glittered and gave color to the scene. The air was humid but surprisingly warm and from somewhere in the depths came the musical sound of running water.

"Horse," said Shalli, pointing to one of the side chambers. Mark went in. The cave he entered was long and well lit. It could easily have accommodated fifty horses. A trough of water ran along one long wall. Mark's horse went in happily enough and stooped to drink. She seemed to be suffering from none of the animal's normal fear of underground places.

When Mark returned to the main chamber, he found the others starting to file in. All of them were quite obviously astonished. He directed them to the "stables" and then turned back to Shalli. The old man had disappeared. Mark felt a momentary twinge of fear. *Is this a trap?* he thought. Then an owl hooted from deep within the mountain and Mark set off, peering into each chamber as he went.

Abruptly, Shalli appeared before him, materializing as he had earlier, as if from thin air. The hermit beckoned and walked into yet another chamber. Mark hurried to follow.

Inside, the illumination was less bright, and it was with difficulty that Mark made out an untidy huddle of rags in the far corner. As his eyes adjusted to the light, the bundle moved and a familiar voice said, "I didn't think you could avoid my friend here for long."

"Ferragamo!"

The wizard raised his head and Mark's jubilation evaporated. The green eyes that looked back at him were the same as ever but the face itself was almost unrecognizable. It was so drawn that all the bones stood out like ramparts. His hair was snow white, almost silver in the magical light, and even beneath his coverings it was obvious that his limbs and torso were shrunken beyond belief.

Ferragamo's head fell back and as it did so Mark gasped. He was sure that *sparks* had jumped from the wizard's hair.

ome while later Mark was sitting in yet another chamber
alking with various friends. They had all wanted to see
erragamo but Shalli had refused to allow anyone else to
nter the wizard's part of the cave. He kept repeating the
hrase, "Too white, too white," and barring the entrance with
uch stubbornness of purpose that even Fontaine had been
nable to pass. As a consequence they all demanded a full
eport from Mark. He had described the wizard's appearance
nd then the way in which he had fallen back to the floor.

"Sparks!" exclaimed Ansar and Orme simultaneously.

"That's what it looked like," said Mark, "but tiny silver
parks, not red ones like those from a fire. I went over to him
nd noticed then that his skin was glowing softly. I don't mind
elling you it scared me."

"I'm not surprised," said Durc.

"I knelt down beside him. He was muttering something
bout 'breathing in sleep,' 'men sleeping for a week,' and
iding in the snow.' It didn't make any sense. He didn't
eem to hear anything I said, either."

"He must have been very ill to lose all that weight," said
ontaine. "Perhaps it was a fever and he's delirious."

"Can't Shalli explain anything?" asked Shill. "Ferragamo
as obviously been here a while."

"I tried that," said Mark. "After Ferragamo had gone back
o sleep, I asked him what was the matter. He just said 'too
hite,' and he's been saying that ever since."

"To the exclusion of everything else," agreed Lomax.

"There's something funny about that cave he's in as well,"
aid Mark. "It's as though there are things in there moving
bout. It's always just in the corner of your eye but when you
ook at it, it's quite still. Made my skin crawl."

"Maybe we should move him," said Ansar. "It doesn't
ound healthy."

"How?" said his sister. "Shalli won't even let us near him."

"Shalli showed me something else," said Mark. "He seemed
ery interested in my sword. He didn't want to touch it but
e made me draw it and pointed to the blade. I didn't know
hat he was doing at first but then I saw something. There
as a luminous pattern in the metal, so faint I could hardly

see it. It seemed vaguely familiar somehow. He seemed very excited about it."

"Let's have a look," said Ansar.

"It's gone now," Mark said. He slid the blade out of its scabbard and let them all examine it. "Perhaps it was the light in Ferragamo's cave. That was odd too. It kept varying."

"The light in this whole place is odd," said Durc.

"There's nothing on this blade that I can see," said Orme. "I don't suppose Shalli enlightened you about it?"

"What do you think?" said Mark. He took the sword back and slipped it into its sheath.

"I stayed for a bit. Ferragamo woke up again and said quite clearly, 'I'm glad you're here. Remember the source.' Then he went funny again. He was asleep when I left him, but he was still mumbling and moving about."

"Nightmares?" asked Orme.

"Something like that, I suppose."

"Well, we'll just have to wait until he's recovered enough to tell us himself," said Shill.

"I wouldn't want to leave in this weather anyway," said Orme. "There's a blizzard raging out there."

"We should be comfortable enough," said Lomax. "Some of the lads have been exploring."

"This place is like a warren," added Durc. "It's a wonder no one's got lost."

"How is it so warm?" asked Mark.

"There's a hot water spring up there a-ways," said Lomax. "My guess is that the water runs through fissures in the rock as well and keeps the whole cave system warm."

"There's cold water too," said Durc. "Melt-water, or a link from a mountain tarn perhaps."

"This cave has better plumbing than Starhill Castle!" said Orme.

"Food?" asked Mark.

"There are stores of dried meat and vegetables," said Durc, "grain as well. The stars know where he got it all from!"

"We could withstand a siege here," said Lomax.

"Speaking of food," said Durc, "most of the others are in the cavern two down on the right. It seems to be the kitchen. We could all use a good meal."

"Don't you ever think of anything except your stomach?" said Fontaine. "I bet you've even got Jani doing the cooking."

"He volunteered," said Durc defensively.

The roof of the kitchen swallowed smoke and steam indifferently. When everyone had eaten their fill of a plain but tasty stew, Fontaine, as usual, supervised the distribution of cake. While this was going on Shalli walked in and nonchalantly sat down beside one of the cooking fires. He beamed at all his guests. Fontaine, intending to be polite, offered him a sliver of cake. This he sniffed carefully. As he did so, delight spread over all his features. He nodded vigorously and said, "Good. Eat," but did not put his portion into his mouth. Instead he handed it back to Fontaine with great courtesy and, with a wave of his hand, indicated all the others in the cavern. Puzzled, she put it back with their stores.

Zunic, who happened to be the closest to him, asked Shalli for news of Ferragamo.

"My brother sleeps," came the reply. "Good. He needs."

Then, without warning, the hermit launched into an oration which sounded very similar to the one he had made earlier from the pinnacle, and which made about as much sense, even though they could now hear every word.

Some phrases sounded oddly familiar to Mark but, like everyone else, he was so entranced by the performance that he could not place them. The spell was broken when, as before, the hermit ended with inappropriate coyness.

"Shall I shut up now?"

Several of the group had difficulty suppressing laughter.

Chapter 27

On the same day that Fe ragamo was reunited with Mark and his comrades, anoth meeting was taking place, far to the east, at sea.

By a series of signals and close observation it had bee established that the newly arrived fleet hailed from Peve On board their flagship was Hoban, the ambassador, and th messenger from Heald, as well as their naval commande With them came twelve fully armed ships, each with contingent of soldiers aboard.

Their greetings and subsequent conference were exchange by loud hailer as the sea was beginning to become rough with a storm approaching from the west. As concisely a possible Moroski outlined the plan and Hoban, acting a Peven's spokesman, agreed to join the party. They had brough some supplies of moonberries, mainly in the form of ancier wine. This had been found under layers of dust in th palace cellars. There was far too little, however, to allow a the men a drink and therefore a landing on Ark was rule out. Hoban also explained that they had sailed directly to Ar because of several delays in their departure and their conse quent fear that they would arrive too late to be of an assistance. Moroski ordered the combined fleets to sail wes ward again.

It was slow going, as they were headed into the teeth c

the storm and icy rain lashed the boats, adding its torment to
the spray from the white-capped waves.

By morning they were in sight of The Shoot and the rest
of that day and all the next were fully occupied with coping
with the storm that raged around them.

———————————————

The morning after they had arrived at Shalli's cave, Mark was
woken by a gentle hand on his shoulder. It was the hermit,
who beckoned him to follow. Rubbing his eyes Mark went
with him to Ferragamo's room, and found the wizard sitting
up and eating. He was still very gaunt and pale but flashes of
the old Ferragamo showed through in his manner as he
spooned porridge into his mouth and waved Mark to a goat
skin-covered chair.

"I'm glad you're here."

"I'm glad we found you. If it hadn't been for our friend
here"—Mark nodded at Shalli—"we would have ridden straight
past. He stood on the rock and made a speech—"

"Don't start him off again," groaned Ferragamo, glancing
at the hermit in alarm. "My head is buzzing already."

Mark smiled, remembering the effect of Shalli's orations.
"Are you feeling better?" he asked.

"Better than what?" replied Ferragamo. A small worm of
doubt wriggled in Mark's stomach.

"I'm glad to see you eating," he said hurriedly.

The wizard's green eyes looked down at his bowl.

"Mmm. This is good. I haven't had food like this since
Koria was here." The worm turned again.

"How is she by the way?" asked Ferragamo, his eyes
softening.

"Koria? She's well. I saw her last when you did."

"Oh yes. How silly of me."

Mark glanced at Shalli as Ferragamo returned his attention to the last of his breakfast but the hermit's smile gave
nothing away.

The wizard put down his empty bowl. "I think we had
better be going now. You *are* going to Starhill, aren't you?" he
said accusingly.

"Yes. Of course. We're all here. Owl gave us your message. But we can't go now. You're much too weak—"

"I'm stronger than I've ever been," snapped the wizard,

his face momentarily angry, before relapsing into a smile.
"We have work to do."

"There's a blizzard outside," said Mark. "We wouldn't
even make it out of the mountains."

"Oh," said Ferragamo. "I'll sleep now then."

So saying he lay down and within moments was sound
asleep. Shalli shooed Mark out and the young prince went to
find someone to talk to. He was badly shaken and needed
some sensible people to reassure him that Ferragamo was not
going mad.

———————————

Mark's anxiety persisted despite the others' optimistic insistence
that the wizard's strange behavior was the result of illness
from which he would, in time, recover. In any case, he
thought, time was something they did not have much of.

All morning the blizzard raged and the travelers spent the
time exploring the caves, swapping tales, and eating.

In the afternoon Shalli once again brought Mark to
Ferragamo's resting place. A little color showed in the wizard's face and his eyes were alert. He smiled at Mark's
expression as the young man came in.

"I don't suppose I've been making too much sense since
you arrived," he said.

"Well . . ."

"You don't have to worry about sparing my feelings. I
know how weird I've been!"

"What happened to you?"

"It's a long story."

"If you don't feel up to it."

"No, I'd like to talk, but I don't want to have to repeat
myself over and over, so you'd better get some of the others
in here."

Mark glanced at the hermit who was squatting protectively
by the entrance.

"I'll explain to my brother," Ferragamo said with a grin.
"You fetch the others."

Whatever the wizard said to Shalli was obviously effective, as the hermit made no protest when Mark returned and
Fontaine, Ansar, Shill, Lomax, and Durc filed in behind him.

"I wouldn't come too close," said Ferragamo, smiling
mysteriously.

For a while he quizzed them on their progress and the arrangements made with Moroski and the Healdean fleet. Then, apparently satisfied, he acceded to requests to tell his tale.

———————————

After he had separated from Mark and Zunic in Ashwicken, Ferragamo had followed four soldiers into a tavern, hoping to pick up some information from their talk. He had heard nothing useful and was about to move on when he had inadvertently become involved in a dispute between a soldier and one of the serving women who was accused of giving short change. He had been grasped by the arm.

"You're a witness, old man. You saw the coin I gave her." The soldier looked into Ferragamo's face and his eyes narrowed. The wizard muttered something about not noticing anything and made his way out. A short while later several men jumped out of a doorway and held him fast. One of them wrenched his staff from his hand and another, the soldier from the tavern dispute, held an evil-smelling cloth to his mouth and nose.

"Breathe deep, wizard," he gloated. "A pretty present you'll make."

Ferragamo had passed out. When he awoke he was in a small, cell-like room. It was almost completely dark and so in his weary state he sensed rather than saw the food and drink that was pushed hurriedly into his room. He could not eat, but his throat was dry and sore and he gulped the water greedily. Too late he realized that it had a bitter taste and he cursed his stupidity as the drug took hold and he fell into a dreamless sleep again.

The next morning, still groggy, he was led out and put on a horse by several expressionless soldiers who, despite his obvious helplessness, treated him with a wariness tinged with fear. Once in the saddle he was trussed like a chicken and then led away in the midst of a large troop of cavalry.

Time became disjointed as he passed in and out of consciousness. At one time he felt the power of Starhill's magic like a probe in his mind. It did not affect him, but he realized that he had no cake with him and, in his weakened state, would not be able to resist for long.

The next day he felt a small object in his pocket pressing

into his skin where his arms were bound to his sides. He soon realized what it was and the seeds of a desperate plan were sown.

Later, his hands were freed for the evening meal, and while he was eating he slipped a hand into his pocket. Quickly he put the whole moonberry into his mouth, intending to break the skin gently and suck the potent juices gradually, drop by drop. Unfortunately, one of his captors observed his action and, stricken by a sudden fear, the soldier leapt forward.

"Poison!" he cried. "He's trying to kill himself."

There was a horrified outcry and several of the group who had been ordered to capture Ferragamo *alive* at all costs made toward him. One of them caught at the wizard and tried to force his jaws open. Knowing he was too weak to resist for long, Ferragamo did the only thing possible and swallowed the raw fruit whole.

The effect was shattering.

He became suffused with power. His eyes shone like beacons, his hair was instantly bleached and his skin took on an incandescent glow. The ropes that bound him fell off and slithered away like snakes. Terrified soldiers fled from the scene, howling incoherently.

Ferragamo blacked out.

He woke up perhaps several days later, literally crackling with magical puissance. Around him, partly hidden by new growths of lush green grass, lay the soldiers. They were still alive but sound asleep. The ropes, having returned to their normal immobility, lay in sinuous curves a few paces away. Beyond that, several trees were in blossom, their scents and color contrasting weirdly with the autumnal scenes in the distance.

The wizard knew that he was too powerful for his own good. He was on the brink of madness, unable to control the potency within him. All he could hope to do was contain it and survive somehow until the magic shrank to manageable proportions. Quite how he was to do this was beyond him at that moment.

A squirrel approached him, its red tail twitching nervously. It lay a nut down by the wizard as if it were an offering, then produced several more from its cheeks, placing them in a neat pile. It looked at him expectantly.

Ferragamo became aware of a terrible emptiness somewhere below his rib cage. With a huge effort he levered himself up into a sitting position and then reached for one of the nuts. His fingers felt thick and clumsy and he found himself quite incapable of breaking the shell. In his frustration he was about to put it into his mouth and crunch it up whole when the squirrel, who was still watching him, picked up one of the other nuts and, with several quick, precise nibbles, removed the casing. It put the kernel back on the ground and picked up another. Soon it had completed the task.

"Thank you," said Ferragamo.

"Don't mention it," replied the squirrel, and bounded off. The wizard stared after it in amazement.

As he ate the nuts, he became aware of myriad tiny conversations about him. They were mainly concerned with finding food and avoiding predators such as the owl in the tree over there, but several of them were about the white man-storm who was regarded with a mixture of fear, awe, and a bewildered friendliness.

Me? thought Ferragamo. And then, *The owl*?

He looked about and saw Owl perched nearby but then he passed out again, his stomach churning at the unexpected arrival of his meager meal. As he slid into oblivion he thought of Koria and experienced a brief vision of her sitting on the jetty at Home, gazing out to sea. She looked up and frowned, but then Ferragamo's world went blank.

When he came to once more the wizard beckoned to his familiar. Carefully tapping a minute fraction of the power within him he impressed a message on Owl and gave him the ability to relay it to Mark. The bird flew off, with Ferragamo hoping that he knew what he was doing. The effort of control had been so immense that he collapsed again.

After that he was aware of wandering, semiconscious, not knowing where he was or where he was going. At one point more soldiers appeared and with a wave of his staff, which somehow was back in his possession, he put them all back to sleep. It was instinctive and the wizard was aware that, although the soldiers would not be harmed, they would sleep continuously for several days.

Time passed in a blur and he found himself in the mountains, unthinkingly fighting his way against the first snow of the year. As he trudged along he gradually became aware of a thin, high-pitched sound that seemed to be

following him. He stopped and shook his head to clear it,
then regretted his action as he felt momentarily faint. The
noise was still there. Turning round, he saw . . .

At this point in his narrative Ferragamo broke off abruptly
and roared with laughter. The others regarded him with
astonishment.

"Oh, I wish you could have seen it," the wizard said.
Sparkling tears ran down his cheeks. "It was priceless." Much
to his audience's frustration he fell into a further fit of giggles.
Shalli began to look quite worried.

"What was it?" exclaimed Fontaine, unable to contain
herself.

Eventually Ferragamo calmed down.

"I turned round," he repeated. "At first I didn't see
anything. Then I looked down. There were all these little
snowballs . . ." He broke off and chuckled again.

"They were floating a few handspan above the snow on
the ground. There were about a dozen of them, bobbing
gently in the air. And they were singing."

There were various expressions of disbelief, but the wizard went on.

"As I watched, one of my most recent footprints sort of
curled up, and rose into the air. Another voice joined the
squeaky chorus."

"Singing snowballs?" said Shill.

"Yes," said Ferragamo. "I walked backward for a few paces
and the same thing happened over and over again. The new
footprints rolled up and joined my flock. Every so often one
of the older ones would sink down and become ordinary snow
again."

"I've heard of following in someone footsteps," said Lomax,
"but never footsteps following you!"

"This magic has a sense of humor at least," laughed Durc.

"I got used to them after a while," said Ferragamo.

The wizard and his flock had walked on. Still he had no idea
of where he was headed. The mountains seemed to mock this
puny interloper. In this cold and unforgiving situation he had

collapsed again only to wake up after another indefinite period to find himself being tended by a white-haired hermit who appeared to be half mad but was eager to help "his brother."

Ferragamo had been in the cave for several days, slowly recovering his sanity and his memory, when the hermit had gabbled something about pilgrims approaching and then disappeared. Ferragamo had called out to him, fearing that it might be enemy soldiers, but he had taken no notice. A short while later the wizard had been vaguely aware of his host's declaimed speech to the newcomers which had ended, "Shall I shut up now?" His mind had been musing over the implications of this when the hermit had returned with Mark.

There was a short silence after Ferragamo finished his tale. No one knew quite what to say. Finally it was Fontaine who spoke.

"Did Owl help Shalli find you?" she asked.

There was no reply. The wizard was fast alseep.

After a quick glance at each other the travelers went out of the cavern leaving Shalli to his vigil.

Soon, all other members of the party knew of Ferragamo's experiences as each of those who had heard it at firsthand related it in their own styles. Mark, who was the only one to see the wizard when his mind was wandering, let the others do most of the talking. Despite his apparent normality in the afternoon, Ferragamo in his present state was still something of an unknown quantity. Mark was worried that the wizard might relapse into the magical delirium and thus become unable to help them on the last stages of their mission. Everyone else was in a buoyant mood and he retreated into his own thoughts only to be brought out of his reverie by Longfur.

You're never satisfied, are you? How many miracles do you want? Against all the odds, Ferragamo is back with us when he could be a prisoner or lost in the mountains or worse.

But—

Longfur would not be interrupted.

And we've found a luxurious shelter with food and drink when we should be stuck out there, freezing to death in the blizzard. And if you stop to think about it, we've got the

*means of communicating with Moroski to tell him of the
delay. And this cake seems to be protecting everyone even
though we are much closer to Starhill now. And if anyone
knows how to deal with what's happened to Ferragamo it's
the hermit. He's been through it all himself.*

Longfur paused momentarily in his tirade.

Shall I shut up now? he added archly, and Mark laughed
out loud. Several heads turned toward him.

"What are you laughing at?" said Fontaine.

"Oh, nothing" he replied. "I just can't believe how lucky
we've been, that's all."

"Aye," said Durc, "somebody must be on our side."

The talking went on and Mark returned to his private
conversation with Longfur.

*About sending a message to Moroski ... did you mean we
could send Owl?*

*I'm impressed. Perhaps you have got more than two brain
cells to rub together.*

I've never seen Owl carry a written note ...

*No, old bird-brain can't abide anything like that. He'd
tear it off before he went a hundred paces.*

*So it would have to be like the message Ferragamo sent to
me.*

Yes. As Moroski's a wizard too it shouldn't be impossible.

*If Ferragamo's strong enough. You heard how it exhausted
him last time. Let's go and find out.*

Longfur padded out and Mark followed.

Ferragamo was awake again and for the first time in the
dim light Mark saw Owl perched in a niche high up in the
cavern wall. Shalli was nowhere to be seen.

"Hullo," said the wizard. "Sorry about falling asleep like
that. I do it all the time. It's most aggravating."

Mark explained about his idea.

"I've been wondering about that. I think I could do it
but..."

He paused and was obviously communicating with Owl.
Mark waited.

"Owl agrees," said Ferragamo, "and he seems confident
that he'll be able to get through the storm. Let's try."

The tawny bird swooped down and settled in front of his
master. Ferragamo's eyes became particularly intense and
Owl's huge eyes widened even more than normal. Tiny

sparks flew from the wizard's hair and fingernails, making a faint crackling sound.

Then Owl blinked slowly and Ferragamo said, "Done."

At the cavern entrance, Shalli's horrified voice exclaimed, "No!" and the hermit hurried toward his brother.

"Send Koria in, would you," said the wizard in a clear but unnatural voice. Mark's stomach churned suddenly. Owl flew out of the cavern and into the blizzard.

And Ferragamo fell back, completely unconscious.

Chapter 28

*I*t took Owl two days to find Moroski and it was a bedraggled bird which was brought down to the wizard's cabin. The fleet was still within a few leagues of Grayrock and all but the essential crew had taken shelter as they rode out the storm. Several of the ships were now in bad shape, especially the Pevenese, who had not been prepared for a long wait at sea. Supplies of food and drinking water were beginning to cause concern as well, although rainwater was collected where possible.

The sailor whose forearm acted as Owl's perch on the way down to the cabin eyed the bird with some suspicion. His arrival had provoked some consternation. Owls do not usually alight on ships and some sailors regard them as unlucky. The bird had persisted in calling attention to itself, and eventually the helmsman had ordered that it be taken down to the wizard.

Moroski sat in the swaying cabin, cursing the weather and hoping the others weren't too close to Starhill yet, as at present the fleet presented a minimal diversion. He tried to interest himself in the game of checkers in which Laurent and Pabalan were engaged. The courtier was easily the better player but, diplomatically, he allowed his lord to win some of the games which were not ended prematurely by a particularly large wave movement. There was a knock at the door.

"What's this?" said Pabalan as the sailor entered.

"That's Ferragamo's owl," said Laurent. "What's he doing here?"

Moroski regarded the bird in silence.

After a few moments he said, "That's a pretty trick."

"Eh?" said Pabalan.

"Ferragamo has somehow impressed a message on Owl here so that it can be relayed to me. Normally he can only converse with his own wizard. I didn't know he could do this."

"What does the message say?" asked Laurent.

"Ferragamo is back with Mark and the others but he's ill or something like it. They are all staying in a cave in the mountains and can't move on because of the weather. It's all a bit vague but basically it means they want us to delay. Any diversion we create now would be too early."

"That won't please Hoban," said Laurent.

"Doesn't please me much," grumbled Pabalan.

"There's no friendly landfall for sixty leagues in any direction," said Laurent. "I can't see the troop ships holding out too much longer."

"I'll have to talk to them," said Moroski. "That's our problem. In the meantime we'll send Atlanta back with Owl to Ferragamo. That way she can act as messenger to tell us when to move."

"Flying into this wind won't be much fun," said Laurent.

"They'll do it," said Moroski.

Later, the wizard gave Hoban the news. They agreed that the Pevenese ships should sail south immediately, making for Heald. No one knew when the call for diversionary action would come and they could not wait indefinitely. If their supply situation was such that a landing on Ark became necessary it was to be as far south as possible and only men who had drunk some of the moonberry wine should go ashore for any length of time.

The next morning Owl, who was well-fed and rested, and Atlanta set off westward. The remaining ships' crews steeled themselves for yet another day of the endless war against the sea and sky.

As far as anyone could tell, Ferragamo remained unconscious for nearly two whole days. They could not be sure as Shalli refused entry to everybody, even Longfur. In addition anyone who tried to enter or even inquire about the wizard had to endure an incomprehensible lecture from the hermit. Eventually even Mark, who was racked with guilt and worry, gave up and waited for events to take their course.

With such a large number of people in the cave Shalli's supplies were dwindling fast. Orme and Durc between them organized some hunting parties but, even though the storm abated a little, their success was limited. More worrying was fodder for the horses. This would run out in three or four days at most.

"At least water's not a problem," said Clowery.

"Then why don't you use some to wash?" said Fontaine, wrinkling her nose.

The outlaw, recalling his last encounter with the princess at the forest stream, wisely refrained from any comments such as, "Only if you scrub my back." Nevertheless, he did take a bath. One of the caves held a large pool which was constantly refreshed with warm water and, once the novelty of the idea of immersion had been overcome, bathing became a popular pastime. So much so that Fontaine complained that she never got the chance to wash with "all you layabouts wallowing around."

When Ferragamo did come round Shalli only allowed short visits by one person at a time. Mark felt sure that the cavern was a different shape from the last time he had been inside but he dismissed the thought as ridiculous. Then he kept sensing unseen movements as he had before and began to wonder. Returning his attention to the wizard, Mark was hugely relieved to find him coherent and, although obviously very weak, regaining his old forcefulness.

After a few inconsequential exchanges, Mark blurted out an apology for suggesting that Ferragamo send a message via Owl.

"Don't be silly. We all have to do what is necessary."

"Even when it means you collapse?" said Mark.

"Mmm. Shalli was a bit annoyed with me," said Ferragamo, "but he'll get over it."

"We need you more than the fleet."

"There are a lot of men out there, Mark. Their lives might depend on us too."

"I hadn't thought of that."

"The effects are lessening now anyway. I can control it better."

"What happened with Owl then?"

"There's a lot of power inside me, Mark. Some of it is still leaking away as you've no doubt noticed." Ferragamo smiled. "All I had to do to enable Owl to talk to you and Moroski was to channel some of that magic into a specific command or spell. The trouble is, I'm not used to this sort of thing, and some of it spilled out of the channel."

"You couldn't control it all?"

"That's right," Ferragamo nodded. "And having random magic sloshing about in one's head doesn't make for good conversation."

Mark noted the glint in the wizard's eye and laughed.

"You didn't make much sense at times," he said.

"Oh you noticed, did you?"

"You kept talking about Koria as if she was here," ventured Mark hesitantly.

The wizard's eyes softened. "Koria is like a touchstone to me. She's the only one entirely dependable source of sanity in my life. Thinking of her helps me and sometimes the words spill out."

Mark felt a lump in his throat.

"The two of you..." he began, then found himself unable to speak. Looking down, he fought the tears that threatened to fall.

"I know," Ferragamo said gently. "I know."

They sat in silence for a few moments. Ferragamo found that talking about Koria, if only briefly, had made his longing for her worse. He closed his eyes and images of her flashed into his mind; Koria watching him approvingly as he tucked into his breakfast; Koria walking along the beach, laughing, her hair blown about all over the place; Koria in his arms, looking up at him, her eyes grown tender. He swallowed hard.

Mark spoke then, with unconvincing brightness.

"Shalli showed me something," he said, "but he didn't tell me what it meant."

"I don't suppose you would have understood him if he had," said Ferragamo, as Mark drew out his sword.

The faint motif was back. The wizard examined it closely.

"What is it?"

"How much do you know about this sword, Mark?"

The prince thought for a moment.

"Only that it's very old," he said. "It was my father's, then Eric's. It's mine now, I suppose." He frowned.

"It certainly is very old, older even than I suspected."

"I know where I've seen that pattern before," exclaimed Mark suddenly. His expression changed and the color drained from his face.

"In your dream?" said Ferragamo quietly.

"How did you know?"

"Mark, it's time I shared some of my thoughts with you. I wouldn't have done this with your brothers but I think you're levelheaded enough to understand."

Just as long as he can cope with the understanding, thought the wizard privately. He cleared his throat.

"The Mirage Warrior was Arkon's eldest son. His name was—"

"Mark?"

It was Ferragamo's turn to look surprised. "Yes," he said.

"I've known all along, I think," said Mark, "but I didn't want to admit it."

"He's not named in the story because all The Servants put their cause before personal glory. He was one of the heroes of the War."

"And this is the same sword?" asked Mark incredulously.

"I think so."

"I always found it easy to handle, even when I hardly knew which end to hold."

"It's special, Mark. Important. And so are you."

"Me? I'm no hero."

"We all serve in our own way." Ferragamo paused, watching thoughts chase each other through Mark's mind.

"You remember that old verse you found back in Home?"

"The prophecy?"

Ferragamo nodded. "*Arkon's heir, first named and last.* It could be you. And *Arkon's blade*—"

They both looked again at the sword which shimmered in the eerie light.

"But you said..." began Mark.

"I don't often admit this," said the wizard, "so don't tell anybody, but even I can be wrong sometimes."

They grinned at each other.

"If . . . What does the rest of it mean then?" said Mark, his face becoming serious again.

"I haven't a clue," said Ferragamo, "but I think we'll find out in Starhill."

Mark shivered and closed his eyes. They sat in silence for a while. Shalli regarded them solemnly from the doorway.

"The pattern on the sword?" said Mark eventually.

"It's a stylized picture of a moonberry tree."

"The source."

"It all comes back to that."

"Which is why we have to go to Starhill."

"The sooner the better," said the wizard.

"Well we'd better get you back to full strength then," Mark said. "Are you getting enough to eat?"

"Oh yes. Shalli would shame any nursemaid."

"Do you want any cake?"

"That's the last thing I need," said the wizard.

Two days later when Owl returned with Atlanta, Ferragamo had recovered a great deal. He had ventured out of his small cavern and met all of the party. Walking awkwardly but talking a great deal he was dismayed at the level to which the stores of cake had fallen. Thus when the two birds arrived he insisted that they set off immediately. After a last wild fling the storm had finally passed away eastward and preparations were quickly completed. A message was written and attached to Atlanta's leg. It informed Moroski that they were on their way and that they expected to be in Starhill in three days. Atlanta could translate that into a time for diversionary action when she arrived.

The falcon flew off as the first of the horses were led out of the cave, blinking and snorting at the unaccustomed light and cold.

Ferragamo embraced Shalli before they left. Much that nobody else understood had passed between these two and it was clear that the parting was painful. Fontaine hugged the hermit as well, much to his surprise, and many of the others shook his hand or touched his shoulder. He would not be forgotten.

The hermit stood and watched them until they were out of sight.

"Remember the source," he muttered and walked back into his cave.

It seemed very quiet.

Chapter 29

A storm is not normally thought of as being capable of spite. However, Hoban found it difficult not to regard recent events in those terms.

They had been sailing south, hugging the coastline for shelter and, hopefully, to further confuse the forces on land. The storm appeared to be abating and, with the ships in the normally placid waters of Ironmouth Bay, it had seemed that the worst was over.

Disaster had struck in the form of a small whirlwind. They had seen it coming but were unable to move quickly enough to escape its path. Dragged along by the tail end of the storm it had turned into a waterspout as it crossed the coastline. Three vessels had almost foundered, several others had sustained severe damage to their rigging, and virtually all of the others had had their already depleted stores damaged even further.

So it was that, with the sky clearing and the sun coming out to mock them, the commanders of the Pevenese fleet came to the inevitable conclusion that they would have to make landfall. They were in no shape to sail far but they put what distance they could between them and the town of Ironmouth and its garrison.

Hoban was a civilian and theoretically without authority over the naval forces but it was he who organized the landing.

A bridgehead was set up by men who had had access to the supplies of moonberry wine.

"I must be the first commander in history to choose his spearhead specifically because they are drunk," said Hoban.

"I doubt it," said the naval commander, smiling.

Once they had a secure base on land, raiding parties were sent out to gather what food they could, and more of the men went ashore. By evening they had a well-organized defensive camp set up and food and water were being ferried out to the ships, which were being repaired as fast as the sailors could work.

Hoban sipped his meager ration of moonberry wine. He felt sleepy and uneasy but there had been no sign of the forces from Ironmouth and he began to hope that they might get away again without a battle.

He was to be disappointed.

After a long, watchful night, the dawn revealed a squadron of cavalry and some infantry approaching from the northwest. Hoban gathered the army captains around him and quickly made arrangements for the scavenging parties to be recalled and for their defensive positions to be well-manned. Several of the soldiers complained of some of their men feeling sluggish, but they went off to organize the defense.

The Arkan forces seemed strangely indecisive in their approach but eventually they attacked. A wave of arrows swept over the Pevenese positions, but because of the careful preparations this did little damage. Then the cavalry charged, but as their route was either uphill or over sand, they were not as effective as they would have wished and withdrew after a few exchanges of arrows and some minor skirmishes.

The respite did not last long. Soon Hoban and his captains were busy following the various movements of horse and infantry as the Arkans moved to encircle their opponents.

The Pevenese were outnumbered and their positional advantage would not last long.

————————————

The news from Ironmouth thoroughly confused Parokkan.

"It doesn't make sense," he said as he conferred with the messenger and his chief of staff. "They sail about all over the place, then divide their forces and only part of them land . . . in a place of limited strategic advantage. What's going on?"

Elsewhere, Amarino, her mind following and influencing the battle at Ironmouth, wondered the same thing.

They were shortly to find out.

———

Hoban was becoming seriously worried. The fighting was into its second day now and slowly their position was being eroded. Casualties were rising and no new supplies were being brought in. The ships were now in much better shape but more work was needed before they could think of retreating to sea.

What was more, some of the men were suffering from a strange sleeping sickness which made them slow-moving and prone to fall asleep at the most inopportune times. Hoban suspected that magic was involved, especially as the severest cases seemed to be of men who had had little or no wine to drink. He sent as many men to sea as he could spare and hoped for a change of luck.

There was little else he could do.

———

Some fifteen leagues to the north the Healdean fleet was faring rather better. The fairer weather and their greater readiness for a long sojourn at sea left them in reasonable trim. Nevertheless, it was a great relief to Moroski when Atlanta arrived, and after reading the message and consulting the falcon briefly, he deduced that Mark and his companions would reach Starhill the next day or, at worst, the day after that. He was therefore able to give his restless crews the orders which meant action—of a sort.

The fleet split into groups and sailed toward various points of Ark's coastline. By morning they were all within the sight of the various lookouts on the shore, who were then treated to a colorful but confusing pantomime as the ships turned back, swapped groupings, sent coded messages, and seemingly switched their attention from Grayrock to other possible landing places and back again. Following their instructions to keep a careful watch for ships flying royal colors, the observers dutifully reported that several vessels showed the ensigns of Ather's Ark—some of them simultaneously—but that the ships concerned kept varying from place to place. No one could make head or tail of it, but the defending forces were kept busy as each landfall in turn was threatened.

――――――――――

Ferragamo and Mark rode side by side. The prince had been very thoughtful for some time and it came as no surprise to the wizard when he started asking questions.

"This magic," he began, "you think it's controlled by a wizard?"

"I'm afraid so. At least someone who *was* a wizard. I would hate to regard him as a colleague now."

"But what has made it happen now? Something must have triggered it off."

"Moroski and I have a feeling that Brogar is connected with it somehow, but we're only guessing."

"Could it go back to the War of the Wizards?"

"It could. There are similarities with the old tales. And the moonberry's involvement makes it more likely. We're fighting the same evil anyway."

"Using people?"

He gets more intuitive all the time, thought Ferragamo. Aloud he said, "Yes. The very thought makes me shudder."

"How does it work?"

"As far as I can judge, the technique, which we blithely assumed had been lost forever, can be used to link directly with another person's mind. You remember that each mind has its own store of magical potential. From that there would be three consequences. The first we've already seen. The wizard using the technique would be able to effectively disable anybody within their range. To us it would appear that the victims had fallen asleep."

"The soldiers couldn't fall asleep or they'd be no use to him," said Mark. "Their eyes were funny though."

"That's the second stage. With a little more power and, especially with those closer to him, this wizard could actively influence people's actions. Turn them into unquestioning slaves."

"He'd be able to read their minds too, wouldn't he?"

"I suppose so."

"What's the third stage?"

"This is where it gets really evil," said Ferragamo grimly.

"Given a certain level of power to start with this wizard could use people to give him more. In doing so he would turn them into vegetables, something not human at all. Their destruction would enhance his power and that would make it possible for him to enslave even more people—"

"And grow even stronger."

"And so it would go on until he was so powerful that no one could withstand him."

They rode in silence for a while.

"It hasn't reached that stage yet though," said Mark.

"No. The further someone is from the wizard the harder it would be. Trying to draw power from somebody too far away would be counterproductive. The effort to set up the exchange would be too great."

"So the people in Home are safe."

"For now," said Ferragamo.

On the third day out from Shalli's cave, the horses finally had level ground to walk on. Their journey had been painfully slow. Although the blizzard had blown itself out there was still a lot of snow lying on the upper slopes and that, with the sometimes treacherous nature of their path, had made Mark and his friends very cautious.

Now that they were well below the snow-line and the foothills had gradually given way to gentler slopes it would not be long before Starhill was in sight. They hurried on knowing that, if all was going to plan, the Healdean fleet would be staging the mock invasion that day.

The night before had seen the last of the moonberry cake distributed and eaten. Nobody knew how long it would be before their immunity began to wear out but everyone agreed that they would rather not find out.

Shortly after noon Mark made out the shape of the wizard's tower in the misty distance, and a strange thrill ran through his body.

Jani says there are horses approaching, said Longfur in his mind.

How can he tell? Mark replied, but before the cat could respond there was no reason for the query.

A few hundred paces away a party of Starhill cavalry came

into view. When they saw the prince's group they immediately charged, drawing their swords as they came.

There had been so little warning that there was no real attempt to organize a defense. Without thinking, the soldiers and outlaws moved together to protect Ferragamo and Fontaine. Then the cavalry crashed in amongst them and all sense of the total picture was lost as each man found his own personal battles occupying all his attention.

Horses wheeled and reared, screaming. Swords clashed and several men went down in the mêlée. Mark found himself strangely unchallenged and sought out Fontaine and the wizard at the fight's center. He slashed out at one of the cavalry guards and missed, but the man made no riposte. Instead he sneered and said, "No, young princeling, we'll not cut you. She wants you alive."

She? thought Mark.

The man laughed but there was no humor in the sound, nor in his hollow gray eyes.

All about Mark the fighting raged, yet to him it seemed that he was the eye of the storm. For some time he was unable to engage anyone and his frustration grew, especially when he saw Fontaine exchanging blows with a burly soldier. Ferragamo, to his relief, seemed to be under the same protection as himself and no one assailed the wizard directly.

Elsewhere it was a different story. Although there were roughly equal numbers on each side, the cavalry were better protected, with chain mail and helmets, and were well versed in the art of fighting on horseback. Mark winced as he saw several of his friends fall and for a while it looked very bad. However, after the initial advantage of the impact of their charge had worn off, the Starhill men found their opponents fighting back with the determination of desperate men. Casualties rose on both sides.

Abruptly the Starhill captain called the retreat and they rode off, leaving over half their men behind, either dead or dying.

When he was sure that there was no longer any immediate danger, Mark quickly counted heads and was dismayed to find that almost half his friends would play no further part in the expedition.

Ferragamo, Fontaine, and Ansar all seemed unharmed. Jani too had escaped unscathed, having used his staff to keep the soldiers at a distance from himself and from Fontaine. Durc

and Zunic were both alive, though the latter was sorely
wounded in the thigh, but Clowery and the other three
outlaws were dead. Only one of the Strallenese soldiers was
still standing. He had dismounted and soon confirmed that
Lomax and his other two colleagues were dead. The soldier's
face was white with grief. Bonet and Richard looked to be all
right but Essan was beyond help, his corpse horribly mutilat-
ed. Mark looked for Shill and saw him kneeling on the
ground, cradling Orme in his arms. Dismounting, Mark went
to them, arriving at the same time as Ferragamo. Shill
glanced up briefly, tears in his eyes. He looked at the wizard
pleadingly but Ferragamo shook his head and the last hope
died in Shill's eyes. Orme's eyes were open, staring at the
sky, but Mark knew they saw nothing.

The dying soldier spoke. His voice was so weak Mark had
to still his own breathing to hear him.

"Shill, old friend?"

"I'm here."

"When this is over, come back for me . . . Bury me in
Starhill. I said I was going back . . . I'd like to stay true . . ."

"You're going back to live—" began Shill, but Orme cut
him off.

"Don't," he said. After a pause, he continued, "You'll look
after Anna . . ."

"Yes," said Shill simply.

Orme coughed. A line of red ran from the corner of his
mouth.

"And the boys."

"Yes."

"Tell them . . ." Orme coughed again, then seemed to
relax. He was gone.

"I'll tell them," said Shill.

———————————

Some time later, with the willing assistance of the able-
bodied members of the party, Ferragamo had done all he
could to heal the various wounds of the survivors. Reluctantly,
they covered the dead, but left them unburied, knowing that
if their mission was to be successful, then speed was now
essential. They could return as soon as their purpose was
achieved, if it was. If not . . .

Zunic's wound make it impossible for him to travel on,

despite his protests, and the last Strallenese soldier, nâmed Ryal, volunteered to stay with him. They were installed in a hiding place far enough away to escape detection should any soldiers return. Then the remaining members of the party set out on the last leg of their journey.

Nine of us, thought Mark. *It doesn't seem like much.*

Ten, came the silent response. *Eleven if you count bird-brain up there.*

Of course. How could I forget you?

Mark looked up at Owl who was flying high above the riders, acting as a lookout.

No more soldiers were spotted and by mid-afternoon they were within bowshot of the walls of the city.

"They'll be expecting us now," said Shill. "As soon as those soldiers got back..."

"Then why haven't there been any more patrols?" asked Ansar.

No one had an answer to that.

———————————

Amarino had in fact known of their approach for some time before the remnants of the patrol returned to the castle. While Parokkan was still puzzling over the confused and contradictory reports coming from the east, she had been using her special powers to tap the minds of various soldiers throughout the city and the surrounding area. When the thoughts of one patrol captain had suddenly exploded with the frenetic action of battle she had focused on him and read his mind.

When she learned whom the patrol was attacking she switched her attention to that small location and in doing so became aware of the peril she faced. Her own soldiers were clear to her, their minds malleable, to read or to influence as she chose. But their opponents were simply not there! It was as if their minds did not exist. All she could detect was the same strange white blankness that had made her so horribly uneasy with Brandel.

Immediately, her opponents' plans became clear and from that moment on she chose to disregard events in the east totally. In doing so, she also relinquished her well-concealed control over the army and its officers. Parokkan especially felt suddenly purposeless, unsure of what to do, and this was reflected all through the ranks.

In Ironmouth the hard-pressed Pevenese forces suddenly found renewed strength and soon afterward their attackers withdrew in confusion. Hoban took advantage of this respite to gather what stores he could and then ferry his men back aboard the refurbished fleet.

Meanwhile Amarino turned all of her formidable magical power toward Mark, Ferragamo, and the others. Despite this, her opponents remained unreachable, as elusive as summer mist. She cursed herself for not following up a report of a capture in the south some time ago. It had subsequently become a mystery, with the prisoner and several soldiers disappearing without any trace.

How can they do this, she fumed. *So close, they should be in my power. Well, let them come! My source is here and theirs is destroyed. They will walk into my trap and then I will control them all.*

She gloated on the thought of the added power that domination of a wizard and a prince of Ark would give her.

Let them come!

Chapter 30

"*I* don't like this," said Shill. "It doesn't look as if the gate is even guarded."

"As if we were being invited inside," said Ansar.

"It must be a trap," said Richard.

"Too obvious," said Durc.

Standing among farm buildings which hid them from view, they all continued observing the Mountain Gate, which was open and apparently undefended two hundred paces away.

"We don't have any choice," said Mark. "We can't hope to scale the walls undetected so it has to be one of the gates. If it's a trap, we have to walk into it."

There was a moment's silence while the others considered this. Then there were nods of agreement.

"We've come this far . . ." said Ansar. He didn't need to complete the thought aloud.

"Let's go," said Shill.

Parokkan felt his confidence draining away. He felt as if he were in a dream. The news from the coast was confusing but posed no immediate threat. His forces on land would be able to cope with any invasion, if it ever came, and the garrison which remained in the city was sufficient to meet any of the enemy that did break through. All this he knew but it was of no comfort now. Suddenly, he had become aware that something was wrong. He felt unsure of himself for the first time in years. All at once he began to notice signs of the problem. He left the castle tower which overlooked the Field Gate road and went down to the Guard House. He passed a soldier on the way and said, "What news?"

He received no reply. The soldier merely went on his way.

What has happened to my authority? thought Parokkan, his mind reeling, close to panic.

In the Guard House he received a further shock. The four soldiers assigned to sentry duty were asleep, slumped at their posts. What was more, he could not rouse them, despite shouting furiously and shaking the crumpled bodies.

Drugged? he thought looking around wildly. *How? Who?*

Cautiously, his sword drawn, he went out and through the small door in the castle gate. The City Square was deserted.

"Guards!" he yelled, and his voice echoed eerily.

No one answered his call.

Then suddenly, as quickly as it had disappeared, his self-assurance returned. He knew exactly what he must do. A small group of the enemy had broken through and were even now entering the city by the Mountain Gate. Among them were the hated figures of Ferragamo the wizard and Ather's youngest son, the pathetic one. Those two were to be lured to the castle. The others were to be harried, tired, and killed if necessary but they were less important.

It did not occur to him to wonder how he knew all this. Soldiers started to file out of the door behind him. He noted without surprise that the four sleeping sentries were among them. Each saluted him as they arrived and awaited his orders.

"You know what to do," he said. "Let's go."

He strode off and the twelve men marched behind him.

"How are you feeling?" Ferragamo asked.

"All right," said Mark. "There's a constant sort of probing in my head but it doesn't worry me."

"Good," said the wizard, then added in a louder voice, "when we go on, everybody keep together as much as

possible. I want us to get to the castle with as little fighting
as possible. We will need all our strength when we get there.
We'll leave the horses here."

The Mountain Gate had indeed been unguarded and the
group had moved inside stealthily and hidden in the nearest
available shelter.

The city was deserted as far as they could see. The normal
bustle which the former residents remembered contrasted
disconcertingly with the ghost town that lay before them.
Ferragamo made them move on before the implications of
this could sink in.

They moved into the back streets but stayed close to the
Mountain Gate thoroughfare and made as directly as possible
for the castle. They relied on Ferragamo's instincts and the
memories of Shill and the other soldiers to choose their
route. Still they saw nobody until, rounding a corner, Shill
saw a soldier at the far end of a small street.

The soldier immediately began yelling to unseen comrades and Shill withdrew. "Back," he hissed. "We've been
seen."

They went deeper into the maze of the quarter. Soon,
however, they heard the sounds of pursuit and then realized
that there were soldiers at either end of the alley in which
they stood.

Shill swore. "That's Parokkan," he said, pointing.

"Let's take them," said Ansar.

"No choice," agreed Mark and they set off toward the
usurper's group. Behind them they heard the other soldiers
break into a run to follow them.

Just before they reached Parokkan he shouted orders and
he and his men melted away out of sight. Forced on by their
pursuers, Mark and his group came to the end of the alley
expecting to be ambushed, but instead found Parokkan some
distance away and retreating. They followed.

This pattern was repeated several times.

"They're playing with us," gasped Shill. They were all
fighting for breath.

"Time to change tactics, I think," said Ansar and swung
round to confront the soldiers behind them. Several of the
others turned with him and within moments the battle was
joined in earnest.

Mark would have attacked as well but Ferragamo, the
strain of exertion showing in his haggard face, drew him back.

"We have to go on," he said. "We're so close now and we haven't much time." The tone of his voice brooked no argument and Mark nodded. With a last glance over his shoulder he ran toward the castle. Ferragamo, Fontaine, Jani, and Durc followed when they saw what was happening. Behind them Ansar and the three soldiers fought on.

Mark led them forward. As they emerged into an empty City Square, Bonet joined them, breathing heavily. "We led them a merry dance," he panted. "Don't know where they are now—" Abruptly he broke off and yawned hugely. Ferragamo looked at him sharply.

At the far end of the square, men came into sight. They were fighting. Mark picked out Parokkan and Shill engaged in a duel. He made to go to his friend's aid but Ferragamo said, "Inside," and pointed to the Castle Gate.

They ran on and were inside before the fighting could reach them. The castle was quiet. Nothing moved.

"The courtyard?" said Mark. Ferragamo nodded.

Before they could go on Bonet yawned again and said, "I don't—" He sat down with a bump and was instantly asleep.

Mark looked at him in horror.

"He's more sensitive than most," said the wizard. "Come on!"

Durc had his hand on his forehead but at the wizard's words he removed it, shook his head as if to clear it, and followed.

There was no need for any stealth now. Mark knew that whatever power they had come to face, it was aware of their approach. Suddenly Mark knew what, or rather who, it was.

"Amarino," he said, and did not wait for Ferragamo's confirmation before setting off toward the tower.

The central courtyard which held the moonberry tree lay at the foot of the Wizard's Tower and was surrounded by a thick seamless stone wall, the last line of defense against invaders. There was only one entrance from the surrounding circular court and this was barred by solid oak doors, a handspread thick and reinforced with metal bolts. In Mark's memory these doors had always stood open, but now they were fast shut.

A short flight of steps led up to the doorway and as they started up them, four soldiers burst from one of the surrounding buildings. Ferragamo raised his staff.

"Save your strength, wizard," said Durc. "We can dea
with these."

Mark, Durc, and Jani took up defensive positions on the
steps. It was a brief but bloody fight and Mark was sickened
to see familiar faces among his opponents, who fought dog
gedly, but who could not overcome their positional disadvan
tage. They all went down, even the last man continuing
against hopeless odds, until the back of Jani's axe caught the
side of his helmet and sent him sprawling.

"They're fighting like men possessed," said Durc, hur
riedly binding a deep gash in his sword arm. "The sooner we
put a stop to this the better."

Mark agreed but he was now utterly weary; the sword
which usually felt so light was heavy in his hand. How had he
managed to swing it?

From the top of the stairs, Ferragamo said, "There's
something wrong within. I can't sense the source."

"The tree?" asked Fontaine.

"Could Amarino have destroyed it?" asked Mark.

"No, she does not have that power. If she did we wouldn't
have got this far."

"You need the tree?" said Durc.

"Remember the source," said Mark.

"Well, we're not finished yet," said the outlaw. "Those
walls are unscalable, so we have to open the gates. Any
ideas?"

No one spoke.

Jani looked from face to face then walked up to the door
and pushed. Both sides swung open easily.

The party gaped, then . . .

· "No!" shouted Mark and Ferragamo together.

It was too late. Jani had stepped inside, his axe held
ready, unafraid. As the others dashed to follow the big man
flames erupted inside their heads, a burst of pain burned
through their limbs, and, once inside, all found themselve
unable to move.

Mark fought wildly to retain his grip on his own thoughts
and on the sword, which seared his hand and had grown
intolerably heavy. A small part of him noted the frozen agony
of those about him and then he saw the direction of Ferragamo's
dismayed stare. In the center of the courtyard, where their
hope should have stood, was an ugly metal dome, big enough
to cover the entire tree. *Iron is impervious to magic*. The tree

couldn't be destroyed, but it had been cut off from the sun, the sky, the air, and from them just as effectively. *It would take days to cut through that,* thought Mark. *Until then, no magic can touch it and its strength can't reach us. We're doomed.*

Amarino stepped from the doorway at the base of the tower.

"Welcome," she said, and smiled. Underneath the smile, Mark sensed the strain that she was under and his heart gave a little jump of hope. *It's taking all her power to hold us,* he thought.

"How nice of you to bring me such a gift," Amarino said, looking at the sword. "You are well named Servant, for you now complete my power. Throw down the sword, boy."

Arkon's blade, thought Mark. *So it is important. The prophecy! What did it say?* He struggled to remember, but could not. Sweat broke from his face as a further blast seared his mind and he fought desperately to stop his fingers dropping the sword, as they tried to open of their own volition. *I can't hold on,* he groaned inwardly, *soon it will be too late. Help me.*

He sensed rather than saw that Jani had moved slightly and at once the fire in his body abated slightly. *The balance is that delicate then. If only . . .*

Still the sword was slipping from his grasp. Slowly his last strength was being sapped. *Has it all been for this?* he thought. *So many people killed and hurt just for me to fail them now?* And what would happen to those others held captive here with him? Ferragamo, who stood frozen, his face contorted in frustrated anger; Fontaine, whom he loved, and who now seemed so small, so vulnerable; the faithful Jani; and Durc who had been given his chance and had proved his worth. Were they all to die or become the mindless thralls of the evil that he alone could face?

It was too much for his mind to bear, tortured as it was. His fingers slipped a little more, the grip now slick with sweat.

The fixed smile on Amarino's face had become a feral grin.

"Why fight?" she said. "Not much longer now." Her voice was hoarse, yet held a note of victory.

A fury descended from the sky. All claws and teeth and bristling fur, screaming and spitting; a sound to rend the

eardrums and raise the dead from sleep; the battle cry of a
cat.

Longfur leapt from the tower window, landed squarely on
Amarino's head, scrabbling and clawing, singing blood.

Several things happened simultaneously.

Jani's great axe crashed down on the iron dome, bringing
forth a dull booming sound but only slightly denting its
surface. Durc collapsed and lay still. Two soldiers charged in
through the door to be faced with Fontaine crouching, knife
in hand, and obviously meaning business.

Before the reverberations of Jani's blow had died away the
air was assaulted with an even greater clamor. Ferragamo
held impotent for so long, almost literally exploded. Power
brighter than the sun, blazed from his outstretched staff
directed not at Amarino, but at the iron dome, which seemed
to disintegrate instantaneously. Mark ducked automatically
but no pieces of iron flew past, none ricocheted off the stone
walls. Jani staggered back, coughing. The air about them
seemed dull for a moment, then a ray of sunlight pierced the
clouds above, and the leaves of Arkon's tree shone green once
more.

Amarino screamed.

Strength flowed through Mark's arm; joy catapulted into
his mind.

Now! came a familiar voice into his brain. *Must I do
everything?*

Mark's body and the sword became one. The mysterious
pattern on his blade shone with a silver-white radiance, far
stronger than ever before. Yet he alone had not moved.

More killing? Must it always come to this?

Before him, Amarino changed. Around her still beautiful
violet eyes her face grew haggard, her limbs twisted, and her
fingers curled claw-like and flailed at the air. She was the very
picture of evil. And yet still he hesitated.

When beauty fades.

He took a step forward. Longfur was flung to one side and
her vicious eyes turned to him.

She changed again.

Her eyes became yellow, her skin grew scales, and her
breath belched flame and smoke. Mark saw again the dragon
that had faced that other Servant so long ago and knew the
price that he would have to pay. His heart shrank and his

whole body trembled in terror, feeling the pain of burning flesh. *They cannot ask this of me.*

He took a step back and Amarino became an inferno which was growing to engulf them all. His mind turned to *ee.*

No! An unknown voice, unworldly and somehow unformed, spoke clearly in his head. *You are one of us. The Servants. You cannot escape your fate. This dragon is a mirage. An illusion. Strike now! The past and future will help you.*

Who are you?

Your son. I am a Servant too.

The voice was gone. Mark was too stunned to try to trace its source. He leapt into the fire.

Then fates decide, he thought. And struck.

The dragon disappeared.

In one flowing movement, balanced and precise, his whole weight and strength unified, Mark drove the sword into Amarino's heart. He met so little resistance that at first he staggered, wondering if he had missed her, fooled by some new illusion. Then he steadied, looked down at the stain on his blade which was already turning black, and at the crumbled thing on the floor. As he watched, the body seemed to shrivel. Soon nothing remained except rags of what had once been a robe.

And battle cease.

Mark turned round to see Fontaine still facing two rather bemused-looking soldiers.

"Hello Gordon, Luca. Put away your swords. Otherwise our future queen may greet you with her knife!"

Chapter 31

The round table had thirty seats, and every one was filled. The three other presences in the room had no need of furniture. Mark had seated himself in his father's old chair with a heavy heart but soon the food and wine and general merriment of all around had started to lighten his mood. He looked around his strange collection of friends and saw also those people who were *not* there. Silently he toasted them.

He felt the pressure of eyes upon him and looked up to meet Fontaine's gaze, her goblet also raised.

Mark found himself thinking back to the plain little princess with the mass of red hair who had arrived at Starhi Castle all those months ago. Quite a change from the radiant beautiful Fontaine who smiled at him now, he thought.

A question of diet, came a feline thought from below the table. *Speaking of which, my bowl is empty. If you haven't scoffed everything, a little more fish would be appreciated.*

Smiling, Mark passed down the food and then looked back at Fontaine who had appeared to follow the interchange with interest.

"Of course, I was thinking all the time," said Ferragamo.

"When you're frozen that's about all you *can* do," put

Durc as, with his left hand, he speared another slice of pie.

"We were not frozen as such. Amarino was using the power she had built up from all those poor people to alter the nature of time for us. I could have lifted my staff, or Jani his axe, but it would have taken a year or two to do it. The sword protected Mark a bit but it took Longfur's surprise attack to break the spell."

It was nothing.

"By then I had realized what I had to do. It was Amarino herself that gave me the idea."

"What I don't understand," said Mark, "is that iron is impervious to magic, or so you've always told me."

"So it is."

"Then how—"

"What happened to the dome was entirely natural."

"What! But it exploded."

"It did not. It rusted."

The entire company were now listening to the exchange.

"All I did," continued the wizard, "was speed the process up a bit. The same trick that Amarino was using, but in reverse. What would have taken many years happened in a few moments."

"Rust. So that was what all the dust was."

"Yes. That was the iron fire of the prophecy. Rusting and burning are very similar processes."

"So the prophecy did apply to us," said Shill.

"Yes," said Ferragamo grudgingly. "It all fits now. It still got us into a lot of trouble though."

"What prophecy?" said Zunic.

"Never mind," replied the wizard. "I'll explain later."

"And time awakes," quoted Fontaine.

"Did it ever," said Durc, still somewhat at sea with the drift of the conversation. *Though I didn't,* he thought to himself.

"Destroying the dome took all the power I could muster," said Ferragamo. "It will be some time yet before I feel myself again." He glanced apologetically at Koria who sat smiling at his side.

"Will someone tell me," said Durc, "in words a plain man can understand, what happened next? I remember Longfur appearing out of nowhere but then the world went black. I know we won but how?"

"Mark," said Ferragamo, "you had better tell the res There's others here besides Durc who haven't heard th whole story."

Mark was silent for a moment, remembering his convers tion earlier in the day with Longfur, which had added muc to his recollection of events—was it only two days ag —and which needed to be included in his tale. With so man eyes upon him he felt embarrassed, as he marshaled h thoughts.

Get on with it, or we'll be here all night.

He began.

"From the moment Jani opened the courtyard doors w were in a trap. We knew it but couldn't do anything about i You all know that the spell which came most naturally an powerfully to Amarino was that of influencing the actions others."

Several people round the table shuddered from person experience.

"Even with the incredible resources she was able to dra on, the moonberry cake that we had eaten made it impossib for her to manipulate or disable us directly, so she had t resort to other methods. She would have succeeded too, b for some things she had overlooked."

He paused for a sip of wine.

"We were invited to enter and once inside she used th time spell to hold all the others immobile while she tried t force me into giving up the sword. She knew it was deadly t her, but it was powerful and had she obtained it she woul have been invincible. She wanted me to reach her but I thin the look of some of my companions surprised her."

Durc laughed and Mark glanced at Jani who sat immobil watching him. The big man smiled.

I'm translating for him, said Longfur, *though he follow more than most people realize.* Mark went on.

"It took her to the limit of her powers to hold us all an she didn't notice Longfur slip round the side of the courtyar and into the tower. I didn't either, though Jani did." An *Longfur didn't tell me because Amarino would have read it my mind and been warned,* he added to himself, wonderin how his subjects would take to the fact that their new kin talked to his cat.

"When Longfur jumped, it was enough to shatter Amarino concentration. We thought the line in the verse, *Whe vengeance screams, no human sound*, referred to the singing of a sword in battle but now we know better. We owe our feline friend a debt we cannot repay. He accomplished what an entire army could not."

Steady on, you'll have me believing I'm a hero, came the complacent thought.

"He was the real hero," said Mark. From the rafters an owl hooted derisively but only Ferragamo noticed.

"Then everything went mad. Ferragamo destroyed the iron dome as he's explained, though Jani all but split it in half with his axe beforehand."

He was ready and we had to try something.

"Fontaine turned to deal with another threat." Gordon and Luca looked hard at their plates.

"And I fainted," added Durc, to general laughter.

"When the sunlight fell on the tree, which was *Arkon's staff* in the verse of course, it released the power in my sword." *And me,* he thought. "And even though Amarino used the last of her magic to try to stop me, I knew what I had to do. I ran her through, though she was so light that I'm sure she had no heart to pierce." He felt cold at the memory.

"And then she was gone. Blown away by the wind. No body, no blood, no skeleton, just a few scraps of cloth. It's hard to believe that she really is dead." He stood, and taking the sword from the scabbard that hung over the back of his chair, he displayed the black stain which ran half the length of the blade. Within the darkness the tree emblem shone white. "This is all that is left now."

"She *is* dead," said Ferragamo. "Arkon's blade has served its purpose."

"While we're on this prophecy business," said Shill, "wasn't there a bit in it about *two that are one* avenging something..."

"*Two that are one call judgment down*," said Mark, and paused.

"Well?"

"I suppose this is as good a time as any," said Mark eventually. "The two that are one refers to me and Fontaine," he lied.

I don't know why you are so ashamed of your litter, came Longfur's thought. *I would be proud.*

You don't understand, and Mark recalled the time immediately after Amarino was dead and all the casualties had been attended to. As soon as it had been possible he had taken Fontaine aside and hugged her to him. Then, holding her shoulders at arm's length he had said, "Just now, in the courtyard, someone spoke to me."

"I heard."

"My son?"

"Yes." Fontaine lowered her eyes.

"Why didn't you tell me?"

"Because you wouldn't have let me come!"

"But—"

"Well, would you?"

"But—"

"No buts. I had to be here. *He* had to be here. You needed us, didn't you?"

It was Mark's turn to lower his gaze.

"I was scared of the fire," he said quietly.

"Fire? What fire?"

"You didn't see the dragon?"

"No," she said and added thoughtfully, "That was your dream."

"Nightmare," he amended.

"Over now."

"Yes."

"For all three of us."

He kissed her then, not caring who saw.

Longfur's voice brought him back to the present. *If you don't say something soon they'll think you've gone dumb.*

"With your permission, sir," said Mark, looking at Pabalan, "I would like to marry your daughter. Provided she is willing, of course," he added.

Somewhat taken aback by this turn of events, the Healdean king took a few moments to realize that something was expected of him. Eventually he stammered, "Well, really, I should . . . my Lady Adesina has always—"

"He means yes!" exclaimed Fontaine.

"Er, of course," said Pabalan and Mark sat down, relieved.

Shill leapt to his feet. "A toast," he cried, raising his goblet. "To the two that are one."

Everyone except the two who were three rose and drank, even Zunic, whose leg was still very sore.

Now can you tell them about your litter?

Eat your fish!

Humans!

Mark looked round the table as the buzz of general

conversation broke out again. So much seemed to have happened in the last two days, so many comings and goings.

Shortly after his fateful encounter with Amarino, Shill had come running into the courtyard followed by Ansar and Richard. The young soldier had come face-to-face with his brother Gordon, and they had stared at each other suspiciously.

Then Gordon had spoken. "Is it over?"

"It's over," Mark had said and the two brothers had embraced. Now they sat next to each other at the round table.

Shill had brought the news that Parokkan was dead, killed by his sword. Shortly afterward he had sought permission to seek out Anna, Orme's wife, and had set off grim-faced. Orme's body had been collected, with the others, the next day, and buried within Starhill according to his last wishes. Anna now sat beside Shill at the table with her two sons on either side of them. She looked pale and tired but Mark knew she was in good hands. Her release from Amarino's domination had been disorientating. It was as if the last few months had passed in a long, featureless dream. Her awakening and the subsequent news of her husband's death had left her in a state of shock from which, with Shill's help, she was only just beginning to recover. Her sons at least were with her. Darin had emerged, cold and bemused but otherwise unharmed, from the dungeons and his younger brother Ashe, whom Amarino had used as a page at several official engagements, was rejoicing in his reunion with his mother. They had not recognized each other for some time.

Bonet, the last of the soldiers, was not there. After recovering from his magically-induced torpor he had gone to seek his woman. He had found her, Mark knew, but she had refused, out of shyness, to come to the castle table despite the open invitation. Bonet had respected her wishes and stayed with her.

Later, there had been other arrivals from the east. All hostilities had ceased when Amarino died and eventually the fleet was persuaded to come ashore. Moroski, Laurent, and Pabalan had come to Starhill and they and several others from Heald, as well as some from Strallen who had rejoined Ryal, now sat at various places around the table. Hoban and two of the Pevenese commanders were there too, having arrived from Ironmouth that afternoon.

Perhaps the most surprising and pleasing arrival had been

Koria who had, on her own initiative, sailed with the fleet in one of the boats from Home. She had made up her mind after a vivid and disturbing vision had come to her as she sat on the village jetty. Ferragamo had made an attempt to remonstrate with her for being so foolhardy but it did no good. He could not hide the pleasure he felt at their reunion and he knew it.

Theirs had not been the only reunion however. The city of Starhill was slowly coming back to life. It was hard to separate the truth from the welter of strange stories but it was clear that a huge number of people had reemerged from the underground catacomb where they had been lying in a living death to feed Amarino with her vile power. Those privileged or necessary few who had been spared this fate felt themselves waking as if from a dream and seeing the silent city before them for the ghost town it was. Then the first of the underground prisoners had stumbled blinking into the light and the news had spread. The trickle of men, women, and children had become a flood as Starhill repopulated itself and began the arduous task of starting to function again. The city was still in chaos but order was gradually being restored as the necessities of normal life reasserted themselves.

Some people did not come out into the sunshine again. They were the ones who, for whatever reason, were unable to stand the unnatural pressures of the demands made by Amarino's manipulations. About thirty bodies had been brought out of the dungeons. Among them was Brandel.

Mark shuddered at the thought. His brother had died fighting, that much was obvious. But what horrors had he seen before he died? *I'll never know,* he thought, and tried to turn his mind back to more pleasant matters. Someone was speaking to him.

"Sorry," he said. "What did you say?"

"Rehan's gone," repeated Ansar. "He was staying here in the castle, we know. His stuff's here. But we've looked everywhere for him . . ."

"I heard it said that someone answering his description fled the city on the day we arrived," said Shill. "He had several chests with him and headed north."

"I'd like to get my hands on that little rat," said Ansar.

"He seemed so honest," said Pabalan sadly.

"I think he met up with more than he bargained for," said Ferragamo. "Don't think too badly of him."

"You don't think we should go after him them?"

"He'll be at sea by now," said the wizard.

"I hope he gets blown to Brogar," said Ansar.

There was a sudden silence around the table.

Then Shill said loudly. "Enough of this. Tonight is for celebration."

"Agreed," said Ferragamo. "How about some music?"

There was a chorus of agreement and instruments appeared from somewhere. An impromptu orchestra was formed, led by Ferragamo, who numbered fiddle-playing among his less well known accomplishments. There was a distinct shortage of female partners but this was rectified later when various members of the castle staff, hearing the noise, approached and were made welcome.

To start with only four couples took the floor; Shill with Anna, Gordon with his wife, Jeanna, and Hoban with Koria, who was sent on her way by Ferragamo saying, "I'm much too weak to keep up with you youngsters. Besides, I'll only tread on your feet."

"You'll not be too weak to play that thing till all hours, I'll wager," she replied, but she had a glint in her eye and smiled warmly as she took the ambassador's gentlemanly arm.

They were led out, of course, by Mark and Fontaine. Feeling distinctly self-conscious, they were awkward at first but soon the music took its hold and they began to enjoy themselves.

Swinging along, their hands clasped together, they found themselves looking into each other's eyes and knew that their thoughts were just about identical. Both of them were lost in wonder, not only at their blossoming love, but also at the remarkable fact that it seemed that they would have a secure and peaceful home in which it would grow.

I can't believe I'm so lucky, thought Mark.

Just wait until she starts throwing up in the mornings, came the sardonic reply from under the table.

Epilogue

$\mathcal{A}$s Mark and Fontaine whirled together in the hall of Starhill Castle, Rehan danced with a different partner. Her name was Death.

Two days ago, he had received a peremptory command from Amarino to leave the city. He was to take six certain caskets and ride north, with an escort if he wanted it, to the small port of Coro. There a ship would await him. He was to stow the caskets aboard and sail immediately.

"Where to?" he had asked.

"Just sail," came the reply and he had been dismissed in a manner that brooked no argument. He had no option but to obey. Defiance would have been as pointless as it was stupid.

He had reached Coro in good time and the ship was indeed awaiting his arrival, but his heart sank when he saw the vessel. It looked hardly seaworthy and certainly would not be even remotely comfortable. Even so, he loaded the caskets, dismissed his escort, and went aboard. The crew set sail almost before the gangplank was aboard.

Now, in mid-ocean, his worst fears were being confirmed. They had been traveling northward, to Rek perhaps, but the ship had been pounded by rough seas and had started taking in water. Soon after that, the idiot helmsman had let the ship be caught broadside by one of the huge waves that were being piled up by the westerly winds. The noise and the shuddering had been terrifying.

From them on it had merely been a matter of time. The vessel was breaking up.

Rehan had shouted to the captain about a lifeboat and getting his precious cargo aboard but the gnarled old sailor had only laughed at him. Rehan thought he was insane.

Suddenly he was in the water, struggling vainly to stay afloat, the sea-cold already numbing his limbs. His last thought was a vision of a horrible face sneering at him.

"Drowning will be easy by comparison," it said.

Amid the wreckage of the ship, six caskets bobbed to the surface. Affected differently by the wind and waves they drifted apart, going their separate ways.

Within one, snugly wrapped and entirely at ease in her cramped compartment, a baby girl thought of her five sisters and wished them well.